What Reade

A Conspiracy of Breath

This book was writte[illegible] a long time, I have ac[illegible] do for the egalitarian [illegible] for the race issue, an[illegible] *Breath* can do this.

Dr. Gilbert Bilezikian, Founder/Leader, Willow Creek Community Church; Professor Emeritus, Wheaton College

Wonderful writing, characterizations that are precise and vivid, excellent historical detail, fabulous prose marked by fresh metaphors and great rhythm, and the description of romantic feelings—so hard to write—rock my world. Beautiful, lyrical.

Rosslyn Elliot, 2012 double Carol Award-winning author

Your writing style is clear and vivid, drawing the reader into the novel, into Priscilla's world … I was drawn into the epoch by your use of language; it was definitely a Ro[illegible] xperience to read the first chapter.

Ruth Hoppin, author of *Priscilla's* [illegible] *uthor of the Epistle to the Hebrews*

Latayne Scott knows h[illegible] u shed light into complex, difficult, a[illegible] s. *A Conspiracy of Breath* is heart stopping, lu[illegible] y real, and very human. Her prose crackles with life, [illegible] nterspersed with poetry both of which will make the reader lower the book, stare out the window, and contemplate what makes us human. What is most astonishing is how Priska's life, 2000 years ago, speaks to our culture this minute. Only a gifted and skilled writer like Latayne could have accomplished this novel. It is a treasure.

Bonnie Grove, author of *Your Best You* and *Talking with the Dead*

I just finished *A Conspiracy of Breath*—in tears.... What a masterpiece! Your skillful use of the Greek translations brings the Book of Hebrews to life in a new way. Your descriptions of the time are detailed and draw the reader into both the inner world of Priscilla and the environment of the time. I share Priscilla's struggle with faith and the call to be a prophet, as well as her dependence on the faith and struggle of others to show the way. Your vocabulary is immense and the writing flows smoothly.

The Rev. Anne O. Weatherholt, Rector Saint Mark's Episcopal Church, Lappans, Boonsboro, Maryland; author, *Breaking the Silence: The Church Responds to Domestic Violence*

I was hooked, and read straight through to the end. It is the best writing I've seen from anyone in CBA: excellent voice, excellent mood and emotion, excellent sense of image and metaphor, excellent sense of historical research that provides a new perception.

Donn Taylor, writing conference instructor and author of *Lightning on a Quiet Night, Rhapsody in Red, The Lazarus File*

It certainly sounds like you have hit the nail on the head with this book. And for many, those "nails" (being confronted with truth) hurts.

Dr. Manfred Brauch Author; Lecturer; Professor Emeritus of Biblical Theology; Past President of Palmer Theological Seminary of Eastern University, St. Davids, PA

I LOVE the book. I love the idea (how fascinating about the baby!) and your writing is strong. I can see what a strong emotional reaction this will evoke in readers, especially while Priscilla waits for them to come get her.

Heather Gemmen Wilson, author of *Startling Beauty*

This is sheer genius. It is, indeed, your opus.

Celeste Green, Academic Dean, Oak Grove Classical Academy, Albuquerque

BRAVO BRAVO! It's fabulous. This could be your best work.

Keith Lancaster, Christian Music Hall of Fame singer and composer, founder of The Acappella Company

If I've ever read more exquisite writing than *A Conspiracy of Breath* I don't know what it would be. Latayne's amazing novel inserts the reader into the ancient world of Rome and Corinth and Jerusalem and lets her feel what it would have been like to live at the time of Paul and Timothy, Aquila and Priscilla, and Latayne's unforgettable character, Cordelia—as an outlaw believer in the Name. The revelation of the book of Hebrews as received by Priscilla is profound, such as I've never experienced it before. This story completely captures the reader. The first chapter is enthralling, hard to leave. Beautiful, mournful writing. Truly, *truly* unforgettable.

Sharon K. Souza, author of *The Color of Sorrow Isn't Blue*

Deeply moved on a personal spiritual level.

Dr. Beth Robinson, Professor of Clinical Mental Health Counseling, Lubbock Christian University; Professor of Child and Adolescent Mental Health Counseling, Texas Tech University Health Sciences Center

I was hooked from the first page. The description of Priscilla walking the streets of Rome, gathering the remains of Christian martyrs, beloved friends and unknown saints, to provide a proper burial, is heart-wrenching. Page one was always in my thoughts as I moved closer and closer to the end, dreading the losses I knew were coming. I was wondering all along how chapter 12 of Hebrews would be woven in. That passage is best understood under hard circumstances and I was dreading it while anticipating it. And when I reached that portion, I felt like I was living it. At the end, I wanted more. What happened to Timothy and Baruch? Priscilla? … It is a wonderful book!

Sandy Denman

A Conspiracy of Breath is a moving account of what it could have looked like for Priscilla to write Hebrews. Long a mystery of the Christian church, Scott paints a highly plausible and engrossing picture of how our beloved New Testament book might have come to be. Scott writes with the detail of a historian and the prose of a scholar, all the while capturing the reader's heart with her gripping accounts of ancient church life in Greco-Roman culture. You will never read Acts or the Epistles, let alone Hebrews, quite the same way after reading *A Conspiracy of Breath*!

Reverend Sarah Ago, Pastor of Compassion, Justice and Missions, Hillside Covenant Church, Walnut Creek, California

I am in awe of the breadth of your knowledge ... of Scripture, of Roman and Jewish customs and life, and of your vast vocabulary! Your words kept moving me forward and at the same time, wanting to stop and just absorb what the words were conveying. It pulled me in to the life of biblical characters I had often pondered. They came alive ... May God bless each word of this book and may all who read it feel that blessing!

Marge Green, author of *A Life With Wings*

In *A Conspiracy of Breath*, Latayne Scott drew me into a world so exquisitely crafted that I felt goat hair between my fingers and the tentmaker's needle-raw fingertips. I could smell dried blood and yeast bread, hear the night sounds and the day's cacophony. I flinched in sync with the characters when danger sparked. But if the book had stopped at authenticity and setting, it would not have had the grip on me that this book does. It changed me, deepened my love for The Breath, and swelled my appreciation for those who sacrificed so much to ensure people like me—millennia later—could turn the parchment pages and read Truth for ourselves. I did not want to leave this story and fear Latayne has spoiled me as a reader. That's how thoroughly it captivated my heart and rearranged my definition of elegant and life-altering storytelling.

Cynthia Ruchti, Golden-Scroll winning author of 20 books, including *A Fragile Hope* and *Song of Silence*

A Conspiracy of Breath is an inspired work that introduces you to the involvement of the Breath of God in the writing of Scripture and instructs you in unknown or little-known facts concerning the Book of Hebrews.... You will discover Priscilla as a courageous and Spirit-sensitive woman whose insight concerning the Old Testament results in ongoing encounters between the reader and the Breath, who yearns for people to know God's determined will to use ordinary women and men in His plan for humanity's redemption.... While biblical scholars have long debated the authorship of the Book of Hebrews, *A Conspiracy of Breath* brings the discussion to a new level. And testimony to the profound influence of this book is that the reader will yearn to revisit the ancient writings and therein find Jesus Christ in the Book of Hebrews, as supreme over all.

LaDonna C. Osborn, D.Min., Osborn Ministries International, Women's International Network, International Gospel Fellowship
www.osborn.org

A Conspiracy of Breath gifts readers with historical characters as authentic, relatable, and relevant as a best friend. Scott's deep knowledge of culture, history, language, and the Bible immerse the reader in Priscilla's life. Scott's voice is lyrical and poetic, drawing the reader from page to page. The plot is compelling and inextricably intertwined with both the character and the culture of 1st century Rome. *A Conspiracy of Breath* is not only a masterpiece in writing, it is a timeless, soul-stirring story that explores the tension of being used as God's instrument while living in a messy, painful world.

Shelly Beach, Author, Speaker, Consultant;
Christy, Selah, Reader's Choice, and Golden Scroll Award Winner

A fresh and engaging approach, which balances vivid imagination and extensive research.

Jeff Miller, editor of *Priscilla Papers*

A Conspiracy of Breath both celebrates and mourns the power and pain of the first-century Church as Jews and Gentiles alike attacked Christians who dared proclaim the Good News. Without the benefit of written New Testament Scriptures and hundreds of years of church history, these hounded followers of Christ lived the truth and preserved it for future generations. Christian readers cannot help but give fervent thanks for the willing sacrifices of Priscilla, her husband Aquila, Paul, Peter, and thousands of unnamed converts to whom we owe so much.

Rachael O. Phillips, award-winning novelist

While *A Conspiracy of Breath* will catch many readers' imaginations because of the idea a woman wrote the Book of Hebrews, I was intrigued by how vividly Dr. Latayne Scott described life in the fledgling Christian church. What would it have been like to live under the constant threat of persecution, dismemberment and the terror of Roman and Jewish authorities? How did believers know what Jesus actually said and did? What stories would people who knew Jesus have shared? … I appreciate how Scott wove the words from Hebrews into a viable story. I smiled at the descriptions of the apostle Peter and swallowed hard at his crucifixion. I walked the Appian Way in my imagination through Scott's description, even as I remembered my own visits to the Catacombs in Rome. This splendid novel will capture readers with its language, its vivid story and its haunting ideas.

Michelle Ule, bestselling novelist and biographer of *Mrs. Oswald Chambers*

Scott writes with a literary sensibility. Those who wonder who wrote the book of Hebrews (it's on my Questions to Ask God When I Get to Heaven list), and those intrigued by the person of Priscilla, will be fascinated with this well-researched, sophisticated read.

Tracy Groot, award-winning author of *Madman* and *The Sentinels of Andersonville*

As one with a weak appetite for most of the fiction turned out these days, I found *A Conspiracy of Breath* to be an utter delight. The writing is a welcomed, refreshing and cerebral gift.... The end result of this fascinating book is the most glorious outcome that any author of any book can achieve: Latayne drove me right back to the Word of God (particularly the book of Hebrews) to further excavate the riches therein, that were endowed to us by the inestimable Holy Breath.

Erin Burch

*A Conspiracy of Brea*th is a profound journey through the corridors of time, back to the days the New Testament sprang forth. Latayne Scott has written a compelling novel inspired by the historical foundation of Scripture. This creative and well researched work causes us to wonder whether Scott's main character, Pricilla, could have written the book of Hebrews. *A Conspiracy of Breath* both captivates and inspires. A must read!

Cindee Martin Morgan, Co-Director of Walter Martin Jude 3 (WMJ3) and Author of *Rescue Me*

A Conspiracy of Breath is a triumph! Latayne Scott writes with amazing detail, creating characters that live and breathe in the reader's imagination. I could not stop reading. Truly the best example of biblical fiction I have ever read. The POV is impeccable, the story world is believable, the story is unforgettable.

Norma Gail, author of *Land of My Dreams,* Winner of the 2016 Bookvana Award for Religious Fiction

Priska brings the Epistle of Hebrews vibrantly to life. Meticulously researched with mind-searing imagery, Dr. Scott's powerful poetry is tucked in the story like hidden treasures.... The humanity, the glorious joy, the tragedy of the early Christ followers are vivid, poignant, and unforgettable. I treasure ... reminders that women did indeed contribute to Holy Scripture, and that the Word is alive.

Texie Susan Gregory, author, *Slender Reeds; Jochebed's Hope*

You will step into an unimaginable period in church history and come back electrified to a new world. Once you've read *A Conspiracy of Breath* you will view the Book of Hebrews—perhaps the whole Bible—and certainly yourself and the world around you with new eyes.

Kathleen Popa, author of *To Dance in the Desert*

With an ache in my throat and longing in my heart, I finished the final pages of *A Conspiracy of Breath*, an exquisite novel that can only be described as divinely inspired. Like her female protagonist, Priska, the author serves as a conduit to bring the message of hope to readers through the age-old device of storytelling. The novel is filled with sensual prose, both lyrical and accessible, and will appeal to scholars as well as laypeople, even backsliders or nonbelievers afraid to open a Bible. Reading this novel was a Holy experience. I have a deeper understanding … a deeper appreciation of what it meant to be a follower of The Way when early Christians were persecuted and killed for believing. The moment I finished the last chapter, I yearned to go back and read the opening chapter again and again and again…

Kathleen M. Rodgers, author of *The Final Salute*, *Johnnie Come Lately*, and *Seven Wings to Glory*

Stunned. Reflecting. Reasoning. Postulating. The presupposition gifted to readers of *A Conspiracy of Breath* is delicious--like the honeyed roll Cordelia made with raisins—especially to the minds and to the hearts of Scripture-loving women. To consider that the Holy Spirit, the Breath, would work through an erudite woman to birth Scripture. Delectable and daring and humbling possibility set during the time and in the places where Christians were devoured by Nero and his lions. Crowning achievement for a genius Christian writer, each word perfectly chosen to mesmerize. Dr. Scott's work offers a salient reminder in a rare virtuoso narrative that we are all vessels of His mercy.

Dr. Lynn K. Wilder, author of *Unveiling Grace: The Story of How We Found Our Way Out of the Mormon Church*

A Conspiracy of Breath clutched my heart in the first pages. Adept at entwining divine moments with common tasks, Latayne engaged my attention long past my allotted time for reading at night. Her mastery of words and lyrical descriptions fleshed out the story to perfection. Priska's world—intense with imagery and emotions—caught me holding my breath at times. She revealed thin places. An awakening to God. A vessel for His use. And she stirred within me a deepening sense of awe for our Maker. Get your hands on a copy of Priska's story, who left me yearning for God, and eager to read more from Latayne C. Scott.

Cathy Messecar, author of *Winning Women Pray Before, During, and After*

In Latayne Scott's moving novel, *A Conspiracy of Breath*, she courageously and masterfully delves into 1st century Middle East … positing that God's Holy Spirit—His Holy Breath—could have worked through a woman, Priscilla from the book of Acts, to produce the book of Hebrews, a Spirit-inspired work whose authorship has confounded scholars for centuries. For those who may doubt whether God's Spirit could have worked through a female jar of clay to construct Hebrews … rethink God's power to work through any and all of us to do His will…. God complicates such narrowness by mandating that, aside from Adam and Eve, humans must come from women's bodies—even the jar of clay that held His blessed Son, Jesus…whether male or female, Jew or Greek, slave or free, all are one in Christ Jesus…. Latayne Scott's novel positions Priscilla as the earthen vessel … through which the Holy Spirit breathed the Holy words recorded in the book of Hebrews…. If you're challenged to rethink that a woman could have written the book of Hebrews, think again…. Why not Priscilla? Why not the book of Hebrews?

Tanya Hart, Associate Professor of History, Frank R. Seaver College, Pepperdine University, Malibu, California

Until I savored Latayne C. Scott's *A Conspiracy of Breath*, I believed the apostle Paul to be the most likely candidate for authorship of the epistle to the Hebrews. Not any more. Scott provides a convincing argument through her use of vivid, page-turning imagery that Priscilla, wife of Aquila, could have very well been this enigmatic New Testament book's inspired author. In the future, I will be reading Hebrews through exquisite new lenses!

Kim K. Francis, author of *His Banner Over Me Is Pursuing Love*

A CONSPIRACY OF BREATH

by

LATAYNE C. SCOTT

TRINITY SOUTHWEST UNIVERSITY PRESS
Albuquerque, New Mexico

TRINITY SOUTHWEST UNIVERSITY PRESS
Albuquerque, NM

ISBN: 978-1-945750-06-9

A Conspiracy of Breath is a Gateway Fiction book
Published by Trinity Southwest University

Books by Scott in TSU's Doorway Documents collection:

Passion, Power, Proxy, Release: Scriptures, Poems, and Devotional Thoughts for Communion and Worship Services by Latayne C. Scott, Ph.D.

The Heart's Door: Hospitality in the Bible by Latayne C. Scott, Ph.D.

Just You, Me and God: A Devotional Guide for Couples Reading through the Bible in One Year by Latayne C. Scott, Ph.D.

The Parables of Jesus by Latayne C. Scott, Ph.D.

Cover design by Noel Green, Park East Inc.

This book is about women, and blood, and words.

I dedicate it to the women of my heritage:
the Huguenots in my ancestry who fled persecution
from France to England to Virginia;

to my grandmothers and aunts and female cousins
and nieces and their children;

to my own beloved mother Rose;

to my daughter-in-law Kimber,

to my female grandchildren Scottlyn, Even, and Judah;

and most of all to my precious daughter Celeste.

ACKNOWLEDGMENTS

This book is the result of almost a decade of research, writing, and development. I am very grateful to all the readers who gave me input, especially Sharon K. Souza and Phil Silvia, editors.

In addition, this book is a patron-funded book. Without the monthly financial sponsorship of the Mountainside Church of Christ, and the great generosity of many, many individual patrons who believe in my work, this book would never have come to be.

"Only God knows the truth
as to who actually wrote this epistle."

Origen (3rd century AD), as quoted by Eusebius, *Ecclesiastical History*

INTRODUCTION

Please, just skip this introduction if you want to. Then, after you've read, you may want to come back for answers to why I wrote it. Or not.

This book came about when several things collided in my life. One was the stored-away memory of the fact that William Barclay—on whom I depended before I began to study Hebrew and *koine* Greek—began his introduction to the Epistle to the Hebrews with the theory that it may have been written by a woman.

The next factor was the situation in my own life nearly a decade ago. I knew a godly man whose family business was failing, and with it the hopes of his employees. I had a good friend with a bizarrely mentally ill spouse. My best friend died still relatively young in a body wracked with muscular dystrophy; divorced against her will, dumped in a nursing home. Other happily married friends endured agonizing deaths from cancer. (Later, my own husband would undergo enjambed illnesses, with unpronounceable names that only textbooks talk about, and those for years and years and years.)

Beginning some time ago, I pondered the statement by Teresa of Avila, who observed with restraint and civility, "If this is how You treat Your friends, no wonder You have so few of them."

And Madeleine L'Engle's letter: "Dear God. I hate You. Love, Madeleine."

(Truly, I never hated Him. I have to say that. But He struck me dumb with what else to say for a while.)

But then ... there was Job, lovely, stunned, innocent Job, scraping the pus off his arms with broken pottery. And Jeremiah, his eked-out writing burned in little strips as he stood in a pit of slime. The patriarchs in portable housing, their situations accidents of their births.

Jonah: "I'm so angry I could die!"

Ezekiel, his joints aching, humiliated as he pantomimes and cooks his dinner on dung.

Daniel with visions that made his eyes ache; an urgent message he can't tell a single soul.

And all the thousands of nameless ones in goatskin tunics, involuntary spelunkers, on the run, their whole lives.

And yet we know about these people because their inexplicable God authorized their biographies, with all their doubts and fears. The Holy Spirit didn't edit these horror stories out of the Record. Preserved them to the syllable, for millennia.

But most unfortunate of all, I think, were the ones who gambled all their lifeblood on a usually second-hand, impossible new story: that a Corpse drained of His blood could live.

Stephen, his chest and cranium caved in with boulders. Paul, shipwrecked or stoned or left for dead, despised with spittle coming out people's mouths when they said his name; with his companion mental sentence of death, an invisible sword at his throat every day. Peter ever in a squabble, or near-death experience, or heartache each dawn.

Everyone in the know, fugitives all, escaping one disaster after another, only to face the wooden fate of all the Carpenter's people: sawed up or nailed to trees or beheaded on stumps.

I thought of those people long ago and realized: The New Testament Christians were the most favored generation of all of earth time, to live on this dirt with God. And yet has God been harder on any other segment of undeserving humankind in history?

What would it have been like, I wondered, to live with the knowledge of the He of Life, and imminent death, both at the same time in your mind: cognitive dissonance of the soul.

But here's the problem I saw. We know what Paul said in his troubles. We know what Jeremiah and Ezekiel and Job thought as they wrestled with cosmic issues of good and evil and the suffering of good people. But though the quotable women of the Bible, Hagar and Mary and Miriam and Hannah and Elizabeth and others, spoke of immediate problems, we have none such correlative insight into how they dealt with long-term suffering. (Well, maybe Naomi. But she settled for a three-word précis renaming herself: Call me Bitter.)

Undoubtedly the Lord heard these women's words, and recorded them, may have even tapped them to say them. And then there's His Pentecost promise: His maidservants and daughters would prophecy. It was specific: all flesh, not just Jewish flesh. Young and old. Men would prophecy. Women would prophecy.

But we have no female Jeremiah or Job, I thought. After

Acts, how many women's words do we have in the Bible at all?

What would it have been like, I wondered, to be a woman to receive words from God, just as the men had, just as the men were promised? To speak them forth like their spiritual mothers Mary and Hannah did, but in a longer form?

My purpose in writing this book was not to convince anyone that Priscilla wrote the Epistle to the Hebrews, but rather to attempt to produce a work of literary merit to show how it might have been for a woman to receive revelation and write Scripture. I also wanted to show how it would play out for such a one—man, woman or child in the first century AD—to deal with the great incongruity between the majesty of their message and the mess of their lives.

We hear that in a letter asking for a winter coat to cover a body that is a ripped tent, the admittedly cheap and temporary clay jar. In a stern quip to two bickering ladies to get it together. In the plaintive, pleading dispatch of the Baptist to his cousin: Clear this up. Are you the One, or am I in this cell waiting for the Next Guy?

My heroine, Priscilla, worries about her best friend's failing health. About the inequalities of a good, plain Jewish boy marrying an educated Roman woman. About what to do with her own past as a patrician—what do you do with those old idols? And who can trust a Gentile with revelation.

About soldiers and a gospel of peace. About births and miscarriages. About sons and daughters. About how to deal with this loose cannon Saul aka Paul. About why the very best people seemed to suffer the most.

Quite surprisingly, as I researched the ancient Roman Empire and struggling lost kingdom of the Jews into which

Jesus was born, I discovered that a Priscilla may not have been suspect as the female recipient of revelation as much as she would have been doubted as a Gentile. Luke, another Gentile, made sure that everyone understood he was just a collator and reporter. He didn't rock the boat with new revelation—and that might tell us a bit about why Hebrews has no autograph to this day.

As a Christian woman, Priscilla would have had rights and honor far above those of Roman women. (And credibility: every time a Rhoda or a Mary Magdalene was dismissed by men, the women were proven right in nearly comical ways.) But some of the infant church's biggest struggles were not gender nor nationality (remember Pentecost?), but religious heritage. Perhaps, I imagine, that would have been her battle; and I have depicted it thusly.

The Holy Spirit (the Greek name can also be translated "Holy Breath," and that is how I name Him) who interacts with Priscilla in my book is not the roaring flames of Pentecost but rather a great, sighing Presence who brings both images and words to this woman's mind. I had originally intended to include every word of the text of the book of Hebrews in this account, but in the end, some of it is paraphrased. After all, part of Hebrews is exposition by the Holy Breath on very unearthly subjects, and part of it is correspondence with more corporeal personalities. Thus, my rendering of Hebrews 5:11-6:12 appears at the end of my book, where the author seemed to me to have inserted instructions and addresses to contemporaries.

When I used to teach biblical exegesis, I repeated what I'd been told: that the epistles of the New Testament were "occasional literature," that is, written for a particular occasion, to a particular group of people, usually addressing a particular set of circumstances. However, I don't see most of Hebrews as instructions for the first century Jewish saints but rather something that, like the Gospel of John, starts out in eternity and shows the interaction of a Divine consciousness with earthly events and people, usually of the distant past.

It's true that in my story, most pericopes of revelation relate to something in Priscilla's life. However, I insist that the situations didn't "cause" the revelations to occur. The revelations didn't arise out of her experiences (and thus cannot be considered purely occasional literature), but come from the Spirit, addressing concepts that weren't time-bound to the first century; rather, eminently generalizable to all readers of the epistle.

I wonder, though, about the convergence of situation to revelation. Did Jesus, who was handed the scroll of Isaiah in the synagogue in Nazareth (Luke 4)—did He unroll it to "find" Himself at the spot to read the passage He quoted, or did He search to "find" it and then preach? In another instance, did He just happen upon a fig tree and teach a lesson about it, or was that fig tree and its fruitless condition divinely prepared for the lesson?

Depicting the exact mechanics of the receiving of revelation was a knotty problem, too. There are many, many ways people received doctrinal messages from God. In a sheet on a rooftop with the explanation later. Fat and skinny cows, hands writing on walls, being picked up and dumped out alongside a riverbed. Warning dreams with angels shaking their fingers at you. Being kicked in the side to awaken someone in a prison. In the temple. On a desolate island. Images sometimes. Other times, exact words and threats if they're not conveyed correctly.

Priscilla, in this book, is overcome, swept away, subsumed by words she dictates to others. The device of an ecstatic trance is all over the Bible. But as the book continues, Priscilla becomes more interactive with the heavenly dispatches, responding to them, pondering them, but always the recipient, crafting but never creating the message.

So yes, I am talking about verbal inspiration; or more accurately, the supervision of Priscilla's mind as she remembered and recorded what was said. This caused two pre-publication reviewers (one of whom said she loved the book otherwise) to refuse to endorse it because they could not countenance the idea that images and exact words came to a person without his or her participation. (My example of Ezekiel 8:3 fell on deaf ears. And then there's John the Revelator and even Paul in a third heaven. Do these people really want to contend that only men can be ecstatic?)

I also imagined that as Priscilla became more accustomed to the precipitous interjections into her life of this Holy Breath, and as she began to share it with others, she might have sent out sections of what would become the letter to the Hebrews. I can't imagine the Gospel writers such as John or Matthew shutting themselves up like Handel to produce a completed document without discussing it with others. My Priscilla doesn't need the approval of others on God's specific messages. But she does crave fellowship as she shares them.

There were other challenges in writing this book. First of all, if there's a timeline of Priscilla's life (especially as it intersected with the lives of Peter and Paul), I couldn't find one. I used a timeline of Paul from a Navarre Study Bible, maps of Paul's missionary journeys, and other documents—all of which I cut up into pieces and posted on a massive four-part room divider screen that I placed around my desk as I wrote. However, if someone finds some blips in my chronology, I beg forgiveness (and welcome correction).

Because of the heavy emphasis in the book of Hebrews

on symbolism, I deliberately used symbols in my own book. Throughout the book, we see Priscilla's beloved friend Cordelia perpetually pregnant with a calcified child in her abdomen. This scientific phenomenon—a *lithopedion* or "stone baby"—has occurred throughout history, but in this case, it is symbolic of something fully formed that would not come to light until after its mother's death.

Some of the poems in this book have appeared previously elsewhere, but always under my personal copyright.

I also deliberately used other literary techniques in this book, most notably a biblical device known as chiasmus. The birth sequence in the book is written in this form. (I know hardly anyone but Bible nerds would care.)

I am aware that someone might object to how a classically-educated Roman young woman would know such Jewish literary devices—indeed, how a Roman woman could write about such things as the furnishings of the ancient tabernacle, or the function of a high priest. (I guess lodging those objections might carry no weight with me, a woman author who co-wrote a book on archaeology without being an archaeologist, and co-wrote another book on Bible marriage customs without researching that subject. In Priscilla's case, I say, if you have the Holy Spirit as your primary author you can write extraordinarily well about extraordinary things completely unknown to you otherwise.)

Bolstering the argument that the author of Hebrews was not a native Hebrew herself, the many Old Testament quotations in the book are from the Septuagint—the Greek version of the Old Testament. Was that Gentile a woman? I admit that I resisted the assertion of others who said there was a "feminine" tone to the authorship; but after I read the epistle repeatedly, with its unique emphasis in chapter 11—

the beating heart of this letter—on women in its "roll call of the faithful"; and when I realized that a mother could identify with the issues of dealing with a son as in chapter 12, I began to give this theory some attention.

However, if you want a more complete explanation of why I believe it is possible, even likely, that a Gentile who was also a woman named Priscilla wrote the book of Hebrews, please see the "Author's Notes" at the end of the book.

In the end, almost nobody believes the book was written by Paul, despite the fact that many publishers of the King James Version of the Bible give its title that authorship.

Paul, a Jew, was called to be the apostle to the Gentiles, not the Hebrews. It seems almost symmetrical that Priscilla, a Gentile, carried the words of God to the Jews.

I wonder if the real controversy may settle out to be, not if Paul had anything to do with the book of Hebrews, but if the author of the book of Hebrews influenced Paul.

My Priscilla, as did almost every Christian throughout history, carried out her God-given tasks anonymously. Think of it: we only have a tiny fraction of names of those who for almost two thousand years held the fort of Christianity. Even more poignant, I wonder if some of what Priscilla taught, like some of the messages of her predecessor Daniel, could have been sealed up against the messenger's understanding; for another time, for other people.

And yet, she listened. And yet, she faithfully wrote.

How it was that we ended up with the book, but not the woman, I don't know.

But on a certain date, in a certain place, the force of irresistible Wind blew into her life, breathed into her mind, exhaled through her mouth, and nothing was ever the same for her, or for us.

A Conspiracy of Breath

Praefatio

I carry the wrapped child in front of me, in the crook of my aching arm, his head above his curled feet, as if he were alive. As if he had ever been born, or named, or drew breath, or saw his dying mother's eyes. As if she had ever seen his.

This is night work, and the mule beside me stumbles in the uneven, now unseen streets that only reveal shadow and character in the light of a doorway, here and there. All around our feet are what people throw away after a spectacle—torn banners, scraps of food, dropped, lost mementos.

Behind me on the creaking wagon are the remains, what I gather after the spectacle: torn things, fallen, saved, remembered.

When I first began this job, I could do it in the daylight. It was a curiosity to those who saw me, a woman who wore the robes of aristocracy and did the work of a ghoul. Most of those who knew me would not meet my eyes, or if they did, it was with a mixture of disgust and wonder. And later, some of them, with triumph, from behind secure windows, around impassable gates.

The first time I gained permission to bring the bodies back from the killing places, Cordelia began to strategize how to borrow a cart and donkey. Many of our friends still lived and had animals then, and she still had a bit of her father's money left.

"We'll need a big wagon," she calculated, counting without knowing it on her crooked knuckles, imagining that the aftereffects of imperial entertainment would necessitate strong beasts of burden, perhaps several trips with several wagons.

She wasn't thinking straight, I should have seen that. There is little left when wild lions are finished with a human being.

I lined the wagon with pieces of old goat-hair tents. People bring me the ripped flaps, snagged beckets, unsalvageable vestibules. When my needle cannot resurrect them, they leave the raveling remnants with me.

At first, I thought my supply was endless and I threw the blood-crusted pieces away. Now I wash them before dawn and let them dry for the next load. My shop, miles away, is where there are no sewers, so my gutters are red ropes each sunrise. My neighbors blink in the sunshine, step over, cross to the other side of the street.

It will take me most of a night-watch to bring the wagon from the circus maximus to the catacombs. I hold my other hand out in front. It is only because I once lived in this neighborhood that I can navigate in darkness so profound I feel blind. The darkness is a covering for me, I must remember that, a veil that keeps me hidden.

In front of me is my childhood home. Though I walk by it often these days, I have not been inside it for decades, since my mother died. I have rounded a corner and candlelight seeps through the doors at the street, the cracked lips shielding the long throat into the house.

In the light, I see my tree.

I named that cypress tree as soon as my child lips could formulate the sounds. My mother, Livia Ocellina, believed it should have a proper Latin name. The tree, she told me, began to grow outside her door the very month she found that I was growing within her. Of course, it never entered her head to name it, only to notice it, and to tell visitors of its coincidence, the tree's and mine. She had the servants water it, and care for it. But when I made its name an issue, she waved it away with those long elegant fingers.

When she finally engaged me on the subject when I was twelve years old, it was with supreme effort, Juno Lucina the light-bringer mother-god, looking down from Olympus.

Was it male or female? she asked me, among her many frittered words. The tree, child, the tree. If it were a male, and of course it was associated with us, it must have the three parts of any patrician name.

I stared at the tree and more heard it than saw it. True, its fronds were the beardlets of adolescent boys, but its sound was that of innocence, of little girls whispering.

Yes, *Arbor puerorum sussorum.* The tree of whispering children. When the breezes came 'round the corner of the villa, its branches murmured secrets and it always had dancing in its voice. It grew with me and though I left childhood, it never ceased its sounds.

Tonight, it looks like a woman bereft, so anguished she holds her hands straight above her head then puts her elbows together and lets her wrists fall behind her bowed head. I have never before known it to be without a whisper. Tonight, it is silent as I pass it by, with Cordelia's child of stone burdening my arm.

Part One:

BEFORE THE BREATH

Chapter One

Though I was born in Rome, my father, a third-son gentleman farmer, moved us to Corinth and then back after his export business failed. He returned with his tail between his legs, so to speak, with my mincing mother and me in tow. That humiliation, I believe, led to his death.

He had been such a braggart—even I, as a young child, recognized it—that failure was all the more bitter, his return not a triumphant standard with rippling banners but a lamprey unnaturally reattaching to the hull of the senatorial family who thought they had shaken free of him.

It was much worse for my mother, Livia Ocellina. She was the only child of one of Rome's wealthiest families which had withered down to her only still-green branch, the daughter of stingy, hook-nosed parents who lived on and on. She couldn't find the Greek myth poignant enough to depict what her husband's social fall had inflicted upon her, though heaven knows she tried. For a while she dressed every day as the eternally-doomed Daphne, complete with laurel leaves in her hair, then as Eurydice of the

Underworld, all in black, and a mercifully short stint as disheveled Achlys of Eternal Night. Finally, the third year back in Rome, with the birth of my sickly brother, she settled with resignation on Hestia of the Hearth.

It was in this phase of our reluctant domesticity that she tried to train me to supervise our single household servant. After my mishaps in the kitchen—all minor, and all involving fire—Mother finally agreed that I was indeed better suited to sewing and linguistics than other tasks. The Greek tutor, hired by my grandparents, instructed my whining brother and me each day. When he left—always shaking his head nearly imperceptibly—my brother would return to his wooden sword and his fuzzy imaginary foes, and I would languish through afternoons in the open doorway of our home's courtyard, reading Homer in the shade of my cypress, watching the street hawkers and the occasional furious chariots that stampeded the pedestrians.

It was on one of those days that Cordelia, my most faithful friend, entered my life. The first time I saw her, she was leaning over a laughing young man twice her size crumpled on his side in a gutter. She punctuated every word with girl-kicks from wiry legs.

"Don't *kick* you *kick* ever *kick* again *kick* treat *kick* that *kick* dog *kick* like *kick* that." Her lower lip stuck out like a drying date. She didn't seem to notice as I approached.

"I suppose those of us who are patrician should consider our appearance," I said stiffly to her and winced as I did it. I sounded just like my mother.

She blew her red hair away from her nose with one blast from the date-lip and glanced down at her expensive dirt-smeared toga. The young man seized the day and scampered off, giggling, around the corner of a building. She winced, too, then gave me an unblinking survey and a caesura of silence that reminded me that my spiked hair, singed in the most recent cooking brazier accident, had not regrown. I must have looked like Helios rising from behind a jagged mountain.

Cordelia shrugged. "It's only my brother."

I nodded gravely. "Well, in that case, it's all right."

We burst into laughter. From that moment on my soul was knitted to her.

When my father contracted a lingering, wasting disease of the gut that had killed his two siblings, my mother's parents relented and sent money so that our family—or more properly, their only male heir, my brother—could remain in our home. All of Rome, it seemed, watched my father's funeral bier carried through the streets, his body propped as if he were reclining at an eternal banquet for which he had regained appetite, followed by my stunned mother as Penelope, almost convincing herself that the funeral and cremation was just a ruse that she could unravel at will.

After his death, I clung to Cordelia. My mother spoke to me only within a lexicon of attire and its necessities: carding, spinning, weaving, stitching, washing, pressing, draping. Our shared cosmology stretched across a loom.

But Cordelia was sanity and health, and I tried to become synoptic with her, to crowd out the other images of my life. I would have made my hair straight and red like hers, adopted her freckled complexion, crawled under the muscles that stretched beneath her collarbones if I could. Each evening we sat beneath the shelter of the cypress that by then was so tall it shaded the whole courtyard. It murmured with us, sharing our young-girl secrets. We carved them into wax writing tablets we carried everywhere, then rubbed them and replaced them and dreamed. I hoped we would never grow up.

Then, two years after my father's death, my mother's

parents relinquished their stern breaths within days of one another. Rome changed. Suddenly, neighbors who once rolled their eyes at my mother were solicitous. Sweetmeats that would have been welcome after my father's death were surfeit in our larder. My mawkish, nearsighted brother became the darling of every society woman who came to pay her respects after the irreparable loss of my grandparents, my wealthy, wealthy grandparents.

My mother put away the widow's weeds of Greek Artemesia and was transformed before our very eyes into her last earthly incarnation, the very-Roman Juno herself, complete with peacock feathers woven into her looped hair like a nimbus, and a nagging rosewater perfume. Before, she had been penurious with words, but now she was extravagant because for the first time in her life people hung on her every aimless circumlocution.

She shielded my pitiful brother as if he were the puerile Mars—which, indeed, she deduced him to be. Though I heard people speculating that she was still a tender limb with fruit ripe for the reaching hand of any number of Rome's men, that limb always swayed just beyond their grasp. As I look back, my mother was infinitely shrewder than any of us ever thought.

I continued to live in different constellations than my mother, populated by Plato (oh, mysterious cave of reality!) and Pindar (how small I was, among the small!) and Herodotus on whose shoulder I rode to faraway lands. Their works—in papyri that were my father's only extant legacy—I both devoured and dreamed. For my mother's part, a daughter who studied logic and rhetoric was, well, rhetorically illogical. I cannot say I blame her for her sighing distances from me. For years, the only touchpoints with the world my body inhabited were Cordelia, and the tactile arts.

To the same degree that I melted into that world, I

became invisible to my mother. For a while I had the secret hope (sparked by my family's sudden prominence) that I might be chosen as a Vestal Virgin, like the daughter of one of our neighbors.

What I saw in my brass mirror—and my mother's fleeting, dismayed glances ratified—was that the virgin part, at least, was assured. Adolescence was unkind to my skin and posture, and I apparently had no counterpart in the pantheon.

Like a poorly-dyed garment laid to dry on a fence, I seeped into the very dun and umber mosaics of the walls and floors of my mother's constantly-redecorated home. By the time I reached 15 years, no one would have recognized either of us.

I would have thought that the cataclysm of my father's death and the later paroxysmal rise to riches would have been the formative events of my early life, before I met Aquila. But two others have that prominence.

The first I recall with shame, because at the time it occurred it seemed to have no impact upon me, and therein lies the shame. My young brother, Publius, died suddenly. I cannot say of what, I have no memory of it nor am I certain if I ever knew.

It was as if he had been only an embarrassing dream from which I awakened to find that my mother had turned into a statue of iron. Neither she nor I shed enough tears to rust her.

Nor did I possess any star that might ascend to replace him. Almost as if I were unaware that he ever existed, I continued my own devolvement into translucence.

The second event was momentous, then and now. My beloved Cordelia who was transiting, as adolescents do, from scatterings to grace, learned of her betrothal to a centurion.

I knew something had happened even before she told me because, approaching my house that day, she whirled twice in the street with her hands in the air. She had forgotten all her market bags. A sly someone now feasted on her fish and olives and onions because Cordelia's dreams had achieved incarnation. Her savior had arrived.

The cypress fluttered with us as we spoke of him, of Caius Clovius, in the days that followed. His family was an old one, his offer of marriage generous. When Cordelia finally met him and saw his confidence like a proud ship that seemed, as she said, to rest on a gentle sea, she drank with him from her parent's finest wine that very day and dreamed even as she was awake. Cordelia was 17 and he was 31 and no one seemed to care. It was indeed his first marriage and his avowed determination that it would be his only union in this life. (I wondered about that …)

His personal name, Cretius, was intrigue itself: He had been to the isle of minotaurs and labyrinths.

My breath drew in suddenly. Could he confirm the myths of my readings? Had he met any real gods, or demigods, or heroes?

Cordelia's now constant swaying slowed as she pondered these new unknowns.

"I don't know. It seems that he has no interest in fables."

I tried to hide my disappointment, sick to consider the possibility that she might be considering marriage to a prosaic man. Nor did my first meeting with him evict that thought.

Even without his greaves and breastplate and helmet (which my imagination supplied and dressed him with), he filled the space between the cypress's lofty bottom limbs and the patterned floor of my courtyard. Beside him Cordelia looked miniature, like a votive statue he had temporarily rested on the floor before picking it up to present to someone. The bottom joints of his thumbs were hams. I could not stop staring at them.

His eyes pleaded for contact and at last I was able to look into them. They were the color of olives stored for the winter. He had absolutely nothing to say and it fell to Cordelia to try to draw him and me—suddenly wordless, me—into a conversation.

Her questions to us each were gentle, designed (I now see) to shine light on intersections. There was of course the favorite topic of Rome, the expansion of the great empire of which he was vanguard. He had served in the army since he was fifteen, and most of that time had been in places that seemed, at least to me, to be exotic. He was willing to describe a Knossian palace—but was steered away from all things gnostic. He spoke with tenderness of his father and his long-dead mother, but I saw a shadow of pain when he said their names. Only when I mentioned a play that Cordelia and I attended did he seem to rise up to meet me, his eyes both anxious and bright and willing, but a glance from Cordelia brought the topic to a close. We ended speaking of the sweetness of the figs we were eating, the stinging richness of the cheese, but I don't think either of them tasted what they ate.

I did not see Cordelia for nearly a week, though one of our servants told me that her mother was parading her through the marketplace fabric shops daily. A few days afterwards, a servant from her household brought me a scrap of leather with a tantalizing message: "Our wedding! Our wedding in ten days! We will come to see you tonight."

I pondered the fact that she had never before announced a visit, and that it coincided with the night of the week that my mother always met some of her many friends for a banquet and gossip. I sent the servants on errands or to the back of the house. When Cordelia and Cretius walked beneath the trembling leaves of my cypress, they seemed *new*.

I struggled with the inexactness of the word at the time but I could not find a better. His soldier eyes had softness. Her soft eyes were resolute. He sat silently as she spoke of the coming nuptials, and she clung to me as I told her how happy I was for them both.

We spoke of details and dishes and times. When they sat, their almost imperceptible leaning toward one another was also a leaning toward me. But once again there were few words as I offered them bread and wine. They looked at each other with a secret look as they ate. They gave each other another look as they finished, a signal look.

Cordelia smoothed her garment with long strokes down her thighs and began to speak.

"Priscilla." She used my diminutive name, the name of tenderness, unlike the clipped *Priska* my mother used.

"We have something to tell you. I am not sure how to start." She looked at Cretius, who held his massive hands in his lap. I noticed a long cut on the back of one of them, and his knuckles were skinned. Even in drills, soldiers get cut, I thought.

"Do you remember the last time we met, when we began to talk about going to the theater?" Cordelia began.

I nodded.

"Cretius told me a story that I want you to hear, about a theater, a different kind of drama …" She pursed her lips and shook her head, not pleased with her own words. She turned to him.

She passed something intangible to him, and Cretius accepted it. I settled back in my chair to listen.

"I have told you that I served in Crete, and that I met many people and saw many unusual things," he began. "But the most unusual person I met was Gaius Rufus Fidelis, like me, a centurion; like me, stationed in outposts for much of his service, most of his early years of service in Jerusalem."

A man of commands not speeches, I thought, as I watched Cretius gathering more words.

"He told me about a crucifixion he once witnessed, one that troubled him for years."

I looked at Cordelia. We would go from talking about nuptials to torture devices? I felt a gag reflex, picturing racked, rotting corpses along a country road. She touched my arm, soothing. Cretius continued.

"I'll just try to tell it the way I heard it from Fidelis. Usually crucifixions are not events, they are processes. A criminal"—here his voice broke—"can die over the eternity of days. But Fidelis was on guard at this particular execution and witnessed something extraordinary. The criminal was a local anarchist, he was told, an insurrectionist who had delusions of royalty; and not only that, people of his own clan hated him for the trouble he had caused, wanted to see him suffer. And suffer he did, but not like others that Fidelis had seen.

"Fidelis helped strip him, but he didn't gamble for his garments because they were too ordinary. Instead, he ripped off the man's loincloth so that everyone could see what all the other soldiers wanted to see, the mutilation those people do to their male children, called circumcision. So, as they pounded the stakes into his wrists and ankles, he wore nothing except his own blood from the flogging the night before and the spit and snot the soldiers had hacked up onto him."

With the crudeness of Cretius' language, he seemed to startle himself, and he looked for approval to Cordelia who to my amazement nodded him on.

"Well, that part wasn't so unusual. That happens a lot

when we crucify Jews. But all people—no matter what their race—die the same way on a cross. They suffocate. The pressure of their outstretched arms squeezes the breath from their lungs and they can only relieve it by rising up on the ankle nails to catch a breath, but that, too, is agonizing. There is no relief, just different kinds of pain, different locations for it, until the lungs fill with fluid and death is welcome.

"But this man had another kind of pain, one that brought the whole regiment who witnessed it to silence, even the most hardened of them. The criminal seemed almost not to notice the nails, so intent he was on something that seemed to hang about ten meters out from his face.

"It was as if, Fidelis said, he was watching something or someone that made him flinch, over and over. Only when his breath became so labored that he had no more air would he seem to rise up on the ankle nails and gasp enough to continue watching, his facial muscles writhing and his eyes blinking as if he were being struck in the face but unable to shut his wide-open eyelids against what he saw. Over and over, it seemed, his cheeks would pale, then become red-streaked, like a blush of shame.

"This went on for hours. The nails and the strangulation of his lungs seemed no more than a distraction to him, if you can imagine that."

I did not want to hear any more about this execution. "So he died, of course."

"Yes."

"As such criminals do, eventually, so let's just …"

"No." Cretius tried to soften his voice. I heard a tear splatter onto the tile. Cordelia was weeping.

"He didn't just die. Fidelis said that every time someone tried to distract him by talking to him or offering him something to drink, he would look away and address them, but just for mere moments, as if he were determined to return to whatever was before him.

"But when he seemed to be sated, wrung out with the searching out of his bloodshot eyes, he shrieked so loudly that it seemed all Jerusalem could hear. And he wasn't speaking to anyone who was there, but to something above his head, beyond, over what he'd been looking at before.

"It was as if at a certain point he just decided to die, and then he did."

We sat in silence. I did not know how to respond, what they expected from me.

"Tell her the rest, Cretius." Cordelia was whispering.

"This memory tortured Fidelis for years. Right after the crucifixion his regiment was sent to Egypt where he worked in a garrison and was promoted to centurion. But could never get that picture of the man out of his mind. It wasn't until he was ordered to Crete that I met him and met another man who explained to us what happened that day in Jerusalem.

"I had just become a centurion, and so was privileged for the first time to take my meals with the other centurions and had heard many of Fidelis's fireside tales of the black men and women who cut themselves for the beauty of a nubbled skin-garment of scars, of Egyptian priests with jackal-head masks, of tombs so ancient no one remembers whom they enclose.

"But under all his stories was a kind of tension, and he would often ask offhandedly of the new officers if they knew a story about an unusual crucifixion in Jerusalem, one that the victim survived. He asked me about that, and I laughed, because no one survives a crucifixion.

"Fidelis was near the time where he would lay down his sword and return to his family's land in Ephesus. He never married and wanted, he said, to live out his days with his only knife the one he used to cut his meat at supper. While we were still in Crete he took a holiday in Knossos and met a man who was speaking in the streets there, a man who to Fidelis's amazement knew about the crucifixion he had been asking about for years."

I sat forward. I have always loved a good story.

"This man, whose name was Mark, knew the criminal's name. Not only that, he corrected something Fidelis said—the man did indeed die, but he came to life again after three days."

I was fascinated. It sounded like the fulfillment of all my aspirations—to know about a legend that might be true. Cordelia and Cretius seemed surprised that I was not objecting, but waving him on to finish the story.

"When Fidelis came back from meeting in Knossos with this Mark, Fidelis was different."

"What do you mean, different?" I blurted.

"I don't know. It wasn't that he was younger, but he moved as if he were. He seemed … new."

I was startled by the word. Fidelis must have looked like what I saw before me.

"Fidelis had become a follower of the man who was executed and then came alive."

"Why would anyone want to be a follower of a criminal that everyone hated?" I asked. "Did he go on to accomplish something extraordinary? Where is he now?"

Cordelia and Cretius looked at each other before he answered.

"He's in heaven. He is the son of God."

"So was my brother," I retorted. "And in spite of that, I can assure you that when he died, he stayed dead."

Cretius looked again at his hands, rubbing them. "Not only did this executed man, Jesus, come back to life, Mark saw him alive. He swore to Fidelis that it was true. He walked and talked and ate with him. But it wasn't the brief time, forty days I think it was, that Jesus lived after his resurrection that convinced Fidelis to," he hesitated, looking for the words, "to, swear allegiance to Jesus."

The mosaics under my feet seemed to undulate. "First of all," I asked, "do you have any idea of what you're saying? That Fidelis became a traitor to Rome?"

"It's a different kind of government," he said. "It's not a competition. And after I met Mark and heard his story, I swore the same allegiance."

I threw up my hands. I wasn't even sure it was safe to have this man in my house. Thank goodness, my mother was gone and the servants couldn't hear.

"So, what did this Mark tell Fidelis, and you, that convinced you to do such a thing?"

"He told us what Jesus saw, while he was being crucified. What he saw that was able to take his attention away from the torture stake. The theaters he saw."

"Theaters?"

"Yes. He explained to Fidelis that when Jesus hung there, what made him flinch and blanch and flush and gasp was that he was looking at millions of scenes in millions of theaters, despicable deeds, deeds of shame and horror. And as Jesus watched those scenes it wasn't just as audience but as if he were himself participating in those deeds, and feeling the shame and regret; lost lifetimes and irretrievable moments of each single willful act. And knowing that this was not just an abstraction of those horrible acts, but he *became* the acts. The realization that he truly was responsible for them, that he had committed every one of those crimes and deserved eternal ruin and hopelessness."

I felt a reeling deep in my stomach. I thought of my brother and I flushed with shame, for sometimes I could not recall his name, the name of an innocuous human being who had lived in my home and I had ignored at best and despised always. I beheld him before the eyes of my mind in my own private theater.

I felt hot tears that I refused to shed. "So how could what this Jesus experienced cause you to want to risk what he risked?"

"Because, as Mark explained, what he saw in some of those theaters was what I have done. And Jesus experienced it and became responsible for it as if he had done it personally." Cretius paused. "Each slave I abused. Every terrified woman whose husband I put a sword into. Each child I left orphaned, or caused to starve. Each son and brother and father *I* nailed to a cross."

I looked at him in horror. "And what good did that do? That Jesus would—as if anyone could—appropriate your very life?"

"We believe that he is God's son. That the great scales of justice were balanced with what he did, a penalty he didn't earn but paid anyway. That we are saved, and that you can be too." Cordelia reached, appealing.

I felt wrath, fire-anger, fear-rage.

"You are lost to me." Even I was startled by my bitten-off words in the stillness of the courtyard. "Not saved, lost to a foreigner. A dead foreigner. Do you not know—have you forgotten? That Rome's only safety, its only protection are the gods. And if they do not strike those who forget them, their citizens will.

"I shall come to your nuptials, Cordelia. But you, Cretius, are putting the dearest person in my life in mortal danger, and I will not forgive you for that."

I did not know, the day I saw the sacrifice of the heifer at Cordelia's home to celebrate her wedding, that it was a portent of much more blood to come. Cretius was assigned to a garrison away from Rome and her parents' great wedding gift was that they would pay for his new wife's trip to accompany him and her lodgings close by, he announced to all the guests at the nuptials.

I did not know that when I saw Cretius put a ring on her finger and carry her across a threshold that I would never see him again.

Chapter Two

I know now that it was dead men who brought me to Aquila, and I am not sure how to think about that, even now.

A year after Cordelia and Cretius left, one morning in the marketplace I heard the sound of a child-like screaming that drew my eyes away from the marred figs and pears on which I was considering granting the mercy of adoption.

Across the way, three men held a pig while another attempted, and finally succeeded in, slitting its throat. The slaughter-sound pulsed through the air like the blood from its neck and then stopped in mid-note. I walked nearer. I could not take my eyes off the clouding irises, the suddenly-prim hooves, the ruddy flesh that slowly drained to waxen.

I began to tremble, veering on cramped, numbed feet into bolts of rough cloth stacked fortress-like against a cart.

I knew the sensation of colorlessness, lived as emptied-out as the veins of the hapless animal. I began to sob into my elbow, my forearms crossed and fingers of one hand weaving themselves into my hair.

One of the bolts fell over onto me and enveloped my shoulders and neck and that feeling, too, was familiar: being enveloped and made invisible by my surroundings. I believe I might have stayed there for hours insensate of the din of the market and its denizen had not one of them—the owner of the cloth, in fact—sat down beside me, wordless but present, for what must have been nearly an hour.

When I became conscious of his lingering presence I quieted myself, hoping that he would see the quality of my clothing as compared to his crude cloth scratching my cheeks, and my embarrassment, and would leave me. He did not. As I began to stir, he stood and brushed the dirt from the backs of his thighs and then with thick index fingers and thumbs took the now-tangled cloth from my shoulders.

When I looked into his face my revulsion must have shown because the brightness of his eyes went as dull as those of the butchered animal. When he turned in profile—lingering, it seemed to me, so that I could look—his remarkable nose came more clearly into view, flaccid as a piece of raw meat on a skewer, and nearly as red.

Two giggling women came around the corner from his cart, bumping their hips against one another. One let her hand travel over the rivulet of an outstretched piece of fabric and turned to see it better, then met the merchant's eyes.

She was my mirror: first staring and then blinking and blushing, withdrawing her hand as if she had sent it afloat onto the river of Phlegethon in Hades and could snatch it from its flames. Her friend stood openmouthed.

"Fabric, ladies?"

The two shook their heads vigorously and turned to leave.

"It's my nose, isn't it? You don't want to buy my fabric

because of how I look." His voice was low, injured.

"Oh, no," the first woman said. "In fact, I was just … thinking how … pretty this piece was."

"Yes," said her friend. "We both like it, don't we?" They both bobbed their heads up and down again, this time looking with wide eyes at each other. "How much is it?"

I was a seamstress and I would have wagered my best tunic that neither of them was; and yet, they paid twice the price for the nubbly cloth—the whole bolt of it—and hurried off.

He was counting the coins. Inside his closed mouth, his tongue cleaned his own top corner teeth, searching out errant scraps of food perhaps. Then he grimaced and his long tongue licked his front teeth, like a cat cleaning its paw. With a start, he seemed to remember I was there and hastily put the money into a pouch.

"What are you looking at?"

I inclined my head and shrugged, then got to my feet.

"Wait a minute." His voice was softer. "Since you wrapped yourself in my best fabric for a good part of the morning, the least you can do is tell me, are you afraid of blood? Tell me why you nearly fainted watching that pig die."

"It wasn't the pig, exactly."

"What was it, then, exactly?" His voice mocked mine.

I looked at him directly and told the truth.

"I felt like someone had let my blood and emptied me."

He looked down, considering.

"And what has made you feel this way?"

I wondered if his nose had ever had a real conversation with anyone.

"My best friend has moved across the world. And what's more, she and her husband are probably going to die because they have abandoned all the great gods, all the

Roman ways …" I felt a sob in my clavicle and swallowed it away. "And she believes that some corpse is her god."

I looked up to see him nodding.

"So, they are followers of that Christos. I'm just surprised that they told you about him. That's not a very safe name to be using in some quarters."

I noticed that his voice had become very soft, and I matched it.

"So, are you one of them, too?"

His scoff was sudden—and flabby. The nose.

"Not at all. Well, not really."

I raised my eyebrows and he looked away.

"Some of my customers are. And they talk to me about … things, about him. Philosophy."

"And you think it's outrageous too."

"They're good people. It's just that this religion requires things that I don't want to give up."

I tapped the side of my head and widened my eyes, then straightened my garments and turned to go.

"Oh, so you're leaving?"

"Yes, I've been gone too long."

"It's because of my nose, isn't it?"

I jerked to respond then saw the shadow of a smile on his lips.

"I'm getting used to it," I said as I walked away, and I heard his laughter follow me through the rows of the marketplace, even over the clamor of the other merchants, as if it were the tail of one of his remnants, clinging to my hem.

When I returned home a letter awaited me: my first from Cordelia since she left. I took it into the street and sat under the whispering tree for a long time before I unfolded it.

Cordelia, wife of Cretius to my dear Priscilla. Grace and peace to you.

Cretius has been assigned to the garrison on Cyprus, in the city of Salamis. Oh, think of it, dear Priscilla—does not even the idea of living on an isle of the sea sound like the legends we loved? I live above the bay, in the only house with a blue door atop the crest of the rim of land. There are wonderful trees here and sometimes I hear your name when their branches whisper to one another.

I am gloriously happy. There is a small community of believers here and Cretius and I feel we have a dual citizenship—as Romans and also of a higher, more wondrous place.

I know that we parted on such bittersweet terms. I want you to come, to be my sister, and to help me. I have wonderful news. Cretius and I will be parents in the spring. Will you not come?

I bid you farewell in the name of Him in whom we trust.

I sat under our tree, weeping, the parchment crumbled at my feet.

"May I help?"

One of my mother's ubiquitous, overworked personal maids stood near me. I did not know how long she had been watching. She looked with tender eyes at me.

"Oh, just a sad letter."

She stood respectfully.

"My friend Cordelia—you remember her of course—is living on an island, oh, somewhere, I don't know where, and is going to have a baby."

The maid raised her eyebrows. "That is sad news?"

"She's lost her mind. She's taken up some strange religion and I can't even think of how to write her back."

"What strange religion?"

"Oh, that Christos craziness. Resurrections. Jewish-ness." I found myself spitting the first letters of the word from the back of my palate.

Again, she stood silent.

"And it's the second time today I've heard about it. Even a fabric merchant was talking about them. They're everywhere. They're going to take over. This is a real threat to Romanness." I realized how silly I was sounding. "I mean, I'm all for religions. Look, I live with Juno."

I could see that she was trying not to smile.

"Perhaps all religions are unreasonable," she said slowly. "After all, do they not require us to believe in things that could not otherwise be true?"

I looked at her. I realized to my shame that I was not sure of her name.

"But this one's crazier than most," I reasoned with her. "It's not based on things far in the honorable, foggy past. It requires belief in a man who was alive just a few years ago—and then dead—and now supposedly alive again. What possible use is that? No heroic battles. No possibility of bribing with sacrifices. No charms and magic powers."

"I wouldn't be so sure about the magic powers part." The maid—ah, yes, her name was Miriam—looked from side to side on the street. "I've seen some of them."

"So, you're one of the followers?"

Her fear put a white ring all around her brown eyes. She did not speak.

"So, who does he help, this Christos? You? You don't even have your freedom and probably never will."

I realized the edge of my words. "Look, I won't tell anyone. Just answer me one question. Why believe?"

I could barely hear her voice.

"Tomorrow is what we call the Lord's day. Your mother allows me to go and worship—of course she has no idea whom. She thinks I go to one of the temples. Will you go with me?"

"Of course not."

She looked at the ground. I did not think she was breathing.

"This fabric merchant, I think I know the one you spoke

of, he comes sometimes," she whispered.

"He's one of them? One of you? The man with the nose?"

She sighed. "Mathos. No, he has not yet claimed the Name of Christos. He wants to believe. But he knows that he can't keep taking advantage of people if he does. I think he loves embarrassing and cheating people—and doesn't see it as anything wrong."

I thought about it for a moment. It did seem like an apt compensation for such a prodigious nose.

I stood looking out on the street where rotting vegetables and the heavy sordid smell of meat gone bad tickled my throat with a gagging. Suddenly my own nostrils seemed so full of the hot thickness of the air of Rome—its people, its tangled legends—that I felt my chest would never accept such air to its fullness again. Behind me, I felt the weight of hundreds of gods that had their life in my mother's mind if nowhere else. I turned to Miriam and grasped her tunic.

"I can make a lot of trouble for you."

She nodded, mute and slack.

"I want you to find someone who will get me to Cyprus. I will pay whatever it takes. But no one must know. Your secret for mine."

A week later, the turgid black air of Rome seemed strapped to my chest as I approached what looked like a bundled-up old woman who had appeared on the corner near our house at a time arranged by Miriam. My guide hobbled toward me, saying nothing, then turned and with syncopated steps led us through street after street to the dark harbor. At last we stood beside the swaying hull of an Alexandrian freighter whose outline faded into the moonless sky, the peaceless sea. Close to our heads, a roughly-painted *udjat* eye of Horus promised protection. I shuddered, knowing that Egyptians painted those on the sides of their sarcophagi too.

I wondered if the Christos of Cordelia could forgive a daughter who stole from her mother for ship fare. The waves lapped at the ship's bow and I thought of the stories of the Skylla and Charbdis, of sea monsters and the precipitous edge of the world.

I turned to press upon my guide some coins and to take my bundle of possessions but instead felt my forearms grasped by strong fingers that pushed me along, ahead, onto the gangplank, into the crowded ship.

If Rome's ethers had seemed insufferable on land, they were condensed within the ship's narrow entrails. Passengers were an afterthought, it seemed, to be wedged between bales and barrels and casks. My guide turned to me and removed a head covering that showed me grizzled hair and a beard. I had been following an elderly man all this time.

"You are my daughter, Hestia." He spoke in an urgent whisper.

I nodded, understanding the subterfuge. "But why didn't you tell me before?"

"Because you wouldn't have let me come with you onto the ship. And it is not safe to travel alone. And because you trust no one."

With that he put our bags into the hammocks in the slit of the sleeping quarters and went upstairs. I did not see him again until morning, and then we were on the open sea.

And I, I was sick.

There were only ten passengers on the ship. Seven were members of a rich family, I learned, exiled by our Tiberius Claudius Caesar Augustus Germanicus. This I learned from a chance remark by one of the crew members, though I never learned why they were exiled. The family had come from the northern provinces, judging from their accents; and they would not speak to anyone else, even the crew members, except through a spokesman whom I thought to be the oldest brother. The rest of us they treated as if we were invisible.

My traveling companion identified himself simply as Nicanor. It was not difficult to relate to him as a father, because he brought me all my food and drink and never left me alone after that first night. By the time the first week had passed I had not the strength to leave my bunk and could feel the hard ridges of my ribcage beneath my breasts when I passed my hands to my convulsing abdomen.

The seas were cyclical, eternal barrages of motion, and time had no meaning. Sometimes I rolled and heaved, a sister to the unseen waves, on my bunk; other times I felt like knucklebones rattling in a metal cup, my insides barely contained by my taut skin.

I dreamed of this Christos, riding high and triumphant on a ship that passed us in twilight, and when I called to him, he looked only ahead. I dreamed of Cordelia, a baby in the crook of her arm, and the sword of Cretius across her lap. I dreamed of the Nyads, swarming beneath the ship like eels.

Sometimes I heard Nicanor speaking to someone else, whose name I learned to be Quinta. Apparently, she was also a convert to what Nicanor called the Way. As I began to open my eyes again some days, I saw that her voice belonged to a rangy-boned woman whose eyes were desperate. Because of her well-patched clothing and callused hands and some whispered words, I perceived that my passage money had covered both her ticket as well as that of Nicanor. I didn't care and do not to this day.

As my strength returned I began to listen as the passengers spoke to each other. Nicanor had a scroll from which he read some of the sayings of this Christos, translating them from the *koine* Greek for his companion. Quinta, though, would listen respectfully and turned every conversation to one urgent subject only, a theme with infinite variations but still a cloth of only one hue.

"Will I recognize my husband in the heaven?" she would ask. "Will he know me? How will we find each other? Are there promises about how we will look? Will our bodies be the same? What about the scars? In the scroll, are there answers? What did the Christos say about it? With so many saved ones, how will they look for their loved ones? Will we be young or old? We did not meet when we were young. Who knows these things? Who can tell me these things?

"And will he," here she would begin to cry, "will he still love me? Will we remember our love?"

When I was able to sit up, I listened to the words on the scroll. Late on the twentieth day aboard the ship, I asked to hold the scroll and, to Nicanor's obvious surprise, began to read some of its *koine* Greek words aloud.

I am an old woman now, and I can say with truth that I have never been ravished as I was by those words.

On the roiling surface of the Mare Nostrum the planks of that ship became a stage on which I, with unflinching gaze, became the sole audience to the theatre of my own pettiness, arrogance, self-focus and deceits; the stage the exact shape, the place of the skull. I could hardly bear the thought of what I had imputed to a man I had never met.

By the time we neared the coast of Cyprus, I had learned many things.

I learned that there is no idea as intimate as that of blood on beloved skin.

I learned that death on a cross is a martyrdom, but that resurrection is a gospel.

I learned that if there is such a thing as a resurrection,

nothing else matters.

I learned that if there is no such thing as a resurrection, nothing else matters.

Thus, I came to know this Christos and welcomed him as driver and lover of my soul. The vast sea was our common sepulcher, our lives renascent together.

The last night on the ship, I dreamed of the old heroes and gods. I saw them one by one fade like shadows into the glare of a sandstone cliff. I looked around for them and they were no more. There was only the cliff, and sand stretching without horizon in every direction.

Atop the crest of the cliff was a standard, and on it was a long, swaying, gauze-like scarf. At first I thought the wind caused its motion. Then I realized that it caused the wind.

Chapter Three

We arrived in Salamis at dawn.

I went alone to the house of Cordelia, the utterly silent house of Cordelia. I found her sitting in a garden beneath a trellis, slats of light on her face. She was holding grapes in her hands. Some had fallen through her fingers and lay on the pavement beneath her chair, but she did not seem to notice.

It was summer, long past the time of her baby's birthing date, yet her stomach rested on her thighs. She looked up at me with eyes grown ripe with tears, and she did not need to tell me that Cretius was dead.

She did not rise to meet me, and I sat down beside her. Far in the distance, a sinuous line of clouds stretched across the horizon, obscuring some distant mountaintop, looking like a snake which had swallowed the peak and in a feather-edged lump was digesting it. Neither of us spoke until the sun was high and hot and the clouds consumed by it. And eternities passed between each of our speakings.

"They said it was an accident but I know that it was not." Her voice was delustered.

I did not know how to begin with my questions.

"When?"

"Two weeks ago."

"How, Cordelia?"

"He was stoned. A fall from a rocky slope, they said, on horseback." She nodded her head toward the mountain we had been facing, and I was speechless, ashamed for having looked at it so long, without knowing.

"We both knew it could come to this. I had hoped when he was transferred here that the pressure would stop, or at least ease. But I knew he would not deny the Name."

I remembered the many fresh wounds on the hands and arms of Cretius that first night I met him. From parrying, not thrusting.

"There was protection, we thought, because he was an officer. But he had officers above him. Cassius ..."

She sat staring again at the mountain.

"And when someone asked Cassius his general about the accident, do you know what he said?"

I waited.

"'There's one thing you need to remember about a horse,' he said. 'A horse can *kill* you.'"

Above us in the air, a pair of hawks careered on an unseen wind.

Cordelia brushed her hand indolently across the knoll of her abdomen. "And then there was my unbirthed child."

Once more I was speechless. Many minutes passed before she spoke again.

"When my time came, it was late winter. The baby did not want to wait until spring. My pains began and Cretius and I were so happy.

"At first the surges were disorganized, I thought, like a

bunch of boys playing storm the city. But then they lined themselves up, like phalanxes in tight rows, determined and faceless and implacable. Again they came. And again.

"Even when the surges took my voice away and only the women were there, I did not cry. But a day, and a night, and a day went by.

"One by one,"—here, Cordelia's hands flitted away the women—"they all went outside the room and it was only Cretius, come back to comfort me. The baby turned stiff within me."

Cordelia's eyes were dry, scanning the wall before her as if it held a secret.

"And he—or she—is there still."

For all my learning, I knew nothing of the ways of birth. I could say nothing.

For the first time, Cordelia let me embrace her. The child was insistent, unyielding between us. So she sagged, her back rounded with yearning and loss, into my arms, and wept until the trellis cast stalking shadows into the furthest wall of her garden.

The days that followed were days of change and fear. Nicanor appeared at the door of Cordelia's home the next morning, his eyes downcast. I realized when he finally looked into my eyes that he had known about the death of Cretius, and the child, before he let me come alone to Cordelia's home.

All Salamis knew of the widow who was a perpetual mother. The Cyprian women said she was cursed. Her rented house was suddenly no longer available, so Nicanor came to take us to the home of a middle-aged Greek woman named Akantha: like ourselves, a convert to the Way, like Cordelia, a military widow. When we arrived at her home, all the earthly possessions of us two women on one cart Nicanor pulled behind him, our time of wordless communion came to an end.

I cannot weary myself with recalling the endless circuitous words of Akantha. All conversations with her were as unbalanced as a man with toes on only one foot. She would describe people, situations, histories in numbing detail, and when someone would try to restate what she was saying so as to move on to another topic, she would say, "Well, no, it's not exactly like that," and would launch again, this time mining all the particulars so as to extract other nuances of each aspect that no one cared about in the first place.

Fortunately, Akantha's great heart outweighed her many words. She and her husband had invested in a herd of milk cows before his death, and she used her time and resources to care for the cattle, humbling herself to become a kind of shepherd woman of the cattle kingdom. Through the sale of milk and meat and hides, she provided for many others in the community of believers in Christos there in Salamis.

"My service to others is the rent I pay for the space I occupy on earth," she often said, and when a recipient would respond, she would shake her head. "No, actually, if you think about the philosophy of service, it occurs to me that …"

Nicanor and other men who were believers watched after us. Cordelia, who resisted all her mother's efforts at teaching her tomboyish daughter sewing and most other household arts, was ill-equipped to be a self-supporting widow. But she was a good cook; and between her culinary support, my burgeoning weaving business (first financed, I am sorry to say, with a number of my mother's faience brooches which she said came from the breast of the mummy of an Egyptian princess, sold quickly before I ascertained the commandments against theft I had suspected) and Akantha's dairy, we three supported ourselves with no contributions from the others, although they helped us sell our wares in the market.

There was a sizeable Jewish component in the city of Salamis, a fact I found both odd and comforting, for it boded well for the tolerance of the rest of us. Its synagogue often hosted scholars and thinkers from faraway places, and as soon as I learned this, my heart yearned, homesick for the language of books.

Most of the believers in the Way in Salamis had come, one person, one family at a time, as refugees from an increasingly-inhospitable Jerusalem. Some brought seeds of the plants of their homelands and mourned when they withered in the Cyprian soil. Others spoke haltingly of their struggles with a spiritually-indentured life. Others seemed to ignore it in the marketplace and byways, bringing out their faith once a week like something purloined that could be shared only with fellow thieves.

But one thing equalized us all: each Lord's day we sat in stunned intimacy as we ate the flesh of this Christos, trembled at the drops of his blood on our tongues.

Among them they had a few scrolls like that of Nicanor, from which they read at the fellowship meals. I craved the sayings of Christos which my ears devoured, my mind digested, and whose razor edge both put inscription and lesion onto my heart.

Many of us were women, a few widows, but many wives and daughters as well. Though my mother had often thanked all her gods for the fact that Roman women had freedom unknown in the rest of the civilized world, in contrast the Jewish women, even those from wealthy families, seemed to my proud young eyes to be backward and unlearned. In my visits to the synagogue my interest in philosophical discussion was met with degrees of disdain that ranged from condescension to thinly-veiled hostility from the men with swaying tendrils of forelocks, perhaps because we had no common language. My best efforts to decipher the mysteries of the three-legged vowelless Hebrew language left me frustrated and even more hungry for its content. Apparently, the women could not read Hebrew and the men had no interest in teaching a Gentile woman.

Even in the fellowship meetings of those who followed Christos I felt of a class lower than even the least-educated and patrician. It was not because I was a woman but—like many other converts to the Way—because I was not Jewish.

After I was in Salamis for three months I began to wonder if my life would forever continue on this way, stitching and measuring, as if my life were fabric I was cutting off from a shrinking bolt, piece by piece, day by day.

Everything began to change the day that a group, including a woman named Havah, came from Jerusalem to Salamis. To say that she arrived is too mild—her first entrance into our Lord's day meal was one of flourishes, salutes, and subsequent crashes of a lamp and a bowl in the room. Even in the rare instances that the slight wiry-haired woman stood still, there was a wake of sighs behind her, both of admiration and relief.

"I am an eyewitness of the rising of the Lord Jesus," she introduced herself, her eyes wide with appeal to the room she surveyed. She met the eyes of each person there before she went on. "I saw him risen, saw his scars, saw his works."

Akantha, Cordelia, even Nicanor and his friends like me knew the Christos stories, but no one of us met him. *This woman saw.* And to my surprise, she pointed to us three women as she continued.

"Look how he has honored us! It was women who were the first witnesses of his rising—and they were not believed. He entrusted them. You have heard the stories." She pointed to the small stack of scrolls that lay on a blanket in the corner. "But it was women who saw before anyone else. They witnessed before anyone else. We are the heralds of all. And we stay faithful."

I must confess that I felt swamped by her sheer, barely-contained motion—that of a sack of cats in a pond—and was repelled even by her frankness, by the smell of earth that rose from her clothes.

But I sniffed my own sleeve, and there was garlic, and there was hay.

"This is the day the believers in Salamis must turn their purpose from being just a refuge to each other, from hiding out here on Cyprus," she said forcefully. "To being heralds, too. You can go to our Jewish brothers and sisters with the good news. Look at the gift I have brought you."

With difficulty Havah, aided by a tall passive-faced man with straight sidelocks and heavy lank hair, hefted a fabric-wrapped bundle to the table that Akantha wisely and discretely emptied of all its vessels. It was as big as a Torah—in fact I thought it must be a Torah—but to my delight, when Havah unrolled it, I could read the *koine* Greek. The Old Law in a language I could read! As I leaned to see, my legs seemed to lose their strength.

I began to read aloud, unconscious of the fact that the room grew still:

Now it came to pass in the thirtieth year, in the fourth month, on the fifth of the month, as I was among the captives by the river Chebar, the heavens were opened, and I saw visions of God. On the fifth of the month, (it was the fifth year of king Jehoiachin's captivity,) the word of Jehovah came expressly unto Ezekiel the priest, the son of Buzi, in the land of the Chaldeans by the river Chebar; and the hand of Jehovah was there upon him.

I looked around. Nicanor was nodding.

"Can this be? How could the heavens open? When did

this happen?" I asked. This was not the words of the Christos, not his time, yet it spoke with his same accent, like a family member or a neighbor.

"Read on," said Nicanor.

And I looked, and behold, a stormy wind came out of the north, a great cloud—

And the cloud raptured me within it.

and a fire infolding itself—

And I was set ablaze.

and a brightness was about it, and out of the midst thereof as the look of glowing brass, out of the midst of the fire.

And my eyes became greedy.

Also out of the midst thereof, the likeness of four living creatures. And this was their appearance: they had the likeness of a man.

And every one had four faces, and every one of them had four wings. And their feet were straight feet; and the sole of their feet was like the sole of a calf's foot; and they sparkled as the look of burnished brass. And they had the hands of a man under their wings on their four sides; and they four had their faces and their wings: their wings were joined one to another; they turned not when they went; they went every one straight forward.

The images overlaid themselves on me.

And the likeness of their faces was the face of a man; and they four had the face of a lion on the right side; and they four had the face of an ox on the left side; they four had also the face of an eagle.

No matter which way my mind turned I could not hold these visages all before me at once.

And their faces and their wings were parted above; two wings of every one were joined one to another, and two covered their bodies.

And what whispered within me groaned, *holy*.

And they went every one straight forward: whither the Spirit was to go, they went; they turned not when they went.

And those words seized me, that Spirit conscripted me, and I felt I must put the scroll down.

The room was vacant of sound. I could hear only my heartbeat in my ears.

I sat down. My eyes came back to focus as if accustoming themselves to a dark room on a day of glare. Havah's face was bright and she was nodding. All my friends sat stunned and uneasy, each face an abacus in motion, calculating rigors and risks.

The man with the lank hair stood and crossed the room. He took one of my hands and turned it palm up and looked intently at the stubble of needle pricks on my fingers.

"I am Aquila of Pontus," he said. His flecked eyes were the colors of grape harvest and he smelled of leather and wax. He placed my hand gently onto my leg and then turned his scarred fingertips up for me to see. Then he walked back across the room. He picked up the Old Covenant scriptures written in our common Greek—what a wonder! what a treasure!—and swaddled them like a child. With a wordless assent from Havah's eyes he brought them to me, standing them against the leg of my stool.

"Prepare the others," he said. Then he left the room, into the night, followed by Havah and the other newcomers.

I did not see any of them again for two months. During that time our group of believers became a structure, of rocks so perfectly chased as to need no mortar, housing a treasure and that treasure was seeing the Christos in those Greek words. We read it all, that is, I read it all to them, from Genesis to Malachi and found him there:

serpent crusher
the root and branch
father and child
stone and fountain
servant and ruler
lion and lamb …

And now there was a New Covenant and there were people living, even now alive, who had known him both as Bethlehem baby, and criminal outside the walls.

Daily, each stitch I took, counted time until each evening I could read the ancient words that said he would come. I mourned that I had walked around on the same earth at the same time that he did and never met him and now he was irretrievably gone. He became mine through words. I could not, I was convinced, have loved him more if I had seen his flesh.

Did we take for granted all the ways that those words were confirmed? I heard almost daily of hands restored, demons cast out of shuddering victims, people rising from hopeless beds. But it was by no means universal. Late in the fall, to our sorrow, our sister Quinta became very ill when a wound on her foot poisoned her blood. All her eternal questions were finally answered one gold and crimson evening.

"We'll see her again," Nicanor told me. "We'll see her again," the others reassured each other.

Outside of Cordelia's omnipresent double sadness—and she, one of the notable unhealed as well—I had never seen how these followers of Christos reacted when one of their own died. I don't know if I expected the kind of pomp that had accompanied my father's funeral, but in the simplicity and grace of the commitment of the body of Quinta to a tomb I was surprised to discover that this was a religion that robbed death of its solemnity.

However, newcomers from Jerusalem brought word of the suffering of other Way-followers there. With this came the forming of my realization that, in deciding to follow and suffer for this Christos, a new dynamic takes shape. Without fail, we create a vortex in which those who company with us—whether involved by choice or by chance—are sucked toward the center of our decisions, and all are changed forever.

As winter rains came to the dry grasses of Cyprus, Havah and Aquila and the others returned. We broke bread with them and discussed if any of us should go to Jerusalem: a council of words and worries and schemes. Havah spoke of a man named Paul who would come soon, one who had seen the Christos even after he returned to heaven; and no one could answer my questions about this conundrum except to say that there was a road, and a day, and a time.

Our meeting stretched far into the night. Afterwards I rose to go home with Akantha and Cordelia, but Aquila nodded to them. We followed in silence until we reached some stone benches outside my home. Cordelia went inside, but Akantha's cows awaited their relief.

One of my most enduring memories is of the rise and fall of the voice of this woman in the distant lean-to barn in the still of that salt-air evening, correcting the cows as she milked them. When one would protest the rough pulling of a teat, or lament the lateness of the hour, the sound of Akantha's persuasions drifted to us.

"Oh, no my dear heifer, it's not that at all. There are other factors at work here. You see, you have not considered …"

Outside on a bench we shared, Aquila clasped my forearm with his hand and looked into my eyes.

"I will never see the way you see." His words were toneless but with force, as if they had the weight of great waves of water behind them. I felt more than heard his voice.

Then I looked into his eternal eyes and I saw horses running, their manes streaming behind them, on a vast open field; I saw courses of water churning and roiling over rocks; I saw great stone buildings that lost themselves in the sky.

At that moment I knew that I would marry him.

I am old. I know that Aquila was with me from my birth, in my mind.

He was the ache I always felt each time my breath was taken away by the sudden drop of shadowed, bottomless canyons, by the pure pleasure of a wheat field rippling through the wind's fingers, by the glint of a mountain stream through pine needles and rough bark.

And now, all these years later, he is the heartsick dreams I dream and forget upon waking because their fulfillment has moved forever beyond my grasp.

"Come with me to be my wife," he said to me that day. "Together we will make tabernacles."

And now I cannot bear to remember the tenderness of his touch.

Chapter Four

I did not see Aquila again until the Sabbat service at the synagogue.

As I entered, I heard his voice, flat and dimensionless like hanks of cloth slapped up against the stone walls. He read from the Isaiah scroll and Nicanor translated in a low, urgent voice, stumbling over unfamiliar Hebrew words and looking to the other men.

"Who hath believed our report?" Aquila's eyes searched the clumps of listeners. "And to whom hath the arm of Jehovah been revealed?"

His words floated above me, seeming to take form as a mountain emerges from auroral indeterminance.

Tender sapling … root out of dry ground …
no form, no lordliness,
no beauty at all …
Despised. Left alone. Defined by sorrows. Companied by grief.

Hide your face from this awful sight, I told myself, but I could not, for it was not my eyes which saw it.

Grief bearer. Sorrow carrier. Stricken, smitten, sickened.
Wounded, bruised, peace-streaked.
Weight-sagging, despairing.
Voiceless.
Cut off.
Graveless.

I could hardly bear to hear it: a God who was pleased to bruise.

I could hardly bear to believe it: a God who was satisfied with a substitute.

"This is Yeshua ha Meschiach." Aquila's voice had deepened, for what he was saying was more shocking than Isaiah's words.

Yeshua of Nazareth was Messiah? As soon as he finished, rolling up the scroll and placing it on the lectern, some of the Jewish men who knew him cornered him with questions. *Prove it. Prove it.*

"The great rabbi Saul of Tarsus is coming. He will explain it to you. He has learned from this Yeshua," Aquila repeated. Nicanor stopped translating and went over to Aquila's side.

Within the women's enclave the Jewish women with yearning faces stirred and murmured. Some leaned toward husbands and brothers and sons as if the streams that arose in their breasts for this suffering One could be transfused across the room, and some cried softly when they saw sidelocks no longer swaying from side to side, but soaked with tears.

But others of the Jewish men began to argue in voices that steamed in the cool night air, pointing toward the Torah scroll at the front of the room. Aquila and one of his friends were the objects of the wrath of one elderly man who pushed them, one at a time, up against the wall, weeping and muttering. He grasped Aquila's beard between a long-nailed thumb and crooked forefinger and shook it. I could not understand what he was saying in Hebrew, but it was obvious that he was trying to pull it out.

Aquila winced and X-ed his forearms in front of himself but did not fight back. At last the elderly man collapsed in tears and was carried from the synagogue by some younger men who glared and muttered at Aquila.

All the Christian men stayed behind, talking in earnest tones to the Jewish men who remained, while all the women were dismissed.

Saul of Tarsus, Saul of Tarsus, Saul of Tarsus, we whispered, all the way home. The havoc-wreaker, the word-receiver. He would come and explain.

The next morning, though it was still Sabbath for the Jews, the rest of Salamis rose to the rhythm of the ordinary: unrepairable rips and surrendering patches and tunics that could no longer be stretched over an oldest child's shoulders. I awaited Nicanor's arrival to take to market three garments I made, along with Cordelia's moist salted cheeses, and was startled to find not only Nicanor but also Aquila and one of his friends outside the door with him. Behind him were three of the Jewish women I thought I recognized from the synagogue who sat murmuring and fidgeting on the bench where Aquila had spoken to me. The older woman was veiled—a married Jewish woman—but the two unkempt younger ones bore broad smiles and nudged each other repeatedly.

I began to move toward them, to offer them another seat, to tell them that those wooden slats and posts marked a sacred place now.

But I confess it was Aquila who captured and filled my eyes. Pressing errant hairs back behind my ears, I was suddenly consumed with the thought that I couldn't remember if I had washed my face. And then there were my eyebrows. All my life I wished I had proper eyebrows.

"This is Tertius. He will take your goods to market." Aquila's voice was stiff as wind-dried rags. There were places on his face with fresh scabs where his beard hair had been pulled out by the roots, taking flesh and all.

I thrust the basket of woven goods and fragrant cheeses at the young man Aquila indicated and Tertius put it under his arm, turned, and began to lope away from the house as if it were on fire.

I looked at Aquila but he would not look at me. I wondered if this were the same smoldering brand who spoke fire into my soul on the bench two nights before. As if he read my thoughts, he gestured toward the women.

"They have come to help prepare for the wedding."

He signaled to the older one, a thin woman of all joints and elbows who rose from the bench, carrying a square of linen. With great ceremony she shook it out, snapping it in the air as if to frighten out every wrinkle that might think to inhabit it, then presented it to me on stiff outstretched arms.

"I am Milcah," she said dramatically. "I am your stand-in for your parents, who are absent."

"Absent? My father is dead …"

The two other women jumped to their feet and grasped corners of the cloth, giggling, and lifted it above my head, wrapping one end of it around my nose and mouth until only my eyes could be seen. I confess that I did not fully cooperate with the swathing of my face. I could see lumps and knotty folds out of the corners of my eyes.

"What is this?" I asked, my words muffled through the cloth. I hoped that my eyes had an efficacious pleading in them as I looked at Aquila. He stole a glance and then looked away. I could not interpret the look in his eyes.

At that moment Akantha came around the corner of the house from the field and looked at me and burst into laughter.

"Are you practicing to become a mummy?" she asked between the hands she clasped over her mouth, but then she could not resist the self-correction. "Well, no, actually, one could not practice for that event since one would be an inert *recipient,* of course, of the mummifying process, one's brains having already been drawn out through the nostrils with one of those disgusting hooks the Egyptian priests use ..."

"It's not that at all, dear sister." Nicanor's stanching voice was firm.

"I have not been true to my heritage," Aquila said, and I wondered why he could speak so clearly to her and not to me. "I want to have our marriage performed in the way of our fathers. So Nicanor now stands in for my own father who is dead, and Milcah for Priska's parents, so that we may mark the beginning of the betrothal in the traditional way."

"Betrothal?" I protested, spitting out a fold of the cloth. "I thought our marriage was going to be next week. Or," my voice faltered, "or at least very soon."

Just that morning, earlier, Cordelia and I had begun making a list of what would be needed for a wedding; and since every wedding she and I had ever attended was done in the traditional Roman style, we speculated. Aquila would provide the ring I would wear on my third finger left hand. After all, had he not kissed me that night? And that, if not an ironclad Roman promise, was certainly more than just a suggestion of an oath. We would need the special nuptial bread, a fine animal to sacrifice (Akantha was already eyeing a possible candidate if she did not talk it to death before its time), the wonderful diaphanous red veil that would be just anchored to the top of my head with a wreath of flowers and allow me to float radiant and smiling among the guests at the wedding celebration ...

Not like this linen wrapping that immured my very breath.

"She doesn't have to wear it before the cup, does she?" Aquila looked from Milcah to Nicanor, who shrugged and looked into the distance as if something there might command his attention.

"Cup?" I asked.

As if on cue the second of the women ran back to the bench and opened a floppy-lipped basket, producing a wine flask and a thick-stemmed metal cup.

"And we won't just do it out here in the open, will we?" Aquila looked nervously at Nicanor, who shrugged again, this time apparently intrigued by the dust on his sandals.

"He's quite right," said Milcah in a voice like from Sinai. "If we are to do this properly, and we certainly shall, we will remove this veil until after the cup." She began to unwrap my neck.

"And inside. You." She pointed to Nicanor and Aquila, who with raised shoulders turned and walked into the house.

"And you three stay outside on the bench." Milcah took the cup and flask from the second woman, who sat down between her companion and Akantha on the bench.

"And you come with me inside."

I tried to rearrange my braids that the cloth had dragged as we turned toward the house, but looked through a halo of hairs that radiated out from my forehead, full of static, each a hovering rod of sunlight.

We met Cordelia coming out the door, her eyes wide. She walked past me without a word, and as I turned one last moment before entering I saw the three women wriggling to make room as Cordelia wedged herself onto the bench. Akantha opened her mouth several times, but no words came out at first.

"Well," she said finally.

My sun-blasted eyes could see only shadows in the room. Nicanor sighed, reached out toward me and guided me to one of the three stools.

"I wanted to be *your* father-proxy," he muttered, loud enough for all to hear.

The first thing I could see were Aquila's eyes, and I realized that he was sitting on one of the other stools. As if emerging from a mist, the wine bottle and cup came into my peering view, sitting on the third stool between us. I looked again at Aquila and wondered if his eyes would drink me up before he touched the wine.

Milcah poured wine into the cup.

"Your parents, Aquila, have gone to the grave. Yours, Priska, are … are not here," she said. "So Nicanor speaks for your parents and I for Priska's."

She paused, ignoring Nicanor's exhalation. "And so it is that we have agreed to the upcoming marriage. To signify the betrothal, you will drink from the same cup. But before you do, I must explain some things to Priska."

I pulled my eyes away from Aquila's devouring and looked at her.

"Everything is in order. Later, the other women and I will explain to you the *mohar* and the other gift that Aquila has for you. And the *mattan,* the gift that we your parents"—here she looked at Nicanor, who began to shift his weight from leg to leg—"the gift we will give you."

Their eyes turned toward a basket that lay on the floor beneath the stool holding the wine. My foot was touching it and I withdrew it as if the basket contained an unknown danger. I tucked my foot beneath my robe as Milcah continued.

"Once you drink from this cup, you show your willingness to be Aquila's wife. Once you drink from this cup, you are Aquila's wife."

I looked again at Aquila. So short? So soon?

"Perhaps you should explain a bit more before she drinks," said Nicanor.

Milcah nodded. "You are legally bound as his wife with this cup. However, you will not be able to … to … come together until the day he comes for you."

"I don't understand."

"In our ways, in the Hebrew way," said Aquila, his voice husky, "once we are betrothed, it is as binding as a Roman marriage. We cannot consummate our marriage until the betrothal is over. But we will be married."

Everyone was looking at me.

"What did she mean about 'until the day' you, you, come for me?"

"It's part of the custom," he answered. "It's a good custom. I have to build a home for us. And make other preparations. But I won't be able to see you until it's done."

"So when will it be done?" I asked.

"In a normal situation, the bridegroom's father—and in this case, that would be Nicanor—watches the construction and when he says it's done, the marriage can take place."

Nicanor shuffled in a corner. "In a normal situation …" He began, echoing Aquila. "A betrothal takes near a year. But this is an unusual time. And the home Aquila will build you symbolizes your future with him. He is a tentmaker."

"Let me speak for myself." Aquila's flat voice rose. He looked into my eyes and began.

"This is a perilous time for all of us who follow the Way. Those of us who are Jews must show our brothers who still are under the Law that we do not reject the Law, nor the old ways." His hand strayed up toward his mauled beard. "We must do what we in conscience can do. But we cannot wait a year."

"So when is the day? The day of the nuptials?"

"I don't know." Aquila looked pleading at Nicanor and Milcah.

"You won't know when your bridegroom will come for you," said Milcah. "You'll have to be ready every night."

I looked at Aquila to see him laugh. He did not laugh. But one corner of his set lips moved.

"Very well," I answered. "Just so he comes. I will wait. Give me the cup."

And drink it I did.

After one lingering look across the cup at me, Aquila rose and left the room. The Jewish women and Cordelia and Akantha came in from outside and tenderly veiled me, a married woman who could only be seen by her husband, and told me what must be done.

And wait I did.

The first night, the three women returned at sundown, carrying the basket that had lain at my feet beneath the betrothal wine. Milcah introduced the other women as her unmarried twin daughters, Tirzah and Shiprah. They were not mirror-images, but as if they were poorly-drawn portraits of one another; women so lumpy, of hair in ill-contained spikes and jagged corollae, in clothing so coarsely-woven and fraying, so as to be in appearance as much haystacks as persons.

I stood in the convulsing lamplight wearing the garment I made that very day, out of the finest fabric I could afford. At the market, I spent the last of the money from the sale of my mother's brooches for it, one inlaid with both gold and silver. When it slipped through my fingers to the merchant it pricked my finger and had I not drawn it to my lips, the blood would have stained the precious fabric.

I wondered then, and I wonder now, if I were meant to remember the theft that allowed me to have the brooch.

And yet I knew my mother, and she would have suffered the secret theft of a thousand brooches rather than have her only daughter openly shame the family by marrying with no wedding garment.

The folded piece of fabric was so white that it hurt my eyes when Cordelia and I saw it lying in the sunlight in the market and I could hardly bear to put a stitch into it. I bandaged my finger and worked carefully all through the afternoon on the Hebrew-style tunic and draping shawl. By the time the Jewish women arrived, neither Cordelia nor Akantha—they who had swept the stone floor over and over so that no dust would touch it—could stop moaning over its brilliance that seemed to outshine even the oil lamp in the dusking evening.

We watched soberly as Milcah and her daughters commandeered our few furnishings and began arranging our small living space as if it were a stage. Our three sleeping mats were piled atop one another alongside one wall and covered with an embroidered shawl whose tiny glass beads glistened in the lamplight. Milcah took me firmly by the shoulders and backed me up to the mats and sat me on them, spreading my garment around me. Her daughters arranged our three stools and two more they had brought with them in a semicircle before the mats.

This seemed to me so contrived that I attempted to rise but Milcah firmly pushed me back onto the mats. Cordelia and Akantha were so cowed by the proceedings that when I appealed with my eyes to them, they looked away, sitting stiff-spined on the stools pointed out to them by the twins. Milcah produced the basket of the night before and I expected that she would draw out the goblets and more wine and I felt my mouth begin to water. It had been, after all, very good wine.

Instead she brought a small wrapped parcel and put it

into my hands. To my astonishment, I found that it contained the brooch I had exchanged for the fabric. I looked to Milcah for an explanation.

"Normally, a bridegroom would pay the bride's family what we call a *mohar*," she explained. "You know the scrolls of the law and the prophets. Remember when Abraham sent his servant to get a bride for his son Isaac? The servant took gifts for the family of Rebekah."

"Why, mother, explain why," said one of the twins in a singsong voice. I turned to her in surprise.

"Because, my daughter, a bride's family must be recompensed for raising her. Though she might be a great beauty" (here Cordelia and Akantha murmured but I knew better), "even the most lovely daughter cannot work in the fields to support the family as a strong son would. So the groom gives the bride's family a gift to thank them."

"What types, Mother, what types of *mohars* are there?" the other twin's voice chanted. I began to realize that this was part of some ritual.

"A rich man gives jewelry or other valuables. A poor man like Jacob might work fourteen years for his father-in-law to earn his bride. And someone like David might kill hundreds of Philistines and bring their foreskins as the *mohar*."

Akantha and Cordelia looked at each other and raised their eyebrows.

"And why else, Mother, why else?"

"Because, my daughter, the groom wants to assure his bride's family of the honesty of his intentions. It is like the earnest money on a purchase."

The room was silent as my friends and I absorbed this information.

"Well, in a technical sense, if one were to be completely accurate, since she is a Roman citizen and cannot be purchased …" Akantha began.

"Quiet," Cordelia and I said in unison and then looked wide eyed at each other, daring our twitching lips to release the laughter. But Milcah silenced us with an upheld hand.

"I stand in proxy for your mother," Milcah said, obviously beginning to reach a satisfying rhythm to this whole procedure. "And I give you this brooch which Aquila bought back from the fabric merchant."

"Aquila was there?" I asked. "Why did he not bring it to me?"

Milcah, Tirzah and Shiprah turned openmouthed to stare at me.

"You will not see your husband until the day of your nuptials," Milcah said. "Did you not understand? Your veil and this *mohar* are the only assurances you have that he will return for you."

Again our little house was silent.

"The brooch is the *mohar,* the bride price. But now I, as countless mothers in Israel before me, I turn the *mohar* over to you as a *mattan* gift, a dowry.

"This brooch is now your exclusive possession. The *mattan* is the bride's, forever. No matter what happens in your marriage, it can never be taken from you. It is a symbol of your great worth to him. Should your husband divorce you or abandon you or try to take it from you, our law says it is yours and yours alone."

This time the silence darkened the room.

"But your husband Aquila loves you …"

"Tell me, Milcah, why you call him my husband?"

"He is your husband. If either of you break the betrothal, it would have to be through our synagogue leaders, with a divorce. As I was saying," she gave me a sharp look, "your husband Aquila loves you and so he has sent you a gift from himself, the gift of Isaac who sent gifts to Rebekah, who stood in the field looking for her as she arrived wearing his jewelry, and took her into his tent and was comforted."

She took another fabric bundle from the basket. It made a faint clinking noise as she handed it to me.

I was surprised at its weight. Its contents snagged on the lamplight.

Milcah was taking it from me before I knew what she was doing, and placing it over my headcover.

I heard Cordelia murmur, "What woman, having ten silver coins, if she loses one coin …"

But I was the woman of ten gold coins, and here they were before me, suspended from a chain, mounted on a headband. I could see the edges of coins sway above my eyebrows, hear the ones on the sides of my head make the music of a bride's security. Akantha brought our brass mirror, and in its yellow surface I saw the gold of the coins, the gold of my eyes.

Everything was golden that night, even when I looked away from the mirror.

Chapter Five

It was months of golden nights that followed.

By day I was Priska the seamstress, stitching together the coverings for other people's bodies and possessions. I strained my eyes with the needle and in the marketplace, yearning for even a glance of Aquila, but I heard from Akantha that he was called away to outlying areas of the island of Cyprus to prepare some other synagogues for the arrival of Paul.

I wondered if his beard would survive.

But each night after our evening meal, Akantha, Cordelia and I prepared our home: three women who had once been wealthy, but who now had not much more than when they were born. First, aging Akantha with no hopes for a husband that her incessant talking did not drive away. Me, lovesick and often wondering if I had dreamed the absent Aquila.

And then my Cordelia, perpetually pregnant, yet her mind birthing ideas.

"Well, of course," she said, "we are all a body, just one body, with all our brothers and sisters, waiting for Someone to come for us."

Akantha and I turned openmouthed to her. She continued sweeping the floor, her fingers twisted around the broomstick.

"And He paid a *mohar* for all of us already."

Only the brush, brush sound.

"It was His blood. More treasure than any jewels. More costly than foreskins won in battle, more dangerously won. Everything He was and had. That was our *mohar*, our bride price."

The brush, brush. Two women with no husbands, no hope of husbands. One woman yearning for hers, unseen.

"Actually," said Akantha, then stopped.

"I never saw that blood," I said. I hated myself for contradicting Cordelia, so intent she was, so carried away in her thoughts. "Do we just live on that hope? I mean, I have the brooch and the coins." I touched my shoulder, my temples. "What do those of us who never saw the Christos have to assure us?"

"Don't you remember what Nicanor told us the Christos said? About the Holy Spirit?"

To be honest, I had not thought much about this. And I saw little connection of a forceful unseen Personality to what we were talking about. Surely, He made His presence known in the healings, and we who carried Him within us had become accustomed, I suppose, to his inhabitance.

"He is our down payment. We wear Him, breathe Him."

Brush. Brush.

"He is the earnest on what we shall receive."

I felt a great opening of my lungs. "The Spirit guarantees that our Yeshua will return. And no one can take Him from us."

Sighing, sighing.

Then in silence the two women put their rings on my fingers, their necklaces on me, pinned their earrings and nose rings to my belt, lined my arms with their bracelets. I heard Milcah and her daughters at the door.

Shyly, yearningly, each woman put her own jewelry on me, then Milcah led me to the seat with the embroidered shawl. She produced another basket (and though I tried, I could not exorcise a mental image of her home with scores of wildly-colored baskets on every wall and bits of hay on the floor). From the basket she pulled a scroll.

"These are the love songs," she said simply. "In Greek, they are called the *epithalamia,* I think you call them."

Nuptial chamber songs. I felt my cheeks redden and looked to see both my friends blushing as well, but Tirzah and Shiprah seemed to relish what was coming. They sat close to their mother, looking over her shoulders.

The three of them began to sing in the pendulous rhythm of Jewish song, one girl stopping to giggle or the other putting her hand over her mouth as she sang.

Not knowing Hebrew, we Roman women had absolutely no idea what they were singing. We sat politely for a long time, until Tirzah began to pantomime as she sang.

A table for eating …

Something hanging above …

Raisin cakes (which Shiprah produced from yet another basket and ate with gusto) …

Apples …

"I know!" I shouted. "It's the Song of Solomon."

The women nodded, smiling now, but did not stop singing. I began to recite in Greek to Akantha and Cordelia:

Like an apple tree among the trees of the forest,
so is my dearest compared to other men.

I love to sit in its shadow,
and its fruit is sweet to my taste.
He brought me to his banquet hall
and raised the banner of love over me.
Restore my strength with raisins
and refresh me with apples!
I am weak from passion.
His left hand is under my head,
and his right hand caresses me.
Promise me, women of Jerusalem;
swear by the swift deer and the gazelles
that you will not interrupt our love.

They came every night but the Sabbath, and sang the same songs, until our necks jerked us awake again and again and the Jewish women, yawning and stretching, gathered up their baskets and went home in the darkness, carrying their tiny oil lamps out in front of them, in their outstretched palms.

I dreamt each night of gazelles on mountaintops, of turtledoves seeking their mates, of lilies and honey and milk; of furious north winds and spice breezes;

Of ornaments of silver set with studs of gold, of cedar and fir rafters high above my head;

Of eyes at a window, looking through a lattice;

Of green grapes and their perfumes;

Do not stir up nor awaken love, the women sang to me in my dreams, *until it pleases*.... They murmured of secret places of the cliff, of sealed fountains and enclosed gardens scented with calamus and cinnamon, of little foxes running.

I dreamed melodious dreams of hair black and iridescent as raven wings, of eyes like doves by rivers of water and cheek-banks of scented herbs; of hands like rods of gold set with beryl and legs as marble pillars;

Of the excellence of cedars;

Of the handles of a lock on a door, dripping with myrrh,
His mouth most sweet,
Altogether lovely
My beloved
My friend

Chapter Six

One evening in the late winter the Jewish women arrived earlier in the evening than usual. At first it sounded like one of them was keening and I ran outside half dressed, wondering if someone had died or some other misfortune occurred. The sound came not from one of the women but from a knee-high lamb they were pulling toward the house with a rope around its neck.

"Is this part of the marriage ritual too?" I asked. I dared not touch it for fear its mud-spattered wool would rub something off onto my wedding dress. Akantha stood in the doorway, her face showing the native suspicion of every dairy farmer toward a sheep or goat. Only Cordelia moved toward the lamenting little animal with hands of compassion.

"Marriage? No, not the marriage," said Milcah. Her two daughters looked at each other and shrugged. One of them was trying to tie the wriggling lamb to the tree outside our door. "This is another gift from your husband."

"So … we will begin our married life raising a sheep?" I asked.

Again the daughters looked to their mother, who shook her head.

"It's a Passover lamb," she said. "This is your first Passover, so I suppose you couldn't be expected to know all this. We will celebrate next month. Each household is supposed to have a lamb."

The daughters went into the house and we followed them. Though Akantha, Cordelia, and I had not yet mastered Hebrew, we had learned many of the phrases:

Let him kiss me with the kisses of his mouth, we sang;

Behold, you are fair my love, we sang;

Everyone bears twins (here Tirzah and Shiprah would giggle);

And, *return, return O Shulamite,* and sometimes we wept.

But as the evening went on, the lamb moaned and keened so loudly we could hardly hear ourselves. One could hardly feel festive and passionate with the rising and falling of its cries.

"I'm pretty sure that Aquila won't come tonight," said Milcah finally. "He said as he gave me this lamb that Nicanor insists there are many more preparations to make. So we will retire early tonight and come back tomorrow. I'm sure the lamb will have settled down by then."

But by the time they returned the next night the lamb was nearly hoarse from crying, now screeching out cries like a tired old dog barking.

"I don't know how to do this, what's proper, that is," I said. "Can we just give the lamb back until Passover? It obviously misses its mother, and though I tried to give it milk from a leather bag, it refuses to eat. It wants to go home."

"The lamb stays with the family that will slaughter it."

"Slaughter it? I don't want to watch this poor thing for a month. And I couldn't dream of killing it, now or later. Look at its face. It's perfect. Who could do that?"

"That is precisely the point," said Milcah. "It is perfect. It was bred for this one purpose only. You will look into its face every day, and learn to love it as it nuzzles your hand and looks to you for food. You will know that it will not deserve to have its young life cut short. But on the appointed day, with your own hand you will take it to someone with red sleeves and watch him slit its white throat."

I felt horror, remembered the pig in the marketplace. "I could never do that."

"You can and you will. And as you do it, you will remember that escaping from the Death Angel always costs someone. Redemption and sin—each always has an implacable price."

There was no giggling that night. We sang the songs with somber lips. I began to wonder if Aquila had been right to insist on this wedding with no wedding date. The customs of the Jews seemed no longer quaint, but barbaric. Perhaps this waiting every night was a kind of test, even a joke, to ascertain if a woman really wanted to marry a man. Perhaps everyone knew it but me, and they were as weary as I, and only waiting for me to say I refused to do it any longer. Perhaps Aquila himself had sent me the lamb to hurry the process.

The next day I stopped Cordelia as she fastened her sandals on her feet. I could see that some of her toes were beginning to curl and cross over others, but I knew that she did not want me to comment on it. I waited until she straightened up from her task.

"I don't know about this waiting. It seems pointless. Is there anything you know about how long this might last?"

I began to cry. "If you know, please tell me. Don't let me be taken for a fool."

She embraced me, standing sideways as she did when she was close to anyone so as not to offend them with her belly. I was ashamed, for I did not want it to touch me, either.

She didn't seem to mind, and then sat me down.

"I have inquired on your behalf, dear sister. Part of the custom is the tension of the waiting," she said. "And in normal circumstances, there would be clues. If Aquila were building you a house beside his father's house—for that is the Jewish custom—we could hear the hammering or see the supplies being taken there. But of course, Nicanor told us that your house, for now, will be one of Aquila's tents. And if Nicanor were indeed Aquila's father he would have been saving all these years for the wedding feast, and we'd know about preparations. But even I who make my living with preparing food for others have heard nothing in the marketplace about a great feast."

"So you don't know when, either."

"Not exactly. But I do know that he promised you he would come for you."

"And I'm supposed to learn something from that, as a good Jewish wife?" I couldn't keep the bitterness and fatigue out of my voice.

"No," she said with a sweetness that made me ashamed of myself again. "As a follower of Christos, you are learning something quite extraordinary. Remember that Nicanor told us that Christos said He was going away to prepare a dwelling place for us. And that the assurance of that was His word on the matter."

She arose and struggled into the sling that carried her basket of baked goods. She kissed me and left for the market. Outside, the lamb whimpered, its eyes closed.

That night I dreamed of the lamb with a human face. It spoke to me, but I could not understand what it said.

I awakened and the lamb was still crying. It was days before it stopped.

In fact, the night that Aquila came for me, one of my most vivid memories—and my last of the home where I had lived—is of the lamb who sat silent at my doorway as the men stormed my house and abducted me.

Now, the abduction happened on this wise. Cordelia and Akantha and the Jewish women and I were singing when we heard the racket outside. Milcah moved quickly to veil my face while the other women scrambled for their little oil lamps and bags of oil.

The men, Jewish and Christian, who came with Aquila pushed him into the doorway. He stood and waited for us to still ourselves and then, with his quiet voice, he spoke, looking down.

"You have ravished my heart, my sister, my spouse. You have ravished my heart, with one look of your eyes." The Jewish women began to sing the words in Hebrew as he said them.

Then he looked into my eyes and said, "Come, my beloved. Let us go forth to the field." That apparently was a signal for the joyful pandemonium that ensued.

The entire Jewish quarter of the city awakened to the sound of the wedding drum. Dogs howled, sleepy-eyed children looked out doorways from behind their parents' legs, and men and women looked at each other with softened eyes. It seemed to me that the men who bore me on their shoulders took a route that threaded through every seam of the Jewish sector, shouting and singing.

We arrived at last at Nicanor's house with an entourage of neighbors and friends. Our new brethren and sisters from the synagogue brought a *huppah* canopy that represented the promises to Abraham of progeny like the star-filled skies above his head.

Aquila and I stood beneath the canopy and shared the same cup of fragrant wine, me lifting the edge of my veil to sip beneath its edge.

To no one's surprise, Akantha reprised and expounded on Rachel's blessing:

"May you, sister, become the mother of millions!

May your descendants conquer the cities of their enemies!"

Her explanations faded into the other sounds. I could hear nothing but Aquila's voice. At that point he introduced his childhood friend Jacob to me, who was one of the men from the raucous wedding party whom I had not recognized. He had come from Pontus, he said, for this occasion, and he was the *shoshben,* or friend, of the bridegroom. He stood beside me like a guard and Aquila turned and walked around the far side of Nicanor's house, away from us.

"That is where your dwelling place is," Jacob said, pointing to a goat-hair tent that was pitched at the side of the house. "Aquila is making sure all is ready for you." When Aquila returned, his face glowing, everyone cheered as the three of us walked back to where the tent wall rippled and pulsed in the night breeze.

I looked at Aquila and then at Jacob. Surely, I thought, he would dismiss him now. But Aquila shook his head. "He stays outside the tent and awaits the signal."

For the first time all evening, the people on the other side of the building were completely silent. I could hear the crackling of the distant bonfire.

Aquila held the flap of the tent open and I walked inside. There on a stool was a plate of figs and ruddy apples and cheeses and steaming meat. A flask of wine and a brave-flamed lamp were partially buried in the sandy floor. The embroidered scarf I had sat on all those evenings draped a double sleeping mat.

I heard in my ears the songs of my sisters as my husband removed my veil and I surrendered to him:

I am a wall
And my breasts like towers
Then I became in his eyes
As one who found peace
And the peace was not broken
And the peace was not broken

And the peace was not broken, even when Aquila rose from the mat, facing the tent door, and shouted.

"Excellence! Excellence!"

I heard Jacob's footsteps departing, and a few seconds later the raucous singing and feasting outside began.

Sometime before dawn we emerged.

Aquila and I sat on little thrones in the midst of all the whirlings and feastings; indeed, wore crowns on our heads. I began to think this was a dream. All the women and Havah danced to everyone's caution (and the loss of only a few earthenware dishes; nothing, really), and Cordelia laughed, really laughed, for the first time since I came to Salamis.

The feasting lasted a full week. The food was sweetness such as I had never known, not even in the house of my mother. Or perhaps it was just the days, and the embraces of my Jewish and Christian sisters who brought their best dishes for my wedding week and watched me anxiously as I tasted before returning to the tent.

I cannot speak of the unbearable sweetness of those days within the tent mansion.

But I learned on that first night that Aquila was a freed slave, on the night that he freed me. I learned that he had been there on the day of the tongues of fire.

I read a poem to Aquila that first night, when we

breathed vows to one another in that peculiar stillness of near-dawn. We wept at its truth.

You have returned as a gift of perfume
That is brought on the wind from a faraway place—

I have a need now for a covenant:
And so I willingly cut this victim, my heart,
And invite you to walk between the halves.

(The pain confirms this love: having this pain
Is far, far better than not having this pain)

Time, that burner and destroyer, laps at the offering.
It is graced by your fragrance
And I am filled with joy.

The *epithalamia* infused every song of my life, all the acuteness of my senses. To this day, I cannot eat raisins or apples without remembering Aquila, nor smell myrrh or cedar without a woman-ache.

The poem is with me still, in a small sack I wear between my breasts. The sack is made from the last scraps of that honeymoon tent, the goat hairs long ago worn away from the tender leather. These and Cordelia came with my husband Aquila and me along with some of the brethren, to Jerusalem. The Greek Torah and our clothing were the only other possessions we brought to Beulah, the married land.

But before that, the Rome I thought I would never return to, summoned me. My wedding week was barely completed when my mother's message reached me.

Aquila my husband, Cordelia my friend, and I sailed in the crisp-dawn before the Sabbath that Paul was to arrive. I thought I would surely die aboard that ship. But I did not.

Part Two:

INHABITATION

Chapter Seven

The last breaths of my mother, Livia Ocellina, coincided with the advent of the Holy Breath upon me. It is with this story that the consummation of symbiosis of my life began.

No, my mother did not exhale and then I inhaled; the Breath breathed, and with that act all air in my life was displaced.

From my mother's first glimmering suspicions of her own mortality—a wasting here, a wheezing there—she began to heap gods to herself. No longer was she merely a goddess herself but she began to crave them, to covet them—and not just Roman gods, any deities she felt could aid her or at least serve as peers. At the end, her house became populated by a jumble of strange-headed statues, standing in groups as if conferring, and noxious, competing incenses curling through the air.

She hired a dozen girls to accompany her at all times, young barely-women who could read Greek and who kept tucked in their twelve tunics tiny pieces of neatly-divided scrolls of the Odyssey, ripped along a knife edge. Thus, she had her own chorus of tragic maidens who, elbowing each other into intermittent unison, chanted her praises in words unintelligible to her and then tittered nervously behind their hands about the fact that the handmaids of Penelope, after all, ended up by being hanged.

The day I went to her in Rome at her behest, the last day, Miriam guided me as I passed through veil after overlapping veil hanging from the ceiling of the great room, diaphanous swaying linen draperies that brushed nearly weightless against me. And yet they had texture, lingered against my skin and clothing like the sigh of a lover, like the first stirrings of a child deep in the belly, like the goodbye kiss of a beloved foe.

When the last veil parted I gasped, because of the wide eyes of the chanting girls behind her, but also because of the tiers of other bodies in the room, as enjambed as the breathless recitations. I was part of an audience.

My mother had been propped amongst peacock feathers and purple embroidered pillows, the golden center of a drooping flower. She opened her eyes and they were the color of old honey. They did not focus on me at first, but upon the curtains as they swayed in my wake, in a look of amazement as if they were novelties to her, hastily hung as she dozed.

To my dismay the surprise faded as she looked at me and the familiar, wearied gaze she had always given me was back as if the three years of my absence evaporated. The other bodies, some spectral behind the veils, rustled, murmuring and cooing at her, reaching out as if to help, *if only, only* they could. I felt my stomach slip.

"Ah, it is Priska," my mother said, her voice the sound of something moving beneath dry grasses. "You have returned as I bade you."

The rustling of the room escalated. Without thinking, I smoothed the front of my tunic, the rough cloth, one of so many symbols of my independence from her riches.

I bowed my head but knew better than to approach her. A maid emerged from a swaying panel and wiped something that looked like olive oil onto her lips and she smacked them, undivinely. Then her fingers waved to me from a boned wrist on the coverlets and I came closer.

"Is that tent tradesman with you?" The whole room inclined toward her voice, then became utterly silent.

"His name is Aquila, Mother. My husband, Aquila."

She closed her eyes dramatically. I looked around to the room but recognized no one except her wizened scribe who sat on the floor, his pen poised above sheets of vellum. The top one had nothing written on it. I suspected none of them had.

So many moments passed that I began to fear my mother would die now just to spite me.

I surrendered this last of so many battles. Clearing my throat, I asked, "May I bring you some wine, Mother?"

Her eyes fluttered open, tiny slits of brass gleaming in the lamplight, and she nodded. One of the chorus women stepped forward with hard eyes and a forward chest. She stumbled over an outstretched foot as she brought me a goblet, engraved with Dionysius and clusters of grapes. My mother drank slowly and noisily from the cup as I held it to her mouth, peacock feathers braided into her scanty hair dipping with each gulp.

"No, my husband is not here."

The room sighed.

"But Cordelia is."

"Ah, another visitor from afar." She panted hard for a moment, and a maid started toward her, but she continued.

"I welcome the widow Cordelia, your childhood friend."

Again, the clawing motion of her upturned hand, bidding Cordelia enter. The hard-eyed woman took the cup away—a cup worth more than Aquila and I would earn in months of work—and I heard behind me the whispering of robes passing through the veils, leaving and returning.

The room inhaled once and hard when Miriam brought Cordelia into the room and then retired behind the curtains. Cordelia wore, as always, the garment of a widow, but it could not hide her pendulous belly. My mother smiled faintly and wickedly.

"Why, Cordelia," she rasped. "We all heard your husband died …" She paused and when Cordelia began to speak, shook her head, forbidding a response.

"Died *over a year* ago."

Cordelia looked down haplessly, her hands sweeping in front of her midriff as if apologizing for it. Gone was the feisty girl my mother once knew. Before her stood a stooping woman whose every introduction begged an explanation.

I had tried to explain this before, to sympathetic people, and then only with great difficulty.

"The child of Caius Clovius—her husband—the child they conceived was never born."

Again, the room was silent except for a lamp that sputtered in the corner. My mother's lips pursed as she repeated the sound. The room began to laugh. My mother closed her eyes as if relishing a sweetmeat. When she opened them, she inhaled deeply as an actor who must deliver his best line to his greatest audience.

"Well, for a believer in that Christos person who was born of a virgin, that must not be so unusual."

My cheeks burned as the laughter erupted, louder than before. I wanted to put my arm around Cordelia but knew that was not what she wanted. Before my eyes, my mother rallied.

"My dear, it is for that very reason I called you here. We must come to terms with our god matters." She straightened her shoulders against the pillows.

I did not know what to say. She had summoned me with a letter saying she was dying, a letter that took weeks to reach me and weeks for me to travel in response. I hardly expected a theological discussion.

"You wrote me that you only can have one God." She spoke the words as if she were biting them off a piece of gristly meat. "And of course, then, there's his … *heir* … his child … that Christos."

The room seemed to hold its breath at the mention again of that dangerous name.

"You know my dear that no one who follows him has any peace."

I began to speak, but her hands clenched and then released.

"Look around you, my dear. No one who follows this Christos will die in bed, surrounded by loved ones, like me."

Loved ones loved ones loved loved, they murmured.

"One god is too few to stake all of one's hopes upon. Surely you see how limiting that is, how foolish."

I stood silent.

"There are so many gods. There are so many ways, so many avenues. They have so many … resources."

"I don't need their resources, Mother."

She sagged back into the purple. Her amber eyes closed again, but only for a moment this time.

"I thought you would say that."

I shrugged.

"For my part, I'm willing to say that your Christos is, ah, a part of the pantheon."

I smelled a trap.

"There's only one God, Mother."

"Yes, yes, you say that." She seemed to be wheezing more. "So I thought of what we could agree on."

My theft from her when I ran away from hope should have cut off all avenues of any future enrichment. I had long ago given up on hoping for her approval. But now, agreement?

"Angels, my dear. Heavenly messengers. Your religion has them, does it not?" She turned her head as if appealing a case to the room. "All religions have them. This other god, Zoroaster, he has angels. And there's the Egyptian Anubis, and our Hermes." She counted them out with finger taps on the thin sheet of air above her coverlet. "And even combinations, like Herm-Anubis—see how people can agree?"

Her eyes darted from side to side, and then I understood.

I was her only living relative. Agreement meant to her not just a compromise on supernatural entities, a settling on one that would not make me an enemy of the state. Such an agreement would make this audience witness that I was her compliant heir.

If I did not claim my inheritance, it was nobody's. And everybody's.

It was the room's. And if I left, the room could swallow her before she even died.

It was at that moment that an experience bubbled up, one that has become as familiar to me as it is inexplicable.

First was a sense of anticipation, a prefix to a word not yet voiced, like hearing—and smelling—a heralding thunder in complete darkness.

Wonder, the soul agape.

And then it began.

It was the clutch in the stomach when you take one poised-in-air pace off a step much deeper than you'd thought. It is what happens in your throat just prior to a gasp, or after; when the lining of the lungs has flattened out and there is no air, anywhere.

And then I inhaled it, the Holy Breath.

I do not remember speaking. I do not remember anything except the breathing in.

Cordelia told me later that I stood erect, alert, my eyes open but unfocused; and with the change in my voice (as if it were muscle, not air, she said) my mother started in her bed and a murmur of *Delphi, Delphi, Delphi* rippled through the room.

The scribe at my mother's side began unbidden to write my words:

In the past God spoke to our ancestors through the prophets—at many times and in various ways,

many ways, many ways

but in these last days he has spoken to us by his Son, whom he appointed heir of all things,

and through whom also he made the universe.

listen, listen, listen

sustaining all things by his powerful word.

words, words, listen to these strange words

After he had provided purification for sins, he sat down at the right hand of the Majesty in heaven.

So he became as much superior to the angels as the name he has inherited is superior to theirs.

the oracle, can she be the oracle

bring more wine

For to which of the angels did God ever say, "You are my Son, today I have become your Father"? Or again, "I will be his Father, and he will be my Son"?

No one else, no one. Wisdom, wisdom—mark it well, scribe!

And again, when God brings his firstborn into the world, he says, "Let all God's angels worship him."

In speaking of the angels he says, "He makes his angels spirits, and his servants flames of fire."

spirits, spirits, flames of fire

But about the Son he says, "Your throne, O God, will last for ever and ever; a scepter of justice will be the scepter of your kingdom."

(Cordelia saw it: Ezekiel among the elders of Judah, she said.)

"You have loved righteousness and hated wickedness; therefore God, your God, has set you above your companions by anointing you with the oil of joy."

(Some actually wept, Cordelia said, upon the words *oil of joy*.)

He also says, "In the beginning, Lord, you laid the foundations of the earth, and the heavens are the work of your hands.

"They will perish, but you remain; they will all wear out like a garment.

"You will roll them up like a robe; like a garment they will be changed."

Like a garment, a worn-out garment, like a robe, like a rolled-up robe …

And then Cordelia knew, because of Pelatiah son of Benaiah, what would be.

"But you remain the same, and your years will never end."

Then I asked questions, Cordelia said, appealing with an outstretched arm and unseeing eyes to the curtains, to the shuddering room:

To which of the angels did God ever say, "Sit at my right hand until I make your enemies a footstool for your feet"?

And then, Cordelia said, my mother's back arched.

Are not all angels ministering spirits sent to serve those who will inherit salvation?

And then she died.

And then vellum sheets slid to the floor.

And then the room emptied, faded away like wraiths in the folds of the whispering curtains.

Chapter Eight

My mother's funeral was the spectacle she wanted it to be—I owed her that much, I reasoned. I exhausted all the marketplaces in Rome of peacock feathers. So many nodding iridescent eyes were on the *lectica* borne on the shoulders of six slaves that they created a breeze on the cheeks of bystanders as her body passed through the listing cobblestones of Rome.

At one point in the procession, one of my mother's hands slipped off the bier. I did not secure it, allowing her fingers to trail for one last languid time through the stream of life all around her. Though born Livia Ocellina, she was now Juno resplendent, Isis rejoining the reconstituted Osiris, All Goddesses Amalgamate hidden forever behind the shades of eternity.

I will never see her again. I wish I could mourn the loss of my mother, but I cannot; I grieve for a sister who never was.

We interred her among her people in the rankness of

her underground family crypt, in the same grotto as my father. The six slaves disappeared as soon as they slid her ashes into the niche. Only a handful of people remained.

Where the Christians at the funeral of Quinta had been clear-eyed because of hope, at my mother's last rites her few mourners were dry-eyed and pragmatic because they had no hope, never imagined a reason for it. With the sides of their sandals they brushed the flower petals and broken peacock feathers to one gritty corner of the small space and emerged squinting in the sunlight with eyes darting toward the marketplace, toward homes and buildings where people lived.

Aquila had conceded to my request that he not attend the funeral and interment. Thus it was that only Cordelia and I and mother's maidservant Miriam stood watching the hurryings away. But as I turned I saw approaching us a very fat woman, holding a child.

"Too late for the funeral, I see," she said. "Just as well."

Panting, she set the young girl onto the pavement in front of me. A girl, wavy brown hair in her eyes, looked unblinking at us three women.

"Who have we here?" I asked, stooping to the little girl.

"No need to know my name," the woman said. "You're Priska, daughter of Livia Ocellina?"

I nodded as she continued.

"This child here, though not your kin by blood, is as near as you have to a relative."

I looked in wonder at the steady gaze of the child. Her eyes had deep corners, her features were as precise and grave as those of a Parthenos pillar: extraordinary beauty framed in the soft contours of cheek and still-baby jawline.

"Your distant cousin Rufus, an orphan, married this child's mother and then they both died." The woman fanned herself. "Her name is Rubria. And she was chosen as a Vestal Virgin, fortunately while she was still eligible, while her parents yet lived."

I tried to make sense of what she was saying. "I did not know the Vestals could be chosen so, so young," I said.

"Times have changed. She's six, not too young. And I thought it only right that she know you, the only person on this earth to whom she now has any family ties."

I took the child into my arms. She looked serenely around at each of us, pushing away from me slightly with the pressure of her palms on my clavicle.

"I have no inheritance, you know. Just some property." My voice sounded harsh, even to me.

"Doesn't matter, not why I am here. Being a Vestal means she wants for nothing, is taken care of better than you or me." The woman was brushing dirt off the rolls of flesh on her arms, then pushing it along with a finger between the folds. "I am her nurse. Best to tell you my name, I suppose, Philomena, you should know. Rubria has begun her actual training, so if you want to contact her, you may write to her through me." She named an address on Via Appia, and then hefted Rubria in her arms.

"It's not good to be seen in your presence, you know," she said, and left as quickly as she had come.

The child looked at me over the woman's shoulder until we lost sight of each other in the dusk and the distance. Even then I imagined I could see her bottomless black eyes. Though I have never thought of myself as having the gift of prophecy, a cold wind blew over me as I watched the child depart, chilling the moving parts of me, deep inside. I cannot to this moment think of Rubria without the fabric of my heart unraveling.

But there were transactions and troubles more immediate to my mind. Cordelia thought it would be difficult to liquidate my mother's estate. No such transaction is hard if you set the price low enough and turn your back on pilferage. I knew which of my mother's servants I could trust—but poor Miriam barely trusted me after all my threats before I left Rome the first time. I tried to convince her that I was now her faith sister. I am not sure yet when she came to believe that.

The proceeds of the estate were a problem. Aquila of course was the legal heir, but he left it to me what to do with the inheritance. Small amounts of money I scattered around with various moneylenders in Rome in hopes it would avert the attention of those who watched my mother's estate. At that point I dared not take any great amount of coin on my person. It was pure subterfuge to divide other monies between messengers who were dispatched to take it to help needy brothers and sisters.

I kept in my name an undistinguished yellow-walled house near the Aventine Hill that my mother's family had owned and Aquila, Cordelia and I moved into it. Cordelia insisted on playing the role of our household servant which humiliated her parents who, though they had disowned her in shame because of her conversion, felt it added insult to injury to see their patrician former daughter barely grasping the wooden handle of a broom on the threshold of such an unadorned dwelling.

Cordelia resumed her trade as baker and the partitioned house was large enough for the three of us and our growing business making tents.

It was in that yellow-walled house that the word-dreams began. Although I have dreamed copious dreams in my life, both visual and auditory, this was the first of a species of dreams, a different race, so to speak, of experiences that were as alive as any companion I have ever had.

They began alike, with a snapping sound like fabric being shaken out. Then I would see a sheet with Greek writing and then Hebrew letters afterwards.

The first one hung suspended before my sleeping sight until I had memorized it all:

speaker
heir
creator
radiance
representation
purification-maker
anointed

I sat upright upon awakening. I never wrote the words down, but they never disappeared from my memory. They chanted themselves inside my head as I ripped, stitched, clipped, bound.

In our yellow-walled house, our proximity to a large estate of a senator named Pudens brought one bright hope to us. Through the growing network of believers there in Rome we learned that this nobleman often invited Peter, the disciple of the Christos, for discussion. Though Peter had lived in Rome several years, I had not yet met him; and though Aquila heard him on the great Pentecost day, they had never spoken either.

"Why did you not seek him out that day?" I asked Aquila one misty evening as we rested, our arms scoured smooth, our elbows and knuckles reddened, from wrestling with goat-hair fabric. "Surely after the miracle of the languages—what I would give for that gift!—and the living fire on their heads, you would want to see such a man up close."

"There were thousands of us that day," he said. "Some say three thousand who asked for baptism. And the others already believing. Everyone wanted to talk to the apostles. And the atmosphere was"—here he searched for words—"unlike anything else. Before or since."

When I asked him for details, I saw his eyes pleading

with me. He was not a man of words, at least not many of them. He was content to answer questions if they were requests for information or the recounting of events but for all his strength and courage, he was a man of few syllables but many resources, I was coming to learn.

A week later he arrived from the market with a just-plucked chicken, a bolt of fine cloth, and news.

"Let us make ourselves new garments," he said simply. "We have been invited to the home of Pudens next week. Peter will be there."

I wondered what Peter would be like. I had heard of his first addressing of that mob of thousands: *You murdered, you murdered, you murdered.*

But even as Aquila spoke of meeting Peter, he whispered, his eyes looking to the shadows of the room, beyond the door. Though we both knew the reprehensible emperor Claudius—that shrewd, gag-voiced limping despot—to be only a man, it seemed that among his deformities were thousands of ears that he could dispatch at will to bring him news.

We scarcely knew what to believe about our safety there in Rome, nor the motives of those who would report to us the reasons for the unrest we felt. Neither our business nor that of Cordelia had suffered; we had more than enough to eat and often harbored newcomers to Rome—and, discretely, natives who were newcomers to Christos—in our home.

But sometimes Cordelia would come home from the market, saying even the friendliest Jewish women whispered to her over her loaves about the anger that was spilling over from Rome's great goblet of wrath onto all that named the Name—Jew and Christian alike—of friends and sons and fathers who walked away to labor and never returned, of women who vanished in the night.

"Those must be just the slobberings of the old women," I told Cordelia, but wondered if the tales were false, why so many people told them with such great relish. The truth was that many believers didn't fear the Roman government nearly as much as they did the perpetual public offendedness of the Roman Jews to the message of the Way, and the unwelcome attention this brought to us all.

But to Aquila and other believers it seemed that the excitement of sparring with words held no real danger. Surely, they thought, great Caesar had no interest in the spats between sects.

We had not learned, children as we all were, that mice may play near the feet of the dog that guards the gate, but when their skirmishes disturb his peace he does not care which set of whiskers took the first grain of barley.

We did not know, we simply did not know.

Chapter Nine

When the summons to Pudens's home came, Aquila and I loaded our arms with fabrics and baked goods, ostensibly tradesmen taking their wares to a rich man's estate, our new clothes covered with old cloaks. I could not decide whether to wear my wedding coin headpiece but finally decided to do so. I heard the voice of my mother in my head telling me to stand up straight, to remember I was nobility, to stare down anyone of lower class who dared to look at me.

If my mother had such a voice, it was silenced in my head not by the success of my actions but by the fact that no one at the residence of Pudens (except the preoccupied slaves who gave us hurried greetings) even noticed our arrival. All of my posturing was wasted.

As soon as we entered its courtyard we heard raised voices, the verbal swat and returns of words. Aquila and I looked at one another, but a grizzled old slave was announcing us to four people who paid no attention at all to what he said. He shrugged and left us standing in the doorway.

Three of the men did not draw my attention but the fourth had a nose. The nose. I knew that nose. And it was saying words of wonder.

"I have read them all. All the great ones. I have spent all I earn on books. I tell you that just because the great philosophers of Greece had similar ideas does not mean they plagiarized from Moses," he said, sweeping his arm in front of him. The speaker was Mathos, the man I had met in the market. He leaned toward one of the men. "You could never prove that."

"I can and I have," said the second man, a bowlegged old man whose sidelocks and prayer shawl contrasted with his Roman-style robes. I recognized that his was the loudest of the voices we had heard, both screeching and groaning at once, like tree limbs rubbing together in a wind. "*Koine* Greek may have been invented by Adonai just to provide the perfect translation for His Word. Did you ever consider that?"

This idea seemed to silence the two other men, if you did not count the fact that one of them seemed reduced to some sort of sputtering. "Well. Well. Well."

It was then that they noticed us: Aquila whose eyes were scouting an escape route, and me, leaning toward the conversation I longed to join. The man who was saying well, well, well, rose and approached us, fussing like a woman.

"Some host I am, leaving you there watching us argue," he said. "I am Pudens. Welcome to my home. My slaves will take your, your wares." He hesitated, looking at our bundles and turning to look for his absent slaves. He clapped his hands loudly. "And give you some wine. Welcome, Aquila. Welcome, Priscilla."

I looked at him in surprise that he would use the

diminutive form of my name upon just meeting me. He leaned toward me conspiratorially.

"My mother's name was Priscilla. I hope you don't mind me using that form."

I was shaking my head, wanting to tell him that my mother had, as she said, "snatched the name Priska out of the divine ethers," when one of the other men rose and hurried toward us. He looked Aquila straight in the face and then embraced him, fiercely. "My brother, I have longed to meet you. I am Peter," he said, then turned to me.

I wanted to look away, demurely, but could not stop staring at him. His hair and beard were a wild thatch that wandered the topography of his head, and his eyes were hooded as if each one wore a helmet visor with a shag of eyebrow atop. But he looked intently into my eyes before returning his gaze to Aquila. I wondered if he would converse with me, or have me sit across the room as Jewish women usually did.

"Ah. So the woman who went away empty has come back full," said Mathos of the nose, approaching us. "Kind of a reversal of the Naomi story, wouldn't you say?"

Aquila looked at me. "You know this man?"

"I met him before I went to Salamis. In the market. Once." I felt disoriented, as if I had walked into a fable of odd-looking people. But the conversation had started up again, and before I or anyone else took notice, Aquila guided me to sit in a chair with the men.

"That's Philo of Alexandria," said Pudens our host, confidentially, leaning over my shoulder and pointing to the man with the swaying sidelocks.

"I know his writings," I said, louder than I should have, to be heard over the men.

At that, the entire room grew still. Everyone was looking at me, especially Philo whose eyes widened in delight.

"A Jewish woman who knows my writings, how can this be? Don't tell me that you can read as well?" he said.

"She is not Jewish. My wife, she is not Jewish, she's Roman. And she can read and write—not only Latin but Greek," said Aquila. "And she knows the Bible writings as well as any of the men. She studies the scrolls all the time." His voice boasted.

Philo rubbed his hands together before dragging his chair next to mine. "So you would appreciate why I say that the Septuagint was inspired." He saw the question on my face. "The Septuagint—the Greek translations of the Hebrew Bible," he said.

The thought had never occurred to me—nor any mental description of any process by which the Hebrew would have been translated into Greek. The scrolls from which I read might as well have sprang, as Minerva from the headache of her father Zeus, fully clothed and equipped. But, of course, someone—or more likely someones—must have stroked, milked those backward-looking Hebrew words.

I looked again at Philo. I had read of this well-known author's thoughts about the Logos—from Plato, but applied to the Hebrew God. His emphasis on allegories. But I had not heard this term, Septuagint.

"Seventy-two men, seventy-two days, translating," said Philo. "All in separate rooms. All emerging at last with exactly the same translation. Had to be divine. Had to be." He was gesturing toward the men, but then faced me again. "So, what have you read of mine?"

I looked deep back into myself for one of my favorite quotes. "'Consider what the figurative allusions are which are enigmatically expressed in the mention of the cherubim and of the flaming sword which turned every way. May we not say that Moses here introduces under a figure an intimation of the revolutions of the whole heaven?'"

Peter touched Aquila's arm, a question for which Aquila had no answer.

"Your work on the Cherubim," I said while Philo beamed and grunted. "But that was before …" I thought of how cosmopolitan I had thought myself years before, reading this Jew who Greekized everything.

"Before she became a believer in the Christos." My husband's flat voice, proud again.

Pudens straightened three brass dishes on the tabletop, lining them up equidistant. I noticed for the first time that one of his arms was withered, like dried meat twisted onto bones, the hand a rubble of tendons.

"A Roman woman who reads Greek and knows the Law and the Prophets. What a treasure you have, you know!" Philo said.

Behind him, Mathos muttered, "Wish I'd known any of this before. We could have had an intelligent conversation which I assure you is a rare commodity in that marketplace …"

"Perhaps our well-read sister can join us in a knotty problem," Peter interrupted. I had heard how this once-unlearned man had devoted himself to instructions and philosophies. "Our brother John speaks often of the Logos, but he says that Jesus was the Logos," he said. "So, tell Philo what you have perceived about what he says about the Logos. Is what Philo says the same as John?"

"John, the apostle? Is that who says that?" I asked.

"The same. The one Jesus loved."

"Did Jesus tell him this?" I asked. "Or he has this," I searched for the right words, "he has this by revelation?"

I saw Peter's visor eyes assessing in arcs between me and Philo, stopping when I said the word "revelation."

"It is my understanding that this was brought to him by

the Holy Breath."

This Holy Breath, I knew. But I dared not say such a thing to Peter.

"I will speak for Philo, only if he is gracious enough to correct me when I stray from accuracy," I said, my eyes down. When I looked up, all the men were nodding, and I continued, my voice low and shaking.

"Philo has said that the Logos—the concept where all ideas, that is, their reality, resides—is the first-begotten Son of God." Philo closed his eyes dramatically, gesturing me on.

"But not God, not the same as God." I finished. Philo sighed.

"I have heard John say this: that the Logos was with God and was God," Peter said.

"And John is beginning to write his account of his time with the Christos," said Mathos. "And John calls him Logos there. And calls Jesus 'God' as well."

"So," my words walked carefully through the spiked lives and barbed years of knowledge in that room, "so if Philo's concept of Logos is not identified with God Himself, as John's is, it is not the same."

Then I recalled the Holy Breath's words to me and I exhaled them to these men:

"The Son is the radiance of God's glory," I said. "And the exact representation of his being."

Peter was looking at me with that narrowed look again.

"About the Son, He says, 'Your throne, O God, will last forever and ever.'" I could hardly speak, my breathing so tightly embraced by my lungs that it barely escaped.

"Ah," said Philo.

No one spoke for several moments. Pudens ran his dried-meat finger along the lip of his wine cup, then curled a drooping grape stem into the middle of a dish: a perfected circle.

I had the impression that they had already settled this among them. But not with those words, with our shared language, the Breath and I.

Now what they had debated, caressed and stabbed with conversation, was ratified by a woman. I wondered what of possible use that could be.

I pondered that all through the evening as the conversations ebbed back and forth through the room. Though Philo and Pudens and even Peter would sometimes defer to me with their eyes and include me in sweeping arm motions as they spoke, I listened only and did not speak again. I hoped, desperately hoped, that a woman's prudence would buy us another invitation to the house of Pudens.

We left late that evening, our fabric hidden in a basket that Aquila carried as if it were only air-filled. It was only a few days until Pudens invited us again, and Cordelia as well. Each time we returned to his home it was with the same ruse: arriving at a different time than other guests, always carrying cloth draped over empty baskets that we would carry out again as if the Jew and his woman and their limping servant woman had sold out their wares.

While we met on the Lord's day in our home with a small (and ever-changing) number of other believers, we could not persuade Pudens to join us. Even though Peter came twice (he and Aquila and many others most often traveled covertly through the city, encouraging other believers also meeting in homes and synagogues), Pudens would not come, even when he knew Peter would be there. I began to wonder if Pudens had absorbed the meaning of his name, his own bashfulness. Or, to my shame, I remember myself thinking if perhaps he were not just timid but cowardly.

Nonetheless our sporadic invitations to the home of

Pudens were honeyed times for me, so much, in fact, that I was unable to eat each time an invitation came, and only for the sake of politeness would partake of what he offered in his home. The feast, for me, was the ideas.

One evening Aquila and Cordelia and I arrived late. Aquila had seen several men from one of the synagogues watching the entrance to the estate of Pudens and so we came under the protection of the darkness. As soon as we entered the great room I felt my pulse rise because they were discussing the allegory we called Plato's cave, one of Socrates' dialogues. Peter sat leaning forward, his hands open and palms upward on his knees.

"Let Priska explain this to you," wheezed Philo. I saw the hurt in Peter's eyes.

"Actually, no good Jew would play the game of Plato's cave like Cordelia and I did, right Cordelia? So he couldn't know." She nodded in agreement.

"A game?" Philo seemed suspicious.

I sighed with relief as I began to explain, and as I did, the tension in the room began to pool in the corners by the door and then slip out into the night.

"When we were girls, we would play a game, acting out the allegory of the cave. One of us would sit, face to a wall, while the other stood behind. Here, let's show them, Cordelia dear." I moved a stool over near a wall, its wooden legs bumping along on the tile floor, and Cordelia sat on it.

"May we extinguish all the lights?" I asked Pudens. "And may I ask you to bring several of your favorite statuettes?" He looked around perplexed and then, with a smile on his face, left the room, returning with a small wooden bust of a woman, a wheeled toy in the form of a horse and a fan in the shape of the wing of a bird which he held away from his body as if disavowing it.

"Would you light our torch again?" I asked Aquila, who

used one of the last lamps to light the still-smoldering stick we brought from our home. In the darkness, I stood behind Cordelia.

"Dearest Cordelia, you get a prize if you guess what I am holding," I said. She laughed, remembering our childhood game. Aquila held the torch behind me and I cantered the horse, casting its shadow on the wall before us. She guessed the horse and the statue in turn, but could not identify the fan until I swayed it in the air.

Philo rubbed his hands together, Peter and Aquila frowned, and Pudens with whispered threats dispatched a reluctant servant who brought a wine flask and a large pair of tongs. Once those were identified, the game was to predict which object would cast its shadow next.

"Splendid!" said Philo. "Now, imagine that Cordelia knew nothing but the shadows cast by the puppeteer on the wall, and spent all her time speculating on which image would appear next. Day and night, it's all she sees and all she thinks about. She would think that is reality, when indeed it is only a shadow of something else. That's Plato's cave. And a game from that, hmm—I never knew."

"But the toys, the statues, they aren't real," said Peter. "You said that before, when you were trying to explain this. They're just depicting something else." He looked for assent to Aquila, who agreed with one deep nod of his chin. They both looked at Philo, who, with a hand, deflected the comment to me.

"We were just children," I found myself apologizing. "We didn't take the game as far as Plato did. His allegory went much beyond just the images and what shadows they cast. In the story, someone who's seen only the shadows his whole life not only discovers the shadow puppets, but climbs out of his cave, into the sunshine, to discover the real objects depicted by the puppets. In our case, he would find the person this bust depicts. He would look at a real horse, and a real bird."

"Exactly," said Philo. "And such a one would have a moral obligation to go back and tell all the other shadow-watchers what he had learned. That what they saw on the cave wall was just a reflection, an image of something. They would not believe him. And they would not appreciate it."

"He would tell them the truth. About what's real." Aquila's voice was prime, unadorned. But he understood. "Like the Christos. He knew what was real. And He came to tell us."

At a shout from Pudens a servant returned and began lighting all the room's lamps again. The men began to discuss this, and I am glad they did not notice me or Cordelia.

I began to turn her chair around and then … felt the Breath again.

It was as if my whole soul were hollow, inside out, bristling neck-hairs in the charged moments just before a lightning strike. Cordelia saw the look in my eye, she told me later, and led me out into another room and began to write what I said:

We see Jesus, who was made some little inferior to angels on account of the suffering of death, crowned with glory and honour; so that by the grace of God he should taste death for everything.

For it became him, for whom are all things, and by whom are all things, in bringing many sons to glory, to make perfect the leader of their salvation through sufferings.

A salvation-leader. A part of me pondered that.

For both he that sanctifies and those sanctified are all of one; for which cause he is not ashamed to call them brethren,

saying, I will declare thy name to my brethren; in the midst of the assembly will I sing thy praises.

And again, I will trust in him.

Cordelia repeated it: I will trust in him.

And again, Behold, I and the children which God has given me.

Cordelia stopped holding the parchment and touched her stomach.

Since therefore the children partake of blood and flesh, he also, in like manner, took part in the same, that through death he might annul him who has the might of death, that is, the devil; and might set free all those who through fear of death through the whole of their life were subject to bondage.

I wanted to escape. What if the men heard me?

The Breath would not stop, insistent as a lover.

For he does not indeed take hold of angels by the hand, but he takes hold of the seed of Abraham.

I looked to the door, toward the men.

Wherefore it behooved him in all things to be made like to his brethren, that he might be a merciful and faithful high priest in things relating to God, to make propitiation for the sins of the people; for, in that himself has suffered, being tempted, he is able to help those that are being tempted.

A great silence followed there in the tiny room where we sat. Then Cordelia and I returned to the great room where for hours the men discussed whether Jesus was the philosopher who brought truth to others. No one had noticed our absence, for women often disappear from where men shout and argue.

We were the weaker ones indeed that night. I could hardly speak any more. I knew that Jesus did much more than what they were saying. I knew there was a depth to the idea of the facts and their representations, a profundity they had not yet plumbed. But Cordelia's eyes warned me, soothed me.

She brought me a plate of fruit and we spent the rest of the evening, grownup girls who played games and now sat forgotten by the men as we looked at a scroll, as Cordelia murmured to me of the vineyards of our childhood, the vineyards of Salamis, the wine of revelation, the annulling of him who has the power of death.

And that night, I dreamed of the sheet with new Greek and Hebrew words:

crowned, death-taster, brother-declarer, tempted atoner.

After that night at Pudens's house, Philo came more and more infrequently, talking less when he did, his phlegmy voice scraping out coughs. I mourned him for weeks before he died, even while he was still coming to Pudens's house, because I could not bear the thought of losing such a mind.

"Lovers are lunatics," he often said, smiling and pointing to Aquila and me, collapsing into airless coughs, and we would look at one another and know there was no argument against that ancient of proverbs.

But increasingly he spoke of himself: "The soul is only imprisoned within the body," he would say, and Peter would tighten his lips and not argue with him though he insisted later that Christos never spoke thus of His own body or that of anyone else, as if it were enemy and captor.

Philo's penitentiary finally crumbled under the assault and when he went to sleep with his fathers, I felt the loss of the ideas that had created such welcome frictions in my mind, almost as if they were living things now extinguished as well; as if I were called to the funeral of a massacre or plague.

Perhaps it was his passing that brought gravity to the mind of Pudens, a kind of weighted consequence in every sense of the word, for his oldest friend Philo went into eternity like a traveler who leaves his knapsack and provisions behind, wagering on the beneficence of an unknown host. I could not speak to the final disposition of his soul, nor did Pudens.

But one immediate result was that it was as if the mind

of Pudens aligned itself, now became ordered and quiescent when he spoke. His face like Janus looked back at his senatorial privileges and life of ease and—quite presciently and pragmatically—forward to the great company of the many fulfillments of my mother's prophecies of uneasy deaths for us all.

For clear-eyed Pudens, we Christians were like signposts at crossroads all of which led only to destinations of suffering; and thus, his decision to ally himself with us was a singular act of fully-informed courage.

His invitation to meet him at his family tomb in daylight unnerved Aquila and me. Shrugging and shuddering, we tried to mentally prepare for what might transpire there. We followed him into the dank guts of the earth, the death-hole that extended under the city wall underground on Pudens's estate.

I was walking behind, my face veiled, and did not from a distance see the sign there that caused my breastbone to sag into my chest as I passed under it. Not until we had gone several yards into the torchlight-swabbed dark did I recover, remembering the name of Pudens's mother, now buried here beneath what he told us lay above: The Cemetery of Priscilla. I was glad that Aquila could not read Latin.

"Come now, this way." Pudens's words were coarse-edged, all but drawn into the walls by the crypts that devoured flesh—the sarcophagi—but seemed to eat sound as well. We rounded several corners, turned back on ourselves, it seemed, enough times to have made two circles, and then suddenly Pudens disappeared behind what looked like a solid wall. Looking closer, I could see that a space had been cut out behind it, like one curved wall in front of another, only visible if you stood just to its side—no small feat in the bowl of space it terminated.

By this time, Cordelia had gotten down from the stretcher and was walking sideways through the passageway. With Aquila and his friend following, I squeezed through and found myself in a surprise of light and space: high-shouldered walls (we must have descended, I realized) and a red mosaic floor with a large reservoir in it. A closer look showed it to be a partially-buried and repurposed sarcophagus with long curlicued wings carved into each corner—Egyptian; prissy and Ptolemaic, I calculated—and filled with water. Gazing into it were Peter and Pudens and Mathos.

"I had this room built for Peter," Pudens said. "Here he can baptize without fear."

We looked into the perfectly still surface that reflected our torches like another watery room below. Pudens turned to us, the newcomers.

"I want to make the confession that others have made, here in this room. I, I cannot make it as publicly as others outside this room …" His voice trailed off. Peter was facing him, and took Pudens's forearm, clasping it with his fisherman's hands. It was so withered that Peter's thumb and longest finger nearly enclosed it.

Pudens stretched his neck and looked straight up for a few moments. Only he, apparently, was unaware of the way that Peter's thumb and fingers were growing apart. The old wineskin of Pudens's flesh was filling up with secret, unseen fountains that made it blush and tighten. Another instant and it settled into raised man-veins and muscles on his arm.

"My Roman citizenship will protect me, at least for a while. I have the resources to help the brothers and sisters of the Way." Pudens was still considering the ceiling. "But first I have to follow the Way, myself."

He looked down at his arm and turned it over, perhaps less surprised than the rest of us.

He turned to Peter. "Peter, I want you and everyone else here to know that there is no doubt that Jesus of Nazareth is very God, only God. I don't believe because you healed me. I believe your testimony that you companied with Him, that you know He died, that you companied with Him afterwards, that you saw the holes in His hands and feet, that you saw Him go back into heaven. I want to replicate that—with my own body, now made whole."

His voice choked. "I want to be buried with him."

Peter looked intently into his eyes, then pulled off his outer garment and Pudens did the same. Cordelia and I both began to turn away in modesty but saw that each was wearing a tunic, and they both began to climb into the sarcophagus and within moments they emerged dripping and shivering. Mathos produced an armful of drying cloths for Pudens and Peter and handed the rest to me.

"You'll need these," he said.

"I have been baptized," I protested.

"I haven't." He climbed into the reservoir and looked up at Peter, who joined him. Mathos continued talking.

"My confession is this. I was born in the covenant of Abraham. I want …" He hesitated. "I want to be a new person. I want to belong to somebody—to this Jesus the Messiah, the hope of Israel. And my hope. And I promise I will follow him no matter what."

Perhaps it was at that point, watching Mathos, that I had the first imaginings of myself as an indexical entity, freed from myself, my being, and able to span the chasms of thought and dreams and philosophies between the Hebrew people and the Savior they hoped for and murdered. It was as if every book I had ever read, every myth I had ever loved, every idol I had cherished dissolved like melting, swallowed-up flesh that night, leaving only their skeletons of usefulness for this task.

I did not know that was the last time I would ever see Pudens, though he lived for many years and himself baptized hundreds with his two strong arms in his covert room.

The next day I went to the marketplace with Cordelia to see Mathos and offer him some of Cordelia's sweet bread, as a kind of new-birth-day celebration.

We could hear the sounds of shouts as soon as we arrived at the market. Approaching Mathos's fabric stand I saw his textiles scattered, one bolt unrolling down an aisle as a young boy with a stick followed, prodding it.

"His own fault," said a man at the butcher shop. I looked up and saw another animal suspended from a hook—this time a goat—with its blood coagulating beneath its head. With difficulty I turned to the man who had spoken.

"Mathos the fabric vendor? His fault? Why do you say that?"

"As soon as he got here this morning, he started talking about that Jew troublemaker, that Jesus person. Good news, Mathos kept saying, good news. But then it went into nonsense, something about rising from the dead. All foolishness, all trouble. About he himself rising from the dead, it sounded like. Ridiculous stuff. Then some of the Jews over there," he spat toward a spice shop, "they asked him to be quiet, to not attract the attention of the guards, but he wouldn't stop. Then the Jews began pushing him." He stopped, looking at something over my shoulder.

Two guards carried Mathos by the arms. His legs moved in the air, his toes pointed, but didn't touch the ground. One of the guards grabbed a bundle of sheer cloth with a spare hand, his thumb stroking it, and tucked it into the front of his tunic. Mathos spotted me, then looked away.

But I heard him, and still hear him, from far away.

"It doesn't matter, do you hear me? It doesn't matter. Jesus is worth it. New body, I'll have a new body. Feet to face, feet to face!"

And now, all these years later, I remind myself that when I see him again, I will look past whatever nose he has, into those true eyes.

Chapter Ten

Though it couldn't have been proportionally causal, the arrest of Mathos was a kind of temporal tipping point. Within a day, the edict was imposed on us all. Claudius, who could not experience any other kind of surfeit, finally had enough of Jews and penis-cuttings and their strangenesses about what they ate; and those other kinds of Jews, he said, with their lurking around and crazy messiah national heroes who they said didn't threaten his Romanness but certainly did.

We had just enough time to distribute the last of my mother's estate money to house church leaders who passed it on, and those recipients who were able bought passage, as we did, on any ship leaving Rome.

The journey to Jerusalem is a dim memory stained as much by the fear of illness as the illness itself that so characterized my first sea voyage to Salamis. This time it was Cordelia who nursed me to a wavering wellness that improved the closer each time we came to shore in our many stops on the way. It was as if the sea's waves entered me somehow through the boards of the ship and bled out and diluted all my strength, but when I saw land I was able to revive, as if the sand and trees were flesh and nourishment.

At long last we arrived: Peter, Cordelia, Aquila and I. Nicanor met us at the port of Caesarea, and warned us of plots against Christians entering Jerusalem. As much as some sought Peter for the grace of even his healing shadow, others sought his life.

We hurried onto two hired mule-drawn carts that took us two days into the Judean desert wilderness. There we met a young, heavily bearded Greek in the bluest robe I had ever seen, who directed us into the narrow wadi he assured us would lead us to Jericho from which we could safely enter Jerusalem. He lagged behind us, swatting at dirt on his hem, fanning himself, complaining of a weak ankle, and to no one's surprise soon disappeared with his pay.

I had the sensation that something fuller, more significant than the occasion I was experiencing was about to happen, that it was a function both of the place alone and no time at all. I looked around for David the King, knowing that this was a land immortalized by his words. I would not have been surprised in the least if he had emerged from a wadi, shepherd staff in hand and cheeses on his back, or swaying with idiot-drool in his beard, or stumbling cold-footed looking for a maiden and warm blankets.

But it was not him but his words that took shape before me.

ἐὰν γὰρ καὶ πορευθῶ *Though I walk*

The sandy bottom of the dry streambed made walking even more difficult than on board the ship, and seemed, like the sea from which we had so recently escaped, to have its own will and motion. Its invisible riptides pulled down at our muscles until they burned with the effort to resist them, and with its ebbing filled our sandals with grit and sharp little rocks as we walked around the boulders.

Then suddenly the wadi opened its wide lap and dug its invisible, distant heels into the surface of the wilderness. Within an hour, the walls of it were tens of feet high, and never branched off once. With no other wadis intersecting, we began to ask one another, first jokingly, if we could be lost in this sinuous canyon that crawled relentlessly through the ancestral land of the Hebrews.

ἐν μέσῳ *Through the valley,* I thought …

Though it was early in the day when we entered the shallow wadi in the morning's glare, soon after noon the slit-like passageway became profound and shadow-jutted, with currents of air that seemed to streak it with cold. We walked like children wide-eyed in a twilight forest, bumping in to one another with fatigue and imbalance and laughing nervously at our missteps, at least at first. After a while, though, the only sounds were our breathing and sighing.

After a long while, Aquila and another of the younger men attempted to scale the walls, hefting one another, pulling up one another, but sliding back again and again. We could see from the growing shadows even at the top of the wadi's rim that the canyon had taken an unnoticed turn to the west, and with a crushing realization we knew that many of the miles we had walked must have taken us not toward, but away from the city we sought. Our cloaks were little protection from the winter's chill, our burdens suddenly unbearable, the darkness infusing, and the brethren's home and dinner we yearned for, an impossibility.

No one carried a firepot nor torch. No one had an alternate plan.

We could not go back: the carts that brought us to the wadi's beginning in desolation were long gone. Like the

Israelites at the Red Sea, we could not retreat, could not veer against the walls that were like frozen tidal waves on each side, could only go forward.

σκιᾶς *Of the shadow*

the light-leeching shadow …

We sat down, and in the gloom ate the dried figs and drier barley crusts from our packs. No one said a word.

A cascade of small rocks clattered down the side of the wadi and drew our attention upwards, and then before our very eyes a young mountain goat slipped on more loose rocks near the top of the canyon and careered shrieking to his death, falling, splaying, splattering, right at our feet.

θανάτου *Of death*

Cordelia groaned, a thick-throated labor groan. Though she had previously said nothing, I could see that the passage had been hardest on her. Since her return to Rome, her finger and toe joints had become more swollen and several of her fingers would not straighten out any more. In the canyon, she lurched from one wooden foot to another as she walked. The men had long ago taken the larger of the bundles that she and I bore, but we were unused to such distances.

οὐ φοβηθήσομαι *I will not fear*

When I saw tears on Cordelia's cheeks, I began to cry too, not seemly and ladylike, but with choking wails and hiccupping sobs. I was filled with rage, not for myself but for this woman whose crippled, death-inhabited body stumbled along on the path of God's favored ones, for whom there was no husband, no healing, no help.

Aquila put one arm around me and vised my upper arm with his hand and I slumped into that force. The heads of the men who walked in front of us seemed to angle forward and carry their drooping necks and shoulders along with them, as if for each the head propelled and feet and body followed and would not look back at us as we wept, only going straight ahead into the deepening darkness.

κακά *Evil*

The men stopped ahead of us in a heap. They were looking straight up and I followed their gaze. There at the canyon's rim a man stood looking down at us. Aquila waved to him and shouted.

"We're lost. We're trying to make it to Jerusalem. But we think we have taken the wrong path."

The man nodded solemnly, and with a gesture of his hand motioned us forward and walked along the rim just above and ahead of us as we kept pace. After another long while, hours it seemed, the walls of the canyon seemed to fan outwards a bit. The man stopped suddenly and began to walk down toward us.

Again we were silent because of the mountain goat, because of its scattered blood and burst body. Cordelia put her knotted hand over her mouth and began to weep again. She refused to look up any longer and sat straight down and began to rock almost imperceptibly. The man continued down, switching back and forth.

As he neared us I tried to identify the fabric of his undulating garments. In the arid murk, they seemed to be made of smoke that swirled around him as he turned. I could not see anything but his eyes above the covering over his mouth as he descended into our darkness.

When he was about ten paces above and in front of us he spoke.

"You must step only where I step."

With that he turned and began to walk back up the way he came.

Aquila led the way, holding onto my hand. Nicanor followed, leading Cordelia, and the others came behind. Again and again the sandy soil gave way at the very crumbling edges of our footsteps. My free arm flailed and grasped at air. Beneath us, rocks bounced into the blackness. No one could look at anything other than the feet of his predecessor and we jerked along, entrained to one another like prisoners.

When Aquila stepped into the narrow hem of sunlight, the man's heel took a last hefting step to the surface. Aquila followed and blinked in the glare of the horizon-cradled sun, shielding his eyes with one elbow and then turned to help me up. When I emerged onto the surface, Aquila stood there alone, turning and looking.

As the others scrambled aloft with hands clawing at the dirt, with sighs and groans, no one seemed to notice that the man was gone.

I knew what I had seen was the ashes of the flames of fire. I felt the winds of unearthly presence departing.

I feared the fate of footstool, I craved the worn-out garment folded up; and the oil of gladness lingered, its last drops suspended, then falling, from the tips of my hair.

I sank to sit upon a large rock and began to speak a continuation.

Therefore we must give the more earnest heed to the things we have heard, lest we drift away.

For if the word spoken through angels proved steadfast, and every transgression and disobedience received a just reward, how shall we escape if we neglect so great a salvation, which at the first began to be spoken by the Lord, and was confirmed to us by those who heard Him,

As I spoke, I thought of Mark and Fidelis and Havah. They heard His voice.

God also bearing witness both with signs and wonders, with various miracles, and gifts of the Holy Spirit, according to His own will?

I wondered, even as I spoke, why none of those wonders were visited on Cordelia. Mercy.

"It was an angel who guided us, surely." Aquila's eyes were searching mine.

For He has not put the world to come, of which we speak, in subjection to angels. But one testified in a certain place, saying:

"What is man that You are mindful of him,
Or the son of man that You take care of him?
You have made him a little lower than the angels;
You have crowned him with glory and honor,
And set him over the works of Your hands.
You have put all things in subjection under his feet."

Was the silence that followed embarrassment? I do not think that it was awe. Yet no one moved to rush me as I wrote down what I had just said.

The handwriting was mine. That is all.

When I finished, I saw that all faces were turned toward a city in the distance—all except Aquila's. He was looking hard at me, as if trying to make a decision to speak. He did not, and we gathered our bundles.

I do not remember the trek to that city.

I wondered about what I had heard about angels who came to Christos when His fate was stripped down to that of Yeshua-man in the abandoned garden, before His death. He didn't want to drink the cup that married Him to His fate. Even He capitulated.

What did those angels say that comforted him?

I looked to Peter for an answer, but he was striding ahead into the sunset, toward the city.

I could not imagine. But this I knew: what the angels said did not prevent the coming horrors for Jesus.

We entered the gates of the city just at nightfall, frantic with fatigue and relief.

Chapter Eleven

We waited there in the city for a week until Passover. The house where we lodged was owned by a man with emptied-out eyes named Caleb ben Azariah. He showed us to sleeping quarters scratched out of the cliff that supported the back end of his house and I began to wonder how large a family he must have had in the past. But they were gone, and any time I began to ask him about the shawl that hung on the wall or why there were so many small oil lamps—the kind you use for walking around outside in the dark—lined up against the wall, Peter's look silenced me.

Twice during the week Caleb herded us into a grotto camouflaged in front as a stable and in the dark we squatted and leaned, legs aching and cramped from the uneven floor and walls. Distant voices rose and fell in the house and when Caleb's hand pushed away the covering we saw that where we were hidden was unfinished, like a partially-eaten melon half for which someone has lost his appetite.

Was it the Jews or the Romans who came searching? I

never knew.

I began to dream, more and more, in restless nights of sporadic sleep. More than once in my dreams I saw smoking altars and slowly-walking lions and gates which creaked and awakened me before they opened, and I began to yearn for Jerusalem.

They became a litany for me, the names of the gates of Jerusalem, the names I had read in the scrolls from Nehemiah and Ezra and others. I do not know what I expected to see, to find, when we were finally able to approach the great city—a yawning, open mouth at the Fish Gate, the brisk-brisk of hoofbeats at the Horse Gate, a Sheep Gate feather-edged with wool drifting in the languid breeze?

Valley Gate, Water Gate, Corner Gate, my mind recited.

Old Gate, Prison Gate, Gate of Ephraim.

I yearned to enter the Gate of the Fountain, had seen it in my dreams with a bubbling and the fragrance of wet dirt and splattered stones. But we came in through the Dung Gate, near the cursed Hinnom Valley whose acrid burnings we smelled before we saw it. I hoped this was not a sign.

I knew there would be a sign. My mind was alerted. I knew that feeling of precursor, of knowing something would be signified to me, and it gathered like chaff blowing into a corner.

At first I thought that this fragrance of augury concerned Jerusalem itself, mingling perhaps with the fact that I read the Law and the Prophets so repeatedly they became oil that entered my pores. From its first mention as Salem, the stone-suckling of Melchizedek's mysteries, I felt exiled from a homeland I had never seen but had been mourning all my life with the harps of my heart. I yearned for the womb of the dawn, craved the dew of a youth I never had.

This was story—story not just of time and people but of place; and before I set foot on the road up that ancient peace-city of kings and priests, I felt the moist sigh of the Holy Breath on my ear.

We entered at night, as if we were tradesmen anxious to be in the market at dawn. But truth be told, because it was Passover time, the city was jammed with strangers and our subterfuge was unnecessary. Lodging with Jewish brethren (how I regret that their names are lost to my memory), Cordelia and I made ourselves colorless and useful: baking unleavened bread, repairing clothing and shoes. In the evenings as we sat veiled on the rooftop, Cordelia and I could hear children still singing the psalms of ascent their parents sang all the way up the winding roads to the Feast.

When the LORD brought back the captives to Zion,
we were like men who dreamed

The children's voices were sharp-edged, like metal rods hitting stone.

Restore our fortunes, O LORD,
like streams in the Negev …
Sow in tears
Sow in tears
Songs of joy
Songs of joy

We stayed in hiding the first week because, we were told, Peter twice had been a wanted man within these walls. From Peter and Nicanor I drank in the stories of Herod Agrippa's dark, deadly obsession with James the brother of the Christos, of Agrippa's hatred of Peter, of the imprisonment and the rescue by an angel so insistent on waking Peter that he pounded on his ribs as one would a locked door. From that gate of prison Peter walked straight to Rome, he would jokingly say.

These memories Peter seemed to relish, but when other

people came to the home where we lodged who wanted to tell the older stories, of the hounding of the believers by the Jewish leaders after the death of the stoned-one Stephen, Peter grew restless. It was as if this part of his life was a great monument where visitors could linger at inscriptions or leave offerings but could not enter. At some unseen cue, something would vacate behind Peter's eyes, as when someone asked him about the great sheet (A sheet? I asked the first time—I knew about sheets) let down from heaven, roiling full of animals. The memory seemed to strangle him.

I thought at first it was that although Herod was dead, some Jews still sought the life of Peter, but I have met few men in my life as blindly courageous in the face of physical danger as Peter. Surely it was not death that he feared from the Jews of Jerusalem. I puzzled over this for many days.

And yet during those first days on days when it was only Peter and Aquila and always-reticent Cordelia and me in conversation, Peter's eyes were direct and clear, undefended and penetrating. Our sequestration in the house of Caleb ben Azariah, the house of the hidden grotto, became a blessing, for within those walls Peter was like a grandfather telling old stories.

From him I first learned of the adversary, the plummeting lightning-become-snake-become-throne-room accuser and earth-roamer.

Resist him, Peter insisted, as person and not just invisible energy. Through Peter's eyes, I began to see this foe as one of penchants and brilliance and unremitting inner famine, as if he were, in Peter's words, a prowling lion.

My Romanness had no language for such utter evil.

"How did Jesus relate to him? Did He resist him? Did Jesus confront him?" I asked.

"Actually, more defied him." Peter told me of the forty thick-tongued desert days, of stones and temple pinnacles and a mountain with a panorama of reigns.

"But he—this enemy—he has limits. He has no ability to see the future, is that correct?"

Peter thought for a moment, then responded. "The old Law tells us that the Christos would crush him. That is all he knows of the future—the account of his own defeat."

"Why then did he try to get the Christos to sin? Why all the charade in the wilderness with the stones, for instance? Why would he rejoice at the crucifixion? Why does he continue to fight us now?"

He shook his head. "For the sake of his own kingdom, I suppose. How else could he spend eternity while refusing to surrender?" He paused and tried to gather all this together.

"All rulers build something," he said.

And it was then I came to understand something about the beings from eternity. Such a one, an angel, can be lustrously evil—or as unremarkable as a visitor from a dusty road.

A lion can roam the earth, voracious; or can swallow you whole and spit you out onto a celestial shore.

But what Peter described that preceded the wilderness tempting most intrigued me: It was the Holy Breath who heaved, shoved the Christos into that desolation-solitude, where both surely knew the adversary schemed to ambush Him.

Perhaps it was Peter's impassioned description—though not just his words—of the Spirit as Holy Compulsion, that made Cordelia and Aquila look at me.

"Tell him, Priscilla." Aquila's words left no room for negotiation.

"I have felt this sacred impelling, this Breath." I had none of my own, the last word coming through my mouth pushed out by my throat and chest muscles, airless.

"The Breath breathes on her." Aquila spoke again.

Cordelia rose to leave the room, returning with one of my scrolls. She opened it and searched while Peter looked at her quizzically.

"Therefore, in all things He had to be made like His brethren, that He might be a merciful and faithful High Priest in things pertaining to God, to make propitiation for the sins of the people. For in that He Himself has suffered, being tempted, He is able to aid those who are tempted," she read.

Peter nodded slowly. He did not speak for a long, long time. He rose and looked over Cordelia's shoulder, reading.

I sought shelter beneath my shawl, my swinging dowry coins, my eyelashes, wanting to be a quiet bread-baking small-stitching innocuousness of Jewish womanhood.

The Breath gave me a hard push in my sternum and the words tumbled out, as uncontrollable as first menstrual flow on a long journey, and at the time it seemed to me, as unreasonably shameful.

Calling, heavenly calling
Jesus: apostle and high priest

Peter raised his eyebrows and I knew his thoughts: Not *apostolos*—no, not sent out; no tribal right to priesthood …

House-builder, greater honor
Than Moses

I saw anger in Peter's eyes.

Do not harden your hearts
Bodies falling in the desert
Rebellion
Declared on oath: God's own anger
Today

I saw fear in the eyes of Peter.

Sabbath rest
Sabbath rest
Sabbath rest

I wanted it to stop. But there was one more exhalation.

The word of God is living and active

And for the first time, the Breath was not breathing on me, He was breathing *through* me

Sharper than any double-edged sword

through me

Penetrating

through me

even to dividing soul and spirit

through me

joints and marrow and I was

Undone

And Peter was angry and I wanted to cower but

It judges the thoughts and attitudes of the heart

Nothing in all creation is hidden from God's sight.

Everything is uncovered

    laid bare

before the eyes of him

    to whom we must give

account

Peter was gone when I awakened the next afternoon. I had fainted again, and I was angry, even angrier than Peter had been. I felt robbed, not only of the time but of Peter's potentials: He left without a farewell, but even more important, without filling my most fervent though unspoken expectation. This man of shadow-healings and *dunamos* words—Words! For heaven's sake!—did not heal Cordelia.

Though she never asked nor even hinted, Peter owed her that, I believed. Were all these healings, dispensed with a liberal hand as if they came from a bottomless purse, were none for Cordelia?

And I felt disgraced, the cause of Peter's sudden leaving,

a belief from which no one could dissuade me even though they told me he was only just outside the city in a neighboring town with relatives. He might as well have been in Achaia or Arabia or Pisidian Antioch.

Jesus had called Peter a rock and for the first time I hated that stone-ness in him.

My secret grief companied with me all the day, until the setting sun made titans of all the shadows. More than Peter's departure, I felt that a day had not just been lost to me but kidnapped and living in the memory of others while beyond any ransom of mine. I grieved that day in which I had been unaware of my surroundings, a forever lost *Today* in which Someone had breathed my breath, steered my life, and I was without say—quite literally—in the matter.

The understanding began to settle in on me. I carried with me for days the sense that I was in an inexorable process of relinquishing parts of myself, as if I were a slack grain sack with a slit through which something unidentifiable but important to me rustled out with each movement.

The next morning Aquila and Cordelia flanked me as we left the house.

"We cannot impose forever on the hospitality of the brethren," my husband said, and while Cordelia and I craned our necks to see past the booths and buildings in the narrow uphill street, he scanned the market and we soon returned with one bolt under his arm and followed by a screeching donkey carrying enough fabric to keep my needle occupied—and bring in coin—for a week.

"But when can we go see the Temple?" I asked. So far, we had only seen a gate, a house, and the fringe of the market. "We have not really seen any of the city."

How true that was became more apparent when we ventured out the next morning to walk again through its streets, this time along its tendons and muscles and veins toward its heart.

In my imagination I had believed Jerusalem to be a goblet of honeyed milk that would satisfy my scroll-dried thirst for this fount, the center of the world.

But other images overlaid one another so fast I could hardly digest them.

I saw Jerusalem as it really was: a vessel emptied out and boiled dry so many times that its unseen fissures were to me nearly palpable underfoot. My eyes ached to look at streets and buildings that Jesus had seen, to see with His eyes, but when I did, the Breath was a draft across my eyes that made them seem to crumble and lay scattered in a great mountaintop field before me.

And then amidst the clamor and commerce I heard it: the gasp of God.

The experience unsettled me so much that I did not share it with Cordelia nor Aquila, at least not at first. While she and I looked, speechless, at the temple—Cordelia with awe, I with dismay—Aquila stood under the awning of a dove merchant's booth and spoke urgently, his voice mingling with the laments of the birds. When he rejoined us, I knew he had news.

"The apostle Paul of Tarsus is here, in Jerusalem. He has come from Antioch, through Phoenicia and Syria." He refused to say any more until we were in the safety of our host's home.

My questions burst forth as soon as the door closed behind us.

"Antioch? Did someone try to kill him again?" Paul's narrow escapes would have been testimony of his favored status even if one could not believe his message.

"Not that." Aquila shifted on the stool where he sat.

"Paul has brought many Gentiles to believe in the

Christos, and that has not set well with some people."

Cordelia and I looked at one another.

"So Romans—and other foreigners—" my voice was acid, "aren't welcome any more among the brethren?"

"No. It's not that." He looked at us, then down.

"It's the old laws. Some say that God said the law would never pass away. And that Jews were his covenant people."

"Yes?"

"So," he struggled to explain, "a delegation went to Paul in Antioch, to try to persuade him to help Gentiles live the old laws, the eternal ones." He blushed.

Understanding dawned on me, why Aquila was choosing his words so carefully.

"He's talking about circumcision," I murmured to Cordelia, and Aquila gave me a grateful look.

"So, Paul and Barnabas his companion have come here, to meet with the other apostles and elders. There is still much danger here, so it is hard to gather such a group. But one of the believers who is of the party of the Pharisees wants to persuade them to obey Moses' law. Even Peter is leaning this way, going back and forth in his opinions."

"When will we get to meet Paul? And when can we hear the debate?"

Aquila looked away again.

"It will only be the men this time." He must have seen my surprise and hurried to continue. "The meeting must take place indoors, and there are few places where a crowd can meet. One of the synagogues where there are a lot of believers, I think."

I pushed my lower lip out and felt my voice tremble. "Men believers."

"I myself will wait outside to see if there will be room," he said.

I sat in silence. Aquila brightened.

"But I have some good news. James, the Lord's brother, will be there."

I had heard of this man, whose vows to not cut his hair left him with dreadlocks that touched the floor (his tribute, he said, to his late cousin the Baptist.) A man who had once accused the Christos of moon-sickness, of lunacy. I yearned to meet this man of such history and will.

"I'm listening," I said after a while.

"And I have heard that he is writing a letter, a general letter, to all believers." Aquila knew how to coax me.

"Yes?"

"And that he has done this under the direction of what you would call the Holy Breath. He has described this, this Holy Breath."

I leaned forward, hardly able to contain myself. Aquila requisitioned the words he had heard.

"He says it is like the carrying-away of Ezekiel."

I knew that feeling.

"And you say he is collecting what he is told, what he hears and knows, to write in a letter?" I stumbled over my own words.

Cordelia and I looked to the corner where a pale earthenware jug held my scrolls, its opening plugged with burlap.

"Yes," he said.

"Just like me."

Aquila looked away.

My anger reeled like a drunkard, off balance and unreasonable.

"Oh, have you begun to doubt me, Aquila?"

His eyes widened and he shook his head slowly but did not speak. Cordelia hurried from the room.

I felt tears corrupting my vision.

"I saw how you looked at me, in the valley, and then

with Peter, when the Breath came to me." I was sobbing.

He reached for me but I pulled away.

"Peter didn't believe me, and you don't either."

"I do believe you."

I could not stop sobbing. I was afraid others would hear, so I tried to quiet myself but choked out syllables without words.

"I do believe you." Aquila's voice sued.

I felt the draining-out feeling again. I gathered all my strength to speak. "Peter didn't want to hear that a woman could have the Holy Breath."

Aquila took the spasms of my shoulders in his hands and straightened me up to look at my face. For some reason, I thought of how the Holy Breath would have cupped the shoulder blades of Jesus and pushed him into the desert temptation.

Aquila's words were deliberate, his eyes on mine.

"No, Priscilla. Peter didn't want to hear that a *Gentile* could have the Holy Breath."

His words stanched my tears. I looked at him in amazement. I suddenly understood the battle Peter was fighting within himself, why he could sit at ease with Gentile believers when he was safely hidden away in an unnoticed house, but within the presence of his countrymen have a return to revulsion of the animals squirming on a sheet let down from heaven.

"You must go to this council," I said, grasping Aquila's arms. "You must go."

But in the end, just as I urged him to go, so equally was I the cause that he stayed.

This time it was not the Holy Breath inside me but someone else, and when I fainted again this time it was days before I saw light.

Chapter Twelve

I heard a deformed man once describe his involuntary celibacy as a whetstone on which all his desires were paradoxically sharpened, so much in fact that he lived to regret, he said, his very man-ness.

In a similar way my woman-ness became an anvil upon which I was hammered out and shaped in Jerusalem; and though I did not regret my gender because of Aquila, in all other areas I have long mourned it.

The purest form of love of another human being transcends the features of flesh: This is a lesson in which age has tutored me. Yet even in such transcendence we cannot escape the very ubiquity of what hauls around our souls from place to place, and that is the shoving ambivalence of *agape* love.

The Breath taught me the perfection of flesh, its meaning as fellowship, in the days after I regained consciousness after the evacuation of my child and quite nearly, my life. For a week, Cordelia said that I seemed a recumbent statue of tallow and blood, and everyone gave up hope except Aquila and she who never left me.

But the Breath spoke before I did, of

a high priest who could sympathize with every weakness,
gently dealing,
with compassion from his own reservoir of loud cries and tears,
the learning of obedience from suffering

—and all these words coming from what Cordelia called my lips of wax.

In the first days of shadow and more and more light, she read me what I had said—what the Breath and I had said—and I began to remember their passage through my throat and mouth.

There was more. With words as delicate as the new growth on a late-winter bush, she told me of the child, too mercifully young to have gender, too bittersweet to have name, who flushed out with my blood and Aquila's tears and who Cordelia washed and wrapped and buried under an olive tree shading a garden tomb, praying the words the Breath had breathed through me:

Let us then approach the throne of grace with confidence
so that we may receive mercy
and find grace
to help us in our time
of need

But this knowledge made me mute. For days and nights I could not count, I was in a place with no syllables of my own. I lived in twilight, fraught twilight, even my mind dumb, grieving the loss of what I had not known I possessed.

Sometimes I stared at Cordelia's belly and wondered how it would be to know and then never give birth, or whether it was worse to have not known and nonetheless delivered a child in a writhing dream.

Days and days and days.

And then a day came when I stretched my arms and knew that they had blood in them again, opened my lungs and felt the air of life. To my shame I admit that my first words then were those of my own needs: of water and food and explanations. And Cordelia could not find enough of any of them to satisfy me because all dribbled out of the corners of my mouth.

It was as if everything had tumbled onto a grate and what fell into the cistern below belonged there and could be measured and gathered and catalogued.

"Tell me of the council, of what was decided," I asked Aquila later that day with a voice that knew its own disuse and proceeded with caution.

He paused from stitching the vestibule of a large tent, wrestling with the coarse cloth over one shoulder, his hair flaring out toward its friction.

"So, what did Paul and Peter and the others decide about us Gentiles? Do Cordelia and I need to prepare ourselves for circumcision?" It was my first attempt at humor and it felt like a foreign language to me and produced only an exasperated sigh from Aquila as he wrangled a failing needle.

"Of course not. It's only for men. And it's not a requirement."

I yawned. "So, you can somehow be uncircumcised? To show fellowship?"

He looked narrowly at me and began to shake his head, then a slow smile lifted the tired corners of his mouth.

"Ah. My Priscilla is back."

I shrugged.

"They tried to decide what could not be bartered or negotiated." He looked toward the distant corner of the room, searching for words. "What was beyond compromise. What carried meaning for Gentiles and Jews alike."

"What was that?"

"They sent out Paul and his advocate and friend Barnabas and two men named Judas and Silas with a message. It was for all believers, Jew and Gentile alike." He put the fabric down and counted off on his fingers. "Don't eat food sacrificed to idols, don't eat blood or the meat of strangled animals, and no sexual immorality."

I settled back onto the couch whose cushion bore the intaglio where I had lain those weeks. "And what about Peter? Is he still here in Jerusalem?"

"He went to Antioch, but it came to light that he was still afraid of the Jews who are of the circumcision faction. He had persuaded Barnabas, too."

"He is a great man, Aquila. We have seen healings—he is a power conduit. Even his shadow, even his sweatband—they brought health. But even more, he is an eyewitness—he walked and sailed and ate and slept with Jesus."

I looked around for some way to say this right. "How can he be so mistaken?"

He considered for a moment in that drying-honey way he had of speaking. "An extraordinary man. But I wonder if his leadership is being passed on to someone else. Or at least distributed. Perhaps that is a better way of saying it."

I waited as he sorted out some raveling threads. "Seems he and Paul had a big disagreement, but Paul prevailed," he said, sorting words as well. "And now we hear news of Paul from Lystra. So many are coming to the light. So many new believers. New churches springing up in homes and synagogues everywhere."

I realized that a teeming universe lay behind that simple account. I was not able to process more than that; in fact, could hardly keep my eyes open.

But the next day I helped him cut the flaps for a tent, and we were partners again.

A veil had descended over Aquila's eyes in Jerusalem, however. It did not leave him until we left that city. I realized that our bodies had occupied the same space when I was ill but that we had not partaken of time in the same way. Perhaps we never did from that point on, and often when I awakened at night and watched him I wondered if that were a token of what he must have experienced and that I now must bear even in waking hours.

It was the nighttime that was worst. Each evening, to Aquila's bewilderment, I would feel myself begin to splinter like wooden table legs when a wagonload is unloaded onto it. I was defenseless against the inchoate darknesses, the sadnesses, the murky irrationality of fears that seemed to partake of my own flesh and make it their substantial own and that in the night watches gathered into a singularity, a faceless entity of dread.

Once when trimming Aquila's fingernails, I accidentally drew blood. For the rest of the night I lay and thought of a hundred ways I could injure my own hand.

I began to wonder if I were losing my mind. Then this substance began to come to inhabit daytime hours too, and within days was so constant a companion that I could see the concern in Cordelia's eyes.

"This is the way of many women after a child," she told me, "and it will pass."

But it did not pass. It grew.

"You have not had a child," I said one day. I knew my words hurt her but I could not stop myself from infecting her with the sickness-dark that was within me. "So how can you assure me, since you have not had a child?"

Her words were quiet and her eyes averted.

"Nor did you experience having a child," she said,

letting her voice linger on what she said. "But you have all the other effects. This is the way of many women, and once you have looked it in the eye, it will begin to leave you."

But this aspect of woman-ness did not leave at once, or all at once. It became a secret, shared companion to her and to me both, an unwelcome guest for whom we set a place at the table of our conversations and looked in upon at dusk and midnight and acknowledged each dawn.

But with each sunrise its once-irresistible pointing finger began to lose its authority to dominate and direct; and one morning we both knew that it was leaving its garments behind and would visit again, but that it no longer resided with us.

Chapter Thirteen

How Aquila and Cordelia and I were able to escape the attention in Jerusalem of the vectors of all the roiling activity within its walls during that time, I do not know. The entire country was under the rule of Roman procurators. There was no such thing as normalcy, I was told. The unheard-of was the expected.

There had been riots in the Temple precinct. Galilean pilgrims were slaughtered, it was rumored that Samaritans were bribing officials. A man proclaiming himself to be a prophet came to the Mount of Olives with 30,000 disciples and when the Procurator Antonius Felix heard of this, he killed 400 of them and crucified anyone he considered to be another imposter. It was not a good time to be a follower of any messiah.

And yet in all this we were untouched. I remarked once that it was as if Aquila and Cordelia and I wore the caps of invisibility of Perseus and passed unnoticed among Pharisee, Sadducee, Roman and barbarian. Almost at once, though, I regretted using the imagery of dead idols when there were accurate words, David's ascent song that Cordelia and I sang in the yeasty air that itself climbed over our bowls and looms and needles:

If the LORD had not been on our side, let Israel say,

and Cordelia and Priska, we sang:

if the LORD had not been on our side when men attacked us, when their anger flared against us, they would have swallowed us alive; the flood would have engulfed us, the torrent would have swept over us, the raging waters would have swept us away.

We sang, we sang, the songs of contravention …

Praise be to the LORD, who has not let us be torn by their teeth.

We have escaped like a bird out of the fowler's snare; the snare has been broken, and we have escaped.

Our help is in the name of the LORD,

… the God of kneading troughs, and weaver's shuttles, and women with burned forearms and hands aching and fingertips scarred;

the Maker of heaven and earth.

The God of a house of tents and bread and peace in the midst of a ripped-open city.

And thus it was that Jerusalem in those days carried all the symbolic weight that it was created to do, for others and for me: opened gates and unused passageways, birth and death, capture and escape.

And prophecy. It was during my time in Jerusalem, and a while afterward, that the Holy Breath breathed on my eyes as well as on my lips, and I saw things that were to come. There were no words to this, no time and times and half times, no unrolling scrolls with writing, just images. I could not understand the meaning of many of them at the time and archived them in my mind.

In Jerusalem, no one was safe. Cordelia and I went nowhere in the city without Aquila. One day we were near the temple and saw a man moving in what I could only describe as a procession, wearing vestments I recognized from the writings of Exodus. Cordelia stared at the man as he paused and turned dramatically in the sunlight so that the jewels on his chest sparkled.

"That apron-like garment on his chest is the ephod," I whispered to her, "and the jewels are in what is called the breastplate—one jewel for each of the twelve tribes of Israel."

The man's blue robe made a faint metallic sound as he moved up to a platform and gazed over the gathering crowd, and I saw the dozens of tiny gold bells and pomegranates on the hem of the robe he wore. He turned again—consciously, I could see—so that people could get a better look at him, and he held one hand out in front of him like a Caesar statue. His head was wound round with a white cloth and blue cords held a gold plate onto his forehead.

Cordelia squinted. "What does that gold plate say?"

I clasped my hands together in front of me. "Holiness to the Lord," I whispered in awe.

Beside me, Aquila spat on the ground. "Holiness? I don't think so. This man, Jonathan, isn't even of the priestly tribe of Levi. He's a fraud."

I had not taken my eyes off the man but the glistening of the colors on his chest dulled like the scum on the surface of an abandoned well. Before my eyes—no, before the eyes of my heart—the high priest seemed to gather within himself and wither like a winter-blasted branch and then disintegrate, leaving his garments and vestments—even his turban—standing as if inhabited only by air.

Behind him, the Temple seemed to melt. Its foundation stones began to tumble as if they were chasing one another in a race to dive from Jerusalem's plateau to the valley below. All that remained was a single room and its ponderous veil moved in the breeze. I could see the glint of gold behind its borders. I began to tremble.

"What do you see?" Aquila's voice was urgent. Behind me, I felt Cordelia's arms circling my waist, protecting. Aquila stood directly in front of me and pulled his tallit, his prayer shawl over both our heads. I felt his breathing on my face.

"What do you see?"

"All that is left of him is the vestments." It sounded impossible, even to me.

"Go on."

"And the temple—

Look, Teacher! What massive stones!

all the stones of it fell down,

what magnificent buildings!

just like Peter said

Do you see all these great buildings? Not one stone here

that the Christos prophesied …

will be left on another

every one

will be thrown

down

"Go on." His voice was tender. He knew the words of Jesus, Peter had told us.

I took courage. Aquila believed me.

"And the inner room, the holy place, is all that is left. And I can see things inside it, but I don't understand what it means."

I paused, trying to put words to the quality of what I saw, discovering to my amazement that I could still view it even inside the covering of Aquila's tallit.

"But I'm afraid to look at it. It isn't made of earth things." I could not find the right words. I rested my forehead in the little cupped space below his collarbone and closed my eyes.

We stood there, the three of us, until the images left the insides of my eyelids. I felt Aquila's tallit falling from our heads, his arms wrapping it around our shoulders. Cordelia's arms slipped away from me. When I opened my eyes, the crowd had dispersed and the high priest was gone.

A mule-drawn cart creaked beside us and we stepped aside to give it passage. Its driver looked at us with no curiosity and continued on. We began to walk back to the house.

"It makes sense." Aquila spoke into my ear as we walked slowly so that Cordelia could keep up. He began to recite something that was familiar to me, as if it were words spoken to me while I was still in the womb, words that were part of me at a time when I could not comprehend them, could only move with their throbbing rhythms.

"Every high priest taken from amongst men is established for men in things relating to God, that he may offer both gifts and sacrifices for sins, being able to exercise forbearance towards the ignorant and erring, since he himself also is clothed with infirmity," Aquila said, his words halting but precise. He considered before asking me a question.

"But this man Jonathan believes he has no infirmity; could you see that, Priscilla?"

I nodded and he began to recite again.

"On account of this, he ought, even as for the people, so also for himself, to offer for sins. And no one takes the honour to himself, but called by God, even as Aaron also." He stopped and addressed himself to me again, and turned to appeal to Cordelia too. "These false high priests were not called. Sometimes they even purchased the office."

He began again to recite. "Thus the Christ also has not glorified himself to be made a high priest; but he who had said to him, *Thou* art my Son, *I* have today begotten thee. Even as also in another place he says, *Thou* art a priest forever according to the order of Melchizedek."

By now we were in the house. Aquila turned to me. "Why is Jesus a priest according to the order of Melchizedek?" Cordelia, too, was looking at me expectantly.

"Why are you asking me that? Why do you keep talking about Melchizedek?" I felt confused. Cordelia and Aquila looked at one another.

"Those are the words you spoke, when you were so, so ill." Cordelia struggled, trying not to say anything about the child. She went to the corner of the room and pulled a scroll from the earthenware pot and, rolling to the end, began to read:

"Who in the days of his flesh, having offered up both supplications and entreaties to him who was able to save him out of death, with strong crying and tears; (and having been heard because of his piety;) though he were Son, he learned obedience from the things which he suffered; and having been perfected …"

Aquila interrupted her—no, he stopped her reading and began to recite from memory.

"Having been perfected, became to all them that obey him, author of eternal salvation; addressed by God as high priest according to the order of Melchizedek."

"You committed it to memory? What the Breath said? What I—we—said?"

Aquila drew himself up and recited, from the beginning, with a light in his eyes:

"In the past God spoke to our ancestors through the prophets—at many times and in various ways …"

I sat in silence, listening to words that had come from my mouth, but not from my soul, and drew my own shawl around me as if swaddling myself.

It was months before I was able to travel. But in the summer as soon as I could, we left Jerusalem. We traveled overland to Ephesus, sometimes on horseback and sometimes in a four-wheeled *reda* carriage. From Ephesus we booked a fair-winds passage to Corinth where many Jews and other believers were coming as refugees from Rome, some having sifted through the sieves of other countries before settling as light as twice-milled flour on the floor of that Greek city.

Corinth was itself a resurrection. It had been destroyed a hundred years before by Roman armies and now rose from its own rubble as an imperial colony. For me, of course, it was once, and for a while, my childhood home. But though I had Roman citizenship and this was a Roman city, it was never my destination.

Just as Corinth was on an isthmus between two seas, so it kept at bay things which could never mix but with which I waged battle there from the moment I arrived.

The first was the prescience of disaster, what I later heard described as the sentence of death on the heart. All must die, I knew, yet I had the sense of an unfilled life, as if something were lacking that might never be supplied. Sometimes I wondered if it were that I would never be able to bear a child. In other moments I took hold of the timbers of my soul and shook them as violently as a person can do only figuratively. I began to feel a homesickness for something lost, and would find myself looking toward the mountain, the Acrocorinth, the pendant on the necklace of Corinth's city wall.

All my life I had heard of the temple that once stood there, the place of Venus, and I remembered its crags, the sense of wonder my child-eyes had bestowed on it, the whispers of my mother's garments as she put on her shawl to leave, and I would know it was to that mountain she would go, and my father too. I thought now of the thousands of women who had served there as slave-priestesses and it seemed their tears carved out the crevasses on the mountain, their lost dreams wandering among the tumbled stones of the ruined temple.

And yet … and yet. I ached for the simplicity and the certainty of the old ways, the chants of sweet-voiced Egyptian eunuchs and sistrums in an echoing hallway, the settling of matters by the resilience and augury of knucklebones, the finality of the shriek of an oracle on a three-legged stool over the fumes of Delphi, of a time when I was not continually bewildered by the gods, nor myself.

More than that, my time in Jerusalem with its ungraven images had desiccated a part of me, the part that has always thirsted for art. I found myself thinking of Rubria, the hems of her robe whispering as she walked among the three Graces: life among stones, youth among agelessness, beauty among beauty. I wondered if I would ever see her again.

In Corinth, the symmetry of sparkling ribbed columns with their satisfactions of dimensions and ratios and curling acanthus leaves, and the yearning twist of a carved marble torso over an invisible axis seen only in the artist's mind—these brought back desires more powerful than those of the body: the yearnings of the eye and mind. For centuries, too, Corinth had been host to the Isthmian Games, the competitions for which it was famous; and I confess that these only deepened my distress. Though the flinging of sweat and saliva in the equestrian and boxing and wrestling events held little allure for me, the urgency of the races with the knot-muscled desperation of the angled plunge forward over a finish line, the sagging under a myrtle-branch wreath—these seemed good and right and just and true.

Most of all, the musical competitions of the games created a well of longing into which they threw stones that never hit bottom. My ears could not hear enough. I felt the ponderance of drums in my footsoles, the sting of bells in my armpits and neck, and the call of a *kithera* harp made me weep, unashamed. I mourned the fact that this music thrived in my soul but would never emerge from my lips nor fingertips. It was a treasure I could touch but never possess.

I heard that the emperor Claudius had an adopted son named Nero, who, though only a youth, loved poetry and music, and I began to hope for a future where music and art could undergird the histories of the Christos. But as soon as that thought became choate, I felt a breeze and saw an image of a young boy with dried blood on his elbows and I knew, even then, who it was and what it meant.

Nonetheless, Corinth was as peaceful a time as we had, Aquila and I, for the rest of our lives. I look back on it as the city we lived in but claimed no citizenship for and looked beyond, the place where I learned the meaning of a race with a prize.

And of course, it was the city where I finally met Paul.

Chapter Fourteen

When we placed our skeins of thread onto the worktable of our new shop in Corinth, each was an egg of promise and new beginnings. After the dangers and tensions in both Rome and Jerusalem, we were freed prisoners and could hardly wait to go to the synagogue for Sabbat services, to walk openly through streets where—at least at first—a believer could greet another without fear.

Though there were hundreds of Christians in that city, not all assembled with the Jews, who had an elegant meeting place and much influence in the polyglot crossroads. Corinth was hope for us, and its synagogue was where we wanted to find a core of people who would provide us with connections with the others.

The first Sabbat, Aquila went on ahead to meet with some of the men. In the dusk, Cordelia and I saw four men who embraced each other—were they weeping?—and then passed behind the synagogue screen that separated the men and women. I strained my eyes to see Aquila. His tallit shawl moved in rhythmic nods, and as the setting sun stared across his back I could see every hair of his beard that protruded from the cloth, every burred thread on his cloak, every suspended dust mote in the air. I could hardly tear my eyes away.

Sabbat shalom, baruch atah ha Shem, I murmured clumsily to the other women, Sabbath peace, blessed be the Name. *Kol ha'Kavod*, they said, all the glory to Him. With them, Cordelia and I entered the synagogue silently, and sat in our section.

Through the Sabbat prayers—words here and there I understood, *Adonai Elohenu, Melech ha-Olam*, the Lord our God, King of the Earth—I speculated which of the men in the audience could be the famous Paul, and was startled when the synagogue leader, Sosthenes—one who had rolled his eyes at my efforts to greet some of the other women in my halting Hebrew—introduced a man as the rabbi Paul and invited him to speak. To my relief, Aquila rose to stand by his side to translate into the commonness of Greek.

I cannot best describe Paul's physical appearance other than to say he looked like a man who had been repeatedly injured. It wasn't scars (although there were those; I saw them later on his forehead in the sunlight) but it was the inclination of his throat, the reluctance of one leg in the process of walking, the nearly-unnoticeable favoring of an arm that required that he coax it upward with shoulder muscles and neck. Nor was his face remarkable except in its—how shall I say it?—lack of classical proportions. Whatever mean there was to his face, it was not golden.

I found myself trying to compare him to any other visage I had ever known before I realized the striking similarity to a statue I once saw of Socrates. His eyes were much too prominent. I would even say they were uncomfortable, though he showed no awareness of it. And there was an unsettling lack of symmetry in his chin and mouth.

If such a man were like Socrates, I thought, surely he would be given a compensating grace.

And he was. From the moment he bent over the Torah scroll he became translucent—not to his surroundings, but to his words. He had one lesson and that alone. It was not the theatre of remorse, but what I can only remember, and describe, as the paroxysm of resurrection. What mild and vague hopes I had from the Old Covenant scroll and the words of Christos on the New Covenant scrolls, they blanched in comparison to Paul's story.

He told of his ambush on a road by an offended Yeshua so kinetic, so dominant of time and space, that the ontology of revivified flesh subsumed every other issue that a human mind could contemplate.

But his own experience he soon dismissed. It happened on a road, but.... *Here* and *here*, he said, quoting from the Torah, peering into its folds as if seeing passage after passage fugitive from his relentless address. He reached in and dragged out verse after verse as if they were organs from a still-living creature: heart, lungs, kidneys, viscera that would only function to their destiny when placed into that resurrected One who, indeed, came to life yet again before our eyes:

As the shadow of the Torah, the manna hidden in the corner of a kerchief,

The inexhaustible light of the menorah;

Ram, lamb,

Perfected corner stone ...

When he stepped back from the Torah stand it was as if he emerged from a mist. Sensing his returning mortality, the synagogue leader and others took courage and began to ask him questions which he answered with the placidity—

perhaps even weariness—of a parent who has been asked the same things again and again. There was none of the iridescence of words we had seen before. There were only questions and answers.

Yeshua, Yeshua, the synagogue murmured.

Yeshua HaMashiach, Jesus the Messiah, others replied.

The other men who had come with Paul began to speak with the Jewish men in clots along the walls. Some shook their garment hems and left. Others showed the anger we by now knew so well. Some—those with the Asian sandals and exotic rings—shrugged their shoulders: room for all, they seemed to say.

But one by one, many of the men brought their wives and children outside to the ceremonial washing pool where Paul continued to teach into the torch-streaked darkness. The *mikveh* was reborn and rebirth that very night.

But it was not until the next day that I finally met Paul, when Aquila left for a while and then brought him into our home.

"Paul has heard of your abilities with languages. He wants to talk with you." I thought I heard something like pride in his voice.

He bowed as he came through our doorway, and then Paul gave me what I realized with disappointment was a hurried kiss on the cheek. He looked so—ordinary.

"I'm sorry that we could not be introduced last night," he said. He looked at me cautiously, as if he were afraid of me. "There were many matters to attend to. It seems I cause a controversy among my fellow Jews just by existing." He spoke to me in Latin, and smiled wryly at his own joke.

I sat down with Cordelia. "I have heard that you are also a Roman citizen," I began.

"Yes. Though it has not proved to be much of an advantage."

I thought for a moment. "And I hear that you have traveled much since your … your … encounter with Jesus of Nazareth."

He sighed and I realized that he wanted to talk about something other than this, but he conceded.

"I first spoke of this encounter in the synagogues of Damascus," he said. "I find that people are often more curious about those times than even the life of the Christos."

I dipped my head in shame but he saw and rushed on to explain.

"Then there were my desert years—three years alone in Arabia, a yeshiva of only one student, you might say. When I had been tutored by that place and that Man, I went to Jerusalem, where my Jewish brothers tried to kill me. An experience they have often tried to replicate, I'm afraid." He smiled at himself again.

"I escaped in a basket let down the city wall, but, like most of my escapes, it was somewhat imperfect." He lifted his hands above his head and as his robe fell away from his arms I saw deep ruts of scars beneath his upper arms.

"Whatever I expected from the other Christians, it turned out to be gold and miry clay, one might say, like Daniel's dream of the unstable statue. If not for Barnabas my advocate, I would not have survived the brethren." He looked around the room.

"Then the Hellenists sought my life and when Barnabas, who went ahead of me to Antioch, called for me I gladly went. And it has been a mixture of great joy and much terror ever since."

This was hardly an account I expected. So much turmoil, so many sufferings! Surely Christos would make the way smooth if he called someone in a manner as extraordinary as Paul's. Not true for me or anyone I knew, but surely for the apostle born out of season, the special witness of Jesus …

I did not know how to respond, so I repeated dully, "A lot of traveling."

Paul looked into the distance through the window of the house. "Traveling. Sometimes I think of the great ocean as being a bare belly, and I must lace all the lands around it together, pull them together."

"So you would stitch the world onto Crete and Cyprus."

Aquila laughed—somewhat breathlessly, I realized—and Cordelia patted me on the arm, then the room was silent again.

"Perhaps there is a reason that you are a seamstress and that Aquila and I are tentmakers," he said. "Perhaps you are to have a part in this. Perhaps this is to what you are being called here, in our affinity of fingers."

Paul leaned his head to one side and a sound like pebbles falling against cement came from his neck. I was filled with disappointment, for I did not want to be the fine-work expert of seams and embellishments. I thought of the Christos with a towel around his waist and it did not help a bit.

"You heard the first of the story last night," he began.

"I want to know what that felt like, the vision," I blurted. "That's what I really want to hear about." Both Cordelia and Aquila looked at me with surprise. Paul, however, didn't seem bothered.

"You mean, aside from being blinded and helpless and without recourse and being told that I would suffer—no, being told *how much* I would suffer the rest of my life for the sake of the One I met?" His voice had risen with something like anger, but now was mild. He looked at the floor for a long while.

"I would have to say that I also felt as if I were in a

dream, dreaming of being awake," he said. "Aware of all around me but unable to interact in any way that could help my own situation."

"And this feeling has happened again, since." I could hardly believe myself, my boldness.

"Yes. Many times. Sometimes I see things. But more often it is just words. Words that are like a movement of air over my mind, and it is stilled and listening and I find that I am able to remember them."

"Do you talk to people about it?"

He sighed. "Not often. I prefer to talk about those things where there were witnesses, such as my encounter on the Damascus road."

I nodded. "People believe you when you tell them how that happened."

His neck took his nod and it revolved into the shaking of his head, slowly, slowly.

"People want to know how it happened. But no person's experience, my sister Priska, is normative. We each have an inventory of events and feelings from our lives. From those facts we choose to represent them to ourselves and to others. But the witness of no single person is worth staking your life on. Unless, of course, that person has come back from the dead."

I was satisfied. I had heard what I wanted to know. I folded my hands and took my gaze from him.

"I have heard that your Latin is impeccable and erudite." He spoke now in Greek, and we both smiled. "And that you have read the classics in both languages and have turned from the dead idols to Life." Here Cordelia dipped her head in assent and his eyes lingered on her for a moment.

"And your Hebrew is, shall we say, yet outstripped by your questions about it." He smiled again and I laughed out loud at the charity of his phrasing.

"It's true. I have trouble with a language where there is not a definite past and present and future," I said, hesitantly. Paul tipped his heavy head to one side and then shrugged in agreement.

"Greek is the perfect language for the Good News," he said. "It allows for the sense of things completed and yet whose influence goes on. In fact, it is about things completed whose influence goes on."

I put a plate of Cordelia's warm, flat bread and a plate of figs preserved in honey onto the table. I dared to speak.

"It's a conserve of facts."

I saw him considering the figs.

"How so?"

"Language is a conserve, so to speak, of the facts that it represents."

"But not the only conserve."

I thought for a moment. "No, an event, for instance, can be conserved in a statue. Or a painting. Or even in memory."

Paul tore a piece of bread and rolled it up like a scroll, scattering sesame seeds onto the table. Then he dipped the bread in the figs and brought it to his mouth without spilling a drop.

"Have you considered—and I am sure you have," he began with a concession to me that made me blush, "that language—not art, and not merely memories—is the conserve that God selected to convey the facts about Himself to people?"

I wondered with sudden panic if he were looking into my soul and was about to expose my lust for art. But when I had the courage to look into his eyes I saw only a welcoming raising of his eyebrows. I calculated how he might respond if I did not agree with him. I looked down again before I answered.

"No, not always."

The eyebrows stayed high. I hurried to explain.

"Take our patriarch Joseph, for instance." I was rushing, but could not help myself. "The wordless dreams he had—of the stars and sheaves bowing down to him. What about Ezekiel's visions, and Daniel's—"

His voice interrupting was soft.

"And how do you know of these things? Is it not because the incidents have been conserved with language? And you may savor them, as did Joseph, and David, and Nehemiah, and all who know of them?" He put another fig-laden piece of bread into his mouth and pursed his lips as he chewed, as if he were afraid it might escape his mouth, and looked toward the dish of fruit again. I was suddenly afraid I might lose him to my own cooking.

"Surely, though," I pushed, "the first recipient of such things, the dreams, the words—such a person would be, you know, special."

"I can only speak for myself, of course. He wiped his mouth and cast a longing look at the food. "I heard the words on the Damascus road. But they were not just for me. I had a sense of that, almost from the beginning. What they signified was for anyone who heard about my experience, not just for me."

I took another piece of bread and loaded it with figs and handed it to him. "Go on."

He cupped the food in his hand. "Not special, my sister, and not just for my benefit." He looked at me and now I feared he saw my greed for my own words, the ones given me by the Holy Breath. Could he know? But he was not looking at me, not accusing. He continued on.

"Not all words are equal, you know." He gestured toward the opened Scripture scroll that lay on a nearby stool. "I may not agree with everything our brother Peter the rock says and does" (here he allowed himself a little laugh, without a tinge of bitterness) "but he is right about one thing. He says that no speaking-forth of the holy Writings came out of human ambition, or even human will. He says, in fact, that such words are an outgrowth—an exhaling, so to speak—of the Holy Breath. And thus, they themselves function differently than other words."

I shook my head. "We have only just met, sir, brother …"

He nodded acceptance. "So speak frankly with me."

"But is not your own experience what you yourself said convinces people? It is because you were there, you saw the risen One. Are you not undermining the weight, the influence of your own experience?"

"How so?"

"You are a witness, first-hand. That's the qualification for being an apostle in the first place, is that not true?"

"It is. And our brothers, John the loved one and Luke the physician, believe that conserving the words of the eyewitnesses is essential. As do I. But you do see, dear sister, that there are only a few of us who were eyewitnesses and some of them have died. Not everyone will have such first-hand experience, nor, even more significant, will most even know an eyewitness."

"That is true." Not even the largest synagogue in the world, not even the greatest stadium, could provide audience to every citizen of the world should Paul and the other apostles preach there day and night until the return of the Christos.

"So all experiences are turned into representations—in this case, words—before they can be conveyed from person to person." He paused as if waiting for me to catch up on a footpath.

I nodded.

"And since no one can go back to any experience—not even, say, could I return to the first bite of your delicious figs—then our only access to any experience, ours or that of another, is through the representation of them. The memory. The words that convey the memory."

He could apparently bear it no longer—the figs in his hand were beginning to drip. He ate what was in his hand with small, slow bites.

"I see," I said. "Thus, the holy words—"

"Why do you call them holy words?" The thought seemed to startle him.

"Because they are the access that others have to essential experiences, experiences from beyond our own knowing. They are bolstered words."

"Bolstered?"

"Peter told us that Yeshua told all the disciples that they would have special help with words in times of trouble." I was thinking this through even as I spoke. "And it seems to me you have been in trouble ever since that time on the road."

"That is true."

"Peter said Yeshua promised that when they went before magistrates or any enemy that the words would be given to them."

"Yes. Peter did report that. And it does seem to fit with what happens with me."

"So these would be a special, shall we say, genre or class of words."

He waited a while to respond. "Yes."

I felt a lightness in my boldness. "And when the Holy Breath is—shall we say—active, they are used to describe things. Then such words are those through which anyone can access the experience. Thus, they would have to be assured of protection. No personal agenda, for instance.

Accuracy."

He was looking at me with eyes that narrowed and widened, narrowed and widened.

I was ready for my summation. "In a way, then, I myself saw what you saw on the road to Damascus."

The silence in the room was like white smoke: nearly opaque.

"Or no longer saw," he smiled. "But I am not sure I can agree with you."

I could not contain my excitement, the thrill of my understanding. "It is like the Passover, the shared experience!"

"What do you mean?"

"Moses taught the Israelites, the children of the ones who had crossed the Red Sea, to each say, 'I was a slave in Egypt.' Even though they never saw a drop of that water, never smelled the stenches of Egypt."

He nodded. "Through these words we appropriate the experience each Passover as if it were our own personal experience."

"Then … we are all equidistant, so to speak, from all these sacred events." I brushed his sesame seeds into the palm of my hand and held them tight. "From Abel. From Enoch and Noah and Sarah and Moses and Rahab."

"This mutual proximity, this way of thinking is the spiritual polity of the church, you know. Its economy is that of words," Paul concluded. He stood.

Suddenly I, who had been a sieve for the thoughts in my mind, could not digest all he was now saying. I hid the words in the grotto of my mind. Even now I am not sure of all that he must have meant by that.

"So you are saying that this levels the ground for all of us, whether we saw the Christos or not?" Aquila spoke, his arms before him, his hands smoothing an invisible flat surface.

"Indeed, level. You are exactly right, my brother. Accessible to anyone who believes. As Jesus said, 'Blessed are those who believe without seeing with their own eyes.'"

Paul's own eyes closed briefly and then he sighed and looked at all of us. "However. It will sound presumptuous, perhaps, but I do have the conviction that even the way I speak of what happened on the Damascus road is not my choosing. And other matters. The words feel … supervised, you know?"

He was wrapping his cloak around him to leave. He did not look only at me as he spoke.

But I did indeed know.

Chapter Fifteen

Because the unwelcome houseguest of my soul had resolutely followed me to Corinth, even supposed safety, and the rhythm of tentmaking, and the consolation of a husband and friends, could not evict it completely.

Sometimes I could see its approach in the distance, the size of a man's hand on the horizon, and like Elijah bound for Jezreel I would gird my soul and sprint, gasping, just beyond its claws until I ran out of breath and sensation on the soles of my sand-worn feet, collapsing under a lone haven-tree in my mind, for I knew, like Elijah, I am no better than my ancestors.

It robbed me of words. That was its greatest injury. It reduced my discourse with others to necessities and my prayers to ordinariness of wells and wishes and driftings off at the ends of those times when I deer-panted for communion.

And yet in the scent before the guest's arrivals, and the lingering wisps when it left, I felt the Holy Breath as unmistakably as I had ever known. It was in those times, especially amidst the goings-away of the guest, that I learned to engage battle with God. I do not know whether to be proud of this or ashamed of it, but it was. And it is even now.

Only in a clawing ascent out of where these feelings took me could I pray what I really wanted to say. And there was no method, no procedure, which could evoke it. Once it happened after feeling the Breath like gauze on my cheek as I dropped into sleep.

I dreamed of Moses wedged into a rock, with Goodness a pendulum passing back and forth before him, his vision obscured by a hand on his eyes, hearing words

Mercy, mercy
Compassion
Compassion
Slow, slow, slow to anger

I cried out on the mountain; Moses cried too, because of the intimacy, and the leaving at last.

Just before waking, I saw a rock and I drank from it, the same rock as Moses, and it was Christos.

And the next morning, I could pray again:

Oh God of silence and of hope
I approach you in that hovering place
between Presence and utter void,
between answer and your backside in departure …

(And then, such absence of everything as I waited …)

Let the accusing mouth of sin become tongue-tied as I come to you

During such times, the reduction of the number of my spoken words unsettled both Cordelia and Aquila, though I felt myself powerless to change this situation. How could I augment from a scorched mind? Day by day, Cordelia baked and swept. Day by day, Aquila and I continued to scrape leather, weave goat hair, stitch and stitch and stitch in our open-air shop in front of our home near the entrance to the bejeweled Corinthian marketplace where exotic goods from the city's two harbors, Lechaeum and Cenchreae, astonished both Asia and Rome. And at that crossroad of pilgrimage they all called "two-sea'd Corinth" everyone, it seemed, needed tents.

I saw Paul and his companions, Silas and Timothy, at the synagogue and in the marketplace, but in these meetings there was no speaking of conserves and words. They looked over my shoulders, urgent to provoke the inflammation of the Gospel onto the Gentile merchants and artists and thinkers of the city with words that pulsed. Nothing but Jesus, nothing but Jesus, nothing but crucified.

Aquila was often gone in the evenings with the brethren taking the embers of Christos into the cooking pits of idols, while Cordelia and I were pots left to simmer unwatched because our flames were safe and contained. I wish I could say that I ministered to the new women converts by teaching them, but, truth be told, I found myself awkward and afraid among them. Perhaps I feared the contagion of the grace of their statuary. (There. There it is. I still yearned, I now say with shame, for the artwork of the old gods.) Perhaps it was that I feared that my old robes of aristocracy peeked from beneath the hem of my rough-spun tunic, betraying me as a counterfeit pilgrim, a sham of the devout.

Only one gift could I give to the women. I could minister with God's words to them, never my own. I was surprised to find that the women of Corinth had not been tutored in the classics; in fact, many could not read at all and only spoke *koine* Greek because they could not barter in the marketplace without that universal language. The Jewish women could read more, but only Hebrew, and nodded with satisfaction as they heard the concepts of their childhood now in Greek. And the other converts spoke languages of other worlds, it seemed, and baptized their newly-learned Greek into a pool of clicks and guttural sounds I had never heard except from birds and animals.

Only when reading aloud the Law and the Prophets did I make peace with this growing, polyglot group. I would look up and see faces of wonder, suspicion, hope, fear, disbelief. But it was the words that wooed them, and many began to memorize sections in Greek, and when we met together they would giggle as they corrected one another. But I was ever the tutor, never one of them.

Perhaps I should feel some guilt about this but I confess that the richness I had when I was alone with Aquila in the perfumed nights, and the days I spent with my beloved friend Cordelia left me with no longing for the company of many others. Aquila I loved more passionately than I'd ever dreamed possible. And as for my friend, part of it was a mixture of pity and love for her, as her body, like an obstructed branch, seemingly daily bent around the unyielding burden she always carried before her, and her hands and feet came to look more and more like the drying leftover lumps of dough she threw to the chickens in our courtyard.

When the guest was not in residence, we often spoke—perhaps with the shame of those who are unsure of themselves—of what the Breath had said to me. I wondered if I would ever receive any more words. Many times I saw Cordelia taking the Holy Breath scrolls from the clay jar where we kept them and reading them in the heat of the day when it was too hot to work. She fretted about the fact that she could not memorize with the ease Aquila had in breathing with me the Holy Breath words, nor the facility the other women had with the Old Testament scrolls.

I would see her bending over her kneading trough with her tight lips chewing out silent syllables and her knotted hands pounding the dough which mutely withheld the next phrase; then she would peel the flour from her fingertips and walk again to the earthenware pot where a section of my scroll lay open, tease it open with her forefingers and then exhale a *ha!* of triumph before walking stiffly back to her bread, her lips working again.

Cordelia and I had no access to any of the poetry that had so absorbed our childish minds in Rome: It was all about heroes whose exploits I now doubted and gods whose very existences I knew to be the vapors of long-dead minds. We began, each of us, to write our own poetry—often without the conceits of rhythm and sound, more the evaporation of our thoughts and feelings—and in the quiet evenings after our time of memorizing from Isaiah or putting our own impromptu melodies to Psalms or other sections from the Septuagint, to share our own writings with one another.

For me, this practice seemed to dull the craving I had for things of my old life. I began to feel the luxuriance of words, words for their own sake. In this other use of words, my own words, however, I knew that while the Holy Breath might swirl around me like a night breeze, He was not speaking through me. It was as if His was a different language inside me when He overcame me with words that came out with my voice; whereas the poetry was something as native to me as a child growing inside me.

One evening Cordelia and I spoke of what Peter had said about the final meal he shared with Christos and the other disciples, and the fervency of Jesus when He spoke of unity. The next evening Cordelia shyly brought from a hiding place a piece of old leather on which she had written:

I in them, He prayed
And Thou in Me
That they may be perfected as one

My Jesus (here Cordelia's voice whispered)
You have been
The answer to my every prayer
May I be
The answer
To Yours?

In the way of women who company together, our bodies achieved a kind of synchronicity that seemed a validation of our loyalty to one another, when our monthly flows began and ended on the same days. We would go together, with the secrecy women know, to wash our cloths in a stream as the women of Jerusalem did, reciting to ourselves the words of Isaiah: All our righteousnesses as menstrual rags.

In fact, six months after we arrived in Corinth and the day came that her flow began but mine did not, I was peeved that we would not be able to go to the stream at the same time. It was not until several days later that it occurred to me that my flow was not going to start at all. Cordelia, who had seemed to search my eyes earlier in the week, had not met them now for days, and I did not know how to introduce the subject for fear of her feelings. As it turned out I should have had no such reservations: Her joy was unselfish and unbridled when I told her of the unused cloths, the chafings on my breasts, the turning away from dawn bread and a growing abhorrence of mutton.

I could not tell Aquila right away. I wanted to wait through at least two lunar cycles to be sure, and thus twice greeted the waxing moon with as much enthusiasm as any pagan worshiper. Aquila did not seem to notice any of this in his comings and goings with the brethren and his haulings-off of completed tents to the market every other day. In fact, though our business was booming, I began to fear that even his great strength could not hold up to the pace he set and the curling piece of vellum nailed by the door with the names of new customers who awaited tents.

One evening he returned home with his dark eyes sparkling with excitement.

"I have such news, my Priscilla." He was struggling to take off his outer garment, soaked with rain. He handed me a sack of cheeses whose aroma made me miss Akantha, and for a moment I thought of how to get a message to her back in Salamis, to tell her about the coming child.

"Such news, such news, you will be so pleased," he was muttering as the cloth stuck to the back of his upper arms. He finished the peeling of it and hung it on a peg by the door.

"I have some news too." I could hardly make my voice behave.

"Ah, but mine you will love." He was brushing a bit of mud off his cloak, then looked guiltily at me as it crumbled to the floor. He stooped quickly to pick it up and continued. "I will not only have help here in the shop, but you will be so pleased with our guest."

"Guest?"

"We will have a partner and friend. A tentmaker with much experience. And the conversations we will have!" He walked to the side wall of the shop and appraised it. "We can build sleeping quarters for him here—see, there is room if we extend the wall a bit into the alley."

"What?"

"Well, everyone else in this city does it, when they need extra room. No wonder you cannot walk through the streets without losing a basket over your arm." He was spanning the wall with his arms, measuring.

"Good. I mean, I have prayed that you would have some help with the tentmaking." I looked down at my own frayed fingertips. "I hope he has a good strong stitch."

"That he does, he does. In cubits and spans, that would be—"

"I will have a guest, too, Aquila."

He bent over a scrap of leather, scratching out figures, and when my words penetrated the calculations he turned with a frown.

"A woman to help, I suppose? Temporarily, I hope. She'll have to bunk with Cordelia. I could not possibly make another extension." He looked at me over his shoulder, gesturing toward the wall.

"This one will have to bunk with us, I think," I said.

His eyebrows shot upward. "I hardly think so."

I looked downward. "It will be a very tiny guest, at least at first."

His hand froze.

And then my man of few words had none.

Though Aquila and I agreed to not speak of my pregnancy until I had passed the time at which I had miscarried my previous child, I found that whenever he greeted a friend, he tugged at the man's tunic sleeve and whispered to him. Indeed, I could not have hidden the situation for much longer because all the women whispered that the child must be in the sixth month by the time I spoke openly about it. For my part, I decided that the God of wonders was also a God of surprises in my life, to have given me a body which could not alert me of a passenger until it had been on board for months.

Aquila's guest was Paul, who after the departure of Silas to join Peter, sought both housing and a means to support himself. He proved to be an expert tentmaker, even more proficient than Aquila, and certainly faster than I. With his help our shop produced nearly enough tents to meet the demand, and of designs and ornamentation (there, I admit, I contributed most) that pleased the cosmopolitan tastes of this city and brought us more customers than we could have sought out.

During the first months of his partnership with us, Paul spent much of his time bending over fabric and pelts, arguing with Jews who came into the shop just to pester him, it seemed to me. He, on the contrary, obviously relished the arguments that often stretched over a morning and in to the noontime period, when all the shops of the city closed until early afternoon.

My memories of those times were of mutterings and shouts and interrupting spasms of quotations from the Old Law, and then more mutterings and shouts. Paul was indeed a vessel of message, one that spilled out at the slightest movements. And as soon as he and Aquila closed the shop in the evenings and quickly supped, they usually left to visit new brethren or attend to the problems of what was becoming a fledgling church in Corinth.

Only once during his first weeks with us was I able to speak to Paul about anything of substance, and then only because of the plaguing dream that had visited me every night for a week. Aquila was bewildered by it, though he held me for long hours into the dawn. I knew I must discuss its meaning with Paul, and waited for a proper moment to describe it to him.

The dream was of a man walking away from a valley in which a vast field of dead bodies lay contorted and drying in a blinding sunlight. Above, circling, ravens called to one another (I was quite certain they were not speaking to anyone else) and I heard the words, *Chedorlaomer is no more*, screeched back and forth between them like a chant as they circled and dived into the field.

Another man in colored robes stood motionless atop a flat plain in the distance. I seemed to accompany the first man and now his army as we approached the plain. The second man wore a helmet-like crown that began to glint and refract light like a rainbow. He piled float loaves of bread on an enormous table until they formed a wall. Beside him were stacks of wineskins, their surfaces taut and bulging.

But the first man refused to eat or drink until the richly-robed man took a blood-crusted sack from his hands. I had dreamed this same dream night after night.

"She awakens in the night, saying 'Chedorlaomer,'" said Aquila to Paul one day. "I remember the name. But this whole dream has meaning. More meaning. Please, my brother, tell her what you think."

Paul looked around our shop and out the front door that framed a scene of constant activity as people passed to and fro. I knew what he was thinking: The Jews of Corinth were even less tolerant of interactions between women and men than those of Jerusalem or Salamis had been.

"The man who walked away from the battleground was our father Abram," Paul said as his awl pierced neat holes in a row on a section of goatskin. "And the man who offered the wine and bread, and accepted the spoils from the battle, was Melchizedek."

I was careful and respectful. "What else do we know about him?"

Paul did not answer for a few moments.

"My sister, you know the Old Writings as well as any Gentile I ever met."

Any Gentile woman, I wanted to say. But I was grateful for the concession. I responded with a section of a psalm from that Old Testament that I was teaching the women to memorize:

The LORD says to my Lord:
"Sit at My right hand
Until I make Your enemies a footstool for Your

feet."

The LORD will stretch forth Your strong scepter from Zion, saying,

"Rule in the midst of Your enemies."

Your people will volunteer freely in the day of Your power;

In holy array, from the womb of the dawn,
Your youth are to You as the dew.
The LORD has sworn and will not change His mind,
"You are a priest forever
According to the order of Melchizedek."
The Lord is at Your right hand;
He will shatter kings in the day of His wrath.
He will judge among the nations,
He will fill them with corpses,
He will shatter the chief men over a broad country.
He will drink from the brook by the wayside;
Therefore, He will lift up His head.

As I recited, Paul nodded and recited softly as well, but not with the exact words, and with clumps of phrases. I wondered if he was translating from the Hebrew in his mind and had not memorized the Septuagint as I had.

"Yes, that is the other reference to Melchizedek," Paul said. "And his priesthood."

"So, since David spoke of his Lord speaking to another Lord, then this must refer to Messiah and His reign."

"Yes." He seemed to hesitate, as if he wanted to retract what he said, then decided to ratify it. "Yes."

Aquila's eyes were fixed on me. I looked at him and he nodded encouragement to me and then he began to speak the same words I first heard him recite from my Holy Breath scrolls:

"Thus the Christ also has not glorified himself to be made a high priest, but he who had said to him, *Thou* art my

Son, *I* have today begotten thee. Even as also in another place he says, *Thou* art a priest forever according to the order of Melchizedek."

From behind him, I heard the voice of Cordelia, reciting along with him. Their words were identical: confident and unhesitating.

Paul looked from Aquila to her and back again, but they were both looking at me.

Paul looked down at his work. His awl punched, punched.

"So, you have come to the same conclusion I have, my sister Priska. Jesus came to claim the throne of the King of Salem. A throne that became David's throne. And now His."

I felt impatient: Surely this great thinker could see more in the conjoining of the story of the king on plains and the psalm that talked of this king.

"More than that, brother Paul. The psalm speaks not only of kingship but of priesthood."

"Yes."

"I hear the arguments that the Jews bring to you every day. They don't believe Jesus is the Messiah. They would never believe that He could hold priesthood."

"That is true. He was not born into any Levitical line. He was from Judah. No priesthood claims." Paul's voice became as rhythmic as his awl.

I pressed on. "But look at what Zechariah said: 'Even he shall build the temple of the LORD; and he shall bear the glory, and shall sit and rule upon his throne; and he shall be a priest upon his throne: and the counsel of peace shall be between them both.' So Messiah must be both king and priest."

I could hear outside our door the sound of visitors. Aquila hurried to the door, loudly greeting two men in

Hebrew.

I held a napkin with a handful of grapes spilling out of it toward Paul and turned my back to the visitors. I made my voice low and almost casual.

"Here is the issue, and we must talk about it. If the psalm talks of Messiah, then He would hold the priesthood of Melchizedek."

Paul nodded.

"And Melchizedek was not part of Abraham's line."

Paul's eyes achieved a blankness beyond sight.

"So Messiah would hold a sort of priesthood that is, technically speaking, *Gentile*. So what would the Jews think of that?"

He held the cloth with the cluster of grapes in his hand, just before his parted lips, until the visitors turned to him and I left the room.

Chapter Sixteen

Once when I was a young girl I held an old wineskin under water to see the bubbles that floated up like a twisting necklace of air from the tiny crack on the flask's surface. But as it became wetter, the skin became slippery and I could hardly hold onto it. The air inside it gained power as I lost the ability to grasp and it seemed something alive inside, mysterious and unmanageable as it shifted and eluded my finger beneath the slime of the skin.

I know that feeling, I thought, the first time the child within me slipped against the wet wineskin of my womb. At first I felt delight—the realization my body was not singular but inexplicably plural—and then a great powerlessness, a now-familiar nemesis: the absence of words.

But as I stitched that day, I began to write a poem to share with Cordelia.

This writhing inside me entreats in silence,
Groping for words through lips that have never spoken.
Child of few yesterdays and all tomorrows:

Through the muffled stillness of the waters
Only the echo of my blood rushes
Through hollowing chambers to you.

("Eye hath not seen, nor ear heard . . ."
And yet, I know you.
Why can you not speak as I speak?
Will your love ever match mine?
Will the light of birth open
Your unused eyes to my yearning?)

I, too, move restlessly through terrestrial waters
As conscious of self as a child.
Above, a Father waits for me, to
See as I have been seen, to
Know as I am known;
Wanting me to
Push my way out of this dark world-womb
Into His light.

I was afraid to read this to Cordelia, but to my great relief she embraced it as if she had written it herself; in fact, seemed to draw it to her own permanently-distended belly as if it were a blessing of oil poured onto her.

"We share our children," she said simply, and at the time it seemed she was claiming an ownership of my child, which thought quite unsurprisingly seemed right and good to me. But later I began to wonder in what way I shared her child as well, a child who rested immobile inside her, a leaden and covert entity that must be accounted for in all matters of daily life though never actually seen, an arrested process with no end result at all.

One Sabbath at the synagogue a brother newly arrived from Ephesus brought some correspondence from others, including a scroll from John. Though I had heard many stories about this man, the one who Jesus loved, he seemed one of the facelessnesses that surrounded the Christos, who walked with Him and emerged here and there on the stage of the drama of His life, but who, I confess, receded after saying their lines and thus seemed to have little relevance for me personally. In fact, since the time that I had last heard of him in the house of Pudens, John had never entered my mind again.

That is, until I heard that he was preparing a comprehensive account of the life of Christos. Though I had spoken in snippets to Paul about whether he should begin writing an account of his experience on the Damascus road, and I knew of James beginning to write, until I heard that John was writing too, these seemed to be pearls drilled for a necklace but scattered on the workman's tray.

When I saw that man behind the lectern in the synagogue, holding the scroll from John, I began to feel a sense of kinship with these men, and almost simultaneously a sense of pretentiousness: Had I seen the sweat on the brow of Christos as he labored up a hill? Had I ever heard Him speaking on a knoll or in a thatched hut? Not even in vision, and certainly not even at a time, and on a road, and in a place like Paul.

"Brother Paul," I said to him urgently the next day. "Tell me of what is on the scroll from John."

"He's writing his account of the Christos backwards, it seems to me." He paused and wiped sweat from his forehead with his arm, still holding tightly to the fabric that threatened to cascade down from his workbench.

"Backwards?"

"Perhaps it is my own training, but I wouldn't do it the way he has."

I waited patiently until, tucking the fabric under his chin and gathering it in his arms to lay on Aquila's outstretched forearms, he was ready to speak again.

"He speaks often of the eternality of the Christos—that He existed outside of time, that He was equal with the Father."

I struggled to remember what Philo said. "Yes. The Christos as Logos."

He nodded. Aquila hefted the tent section and together they turned it over on the bench. Aquila set to work stitching a new section, and Paul leaned back against the wall.

"John has many interests in common with you, Priska. Perhaps sometime the Lord will permit you to meet. He is well-read in the Greek philosophers, and a deep thinker."

I could hardly breathe. I wanted to go find Cordelia, to shake Aquila, to say, "Listen to what Paul just said about me!" But I just looked down.

"John began to write a history of the Christos, starting with the Logos idea. But then he said he thought it was most important to concentrate on the last week of the life of Jesus."

I looked around for some words. "In a way, that is like what you are doing. You never tell about His birth, or His early ministry either. Mainly I hear you speak about His death."

Paul looked up at me. "That is true. And purposeful."

"So, what does that section of scroll say? The one that John sent? Is it a letter, or, or…" I tried to find a proper word, "a chronicle?"

To my surprise, Paul walked over to the earthenware jug in which he kept some scrolls and pulled out a roll of papyrus.

"Read it for yourself, sister Priska."

I could hardly believe it. And as I began to unroll the scroll I saw that it was not written in Paul's looping letters (not a right angle to be found, piled one atop another, as if someone had shorn a curly sheep and left its locks on paper). Instead, the sheet was crammed full of slanting lines of thin letters like a forced-march of war prisoners, starving and bent forward against an unseen torrent.

"Begin here." Paul was pointing to a section near the end of the unrolling. "It is an account of the last time Jesus and the others were together before His death."

"Read it aloud to us, Priscilla." Aquila's voice was quiet but proud.

Many times I had to hold the scroll up to the light to make out the crowded letters and saw again what I often remarked upon about the words of Jesus: They were unexpected and often startling. Aquila and I exchanged a secret-bearer smile over the promise of Jesus that He would build us a mansion; and it was then that I knew of Cordelia's entry into the room as she sighed herself through the doorway.

At one point, I put the roll into my lap—or, better said, onto the mound the size of a washerwoman's bundle.

"How do those who heard these words, people like John, how do they maintain faith when it has been so many years since Jesus left?"

"Many met him right away." Paul was matter-of-fact.

"Like you on the road to Damascus? Were there others who had such an experience?"

Paul shook his head. "No. Well, at least none others I know of. But that's not what I was speaking of."

I was disappointed. I wanted to meet others who had such extraordinary experiences. Would any of them be like mine?

Paul went on. "I mean that they were reunited with Him in the kind of meeting we all will have, someday."

I picked up the scroll and continued to read:

A little while and ye do not behold me; and again a little while and ye shall see me, because I go away to the Father.

Some of his disciples therefore said to one another, What is this he says to us, A little while and ye do not behold me; and again a little while and ye shall see me, and, Because I go away to the Father?

They said therefore, What is this which he says of the little while? We do not know of what he speaks.

Jesus knew therefore that they desired to demand of him, and said to them, Do ye inquire of this among yourselves that I said, A little while and ye do not behold me; and again a little while and ye shall see me?

Verily, verily, I say to you, that ye shall weep and lament, ye, but the world shall rejoice; and ye will be grieved, but your grief shall be turned to joy.

I paused and looked ahead at the following sentences. I closed the scroll, though, because two Jewish men were bursting through the front door. I placed it under the fold of a piece of fabric I was stitching, but need not have worried—it was Paul they wanted, and, along with Aquila, Paul they lured. I knew that they would be arguing for hours, perhaps until the next day. I knew not to ask, as they went out the door, if anyone would be home for dinner.

At that moment, I came to realize that what I had seen as our home was no longer a private place, but an intersection.

An hour later, as Cordelia and I sat eating and poring over the scroll, I turned suddenly in my chair. It felt as if someone had approached me from behind and had reached around and gripped my stomach with insistent fingers. But there was no one there, and Cordelia looked at me with questions in her eyes.

A few moments later the feeling grew fingernails. I jumped to my feet and found that a watery red flower had painted itself onto my tunic and the seat of the bench where

I had sat. Cordelia's eyes widened and she stepped outside into the street, grabbing a young man by the arm and pressing coins into his hand, sending him to summon some of the other women, to find Aquila.

The air seemed thick and suspended in the room. As we waited, I asked Cordelia the questions I had never asked, about the last time I had been in labor.

"How long did it last, the time before?"

She would not look at me. "A long time."

"How long?"

She was shoving all the furniture in the room to the walls. She looked for a measuring moment at the men's workbench, then piled all their tools and fabrics in a heap. And then put her kneading trough on top.

"Three days. But because you were unconscious, you could not help. Your … your child did not want to leave your womb. It will not be that way this time. This child is vigorous, and wants to come out." She looked at my stomach and the fabric of my robe rippled across the surface like an uneasy lake.

And so it began: The ancient fellowship of the deep groans, the unbroken chain from Eve to me.

Cordelia's eyes watching me were full of tears.

"I will tell you one thing that helped me," she said. Then she looked at her own still-ripe abdomen and nearly swallowed a sob. "Who am I to tell you anything?"

My body was, for the moment, placid, and I reached for her arm.

"Stay with me. Tell me what helped you."

She gathered herself and nodded. "I thought of the times that you and I, young girls, sat on the seashore."

"Yes."

"And as the waves came, we could see that the sea was drawing in things, treasures from the deep, we thought, bringing them in the foam to us, and we strained our eyes, remember? to see them from afar."

"Yes."

"But whatever came in, had to stay atop the waves. If it didn't, it sank to the bottom of the sea."

My womb seemed at once to try to wring itself out. I could not speak, could not listen. It was as if I were in the middle of the crackle of a pitch-filled fire, explosions of stars riding on the crests of flaming waves.

Somewhere beyond the heat of that fire I heard voices and knew there were other women in the room. I shaded my eyes and saw tunics and legs and feet.

But I was at sea, again and again. I began to crave for the imposition of a beat that would make the rowing regular, but a thousand oars slapped all around me. Then I could hear only my own breath and began to feel a hoarseness far deeper than my lungs. I gasped, long deep breaths that seemed as if my body were beginning a cough and then changed its mind.

I could hear Cordelia's voice. She was commanding me, and I wanted to listen.

"Priska, each wave will end. The waves will each break on the shore. All of them. Everyone. They do not stay out to sea once they have begun. You understand this? You must remember this."

I nodded.

"You must stay on top of each wave, let it bring you and your child as treasure to the shore."

My lips were too dry to speak, my tongue useless. She brought me wine, dribbling into my mouth. I found some voice there in the moist places of my throat.

"I can do it if you read John's scroll to me."

I heard a rustling, a rearranging of people around me. I saw Aquila's face in front of mine, his black hair hanging straight out from his temples, and I realized he was on all fours beside me on the mat.

"Sit up for the surges, sit up for the surges," the women's voices whispered. I stumbled forward and he caught me as he helped me squat onto the birthing stool. Then Aquila's face receded into the shadows.

Cordelia began to read, but I only heard parts.

A little while and ye do not behold me; and again a little while

The reading stopped—or I could not listen. I thought of Cordelia's birth phalanxes in tight rows, determined and faceless and implacable. Again they came. And again.

But mine were the bright-eyed assaulting ones of Habakkuk: *Their horde of faces move forward.*

Cordelia's voice, reading from John's scroll, would rout them:

What is this he says to us, A little while and ye do not behold me; and again a little while?

Sometime late that night I passed a threshold into a world that was only air. I could hear my breathing more clearly than anything else I had ever heard. Each breath shuddered at its own exhalation.

What is this which he says

What is this which he says

What is this which he says of the little while?

We do not know of what he speaks.

A rooster crowed, and I wondered where Peter the Stone of Jesus was. Would I ever see him again? And did a rooster crow in his heart every day?

But then everything in the world contracted itself into the exact size of my abdomen. There were women's hands beneath the stool.

Cordelia read.

Jesus knew therefore that they desired to demand of him, and said to them, Do ye inquire of this among yourselves that I said, A little while and ye do not behold me; and again a little while and ye shall see me?

Verily, verily, I say to you, that ye shall weep and lament, ye, but the world shall rejoice; and ye will be grieved, but your grief shall be turned to joy.

The world was splitting and ripping. It was dawn.

I heard the voices.

"A son! Aquila has a son!"

I was being lowered onto the mat. There was slipperiness everywhere: on me, sweat-soaked. The hands holding me nearly lost their grip. And then the slipperiness I had felt inside me was on my chest, writhing and crying.

Cordelia was reading, weeping.

A woman, when she gives birth to a child, has grief because her hour has come; but when the child is born, she no longer remembers the trouble, on account of the joy that a man has been born into the world.

For a moment of charged clarity, I felt a joining of eternity to me, stretching in both directions from the first intentions of God to the eschatologies of all things. I sought the haven of these heavenlies, the faraways, under my eyelids.

But my arms lost their strength and I felt my hands sagging over the child.

I could not hold the child, for the implacable sea had returned, and the armies, and the breath as coarse as sackcloth, ripped from my lungs.

I was back on the stool. Women knelt on each side of me, my arms held over their shoulders, their faces next to mine like a line of siege shields. This time the world did not rip.

"Aquila has a daughter, too!"

I was back on the mat and another child was there on my chest, holding herself up on her forearms and looking directly into my eyes, and the Holy Breath said her name.

"Tikveh," I repeated. Hope. She seemed to look behind me then, as if summoned by another voice, and she sighed deeply.

And then she was gone.

The room was thick and still again. I held the limpness, still warm. Cordelia was crying. Outside, someone else was crying too, the first notes of wailing.

(This is what we do. This is what we women do when hope is gone.)

"Read what John saw to me, Cordelia," I whispered. "Read me what else Jesus said."

And ye now therefore have grief; but I will see you again, and your heart shall rejoice, and your joy no one takes from you.

My breaths were like raw edges of fabric, now overlaying one another, searching for a seam.

For the Father himself has affection for you, because ye have had affection for me, and have believed that I came out from God. I came out from the Father and have come into the world; again, I leave the world and go to the Father.

"The afterbirth, only the afterbirth," one of the women was saying. The regiment of soldiers began to break rank, to wander off.

My son and my daughter were in my arms. I could not talk as the shrinking pain hummed, vocalized in my outgoing breaths. I knew that I was being emptied out.

The sunlight was coming in slits through our walls. Aquila was crying, stroking both his children.

I sat up with both children resting on the triangle of my crossed legs. I kissed Tikveh, again and again, and washed her with my tears. Aquila wrapped her stillness with his strong hands in the strips of kidskin we used to make purses for rich people, and then he took her away.

As I lay on the mat beside my son, I wondered at how an unknown universe had been inside me those months. If

I could open myself up, I believed, the entire studded night sky would be there, I was sure. And what Tikveh's bright eyes now saw, was far beyond even galaxies.

I turned onto my side and spat out sea water, and then I fell asleep.

It was evening when I awakened with a pulling on my breast, and saw the boy in the circle of my arm. I looked up and knew Cordelia had put him there, and sure enough, she sat nearby on the bench. She came to me and put a pillow behind my head and pulled my matted hair onto it. She drew a comb from a bag.

Wordless, she began to comb my hair: first the surface snags, working them out so as not to break a single hair, then combing deeper, drawing strands out onto the pillow and my shoulders like a shawl.

"I was thinking, Cordelia."

"Yes."

"About Mary, and the birth of Jesus."

"Yes."

"How she did not have to go through her labor in front of people."

"Yes."

"At the inn, I mean. Where there was no room. Where everyone was crowded in, the criminals and rough men who had nowhere else to stay."

"Yes."

"How gracious God was, to keep her from their eyes, to give her privacy, so far from her home and the women who would have helped her."

"Yes."

"I never thanked God for that."

"Yes."

I fell asleep.

Once I awakened. It was just before nightfall, and I saw

Cordelia rocking in silent grief, cradling my baby, holding my child atop her own.

Chapter Seventeen

It was with the birth of Baruch, and the passing of his twin sister Tikveh, that I went from my past life into another, almost as if the two were adjoining houses, sharing a wall; and as the door of one whispered shut behind me I was already framed by the lintel of the new one.

Paul did not come back for days, kept away, we learned later, first by the heated all-night arguments of the Jews who had come to the shop and taken him away, and then later by the arrival of Silas accompanied by Paul's young friend Timothy. Already there was an uproar in Corinth about this young man. Even Jews who otherwise were sympathetic to Paul didn't know how to relate to this man they regarded as a half-breed.

When I learned of this, I looked at my own son and wondered again about my mother's prophecies.

Somehow it seemed acceptable that Paul was not there with us when we laid Tikveh's tiny body in the crypt; for I had seen the longing way the grizzled man looked at the children of others, and I was afraid that the sight of the burial might overwhelm him. I could hardly bear my own grief and that of Aquila and could not that day, at least, mete out my own finite compassion to one more human being.

That night I had the dream of the sheet again. This time it did not hang passively flat but rippled with an unseen wind. Like Zechariah's scroll, it began to narrow and lengthen, arcing like wings that soared and swooped through the utter stillness. Then it passed close to me and paused and I saw words lining up like tallies on each side: *loud crier, source, designated, priestly.*

We named our sleepy-eyed little boy with the mass of coarse, unruly black hair Baruch, blessing. Aquila's first smile came when he told me that he had seen that this name was one of the few Hebrew words I could remember.

Baruch atah, Baruch atah, I repeated: Blessed art Thou, blessed art thou.

Paul returned a few days after his birth and held the child as one of the priests circumcised him on his eighth day of life, an event which people spoke of with wonder for months afterward. Not only was there just a single drop of blood on the flint knife, but other than a startled reflex of his tiny arms upward, Baruch did not cry out, did not react in any way.

My life became centered around the rhythms of the slaking of urgencies in my breasts, the small satisfactions of the smell of my milk on the sweet sighing breath of my son. For many days there were no dreams, no words from the Holy Breath, no discussions with any of the brothers and others who wove themselves and their lives in and out of our shop.

One day I brought cool drinks to Aquila and Paul during the midday rest, Baruch nestled in a sling across my chest. Since the child's birth I sensed a peace between Paul and me that had not been there before—as if my motherhood brought him a kind of relief. I wondered if, among all the other accusations lodged against him, his living in a household with two women could have caused him problems. But the birth of a child whose burr of black hair stood off his scalp in slivers and boards, just like his father's, must have sealed something in Paul's mind at least. He seemed to welcome my coming into the shop, seemed to actually reach his mind toward mine for discussion.

Any silence in the shop was so unusual that it brought a sense of something off-balance, so accustomed were we all to the ubiquity of voices there. This day I came with a sense that something was wrong but unsure of the cause.

Aquila and Paul both bent over their work, my husband at a large loom surrounded by goat hairs that danced in the light through the door frame, Paul intent upon lining a series of grommets along a hem.

When I entered the room, I felt the opacity of a new silence, the kind that ensues after hard words that hang in the air and cloud it. Neither man looked up at me though I knew they both saw me enter.

"That Alexander," Paul muttered as his thick fingers struggled with the tiny brass circles. "I don't think his metalworking is any better than his theology."

I had heard the men speak of an Alexander, a Grecian Jew who had become an ardent follower of Jesus and then just as precipitantly, his enemy. But somehow I knew that the issue that had caused the tension in the room was not related to Alexander nor to tentmaking. I placed the two cups on a bench and turned to go.

"Paul wants to talk to you, Priscilla." My husband's voice sounded worn.

Paul shrugged but looked up at last. "We've been talking about symbols."

I waited for an explanation.

Paul straightened up and stretched his neck from side to side making the sound of saplings breaking, distant as if buried, arrhythmic.

"I was telling Aquila about my time among the philosophers in Athens," he said, "discussing their gods there. At the Areopagus."

I saw in my mind an instantly-conceived tableau of men with scrolls and outstretched arms, milling around on a hill full of breathtaking statues and felt a lust—a lust not for Paul nor the men nor even for their ideas, but for the gods and their beauty, like a woman overhearing news of a faraway lover. I blushed, but neither of them seemed to notice as Paul continued.

"I told them that one of their altars—one they dedicated to 'the unknown god'—was in fact pointing to the true and living God, the One who set times and places for people to live, who by His very power of creation has made all races of the earth not only related to one another but to Himself as well."

I waited again. The cords of tension in Aquila's neck seemed to soften, and he took a tentative drink from one of the cups on the stool.

"In the telling of this, I am afraid that I made a statement that has disturbed my dear friend Aquila."

The cords in my husband's neck rose again.

"And what statement is that, brother Paul?" I handed him his cup and he seemed grateful, drinking a long swallow.

"I am coming to see everything in the world, the created order as well as those things we humans design and implement, as all pointing to God. If not in their intended purpose, then in some way."

"What he said, actually, was a bit more pointed," said

Aquila. "He talked about people as symbols."

"I've been thinking about what you have said about Melchizedek, for instance," Paul continued. "That his priesthood was a type or a symbol of something coming, beyond himself."

"Are you saying that this Melchizedek did not exist, except as an idea?" I felt my head beginning to fog a bit. I was thinking of shadows dancing on the wall of Plato's cave.

Paul must have known exactly what I saw in my mind, and his response was mild, but firm. "Not at all. Melchizedek existed as surely as Abraham. But his being, his life, his deeds, they all carried more weight, as we consider them now."

I wondered why this line of discussion had upset Aquila so. I was certain that Paul had not couched his discussion in such a way as to emphasize his own rabbinic training and so put distance between my husband and him.

"My issue was this," said Aquila. "I have seen you heal people, brother Paul. And I know that other apostles can raise the dead."

I still had no idea what the connection could be between what happened at the Areopagus, and Paul's healing abilities.

Paul sighed. "I have often considered the way that these healings occur. And miracles in general. It is my understanding that on that Pentecost entire multitudes of people had the same experience. You yourself, sister Priska, are the embodiment of those whom Peter spoke of, the daughters who would prophecy, the handmaidens with the Holy Breath poured out on them."

Again he had acknowledged the Breath in my life.

"And Peter and John—just a glance from them had birth-cripples running and jumping in those early days," Paul said. "Luke, John, others—we have all concluded that these eyewitnesses were given these powers to confirm their witness of Jesus."

He stopped to brush some trimmings to the floor, and I was thinking of Pudens—how his arm grew flesh before my very eyes.

"But such events seem to be—" He searched for a word. "They seem to be diluting now. Somehow the spreading of this message has resulted in fewer of such events. It is as if the message itself is to function as the power."

"I don't see why that would anger you, dear husband." I made my voice soft toward Aquila.

"It's the symbol part." Aquila bit off his words as if they were charred meat. Then he looked at the floor, his face flushed.

"I told him that many people are being called, I believe, to function as did Melchizedek," said Paul. "To be real persons, of course, but also to be symbols for others. And that the message about Jesus is being confirmed by the witness of lives—and deaths."

Aquila stood up suddenly and faced Paul, eye to eye. What did I see in his dark face? Fury? It frightened me.

Then he seemed to relax, as if he knew this were an argument he had already won.

"I asked Paul why he did not raise our daughter from the dead," Aquila said in a crisp, dry voice. "He could have done it. He has done it for others."

I felt as if his words were striking my face.

I turned to Paul. "Yes, why did you not do that for your hosts, the friends who share a roof and bread and labor with you? You might say that you were not here to do so, but has distance ever been an obstacle to God?"

Tears were streaming down Paul's face.

"Indeed. I ask myself the same question. Why am I

called to heal some and not others? Why must I attend so many funerals, say goodbye to so many noble people? Why does not the Holy Breath—this same Holy Breath you speak of, sister Priska—why does He not send that lightning-feeling through my hands to *all* the people whom I must helplessly watch suffer?"

Lightning-feeling. I thought about that phrase. Aquila's face had not softened, even seeing Paul weeping.

Paul turned to his friend. "And the only thing I could tell Aquila, the only comfort I could offer him in such a time of loss, was that this tiny life, your precious Tikveh-hope, was a symbol of something else. That those short moments of looking into your eyes meant something more than just a child's passing."

"Who gets to choose to be a symbol?" Aquila's eyes were glistening and made me want to shrink back from his words. "Can we not just work and help others and just be people?"

Paul stood up, too. I saw something in his eyes like those of Aquila.

"I didn't get to choose. I heard the message of a man named Stephen, talking about this Jesus, and I could not wait to defend my Jewishness—our heritage—against such an insolent upstart. When people started to stone Stephen, I reached out my arms to hold their cloaks so that they could have all the freedom of movement they needed to hurl those stones at his body. With precision. For maximum damage, for corporate punishing."

He was sobbing now, his words barely understandable. "There were so many people vying for the best spots to throw those rocks that I found myself standing surrounded by a mountain of men's cloaks, up to my knees.

"And then when my own eyes were sated with Stephen's blood I wanted more. I wanted to search out more of those like him who would even talk of this Jesus."

He wiped his eyes with a fist, then began to speak faster and with more force.

"I hunted them down. I went into their homes and dragged out fathers and sons and women and children. That you probably know. But what you don't know is that I began keeping lists of the names of those I put in prison and I felt *satisfaction* just reading them.

"And then I met Jesus, and He was not pleased with me."

He hung his head and his crying ceased.

"I started on this journey with Jesus, the rest of my life, with two things," he said, brushing threads and tears off his forearms. "One, the knowledge that I had been chosen to suffer for the excellence of a Name.

"And the second was with an understanding that others would look at me, for the rest of my life, and see me as a symbol. Some might comment on my journeys, on the new believers and congregations and, yes, even the healings and other works the Holy Breath impels me to do."

He put his small hammer and needles onto the corner of the workbench, then walked to the door.

"I threw the lists away years ago, but I can't throw them out of my mind. And every step I take, I feel those cloaks around my ankles. I will never walk anywhere in this life without the certain knowledge that they claw at my ankles like the hands of their owners. For every person who sees my good deeds, there are others who cry all night for the loved ones I—a symbol—led to their deaths."

The door brushed against Paul as he left the shop.

I turned to Aquila. He pushed away his cup of wine, and then we sat without speaking.

"Call Cordelia," he said simply. "Tell her to tell people the shop is closed for the rest of the day."

I do not remember which of us first said that we should go to the cemetery, only that we found ourselves there, sitting under a tree near the entrance to the catacombs where our daughter's body lay.

There, outside the entrance to the underground, the brilliant sky looked as if a weary house painter had wiped the last of his drying whitewash off his brushes onto it, just at the edges, so as not to waste it for tomorrow's work. Cordelia sat a short distance away, looking at the sky.

"I have not questioned you about this before, but I must know. Tell me why you named the child Tikveh," Aquila asked me. I looked at him in surprise.

"You told me it means 'hope' in Hebrew." It was true, he had said that, the day of the funeral.

"Yes. But where did you hear the name before? Your Hebrew has not been …" His voice trailed off. Not successful, he probably wanted to say. Certainly not fluent enough for that word.

"While I was in labor, as she was born, the Breath told me her name."

His eyes sought mine. He had something he had been holding inside and it was working its way out of him.

"It has always been a special word for me," he said. "It is also the word for cord."

Had I heard it in the shop as he and Paul worked? I began to nod, as if I remembered him saying it before, as he continued.

"But this double meaning knits itself together, comes together in the life of the Gentile woman, Rahab of Jericho," he said, his hands making twisting motions. I was grateful that he called her Gentile, not prostitute.

I remembered the story of the taking of that impregnable walled city, of the pagan woman who sold her body but who believed in the Jewish God more faithfully than the people who had crossed the Red Sea believed. The woman who harbored spies, and took the risk of hanging a red cord out her window for their return. A red cord of rescue. A red cord that was in the Hebrew mind, quite literally, her hope, I realized. Her hope audaciously dangling out for all to see.

"But Aquila." I began to sob. I was afraid to speak, afraid of rousing the anger I had seen in him when he had confronted Paul.

"How can I take comfort in knowing that my hope is … is … dead?" I didn't dare look into his eyes. "She's not like Rahab. There's no rescue for her. No rescue for me. What kind of symbol is that for me? Why would the Holy Breath give her such a name if she were going to die?"

I stretched my arms out toward the crypt.

The dry-brush streaks of the clouds gained peaks, as if they were reaching up.

And then I felt the Breath come alongside me with the urgency of a lover:

Like the headiness of wine filling the nostrils, like the spice-mellow of juniper honey, like the dusty memory of pollen;

Like the way of a man with a maiden,
like a snake on a morning rock,
like a ship on the ocean beyond all calling.

I sagged into the embrace. I heard Aquila calling for Cordelia, calling for paper.

The Breath was speaking, I was repeating.

God, having promised to Abraham, since he had no greater to swear by, swore by himself, saying, Surely blessing I will bless thee, and multiplying I will multiply thee;

My mind battled with the Breath, because of the three pregnancies, because of two tiny tombs.

and thus, having had long patience, he got the promise.

For men indeed swear by a greater, and with them the oath is a term to all dispute, as making matters sure.

Wherein God, willing to shew more abundantly to the heirs of the promise the unchangeableness of his purpose, intervened by an oath,

Oath. Power-word. Words that stop events, that change reality.

that by two unchangeable things, in which it was impossible that God should lie, we might have a strong encouragement, who have fled for refuge to lay hold

on the hope

the hope

the hope set before us, which we have as anchor of the soul, both secure and firm,

My Tikveh, my Tikveh, my hope. I cried the next words aloud for joy.

and entering into that within the veil,

where Jesus is

where Jesus is!

entered as forerunner for us,

become for ever

a high priest

according to the order of Melchizedek.

Aquila carried me home in his strong arms, weeping onto my face all the way.

It was with these circumstances concerning the births of the twins that I began to understand that God might want to use me as more than a conduit of symbols, but as a symbol myself.

I wish I could say the thought filled me with immediate and lasting joy. I wish I could say that I rose triumphantly to the occasion of being an example.

Some people told me that I should be grateful that I had a child, a strong, healthy child.

My arms were not empty. But never again were they full.

Chapter Eighteen

I first observed the elegance of siege while watching soldiers drill on the open fields in Salamis, and never forgot its lessons.

The individual men melted away into a roiling sea on an earthen ramp storming a wall, snagged sinuous pivot on an invisible point, voiced a single grunt of effort as they heaved a battering ram. Even now I can feel as much as hear the satisfying rasp of shields conjoining as soldiers disappeared from sight in a tortoise formation, can smell the pitch torches and arrows, can sing with the symphony of crossbows released all at once. But most of all I remember the catapult.

The device itself, I observed, was designed with its own single-minded purpose. Unarmed, it sat off-balance like a poorly-designed toy, its claw and trigger and winches ungainly and mysterious. But once loaded, every ratcheting groan, every squealing timber, each anxiety of the spring, fed the torque of motion suspended in midair: As much marital as martial, a self-awareness that yearned for climax, purpose, destiny.

And then! The snap of the mechanism, the shudder of the pedestal, and the aching grace of the arc of the stone become weightless in its flight, bottomless gravity itself in its destination.

It is against such power that the Spartan general Archidamus once beheld a catapult and said, "Oh Hercules, human martial valor is of no use any more!"

I suspect the general spoke not of the mechanism itself at all, but of the irresistible trajectory of something with implacable will and intentionality behind it. And such was the resoluteness of the Breath, that I felt myself becoming both projectile and besieged city alike.

So unremittingly did He compel me so as to be whole gale, a storm to run before and hide from but never to escape.

"Why is it," I asked Paul one day in one of the increasingly-rare times when he and I and Aquila were alone, "that when the Breath comes upon a person, it is so unsettling? I mean, in John's scroll the Holy Breath is called an advocate, a comforter."

Baruch played at our feet, speaking the language of an eight-month-old to a wheeled toy horse laying on its side on his chubby outstretched legs. He flapped his fingers at one of the wheels that wobbled as it turned.

Paul looked at me with eyes first wary and defensive (too many arguments had calloused his soul, I thought), but then he saw that my question was not an attempt to trap him.

"Since, little sister, you do not know Hebrew I will tell you something interesting. You have noticed that the prophet Malachi described his oracle with a word that can also mean a weight."

I nodded. He was kind enough to refer to the Greek

translation I used. My Hebrew had not yet blossomed. Or budded. Or ever sprouted, really.

"Actually, it can refer to a burden." He pursed his lips, tying off a tent stake holder with too-short cords.

For the first time since the Holy Breath had sighed into me, I felt some sort of fellowship with others He had whispered to. Though I had never felt the fire in my bones like Jeremiah, I did understand the weight of words as they swung pendulous under me. I thought of a basket whose stretched handles threatened to break, of straining fabric of a sling, of aching milk-taut breasts when I rolled over in the night.

With a start, I thanked God that Paul could not read my mind. I struggled for an appropriate response.

"You, my brother, know what it is like to be accosted by God," I said. "And as I think about it, so many of His interactions with people have been …" I looked for a word. "Forceful."

"That is true. Actually, I would use the word ambushed, in my case." He sighed out a laugh.

"No wonder Jacob called the Lord 'The Fear.' And I don't think Joseph asked for the dreams of his parents and brothers bowing down like sheaves of wheat to him," he said, "Or liked the reaction he got from his, shall we say, unconvinced family. Think of Jeremiah and his filthy sash. And poor Hosea and that horrible wife of his."

"And what about Ezekiel—carried away and then dumped days later on a riverbank," added Aquila. He scooped Baruch up into his arms and then bent over, showing him how the toy horse could travel across the floor.

"I wouldn't have wanted to be Ezekiel. I mean, even the food he ate …" I shivered. I would have to be starving to use the brazier fuel he used.

"And yet he knew that he was participating in something beyond himself, beyond the objects God had him construct, the acts he so relentlessly performed."

We were both silent. How could any man obey God's command not to cry when his wife, the desire of his eyes, was taken from him?

The Fear.

I drew in a sigh and asked Paul the question I really wanted to know.

"How do you think they knew what was from God—instead of what was, perhaps, only from within them?"

Paul was looking at me with that narrow-eyed look again. "You are asking me how one prescinds one's own human consciousness from the stream of revelation."

He honored me with learned words. And I understood them. I looked him directly in the eye and nodded yes.

"It is a different class of words. They are distinct. Like a donation and not a creation. Fervent without my own emotion. And often surprising. Sometimes even accusing." He was as matter-of-fact as if he were reading an order for straps from a merchant.

"You are speaking of the receiving of words from God," I said. "But what of the giving of them, to others, I mean?"

Again the constriction of the corners of his eyes, the deliberate attention to clipping a stray thread.

"You mean, in letters, instructions, such like?"

"Yes."

He walked his sore-footed walk to his clay jar of scrolls.

"That is a matter with which I am struggling right now." He unrolled a papyrus. "See, I am writing this letter to our brothers and sisters in Thessalonica. They understand some things very well. They know that although they were baptized, they can't baptize their old gods into their new lives."

His words slapped me. Was that what I had been trying to do?

"They are running away from them, throwing them over their shoulders like our chastened forefathers did," Paul continued. "And while they excel in love, they are torn apart by people who want to rise above others with strange teachings. And because of their love, how deeply they are mourning for those among them who have died. They need to know some truths about their own resurrections. Thy need to know about testing spirits. And as I am writing, I know that the words—even though they are exactly congruent to what has been reported to me, they are accurate, that is—they are not just my words."

"Who will believe that?" My boldness caused Aquila to jerk his head back almost imperceptibly. "What will cause the readers to see that these words are not just from your own mind, sent out so that you can lord it over them, perhaps?"

"To the contrary, dear sister. I warn them not to quench the Spirit."

My mind churned this image: Breath that could be quenched like fire.

"And I have told them not to despise prophecies."

I met his eyes and realized that he was looking at me, talking to me, talking about me, nodding to make sure I understood that. I blanched.

"And I told them to test everything, no matter who says it." He touched his chest as he said it.

"Thus, if the words have a non-natural Source, I would expect that they will have a non-natural effect," he said. "The words will of themselves have the power to convict and persuade."

I heard the Spirit's breathing in my mind: the precision of the double-edged sword that ferrets out the gristle and exposes the meat of the message.

"And besides, not being believed—at least at first—is as near to a badge of authenticity as any prophet ever wore," Paul said.

I saw that he was teasing now, and Aquila was laughing too, wiping his eyes, then clearing his throat to speak.

"I want to return to something we spoke of before, of being a symbol," he said.

This time it was Paul who stiffened, but Aquila reached for his shoulder and touched him with the friendship touch of a man.

"Would it not be true, then, that just as such words carry with them their own power, that the one who speaks them forth is also given some inherent, accompanying power as well?" Aquila said. "The ability, through those words, to stand behind them, to validate them?"

Present circumstances would be absorbed, even perhaps ameliorated by that kind of power, I was thinking, my fingers to my mouth as I worked through the notion. After a while—how long, I don't know—I was surprised to see the two men looking at me. Paul's eyes were soft.

"This path isn't an easy one, sister Priscilla. Especially for a woman who is called to be a symbol. Esther was sold as a plural wife to a pagan king. Jael's one claim to fame was luring a man to his death with a tent stave in his skull. And Hannah spent years being mocked by her rival for her infertility, and then at the moment of her greatest vulnerability—and we have her words as Scripture, you know—a priest of God told her to go away, that she was drunk."

I knew that he was reaching out with encouragement to me, with the wine and gall of this path. It gave me the strength to speak to him in a way I never had.

"I know some things about the Christos, things I think

the Jews need to know."

He set his tools down and drew the stools from the corner of the room where they had been stacked. He sat on one and motioned for Aquila and me to sit as well.

"Why do you always call him the Christos?" he asked.

I felt confused, rebuked. "Because He is the anointed one. To show respect for his authority, His position."

"That is true. But He has a name. When He waylaid me on that road, He used it. He said, 'I am Jesus, the one you are persecuting.' He wanted to make sure I understood this was personal. And since the Breath is speaking to you of Him, does He not use that personal name as well?"

It was true. The Breath used the name Jesus. But it was hard for me to do that, as if I was being too familiar. I swallowed hard.

"I've been told about Melchizedek. That he is a symbol, too, with far more meaning than we have known before. And that he is tied to, to *Jesus*," I struggled with the name, "in a way that Jews must know."

Behind me, Aquila took Baruch and was moving toward the doorway to our quarters. He returned with one of my scrolls.

The night before, the Breath had breathed on me, through me. In the stillness of our resting, Cordelia's and mine, before the cookfire, I felt the approach.

I had a sense that my bones were like the timbers of a ship, with a sudden hollowness within them that was an invitation.

And then, the sense of inhabitation—or perhaps more accurately, a sense of a realignment or reassignment of space within me, to accommodate. And almost, to welcome. My voice participated, and I felt a kind of delight that approached knowledge, that I had never before known; a kinship with Cordelia and with the Breath and with the men and women of the past who had companied in such a way as this, before the cook fires and in the jail cells and in silences and tumults and exiles and deserts and camps. And these were the Breath's words:

Melchizedek, King of Salem, priest of the most high God, met Abraham returning from smiting the kings, and blessed him; to whom Abraham gave also the tenth portion of all;

I felt Moses and the sand of Sinai under his sandals, for he first told this story.

first being interpreted King of righteousness, and then also King of Salem, which is King of peace; without father, without mother, without genealogy; having neither beginning of days nor end of life, but assimilated to the Son of God, abides a priest continually.

The Breath was explaining to me:

Now consider how great this personage was, to whom even the patriarch Abraham gave a tenth out of the spoils. And they indeed from among the sons of Levi, who receive the priesthood, have commandment to take tithes from the people according to the law, that is from their brethren, though these are come out of the loins of Abraham: but he who has no genealogy from them has tithed Abraham, and blessed him who had the promises. But beyond all gainsaying, the inferior is blessed by the better. And here dying men receive tithes; but there one of whom the witness is that he lives; and, so to speak, through Abraham, Levi also, who received tithes, has been made to pay tithes. For he was yet in the loins of his father when Melchizedek met him.

The Breath was reasoning:

If indeed then perfection were by the Levitical priesthood, for the people had their law given to them in connection with it, what need was there still that a different priest should arise according to the order of Melchizedek, and not be named after the order of Aaron? For, the priesthood being changed, there takes place of necessity a change of law also. For he, of whom these things are said, belongs to a different tribe, of which no one has ever been attached to the service of the altar. For it is clear that our Lord has sprung out of Judah, as to which tribe Moses spake nothing as to priests. And it is yet more abundantly evident, since a different priest arises according to the similitude of Melchizedek, who has been constituted not according to law of fleshly commandment, but according to power of indissoluble life.

A life indissoluble … an indestructible life …

For it is borne witness, Thou art a priest forever according to the order of Melchizedek. For there is a setting aside of the commandment going before for its weakness and unprofitableness, (for the law perfected nothing,) and the introduction of a better hope by which we draw nigh to God. And by how much it was not without the swearing of an oath; (for they are become priests without the swearing of an oath, but he with the swearing of an oath, by him who said, as to him, The Lord has sworn, and will not repent of it, Thou art priest for ever according to the order of Melchizedek;)

And I heard the lyre of David, and him singing, *He swore, He swore, a priest forever.* With robes of a priest and David's own crown.

by so much Jesus became surety of a better covenant. And they have been many priests, on account of being hindered from continuing by death; but he, because of his continuing for ever, has the priesthood unchangeable.

And now Aquila was reading those words that Cordelia wrote down for me the night before, and I wondered at Paul and knew why this was personal. I looked Paul directly in the eyes again and breathed the newness of the Breath:

Whence also he is able to save completely those who approach by him to God, always living to intercede for them. For such a high priest became us, holy, harmless, undefiled, separated from sinners, and become higher than the heavens: who has not day by day need, as the high priests, first to offer up sacrifices for his own sins, then for those of the people; for this he did once for all in having offered up himself. For the law constitutes men high priests, having infirmity; but the word of the swearing of the oath which is after the law, a Son perfected for ever.

In the silence of our shop: Yes, Paul said, yes yes: who can deny that the Breath has breathed here.

And thus, the catapult began its shuddering contraction of the eschatology of my life.

The next Sabbath, Paul stood before the spittle-sprayed fury of the Jews in the synagogue of Corinth and told them, over their shrieks and the rasps of their clothes being ripped from their own bodies, that their father Abraham and his descendant Levi had given honor and tithe to a Gentile priest; and that their king David had said a forever-Lord had bypassed Levi and was coming to offer their sacrifices and rule over them:

And it was Jesus, and was always Jesus, and would ever be Jesus, the one they crucified.

Chapter Nineteen

Just as I once had the impression that I walked from one house to another, so quite literally did Paul do so after the inflammation of the Jews that day: The synagogue shared a wall with the house of a Gentile believer named Titius Justus and it was there Paul went.

"He was standing outside his door and pulled us inside," said Paul when he and Aquila returned that night. "He is a good man, a God-fearer. He has offered his home to me as a place to teach. The blood of the Jews will be on their own heads from now on. I will teach other Gentiles like Titius Justus."

I saw the rips in his cloak, and when Aquila shrugged me into silence I knew that he would explain it later.

"Paul is concerned for our safety," Aquila said as he eased himself onto our sleeping mat, turning for a moment to look at Baruch who had pulled his blanket up in bunches to his face. In the lamplight I could see a lump on Aquila's face near his hairline and he moaned, without meaning to, I think, as he turned to me then sank into the mat on his back. On his upper arms fingers of hatred left ghost-marks and I realized that someone had held him from behind: four fingers on one arm, four on the other. There was dried blood on one earlobe.

"Peace on earth, goodwill to men." I tried to keep the bitterness out of my voice but with no success, for Aquila put his fingers gently on my lips and I thought that he had begun a slow caress of my neck when I realized that his hand had gone slack and he was asleep.

The next morning I was awakened by sounds from the shop. Paul stood looking at the writing on the piece of paper by the door that scheduled our projects, and as I entered with a plate of fruit and bread for him, he turned.

"I committed to finish these three tents," he tapped the paper, "Tertius Acaunus, Hostinius Caldus, and Gallipor—heaven only knows where a slave got this kind of money to buy such a tent. Maybe he's going to run."

"Are you?"

He took the bread and spoke through a crust. "Am I what?"

"Are you going to run? You seem to be tallying things."

He shook his head and continued to chew.

"Not that I have not run in the past. But there's no need. The Lord spoke to me last night." He must have seen the surprise in my eyes, and he smiled.

"He said that I should not be afraid and to keep teaching here."

I hated to dampen the moment, for Paul was grinning as he chewed. But I had to know the details.

"Was it with words that He told you, or just ideas?"

"Words. Exact words. In a vision." He leaned his head back a bit and squinted as he repeated. "'Fear not, but speak and be not silent, because *I* am with thee, and no one shall set upon thee to injure thee, because I have much people in this city.'"

"I don't understand. Words. In a vision?" I put my two cupped hands out in front of me, as if balancing shifting weights.

He was not put off. "I saw Jesus again, and as He spoke He looked just the same only perhaps a little less perturbed than on the Damascus road." He smiled.

I nodded, satisfied. "So you are safe here. I am glad. But why are your tools in a bundle?" I pointed to the corner of the workbench.

"Those are not the tools I'll be using from now on. I am returning to my fulltime work for God now that Silas and Timothy are here." He smiled. "I will continue to live here—I can scarcely think of not having the company of you three" (here he gestured toward our living quarters)—"but teach in the home of the Gentile we met last night." At that he turned to look over my shoulder at Aquila, who I saw was walking stiffly, and yawning. Within minutes the two men were poking at the list by the door and rifling through bolts of cloth and folded leather like boys trading toys.

I had my own dream the night before. In the stillness after the Holy Breath had whispered Himself away, Cordelia and I sat pondering high priestliness. I do not know how else to describe our conversation, for it was as much about the role of a high priest as it was any one who held the office.

"I have heard stories about the Holy of Holies in the Jerusalem temple," I said to her. "About how only the high priest can enter there. And only once a year."

Cordelia was brushing a bit of sand from a basket of figs. "I hate to be curious, but I wonder how they clean it, year to year?"

"I have heard that men are lowered into it in baskets that allow them to see only the walls as they clean them."

She considered this for a moment. "But what about the Ark of the Covenant? Who cleans it?"

"It is purified by blood." The image arrested me. I imagined a high priest entering this square room, the bells on his robe hem jingling, the flakes of blood from the previous years' sacrifices drying on the gold surfaces, littering the floor.

"And they tied a rope to his leg so that if he were to die in there, they could pull him out," I told her.

Cordelia shook her head, then rubbed her eyes. I knew that writing down what the Breath told me was nearly as hard on her as for me and left us both spent afterwards. I did not protest when she touched me on the arm: a goodnight blessing. She put away the scroll on which she had written the latest Breathings, then walked toward the curtain that separated her sleeping quarters and disappeared behind it.

I fell asleep right away.

I had two dreams that night. The first felt familiar and was so: the sheet with the writing had another list and each word burned itself into my mind so that I remembered every one, even to this day:

Forerunner
Son of God
Priest forever
Indestructible
Intercessor
Undefiled
Separated
Perfected

The second dream I had that night was one of strophes, like the way that the choral songs of Greek plays were divided, with a strophe statement while the actors walked one direction, an antistrophe as they returned.

In the strophe, I stood before a curtain that was as thick as my upper arm, a wall of twisted and knotted fabric: brooding scarlet, brilliant blue. Worked into its depths (how could a needle go back and forth through that, I wondered, even in my dream) were cherubim, fantastical, their wings and feet in motion and their myriads of eyes that all looked at me. I could hardly bear it, the smoke that rose behind the curtain, the sadness, the glory, the fear.

From beneath the curtain a carpet of blood flowed toward me. I turned to run from it but there was a rope tied around my ankle. I slid feet-first beneath the curtain, pulled on the oil-like blood.

Inside, through the thick smoke, I saw something like a shadow, someone like a man dressed like a priest with embroidered ephod, and bells and pomegranates on his robe; and through the vapors that wove themselves together into their own curtain I saw the shadow turn suddenly toward me, with the robes of tendrils of smoke whirling around as he moved. I could not look up at him, but saw only his feet (and there was no rope on him) as the form passed back and forth in front of me. He was himself both strophe and the antistrophe. And then I awoke.

How can love look like blood? I wondered, when I thought of it the next morning. And then I heard Paul speak of his own dream of Jesus, and I realized once again that he had seen Him and I still had not. This understanding was the epode, the conclusion, of what I saw.

A week later Paul came back to our shop during the daytime. Both Aquila and I looked up in surprise as he entered, followed by a man with swinging forelocks and the robes of a wealthy Jewish businessman.

Paul latched the door behind them, then led him into

our living quarters. Cordelia looked up from her kneading trough and brushed the moist crumbs from her hands, then covered her head as I had quickly done.

"Crispus is now our brother in Christ," he said. We all stared in astonishment at the man who was the synagogue ruler—in fact, who had been in the forefront of those who had cursed and threatened Paul the week before.

"His whole family, in fact," said Paul. Aquila moved quickly to embrace him and to kiss his cheek. Cordelia and I looked at each other and I did not know if she felt the suspicion I did. Could this be a trick? Paul knew about people thinking a conversion was a trick.

"They have come to warn us that some of the other Jews are seeking my life. Of course, I cannot die here in Corinth, according to what Jesus told me," Paul said cheerfully, "but since I would rather not be beaten nearly to death as happened in Lystra, and would prefer that not happen to you, I am taking Timothy and Silas to the house of Crispus for a few days. The other Jews do not know yet of his baptism and this will give us a chance to instruct him."

"He will have the responsibility of teaching the other Jews here, since you will be teaching the Gentiles from now on?" Aquila was nodding.

"Exactly. And he tells me that he believes there will be many from the synagogue who will listen to him. Meanwhile, I came back today to get some of my scrolls, but will leave the others here."

Aquila embraced Crispus and Paul again and just like that, the two men were gone out the side door into the alley. Within just minutes, though, three other Jews from the synagogue came to our door, accompanied by a foppish Hellenized Jew I did not recognize.

"Ah, Alexander, have you come for a new tent? Ready to take a journey, perhaps? Not too far away, I hope. Maybe

Rome would be good." Aquila's voice was terse as he addressed the Greek who stepped in front of the Jews.

"There's the woman Paul cavorts with," the man said, pointing to me. He had a peculiar way of speaking, as if he gagged on every vowel, just barely retrieving the sounds before swallowing them. The Jews looked at me and I could tell that I had been the subject of much discussion. Their hatred of me leaked out of their eyes like tears. I drew my mantle around me.

"And I saw Paul enter here, just moments ago, with someone with his head covered so I could not tell who he was." This obviously annoyed Alexander.

He must have been spying outside the shop and had waited for the men from the synagogue to arrive. I thought quickly of how to buy some time for Paul and Crispus. If the men discovered they were no longer in the shop, they would pursue them and they did not have much of a head start.

On impulse, I leaned against the knee-high stack of bolts of cloth on the floor in the corner, spreading the volumes of my robe across them. Aquila had arranged them criss-cross like timbers of a house to keep the ones standing up against the wall from spilling out over the floor. I put my hand dramatically to my forehead.

"You must excuse me," I said, "It is the time of women for me and I cannot arise." Then I clutched my stomach.

This had the desired effect. The men drew away from me as if I were leprous. If they touched a menstruating woman, I would make them ceremonially unclean for days.

"You may look through our living quarters if you wish." I motioned to the curtain on the other side of the room with a hand that wagged on my wrist. Aquila went with them and I could hear Cordelia muttering as they looked behind her privacy curtain and overturned her big bowls. Baruch began to cry and Cordelia shushed him.

The men were pushing each other as they returned to the shop. They looked suspiciously at me and my spread-out skirts.

"I think she is playing the Rachel for us," said one of the Jews.

"What do you mean?" Alexander's words barely came forth from his sticky palate.

"It's what Rachel did, remember, when her father Laban came looking for what she stole from him. She sat on a saddle that concealed it and he was fooled," one of them said.

The four men looked at me, pulling on their beards.

I had not lied, I was in my menstrual period. And I knew the men could not touch me. I clutched my stomach again.

"I bet Paul is hiding under those bolts," said one of the Jews. "Come out, you coward!"

Alexander came so close to me that I could smell his raucous perfume, could see the drops of preening oil congealing in his curly hair.

"You would do anything to protect that man, wouldn't you?" Out of the corner of my eye I saw Aquila stiffen. Two of the synagogue men grasped him tightly by the arms. Alexander tried to peer over my shoulder without touching me. I raised one arm and he jumped backward.

"I live close by," said the smallest of the other men. "I'll go get my wife Hadassah and she'll drag her off." He bolted out the door of the shop.

The two men holding Aquila pushed him to his knees. One of them with a jerk wrenched his arm behind his back and I could see beads of sweat on his forehead. I began to rise and he looked me in the eye and shook his head almost imperceptibly.

Cordelia came from the back room and stood in the

doorway holding Baruch.

"Cordelia is in her time of blood, too." I made my words menacing.

The men looked doubtfully at her belly and one of them gave an extra jerk on Aquila's distended arm.

"When we find Paul here we will kill you as well," said Alexander.

Aquila twisted his body to look at him.

"And if he is not here, you will of course spare us all?"

The other men looked expectantly at Alexander, who gritted his teeth at him. "I am so certain that he is here, I will spare your lives if he is not." He swept his arm in front of him like a Caesar granting life. "But I look forward to the privilege of attending your stoning today—and that of your lying bitches."

For several minutes we all remained in our positions like pieces on an abandoned board game, waiting for someone to move us. Then the noise of the shop door opening turned all our heads.

The man had returned with his very large wife. She shook his hold off her elbow and fussed her way over to me, rocking from foot to foot as she walked.

"A travesty," she hissed into my ear. She grasped me by the forearms and pulled me from the stack, then with some surprising gentleness backed me up against the wall. I noticed that she stood between me and the men, as if protecting me. The men holding Aquila released him—threw him forward, actually—and as he rose from his hands and knees and passed over to stand beside me, our visitors began clawing at the rolls of fabric.

"I am sorry for this. He does not yet understand." The woman, Hadassah, whispered to me. "I will make it up to you later."

Soon the fabrics lay jumbled all over the floor. Then,

outside the shop, the men roared with rage. She shrugged her shoulders and, after a few moments, followed them.

We didn't see Paul again for weeks, not even when we met with the increasing number of brothers and sisters in homes around the city. There was talk of forming one large group to meet together, and with the increasing numbers of influential people who were following Jesus, some sort of building would be necessary, I thought. Paul and Crispus, we heard, set up a school of sorts at the home of Justus. We heard often of scuffles there, but no stonings nor outright attacks.

In the spring, Paul returned to live with us. In the middle of the night another group of angry young Jews dragged him to the court of the proconsul, Gallio. Paul was back home by midmorning.

"Gallio saw right through this," said Paul. "He knew that this wasn't about lawbreaking; it was about words, and he refused to get involved. The synagogue men were speechless, and I just walked right past them."

"So no one was hurt." Aquila sounded relieved.

"I wouldn't say that. As soon as I was a safe distance down the street I heard loud noises behind me," said Paul. "I looked back and the mob had turned on the synagogue leader and they were beating him. I wouldn't be surprised if they have killed him."

"What did the proconsul do about that?"

"Nothing at all."

We sat soberly thinking about what this could mean.

In the end, it meant nothing to Paul's safety nor to ours. Several more months went by. Threats and skirmishes were everyday events. Cordelia struggled with kneading, Aquila and I made tents, Baruch learned to walk and I weaned him.

The young man Timothy—himself just barely out of his teenage years—came often to the shop and began speaking in Hebrew to Baruch, tirelessly repeating the *Shema* and singing songs that fascinated the child. As I watched them, I wondered if the Way would include more and more half-breeds like them, and thought about how the Jews saw Christianity not as half-breed but bastard, to be cast out on the hills like the Romans did to unwanted daughters.

People came to the shop for information and for tents, and almost every night Paul told us of another Gentile whom he was teaching.

The night before we left Corinth the Breath encountered Cordelia and me on a path outside the city, high on the slopes of the Acrocorinth mountain where we went looking for berries.

I say encountered because we walked around a curve in the path, and where there was silence before, the world was suddenly full of words.

I put Baruch into my sling, his eyes heavy and his fingers and lips stained with berry juice, and he immediately fell asleep. And yet I looked into his eyes and knew, for the first time, that some of what I would receive was for him, and for others growing up all over the world. As the Breath breathed, I spoke these words into my son's ear:

Now a summary of the things of which we are speaking is, We have such a one high priest who has sat down on the right hand of the throne of the greatness in the heavens; minister of the holy places and of the true tabernacle, which the Lord has pitched, and not man.

Listen, my son, to your heritage.

For every high priest is constituted for the offering both of gifts and sacrifices; whence it is needful that this one also should have something which he may offer. If then indeed he were upon earth, he would not even be a priest, there being those who offer the gifts according to the law, (who serve the representation and shadow of heavenly things, according as Moses was oracularly told when about to make the tabernacle; for See, saith He, that thou make all things according to the pattern which has been shewn to thee in the mountain.)

Listen, my son, here on this mountain.

But now he has got a more excellent ministry, by so much as he is mediator of a better covenant, which is established on the footing of better promises. For if that first was faultless, place had not been sought for a second. For finding fault, he says to them, Behold, days come, saith the Lord,

And that day has come! Your eyes see it!

and I will consummate a new covenant as regards the house of Israel, and as regards the house of Judah; not according to the covenant which I made to their fathers in the day of my taking their hand to lead them out of the land of Egypt; because they did not continue in my covenant, and I did not regard them, saith the Lord.

A covenant without lists. And this you must remember and learn from it.

Because this is the covenant that I will covenant to the house of Israel after those days, saith the Lord: Giving my laws into their mind, I will write them also upon their hearts; and I will be to them for God, and they shall be to me for people. And they shall not teach each his fellow-citizen, and each his brother, saying, Know the Lord; because all shall know me in themselves, from the little one among them unto the great among them. Because I will be merciful to their unrighteousnesses, and their sins and their lawlessnesses I will never remember any more.

All can be forgiven, my son! Knowing Him means He forgets all that you want Him to forget.

In that he says New, he has made the first old; but that which grows old and aged is near disappearing.

New, like my son. Me, near disappearing.

Cordelia wrote the words on a scroll she carried everywhere now. We sat silently for a long while after she rolled up the papyrus, looking down and across the city, its ruins and sparkling buildings thrown together like cinders and pearls in the horizontal light of the dying day.

Later we walked home, still in silence, and after we prepared our evening meal Paul and Aquila came into the house and announced that we were moving to Ephesus. Our fabrics had been sold and the money given to the growing number of slaves and freemen who were Christ-followers in the city, Aquila told me; the rented house and shop would be turned back to its owner, and we would leave with what we could carry: our tools and few valuables. Our passage had been paid for by a friend.

People came and carried off our possessions into the dark. We sailed the next day.

My last memory of Corinth was of the harbor, and the pendulous flesh under the arm of a heavy and heavily-veiled woman who stood alone near the shore and waved goodbye to us.

Chapter Twenty

The passage to Ephesus, though shorter than any other sea voyage of my life, was one in which I wasted away physically, the sea like a leech on the soft parts of my belly, drinking long draughts from it daily, stripping my breasts like a milkmaid finishing her task, withering my forearms.

About the voyage itself, I remember only three things other than the sickness, and only know of those of a certainty because Cordelia told me.

The first was a poem I dictated to her. We were speaking in the first hours of the journey about Ezekiel and his visions, about how neither of us could hold a visual picture in our minds of the overlaid images of his visions, of how polyfacet God must be to allow for so many aspects and persons. I remember the rising of my gorge and the telling-forth of this:

Just as He is God
Who is served by
A Spirit

Who is the faces of
Lamb ox eagle lion man

Who is a wheel
Within a wheel
Covered by eyes
All around

I lean now
Upon His breast
Becoming with the church
Myriads of ears
That lie just under
His clavicle
Straining to hear
The comfort of
His beating
Heart

The second thing was a dream of Jesus and the sheet. Here were the words, I have the list: Minister of the Tabernacle, Excellence, Promise-Mediator. Cordelia said that I awakened and begged her to write this. I do not know anything else about the dream.

The third thing I also do not remember at all, and tell with shame. It was near the end of the journey, Cordelia said. I had lost all strength and fell from my bunk, and the storm-pitching of the ship made her afraid to try to go get any of the men who were helping with the sails and riggings. Somehow she managed, frail and knotted as she had become, to drag me back up, amidst the roar of the sea and the shrieking of the ship's wooden parts rubbing against each other and Baruch's terrified sobbing. When Paul and Aquila came back down when the sea had nearly spent itself in its fit of anger, I seemed to have welcomed its departing fury into my own breast and was thrashing in my bunk and screaming, frenzied, for Paul.

Why-why-why, she-said-I-said, can Paul look on at such suffering and not heal; why-why-why; had he no mercy, had we not served, did we not risk, was she not crippled, was I not at the edge of death itself?

And Paul, she said, sat in the corner near my bunk, his vow-shorn head in his hands, and wept and wept and wept.

I do not remember our arrival at Ephesus but have a sense that the sea, like Jonah's great fish, vomited me onto the shore with everything else it had tried to drown.

Paul was gone from Ephesus before I came to myself, so to speak. Aquila told me of Paul's single great confrontation of the Jews in the Ephesus synagogue, how he compared it to wrestling with wild beasts.

I thought of Peter's lion, walking through the streets of Ephesus, among its agoras, lurking in its bathhouses, looking with one eye from behind a statue, the black-edged corner of its mouth dripping.

Paul intended to return, he told the new believers in the synagogue, but he sailed again the next day.

Some grumbled that he got tired of tent making and was taking the easier life of a traveling rabbi. We heard that everywhere he went he had to urge people not to quit their jobs to just sit and wait for the return of Jesus. His own activity became nearly frantic, as if he did not know how much longer he would live. He seemed to become immune to the concept of risk and we heard often of one near-death experience after another: escapes, stonings, riots, wrecks. I wondered how long before it would no longer matter to him when Jesus would return (for the end of the world for each of us is our own death, is it not?); when he would meet Him again and this time on a gleaming street, not a road.

I did not know if I would ever see him again. I mourned for the words I said to him while on the ship. And yet I could not say I had never thought them before that day, nor that I have not thought them since.

In Ephesus, among the constantly-increasing number of newcomers to the Way, I began to see for the first time how the commemorative breaking of bread, as Jesus demonstrated, was losing its ties to the Passover celebration. How many million hours, I saw, have been spent in preparing for, celebrating, writing and teaching about the Exodus, an event despised by its own participants, and the brief meal that commemorated it. And I wonder if this new paschal event of Jesus would in time begin to become something ordinary for those who partook. I never saw it such; in fact, many seemed nearly greedy for all it said and meant. Though when Jesus first ate it, He was anticipating His own death, we in wonder anticipated a never-ending life: a split-second of cessation of one life and then, the on and on of delight.

We heard news, too, of the continuing unrest in Jerusalem. I wondered about the fact that when Jesus cleansed the temple, it was in the court of the Gentiles that the merchants had put access to God up for sale. Did they not know, I wondered, that it had been overrun with corruption long before Antiochus Epiphanes sacrificed a squealing hog on its altars? Though I had never entered the temple gates, I roamed through them every night in my dreams, a voyeur like Ezekiel of its losses. I was never as close to it as when I lived in Ephesus, not even when I lived in Jerusalem itself.

As to our daily lives, we soon settled in making tents and had no lack of business because of the city's crossroads. Cordelia's hands, however, became frozen and unusable, in a permanent position as if each could imitate only a swan's head while casting shadows on a wall. She became adept at picking up objects with her upper thumbs and wrists and was quite proud of herself for an ingenuity that nonetheless broke my heart. She had listened as Timothy began teaching Baruch Hebrew and could now communicate with Jews who came to the shop when Aquila was gone and often spoke to Baruch in Hebrew.

She spent much time in teaching young women how to bake and many of them were able to help support their families with what she taught them. A considerable number of the older unmarried women who were believers in that city had come there with Jesus' mother Mary, some said.

A few of these women had actually known Jesus. I never tired of asking them what they remembered, and they patiently obliged with stories of parables and miracles and persecution and dinners on the run.

Some cooked for him. Imagine.

But no one I talked to knew of sewing for him, repairing his clothing.

Others of these women were former prostitutes and all had a story of being rescued from their own lives. Many were too old to do more than just help the younger women. They came and went through our home and shop—once again, a crossroads in the crossroads; so many that they became nameless to me, but Cordelia loved them and they loved her.

Our home was thus much like a tablecloth shaken out each morning: to the outsider, a mass of faces that changed as people moved out of Ephesus to tell others of Jesus, yet constantly replenished by new faces.

One evening after dark a young man came to our door, bearing a bent-over old man whose arm he had wrapped around his neck. The young man, Jehu, was unremarkable in his appearance. To this day I cannot remember a single distinguishing feature of him, but more how he moved with a steady caution as he steered the old man into our shop.

"We need lodging and help." His voice too was unmemorable. "I am Jehu and this is Uncle Aaron."

"Of course," I said. Cordelia hastened to the living quarters and brought out a plate of bread and olives and cheese.

While the young man was unremarkable, the old man was not. He looked like a wax portrait of a man standing, one whom the artist had tired of and began to rub it out, stroking a long, slow pass across one side of his body, top to bottom, blurring it. His face sagged on the right side and his right arm hung limp. He dragged his right foot, hopping along with the younger man's steps. He looked up only once and when he spoke he seemed always unsure of himself.

"Uncle Aaron," he said, the words leaking out one corner of his mouth. He lifted one arm and placed his hand on a sunken chest. Then he looked at the younger man as if for confirmation.

"We are believers in Jesus," said Jehu. "We came here from inland and I hoped to find help for him. The rest of the family is gone, all dead, and there is no one else to help him."

Aaron held his grey hair back from his cheek as he ate the food and some of the wine dribbled out of his mouth. Tears spattered his lap. He didn't seem to notice. When he finished eating, he grasped his limp hand with the other across his lap and nodded with fatigue. Cordelia touched him awake and Jehu helped him to an alcove of the shop where she had made a pallet for him.

I could see that the patches on his clothing, held on by the tiniest stitches, had begun to fray, and my throat tightened with sympathy for the stilled hands that had sewn them there.

"He is ill." There was no need for a question.

"Yes, in many ways." Jehu was relishing a kind of honeyed roll Cordelia made with raisins and only reluctantly offered more information. The old man's soft snores filled the air.

"He has some sort of consumption. He used to be a very strong man but in recent days he loses weight no matter how much he eats."

I nodded with sympathy.

"But the other illness is worse. When his wife died a month ago, the next day he fell into a kind of stupor, for two days. They thought he would die. But when he began to regain strength and was able to sit up and talk, his mouth and his right side would not function. His first question was about his wife. He did not remember that she had died. They had to tell him again."

I nodded again.

"But every day it is the same. He awakens and looks for her everywhere. He calls, then screams for someone, anyone, to help him find her because she's missing, she's in danger, she is old and cannot protect herself. The only way anyone can stop him from tearing apart the house or from screaming to summon a magistrate is to tell him that she has died."

"Every day?" Cordelia put her hand to her throat in horror.

"Every morning," he said soberly. "It is news to him every morning. He begins it with panic and then plummets to mourning, inconsolable, as if it just happened. And by evening each day, he is spent and hopeless, as you see him here."

The old man moaned in his sleep. He was crying again.

"I can mourn with him," said Cordelia. "I know how to do that." Her cheeks were wet but her eyes were clear.

To our surprise, the young man was gone the next morning when we awakened and we never saw him again. For several months Uncle Aaron lived on, shrinking before our very eyes and beginning each day with Cordelia's arm around him, offering him wine, a tidbit of sweet bread, glistening grapes.

"I know where she is," Cordelia would say as Aaron ate his breakfast. "Do not worry, I know where she is. She is safe. We will talk about it after you eat."

Our home, like the camps of the Israelites in the desert, had the sound of a funeral in it every day, as he learned afresh of the death of his wife. Each time Cordelia told him with the tenderness of a first time. Her mercies to Aaron were as new every morning as those of God, as she wept with him, sat with him, washed his hair and his hands and his feet.

One morning Uncle Aaron did not awaken asking for his wife, because he had joined her. We washed his wasted body for the last time and saw the faint smile on his face—straight across it, not crooked anymore. As Aquila and another brother bore his swathed body outside the city, Cordelia and I followed behind on horseback.

"I wonder how we can contact his nephew," I said to Aquila, stroking the hair of Baruch who rode before me.

"What nephew?" Aquila was steadying the cart and did not look up at first.

"His nephew. You know, Jehu, who brought him to us."

He looked at me with a long slow look, a lover's look, a look that said more, more. "He has no nephew."

"But he brought him, called him Uncle Aaron. You remember?" Cordelia was agreeing with me.

"Here is what I learned about our Aaron from a group of women from his village." Aquila pointed up beyond the cleft of the cliffs to the hill country. "They came to the synagogue looking for Aaron, the man who moved with only half his body and who discovered grief every day. Some of their men told them we were caring for him."

"His relatives?"

"No, he has none. He was the last of his family, both sides."

"So why did Jehu call him Uncle?"

"Everyone called him that. He was loved by many."

There was no sound except the horse's hoofs and the protesting of the cart. I lowered Baruch by one arm to the ground and he ran alongside, chasing and retrieving a leather ball Aquila made him.

"Now, here's the interesting part," Aquila said. "The village women were caring for Aaron but were just … undone by his suffering. Not everyone has the kind of stomach Cordelia has to break that kind of news to him every day."

Cordelia's head bobbed in recognition. She alone of all of us had not cried when Aaron died.

"One morning they went to his home and he was gone," Aquila continued. "No one knew where or how; he could not walk alone, of course. And when I told them about Jehu who brought him to us, no one had ever seen such a young man."

I felt a wind on my neck, soft, warm, as my skin shivered beneath it.

I remembered what some of the women who had been friends with Mary, the mother of Jesus, told me what she often said, about pondering secret, inexplicable things inside her. And the mystery of Jehu was one that found haven in my heart.

One warm day Cordelia and I took Baruch to the barley fields on the edge of the city. I stood at the shore of the vast golden sea whose tides followed the wind and felt panic at first, nearly losing my footing at the sight of its rhythmic crests. But just as the walls of the temple in Jerusalem contained a space that became holy because of their stony embrace, I knew that this was to become a holy place.

And Cordelia knew, too. As she stroked Baruch's hair into slow-surrendered sleep, I lay on my back, my arms outstretched, under the cloud-brooding sky.

There in the cleft of Ephesus's valley, where the mountains came together like the warmth of two breasts lying against one another, the sun emerged from behind the opacity of a thundercloud and I felt it, the coming power. The sun began to warm my eyelids and the colors I saw there went from sparkling black to maroon to red then golden.

I felt the ancient fellowship of this recognition. I wondered if Abraham, on the mountain with the knife above his head, his wrist nearly broken in mid-flight by the angel, thought first, "I know you. You ate at my table. And now you are back."

And now it was back, the Holy Breath whom I, like Archimedes, best knew not just by what He brings but what He displaces. There on the grass I was submerged and emptied out, my self-caving in until filled again.

And it was the temple that had been the architecture of my dreams, it was the truth of the temple again, the temple of the Lord, the temple of the Lord:

The first therefore also indeed had ordinances of service, and the sanctuary, a worldly one.

And if it were the first, there must be a second …

For a tabernacle was set up; the first, in which were both the candlestick and the table and the exposition of the loaves, which is called Holy; but after the second veil a tabernacle which is called Holy of holies, having a golden censer, and the ark of the covenant, covered round in every part with gold, in which were the golden pot that had the manna, and the rod of Aaron that had sprouted, and the tables of the covenant; and above over it the cherubim of glory shadowing the mercy-seat;

And I walked through this room, seeing it all but could not speak of it all: *concerning which it is not now the time to speak in detail.*

Now these things being thus ordered, into the first tabernacle the priests enter at all times, accomplishing the services; but into the second, the high priest only, once a year, not without blood, which he offers for himself and for the errors of the people:

("Slow down, can you slow down?" said Cordelia. The flood of words did not.)

the Holy Spirit shewing this,

Yes! The Holy Breath was tutoring me, had tutored others, and was now showing that the buildings the Hebrews had so long loved, to their teeth-gnashing surprise, had been designed with one aim: to instruct about Jesus.

that the way of the holy of holies has not yet been made manifest while as yet the first tabernacle has its standing; the which is an image for the present time, according to which both gifts and sacrifices, unable to perfect as to conscience him that worshipped, are offered, consisting only of meats and drinks and divers washings, ordinances of flesh, imposed until the time of setting things right.

And the time was now, set aright.

But Christ being come high priest of the good things to come, by the better and more perfect tabernacle not made with hand, (that is, not of this creation,) nor by blood of goats and calves, but by his own blood, has entered in once for all into the holy of holies, having found an eternal redemption. For if the blood of goats and bulls, and a heifer's ashes sprinkling the defiled, sanctifies for the purity of the flesh, how much rather shall the blood of the Christ, who by the eternal Spirit

Ah! Holy Breath! You participated there, too? Yes, He says, yes, yes.

offered himself spotless to God, purify your conscience from dead works to worship the living God? And for this reason he is mediator of a new covenant, so that, death having taken place for redemption of the transgressions under the first covenant, the called might receive the promise of the eternal inheritance. (For where there is a testament, the death of the testator must needs come in. For a testament is of force when men are dead, since it is in no way of force while the testator is alive.)

And I thought of coming deaths.

Whence neither the first was inaugurated without blood. For every commandment having been spoken according to the law by Moses to all the people; having taken the blood of calves and goats, with water and scarlet wool and hyssop, he sprinkled both the book itself and all the people, saying, This is the blood of the covenant which God has enjoined to you. And the tabernacle too and all the vessels of service he sprinkled in like manner with blood; and almost all things are purified with blood according to the law, and without blood-shedding there is no remission.

And I stand for my redemption in a sticky pool.

It was necessary then that the figurative representations of the things in the heavens should be purified with these; but the heavenly things themselves with sacrifices better than these.

I felt an old, familiar echo. Things that were real and beyond us, invisible; and reflections of them we can see, not on a cave wall but moving all around us.

For the Christ is not entered into holy places made with hand, figures of the true, but into heaven itself, now to appear before the face of God for us: nor in order that he should offer himself often, as the high priest enters into the holy places every year with blood not his own; since he had then been obliged often to suffer from the foundation of the world.

Suffering? Since the foundation of the world? Can it be? Has it been? Always been?

But now once in the consummation of the ages he has been manifested for the putting away of sin by his sacrifice. And forasmuch as it is the portion of men once to die, and after this judgment; thus the Christ also, having been once offered to bear the sins of many, shall appear to those that look for him the second time without sin for salvation.

The words faded like a mother's, shushing her child to sleep.

From that moment in the barley fields, the mill of my life ground some things fine as dust.

I began to realize that I would walk with a spiritual limp the rest of my life, because my words had wrestled with His.

I knew that I had received a commission: to hoard the true meaning of the temple, and to tell the Hebrew people what it was. And as I looked at the face of my Hebrew son, I saw the conserve like that of figs in honey, dragonfly in amber, life preserved beyond its own.

And that night I sewed myself a bag of scarlet wool, and put in it the flowers of the hyssop, for its red spattering on the lintels of bereaved Egypt, for its stalk lifting of the sponge of vinegar wine to Jesus on the cross, and for the blood, for his blood flung into the smoke-infused holy place.

And for my blood coursing under my breastbone, where the bag hangs now.

Chapter Twenty-One

Baruch began to read, both Hebrew as instructed by Aquila, and Greek that I taught him using the Septuagint. He seemed a miniature man, pushing his hair out of his eyes with one hand as his other pointed at letters. I had hoped that by watching and listening to the Hebrew I too would master it, but it was a silver-finned fish that wriggled always beyond my grasp.

"How odd," Aquila said, trimming a lamp wick to coax it to give us one more hour of light late one evening, "that you have been called of God to seal up the understanding of centuries of Jewishness for God's people—and you are a Gentile who cannot—" He looked up quickly at me as if he were suddenly afraid that he had said the wrong thing.

"No worse than Paul, calling himself a Hebrew of Hebrews, traveling the world teaching only the barbarians now," I retorted. He did say something wrong, something very true.

I was still smarting from his unfinished sentence—

perhaps as much from the unspoken part of it as from what he said—when I awakened the next morning and found him gone from our bed. Cordelia was whispering to a young woman who held a tightly-knit basket with its lid open.

"See," she said, "what luscious things our new friend Ulpia brought us." Inside the basket were some of the largest dates I had ever seen, as shiny as if they were made of glass, fragrant and moist.

I nodded to the young woman—a young face filled with old, old sadnesses—and looked around in the shop for Aquila.

"He is not here," said Cordelia. "Ulpia is one of a group of people just arrived here this morning from Alexandria, and Aquila has gone to arrange housing for the men."

"Welcome to our home, Ulpia." I murmured, still yawning. "Aegyptus. The libraries, in Alexandria."

Cordelia looked at me blankly, but the young girl spoke up.

"The library? It burned in my great-grandfather's day."

"The great library, I know." I fumbled for a date in the basket and smiled at the girl. "But the other two, they are still there, yes?" In my mind, anyone from Alexandria must come carrying the dust of papyrus and the musty scent of vellum. But by this time Baruch was showing the young woman some seashells and the conversation turned. Though this young woman smelled only like her dates, the thought of others from that city of learning intrigued me.

By midmorning I had thought of nothing else. I listened anxiously through the morning for Aquila, and when I stepped outside the shop to throw some garbage onto a pile in the alley I heard the sound of voices.

"I want you to meet my wife Priska, and then we'll go to our brother Dan's house where you'll be staying." It was the voice of Aquila. "She is a very educated woman. She knows the Septuagint better than almost any of the men. You will have much to talk about, perhaps next week." I heard the pride in his voice.

"So you are the Aquila who is married to her," another voice said. "I did not realize the connection. One of the other men was speaking just now of her great learning. How she knows the old Greek writings and all of the Roman ones too; how she has great insights, such that even men listen when she speaks."

I lurked like Sarah behind a wall, listening.

"A veritable *hetaera* of the ancient tradition," said the man.

I froze. He used an old Greek word that I hoped Aquila did not understand.

Unfortunately, Aquila had heard the word, but understood it in a more modern usage, one stripped of any nobility it may have ever carried.

"Did you just call my wife a *hetaera*?" Aquila's deep voice rose in anger.

"Well, only in the sense of how she speaks with men …"

I heard the sound of flesh hitting flesh, deep and painful, and then a loud cry. Two other voices rose in protest and then, the sound of a scuffle and shouted words about blood and welcomes and crazy and leaving.

I hurried into the house and waited, my eyes wide, for Aquila. He did not enter right away but must have stood for a while in the street. When a customer arrived, he came in with him and began showing him a repair, rubbing his hand but speaking as if nothing had happened.

I whispered to Cordelia what I had heard as she sent another young woman home with the dough she had kneaded. Ulpia continued to play with Baruch, and watching her I realized that her mind was a simple one and that she was not interested in what we were talking about.

She giggled in a series of high-pitched squeaks that no one could hear over anyway.

"*Haetera,*" said Cordelia. "Aquila doesn't know what someone with classical learning would have meant by that."

Aquila called for me from the shop, asking me to evaluate whether the tent flap in the hands of a customer could be saved. By that time another customer, and then another came to the shop to speak with Aquila until the sun became low in the sky. While Cordelia and I supped with Baruch, Aquila continued to talk tents as he chewed bread with customers. At last the shop cleared of people.

"It is time to go to synagogue," he said. He wouldn't meet my eyes. Though we met with other Christians on the first day of the week, we still continued to go to the synagogue regardless of the animosity with which many of the Jews regarded us.

Once in sight of the building Aquila walked on ahead and Cordelia and Ulpia and I went into the women's section. Ulpia and Baruch stumbled into each other with mock clumsiness and I realized that at least temporarily we had two children in the house.

Near the end of the Sabbath service one of the synagogue leaders arose and said that we had guests newly arrived from Egypt, and that one of them would address us, Apollos of Alexandria.

I heard a gasp from the other women when the speaker turned to face us. One eye was swollen shut, but this seemed of no consequence to him. Without seeming to look at anyone, he fixed his gaze on the back of the room and began.

"I call you, sons of Abraham, my brothers, to alert!" His voice was light itself if such a thing could be, reflecting off the walls and returning to his face, and it was as if the bruises and the dissymmetry melted away into that honeyed voice, the voice I had heard in the alley. I looked toward Aquila. He tossed his head back and I saw cords in his neck, the size of fingers pointing to the base of his skull. One of the other men next to him looked strangely at him and Aquila looked down, glaring at the floor. But the voice was continuing.

"The voice of God speaks forth in the call of the *shofar* trumpet, like that of Joshua, like that of Gideon, after four centuries of silence. The moaning of the *shofar* has been carried on the winds across oceans, across land.

"No, it comes to you not through me, but through one who bore the real marks of a prophet: one who like other sages sought the solitude of the sere desert, eating its winged food, wearing its gritty garments.

"You know of washings, my brothers. Our bodies stay moist, do they not, with the mysteries of the *mikveh* bath? But the washing of this one hearkens to eternal realities: not the removal of earth-stains, or even the compliance or completion of vows. This bespeaks a demarcation, a frontier of the faith of our fathers. And John son of Zechariah of the desert was its herald, the rivers of the holy places of our ancestors, his fonts."

Men in the synagogue were looking at one another, a churned lake. Women of the synagogue were looking at Apollos, a single-eyed wave suspended in the air.

"I bring to you news of tortured roads jerked into a gliding highway, news of ancient valleys heaved up and mountains like meal in a cup leveled with a knife's edge, of the overturning of old tables and the upending of full vessels and the treading-down of vaunting people.

"Turn yourselves inside out, my brothers!" There was utter silence in the synagogue, and each time he began again someone's shoulders startled.

"You cannot escape this, though you like serpents

would seek shade from its blinding heat under the rocks of your heritage. Can you not feel the breeze on your cheeks from the winnowing fan? Are you chaff or grain? Will you fly or feed?"

Now the room had a warp of murmuring as the shuttle of his voice worked. "I bring you a message of no comfort, none at all: of axes resting at your roots, of coming wraths and all the sins of all of Abraham's children coming home to roost. I bring you the only way of consolation: I say again, turn yourselves inside out and be washed clean of yourselves!"

Now men were charging toward the place where he stood, but Aquila stood as if paralyzed.

The synagogue leader stood in front of Apollos. His outstretched arms quelled the oncoming rush of men who stopped short, stumbling into each other, in front of the invisible barrier a foot in front of him.

"How dare you bring up that false Christos to us!" one of the men shouted over the leader's shoulder. "If you weren't a newcomer I'd stone you myself."

Apollos had a puzzled look on his face.

"Christos? I never said that John ben Zechariah, the baptizer, was *ha Mashiach*. I, like you, am awaiting the Anointed One."

The leader turned to him. "John? You were not speaking of that renegade Jesus of Nazareth, then? We will not hear that here."

Apollos frowned and shrugged. "I don't know the man, this Jesus."

"Of course you do!" shouted another.

"I never heard of him."

"You liar. One of the followers of Jesus denied him too so that proves it. A lying follower of liars."

"I swear by the temple ...."

"That proves it! Three times he's denied it!"

Before I knew it, Aquila was standing next to Apollos.

"He is a friend of mine, and if he says he is not a follower of Jesus, he is not," he said, his voice smothering the others. "You allow those of us who are His followers here, anyway, just as long as you can control what we say." His voice sounded bitter and weary.

"That's right. You keep your dead-man Jesus to yourselves," one of the older men said, his voice falling off as Aquila pushed Apollos roughly away toward the door. A little more roughly than necessary, I thought. The young man seemed bewildered.

Cordelia and I pulled Baruch and Ulpia with us, stumbling past the rows of women in the synagogue. By the time we arrived home, Aquila and another man were sitting down, stony-faced, in front of Apollos, who leaned with his elbows on his knees, holding a cloth to his eye which had begun to bleed again. The oil lamp Aquila trimmed the night before held a steady flame.

"I told him we'd wait until you got here," said Aquila to me. "I couldn't understand a lot of what he said, but I think he needs our help." I nodded to Cordelia and she took Ulpia and Baruch to our living quarters to prepare for bed. I brought in a flask of wine and cups, then I sat down on another stool, my eyes downcast and my head covered.

"You heard what he said in the synagogue, Priscilla my wife," said Aquila, his voice lingering on the last word. "What would you say to him?"

I drew in my breath and thought. Just the name Apollos had entranced me. I looked all the way home for hawks and ravens and crows in the moonlit sky, stepped lightly fearing snakes, listened for cicadas and kithera music, knowing those were the attributes of the god of the arts, the speaker-forth of beauty Apollo, knowing my own idolatrous heart had never turned completely inside out, either.

"Apollos of Aegyptus. You are of the race of Israel? Why did your parents name you after a god of the Greeks?" I asked this flatly, like an interrogator, as if I were disinterested.

This was not the question any of the men expected, and Apollos coughed before answering, buying time, perhaps.

"My parents were not practicing at the time, so to speak. And they thought it would go better for me growing up in Egypt if I had a Greek name since that was the lineage last of the ruling ones there, the Ptolemies."

"Well, that settles that," said Aquila sourly. "Just what we needed to know."

I dared not look at Apollos directly yet.

"What I think my good husband wants to know first of all, then—since I have my questions answered—is why you called me a *hetaera*."

I heard the other man make a choking sound. I looked up and Aquila was staring at me.

"I meant it only in the classical sense, of course," said Apollos, his words no longer measured and sure as in the synagogue, but tumbling out like rocks from a sack. "I meant, as a treasured and educated woman, a resource"—here his voice faded as he searched for the right word—"a resource for the mind. For knowledge and understanding."

No one spoke.

"It was an unwise choice of words." He tried again. "I did not consider that its usage here meant more of—"

"A courtesan?" Aquila asked.

"Yes. No. That is not what I mean. Not what I meant," said Apollos. "I was thinking of the great women who have advised men. Why, even the great statesman Pericles had his Aspasia, who wrote his greatest speeches."

All three turned to me for verification. I found myself

blushing but proud.

"That is true," I said, "from all I have read. It is said of him that he would never have been known as a great orator had his woman companion not given him the right words to move the people."

"Yes," said Apollos quickly. "She was more than, shall we say, a Muse to him; she was the source of words. And I've heard that you, Priska, wife of Aquila, are also a woman of great learning and the source of words, as well."

I nearly missed what he said in my rush to continue the discussion. I leaned forward. "You might know as well that some believe the writer of the Odyssey not to be blind Homer but a woman, you know, because of all the tricks women play on Odysseus, how the armor-clad Athena decides his fate, all seemingly from a woman's point of view …"

Aquila reached for my arm, slowly, touching me under my sleeve.

"Oh," I said. "I do not think of myself as a source of words. I am more a recipient of words." I thought for a moment. "Maybe even a participant in words."

Apollos nodded, then folded and put into his lap the cloth he'd been holding over his eye. He looked warily at Aquila, then spoke again. "We'd have to say that about any woman whose words are recorded in the holy Writings, would we not? Women who were participants in words that are Scripture? Were not Hannah? Miriam? Rahab?"

I had never thought of myself in the same way as those women. Well, Rahab the harlot maybe, I thought; she was a Gentile too. I started to ask him about others who had not spoken in faith and yet we had their words as well: Sarah pushing Hagar forward, Delilah's words through a pouting lower lip, Jezebel's mathematics, then thought better of it. Best to leave well enough alone.

"The Holy Spirit has been poured out on all people, young, old, men and women," I said. "We live in extraordinary, favored times."

"Does this have something to do with what the men at the synagogue said? About a Messiah?" asked Apollos.

"It does. Messiah has come and he, too, has a message and a baptism. There are people here in Ephesus who saw him, who knew him." Aquila spoke with a firm voice.

"I don't want to be disrespectful," said Apollos. He clutched the bloodstained rag in his lap as if it were a shield he might need to quickly employ. "But Messiah would have to fulfill all the prophecies, and if he's come, well …"

"Well, what?" Aquila's voice was tempered, sweet.

"Then why is the homeland of the Jews under Roman rule? Where is the kingdom?" He looked warily at Aquila as he spoke.

Aquila rose to his feet and Apollos flinched but did not look away.

"Here," said Aquila, touching his chest. The other man did so as well.

"And the proof of that?" Apollos asked.

"A descendant of King David who rose from the dead."

Chapter Twenty-Two

For seven things I remember the last years in Ephesus: seven, the Jewish number of perfection and completeness.

First was Apollos, the man with a pagan god's name who helped me put to death idolatry in my heart.

In him I saw myself, in his choosing of heritage of Jewishness, and the art and the orderliness of the *ma'at* of his Egyptianness, and his citizenship of Romanness, and the Greekness of his very speech—and then this complexity one pivotal day confronted with the offense of a humiliated God then rose to reign.

"We are second-generation witnesses," I told him one day. "The most important event of human history—when a man got up out of a grave by his own power, undecayed after days insensate—was not seen by anyone. But all must live by the aftermath of that unobserved occurrence. Even those who saw Him alive after that did not see the event itself. They saw aftermath, and in the process they became aftermath. And now we all live by words about the event."

Like Plato's cave, he told me to my delight, like Plato's cave—a man comes back to tell those who only see shadows that there are real things. "Jesus came back with authority to tell us what is real?" Apollos asked.

I looked at him and then at Aquila—for permission to speak, perhaps, for reassurance. It was one thing to help instruct a man of such intellect and eagerness to learn. It was quite another to ask him to embrace, or even consider, that the Holy Breath had instructed me.

"Jesus once said that rocks would speak if people refused to do so," I said, by way of introducing the subject. My attention was arrested by a striped stone propping up a wooden tent frame where Aquila stitched a repair and I wondered what songs might be trapped in its strata.

"And you know if God could enable Balaam's beast to speak, then He can give words to anyone." I picked my way forward culling words like shriveled dry beans. Apollos and Aquila both turned to look at me, then my husband shrugged and smiled and turned back to his work. He spoke over his shoulder, as if he were tossing out a suggestion for items he needed from the market.

"What she is trying to tell you, dear brother Apollos, is that the Holy Breath has spoken to her directly. I am convinced of it myself. And Paul, the Gentile's apostle, knows it as well."

I rushed to take the attention off myself and to put it onto the Breathings. I told him of a heavenly Holy of Holies, of whose furnishings those in the holy cube in Jerusalem were only representations.

This I treasure as I think of it now. This is the second wonder of my Ephesus world.

"So the golden lampstand the priest sees is like the shadow on the wall of a cave," he said. "What is in the heavenly sanctuary is what is real." I wondered if this could be accurate. I wondered if the Breath were the coming-back and forth of One who could see reality.

I took a worn pattern off a hook on the wall and showed him how every linen garment I made using it would carry its shadow, its likeness, no matter how far away its wearer took it. And that even words describing it can carry its essence when it no longer exists: the memory, the telling of something long frayed away.

He listened, first with respectful disbelief and many questions, then with impatient curiosity, and then (when Cordelia brought in the scroll and read to him), as a man suddenly famished at the first taste of new food. I found that in explaining I found my own clarity.

"It seems that the process has three aspects," I reasoned out loud. "First there is the mind of the Holy Breath, for He has purposed all this with His own logic. Then there is the vessel into whom He breathes. And this occurs on earth, in time, not in eternity—I mean to say, as an insertion into history."

The eyebrows of Apollos rose, then furrowed as he considered this.

"And in the case of prophecy, then, there would be another insertion into human history—when something is fulfilled. A fourth aspect." His face flushed with the thought.

"And that again, by the agency, the power of God," I responded.

And thus it was that the next time the church in Ephesus broke bread, their new brother Apollos, his face with a Stephen-glow, spoke of the antitype of a heavenly altar, one which could not be corrupted with pig waste nor carried away by Philistines nor sacked and ruined.

What the high priest spattered with blood each year,

Apollos said, was only a shadow of a reality rampant in front of blinding heavenly light. And should the metal copy be destroyed, there were words that were a more reliable replica, an even truer type, than what hid behind the embroidered veil atop Salem's summit.

I listened as he read the words from Cordelia's Breath-scroll to the listeners.

Each owned these words, he said. You and you and you, he said. Hebrew and Hellenist, priest and pagan.

Some of the Jewish converts, the men, sobbed—for the first time in their lives freed from the fear that the great Temple would be destroyed and all would be irreparably lost. Some of the women held their hands to their breasts and repeated words as Apollos spoke them. Some of the old ones said that Stephen had come back from the dead, for he too spoke of the tabernacle as a pattern and witness, his face glowed too.

It was during that evening that the fourth wonder of Ephesus happened, the night when the old gods left me forever.

For some reason my mind had been mulling over two images. The first was a painting on a papyrus that my mother once had, of the Egyptian goddess Newet. Her blue body was elongated like a great bench hovering over the world, her head and hands on one side of the land, her legs and feet on the other, her star-studded torso spanning all the created order.

The second was the image of the two-countenanced god Janus, who looked forward and backward. And I felt my two faces, looking back at the old laws and forward to their fulfillments in Jesus.

But this still night in Ephesus these images seemed to fade, as if someone were painting over them with stronger colors.

With that, I knew that I had been given the role of bridging two worlds: the invisible one of true reality, and this sod-anchored place where shadows meet shadows and call themselves real. And I felt myself becoming transparent as across me, through me, shone light.

The last instance of this perforation of me in Ephesus took place the night Apollos spoke my Breathed words in the synagogue. Later, Baruch and Ulpia—for two years now, Cordelia's assistant—walked with Cordelia and me in the still night back to our home.

When I stopped in the street and grasped Cordelia's shoulder she looked into my eyes and reflected back my urgency.

She sent the others on ahead home and Cordelia and I sat on a bench, beneath a cypress tree that felt like home to us. There, for the last time, my precious friend was my scribe, and this time, this fifth Ephesian wonder, the Breath was as patient as a child's tutor, and as rhythmic as dance.

For the law, having a shadow of the coming good things, not the image itself of the things, can never, by the same sacrifices which they offer continually yearly, perfect those who approach.

I understood that the law was only shadow, and this truth: Just at the moment a shadow is longest, then it fades and disappears.

Since, would they not indeed have ceased being offered, on account of the worshippers once purged having no longer any conscience of sins? But in these there is a calling to mind of sins yearly.

I thought of the women, their hands to their chests, memorizing.

For blood of bulls and goats is incapable of taking away sins.

Wherefore coming into the world he says, Sacrifice and offering thou willedst not; but thou hast prepared me a body. Thou tookest no pleasure in burnt-offerings and sacrifices for sin.

Then I said, Lo, I come (in the roll of the book it is written of me) to do, O God, thy will. Above, saying Sacrifices and offerings and burnt-offerings and sacrifices for sin thou willedst not, neither tookest pleasure in (which are offered according to the law); then he said, Lo, I come to do thy will. He takes away the first that he may establish the second; by which will we have been sanctified through the offering of the body of Jesus Christ once for all.

Of course, of course. This is what the eternal Melchizedek must do, had done: a single faultless sacrifice.

And every priest stands daily ministering, and offering often the same sacrifices, which can never take away sins. But he, having offered one sacrifice for sins, sat down in perpetuity at the right hand of God, waiting from henceforth until his enemies be set for the footstool of his feet. For by one offering he has perfected in perpetuity the sanctified.

And the Holy Spirit also bears us witness of it;

Yes! Witness. I take it, I bear it as well.

for after what was said: This is the covenant which I will establish towards them after those days, saith the Lord: Giving my laws into their hearts, I will write them also in their understandings;

I danced with the Breath

and their sins and their lawlessnesses I will never remember any more.

Freed, I danced with the Breath!

But where there is remission of these, there is no longer a sacrifice for sin.

I waited until Cordelia finished writing.

Then we walked back home, and with Baruch listening intently, Cordelia read what she had written to Aquila and Apollos.

Apollos paced and wept.

It was only a few months later when Baruch summoned me from the back of the house to the shop.

"Father said I should watch the shop, and I've been practicing stitches," he said, and proudly showed a fingertip bleeding beneath the nail. I took his hand, made a mental note to get him a new bronze finger stall because he'd outgrown the child's version we first gave him, and poured water from a pitcher over his hand.

"Who is it in the shop? Do you recognize the customer?"

He shook his head and squeezed his finger to extract another drop of blood.

"No. But he sounds like he's strangling when he talks."

I felt coldness behind my ears.

"Get back into the back with Cordelia and Ulpia," I whispered. "Stay there until Father returns. Do you know where he went?"

Baruch looked frightened and suddenly small enough for the old finger stall. He shook his head and walked backwards into a corner of the living quarters where my sisters were kneading bread. I gave Baruch a hand-sign of silence, and he nodded. The two women seemed at first not to notice, but then Cordelia began to watch my departure with anxious eyes. After a moment she patted Baruch and Ulpia and followed me out into the shop.

I could smell the rankness of the oil on his hair before I saw him. Alexander stood behind two older men, Pharisees judging by their garb, who shifted from foot to foot and would not look at us.

Both Cordelia and I pulled our headcoverings across our faces so that only our eyes showed, and the men began to cast furtive glances at us.

"Aquila's two women, eh?" The last syllable seemed to linger on his uvula and made me want to cough.

"And there's another one, I hear," he continued. "A younger one, for Aquila's desires. How does that make you matrons feel?"

It took me a moment to realize that he meant Ulpia.

"You think yourself a prophetess, is that it? I hear that

you, dame Priska, now lead three men by the nose."

Again, I did not know what he meant. He was gagging out, "Three dupes: Aquila, that heretic Paul, and now this fool Apollos."

Cordelia stepped forward and reached for the spirals of his beard. He grasped her hand in his and turned it over, bending her wrist back. I heard Cordelia gasp in pain and before I knew it one of the older men moved aside and there was a series of cracks.

"You will not … think to touch me … with those crooked hands!" hissed Alexander.

Cordelia was screaming now, bending over, and the men were climbing over each other to escape when Alexander released her. He had broken three of her fingers that now hung at sickening angles from her hand. Baruch came running from the living area and I caught him by the edge of his tunic just before he disappeared out the door after the men.

"I cannot have you do that, my son," I said to him. "There's nothing to be gained. We must wait for your father."

Thus it was that Aquila entered a house of weeping an hour later, and his face flushed with dark, old blood as we told the story. When he looked at Cordelia's bandaged fingers I saw him cry for the first time in our lives.

He turned to Baruch and drew him close. "Only seven years old and ready to go after those men," he murmured.

"Nearly eight, Abba."

"I have to tell you that starting today the synagogue leaders have decided we may no longer attend there," he said. "Undoubtedly coinciding with the arrival of that Alexander from Corinth." He pulled his head from side to side, stretching his arched shoulders. "You build a nation of zealots, you shouldn't be surprised when they do zealous things."

"What grounds?" The voice of Cordelia startled me. "What do they accuse you of?"

"Alexander brought up charges of immorality," said Aquila, "but even the Jews here know that is not true. So they have accused me of the two things I cannot defend myself against."

"What are those?"

"They say I manipulate people's hopes. Actually, that you and I do that."

"And?"

"They say I am prideful."

My face flushed now. "Now, that is remarkable. Pharisees who would think humility a virtue. And how are you to answer that? To say, 'Yes, I am, I am very humble, everyone knows that?'"

He brushed something off his sleeve. "You see the difficulty."

With the sound of people entering the shop, he arose and left.

But I was not seeing anything, for I heard in the rug-hung walls a whisper, and then knew the great, sighing Presence was announcing Himself, and all that was within me turned to listen.

I heard the deep-sobbing of Cordelia, the whisk-sliding out of a scroll from the pot in the corner, and Baruch settling in to write: the sixth wonder of Ephesus.

And as the Breath began, I felt parts of me stinging inside.

Having therefore, brethren, boldness for entering into the holy of holies by the blood of Jesus, the new and living way which he has dedicated for us through the veil, that is, his flesh, and having a great priest over the house of God,

The cadence was the Breath's slowest of solemn

marching.

let us

Your father and I, and you my son

approach with a true heart, in full assurance of faith, sprinkled as to our hearts from a wicked conscience, and washed as to our body with pure water. Let us hold fast the confession of the hope unwavering, (for he is faithful who has promised;)

This remember, my son: The giving of a promise requires fulfillment.

and let us consider one another for provoking to love and good works; not forsaking the assembling of ourselves together, as the custom is with some; but encouraging one another, and by so much the more as ye see the day drawing near.

For where we sin willfully after receiving the knowledge of the truth, there no longer remains any sacrifice for sins, but a certain fearful expectation of judgment, and heat of fire about to devour the adversaries.

I saw flames licking at the oil on a curlicued beard, and I understood that this man was a type of many more, an antitype of the father of lies.

Any one that has disregarded Moses' law dies without mercy on the testimony of two or three witnesses: of how much worse punishment, think ye, shall he be judged worthy who has trodden under foot the Son of God, and esteemed the blood of the covenant, whereby he has been sanctified, common, and has insulted the Spirit of grace?

Sweetest Spirit

For we know him that said, To me belongs vengeance; I will recompense, saith the Lord: and again, The Lord shall judge his people. It is a fearful thing falling into the hands of the living God.

And from that day on, until the Breath no longer breathed words on me, Baruch my son was my scribe in those times when I needed one: the vessel of my blood, the vessel of my breath, the vessel of our Breath.

Just a few months later, in the dust of an autumn of

filtered umber lights and skittering leaves, Apollos left without ever meeting Paul, a conundrum about which the Breath would not speak.

Nor did I ever see the face of Apollos nor hear his voice again. Never before or since has my life known someone who I loved in the way I loved Apollos, his perfections, his completeness. His loss to me was ocean-deep, profound in my bones, inestimable.

About this I can no longer speak.

Chapter Twenty-Three

The last time Paul said that Aquila and I saved his life I am not so sure he was correct.

Paul called the men a posse who arrived from surrounding city synagogues to take him back to Jerusalem, or stone him, or hire Romans to flay him or throw him into the ocean—no one was quite sure if they ever colluded on an outcome, only on their hatred for him. When one of them accosted my husband, Aquila, in the market with the mistaken impression that he was Paul, the man's youthful companions gleefully beat Aquila nearly to death, their sidelocks swinging as they struck again and again. I did not see this happen, but those who witnessed it said that the attackers wrapped themselves in their cloaks as they walked away, but droplets of blood clung to the wisps of their beards like accusing jewels, walked away from the red pool around Aquila like a lake of fire from which every passerby quickly stepped aside.

And then they were gone, out of the city, before they

ever knew that they had attacked the wrong man. Aquila could not work for months and Paul again became a tentmaker until Aquila recovered—if the limpness of his left hand and his twisted leg and scarred face and pitted scalp was a recovery.

I began to struggle with things I could see and touch and yet could not reconcile in my mind. This very Paul worked with us, as unremarkable as hanks of flax, and yet one evening he arrived from the countryside mauled by a wolf that had, according to Timothy, lost interest in him when he began to preach to him.

Another time Paul disappeared for days and when he returned his entire back was a scab from lashings, forty less one. I watched Cordelia weave a cloth through the skein of her own overlapping fingers and dip it into salt water and bathe the ribbons of flesh. Then she sat by his side through a day and a night while the delirium took him, and he cried out, "Sentence of death! Sentence of death!" in a voice gone to whisper until at last the wracking fever misted away with the steam around his forehead.

Meanwhile, I watched Aquila's flinching efforts at everyday life. Everywhere he walked was uphill. Many a day I saw him heft a bolt on his ravaged shoulders when his arms seemed to melt from the bolts he'd lifted moments before.

(Yet the touch of Paul's workman's kerchief, still damp with the sweat from the heat of our shop, healed a beggar outside the door. Just like that.)

Nonetheless, Aquila's body, the cargo of his inestimable soul that was his Aquila-ness, was more winsome to me than ever. More than ever, I looked into his eyes and lost myself in the richness within him, like descending into a cellar of cached, ancestral treasures.

These were the realities of Ephesus and they became

such a part of our lives that we no longer saw our bodies as anything other than what Paul called our letters of flesh, daily inscribed into us so that anyone could read.

Both Paul and Aquila mourned the news from Corinth that the believers in that city were fighting amongst themselves, and I believe knowing this wounded the men more than those who beat them ever had.

"Let me take a letter from you to Corinth," Aquila begged Paul one day. "They will listen to you." I heard the men talking about Corinth, all through the evening, all through the night.

That night I dreamed of the cemetery in Rome where the other Priska was interred, where Pudens and Mathos were baptized and where Pudens, for all we knew, might now lie as well. In my dream I saw in the midst of those catacombs a cube of space, a holiest; and past its curtain, into its shadowed depths, I heaved an anchor of hope.

At the end of its rope were the children I would never have, the residence that would never be, the lost people and things, the lost and unrecoverable years, my knowledge of the erosion of what carried the cargo of my soul. And those things stayed at my feet and I stared at the rope that now disappeared behind the curtain.

But the curtain of the holiest became the long cloth with writing I had seen in so many dreams, and now these words were added:

Flesh pathway
Blood-dedicator
Faithful provider
Savior underfoot
Living Judge
Recompensor
Vengeance owner

And in my dream I wept because I could not see my

Lord, just the cloth and the rope and the ruins at my feet.

The next morning when I arose, Paul and Timothy and Aquila sat with their heads together, as Timothy read from the chronicles, of the prayer of David the king before his death, his giving-over of immeasurable wealth for the temple. In my mind I could see the stockpiles of wood, the caches of silver's coolness, the glimmering brass and glinting jewels, the heart of the gold of Ophir still trembling in hidden darkness.

Finished, the men looked at me as I stirred and coughed.

Paul leaned back and stretched. "And what does the great lady Priska have to say about this?" His eyes were soft and welcoming.

I reached over to the scroll they had been reading from, carrying a kiss from my lips on my fingers as I touched it.

"The Holy Breath has taught me that the temple existed in the mind and purposes of God before men ever put stones together to frame it."

Timothy was nodding. "Yes. And that was true of the Tabernacle that preceded it, for Moses was told to build it according to a pattern given to him on the mountain."

"And so, such things are built not from a plan outward but from the mind of God outward," I said.

The men listened and I could hardly keep my breath. I reached for one of the Holy Breath's scrolls but Aquila stopped my hand and recited its words. I rubbed my hands together over and over as I listened. Paul nodded as he spoke and Timothy leaned forward, keen.

"So what the Holy Breath has always intended," said Paul, "was that the temple, and every meaning-drenched object in it, come to be known as a symbol of something beyond themselves, meaning eternal, in the heavens. And it is at that indestructible altar the indestructible Priest has made a final offering."

"Of Himself …" Timothy's voice trailed off.

"Priska, what will you do with your scrolls?" Paul's voice expanded, pushing all other conversation out of the room.

I had not thought much about that—except that as I feared for Aquila's safety, and that of anyone in our household, I also feared for the scrolls.

"I … I don't know. I do not know their purpose."

"Apollos and Aquila and I now preach what is in them. You know that. The new believers who come out of our Judaism find great hope and meaning in what the Breath has taught you about the old covenants and ordinances. It frees them."

"And I have thought that this must be their purpose." I felt as if a child of mine were being examined, suddenly defensive against some coming charge of wrongdoing. "I mean, to help you who preach."

No one spoke.

"What else could be their purpose? I do not claim to be an eyewitness, like you, brother Paul. How could I presume the authority to press this on other people? I could not imagine anyone outside of this circle reading my scrolls. I am honored when you memorize them"—here, I looked at Aquila—"but they seem idiosyncratic to me."

Paul rubbed his chin. "It is true that authority comes from apostleship, and apostleship only from being an eyewitness," he said.

I looked down in silence. I did not tell them about my dreams. I knew they were for me only.

"Our brother Luke the physician cannot claim to have seen the Lord," said Paul. "But he is collecting all the stories, investigating everything, to write his own account. And he says that he feels the—what word does he use?—the *supervision* of the Holy Spirit as he works."

"Surely you can see that what the Breath has told me is

not an account." I bristled at the word, and then pointed at a scroll. "And this is not a collection of anything. In fact, it feels many times like I'm hostage to it. I'm the one being conscripted to do what it wants. Only in some of the recent episodes," I said, flinching at the utilitarian manner of this word, "have I even felt that I was being allowed to participate in what was happening to me."

The men looked at me, each showing a different demeanor of surprise. I felt that I had crossed an invisible line and I began to turn to leave the room, to let the men speak of the weaknesses of vessels and the ancestral quandaries with Eve's daughters.

"No." Paul's voice was firm. "The scrolls are witnesses themselves. And the Breath has told me so."

I turned and hardly dared to look at him as he continued.

"They must be preserved, because they are not finished."

I don't know if I felt relief or dread as I heard his words.

At that moment, Baruch entered the room and came to stand with one arm around the shoulder of his seated father. With another hand, he reached to touch the arms of Paul and Timothy in greeting.

"My friend Aquila," Paul said softly, "it is into the hands of these young men that the scrolls will be entrusted. What Priscilla will continue to take delivery of, will someday, and that day soon coming, be taken away by Baruch and Timothy. They will escape, as through flames, with the scrolls and their lives alone."

While I exhaled with relief to hear that my son would survive me, it is nonetheless a sobering thing to hear prophecy of your own death. Even after Paul and Timothy left that day, Aquila and I could not find the courage to talk about it. This knowledge hung like trapped smoke in rafters above our heads. And then he and the men left for the evening.

The events of the day troubled me so much that I could not even tell Cordelia. How does one introduce the announcement of utter loss? I felt selfishness that I had not asked Paul about Cordelia's future. Who would protect her, provide for her? From across an evening-streaked room I watched her patience with the chattering reveries of Ulpia who finally nodded off to sleep in slurred mid-sentence, and only then did I see that Cordelia was carrying a burden of her own.

"I've written another poem," she said, her voice plush like lamb's wool in the warmth of the room. With writhed fingers that held the paper in tiptoes, she handed me a scrap of vellum and I saw the childish writing of Ulpia. I felt a stab inside as I envisioned Cordelia dictating a poem to the drifting attention span of the young woman. Where was I when this happened?

I began to read her words.

You are the mist that seeps
Under the Egyptians' door
But is held at bay
By lintel-blood

You are the mirror-imaged
Cloud that burns at night
And towers by day

And You are a pillar to me
Where I chain myself
Against the winds
That would drag me away

You are the fire within me
That must be contained—
And shared

You creep into my crevices
Bringing life, not death

You invade me, storm me
As a walled city;
And I surrender to
Your presence

Her face was eager as she looked for my approval.

"It's really a good poem, Cordelia. Very strong images." I rubbed my knee and inspected an imaginary spot on my tunic.

"But—the feelings, what about that?" She who was so articulate was struggling with words and I refused to give her more precision so she could ask what she wanted to know: Did I ever feel that closeness to Jesus?

And the answer was no. Never. And I did not know how to tell her that.

"The idea of surrender, where did you get that?" I asked her, deflecting.

"From what the women who knew Him said. And the men. How he invited intimacy from anyone who was humble."

I hesitated. What she described I craved.

"How does one feel that kind of closeness?"

She looked puzzled for a moment. "You mean because you cannot see Him or touch Him?"

No, I thought, not that. I searched for words and she looked at me suspiciously.

"Now, Priscilla," she chided. "Do you not, have you not

heard the very voice of God in your own ears?"

I dipped my head to one side in acquiescence.

"But it is not the same."

She held her inner wrists to the ceiling in question. A long and uncomfortable silence ran like a freezing river between us. She waited me out.

"Cordelia. You are a woman."

She nodded and dropped her eyes to her still-full breasts, her arced body.

My cheeks and eyes burned with shame. I could not say it to her until it burst churning from me.

"He's a man, Cordelia. I don't know how the women who followed Him around dealt with all that means."

She shrugged. "They cooked for Him and helped in the way any sister would."

"Granted. But He was resurrected with a body. Does He still have that, somewhere in the heavens where He ascended to?"

"What is the problem with that, my sister Priscilla?"

My tears seemed to scald my cheeks as they flowed down, and I could not tell if they emerged from dishonor or disgrace. No, it was anger.

"We keep ourselves pure. We don't touch anyone but our husbands and you can't touch any man at all. So how do you dream of surrender? What does loving Jesus mean to you?"

Her body made a slow, backward-leaning motion, until I was afraid that she would lose her balance on the stool where she sat; but her eyes never left mine, piercing me to the innermost of myself.

"Ah," she said, "ah."

Then she arose and came around to my stool, and stood behind me with her arms atop mine, folded across my chest.

"I will let you dream my dream with me," she said. Her

cheek was warm against mine, her breath like the Breath.

I waited.

"Jesus said that we must come to Him like children," she said. "So I want you to see what I see when I love Him."

I waited.

"Remember when we were young girls? We didn't know each other then, when we were very little. But imagine that we are so small that we would have to be lifted to be in someone's arms."

I waited.

"And now we come running to Jesus, and He is sitting, and He turns to us with bright teeth and tender smiling eyes. And now! Look! With strong arms he lifts us up, one at a time. And we each put our heads on His shoulders—really, just onto His chest, because we are only toddlers, we are so small. And we can smell field lilies and cedar shavings and salt air.

"We look at His hands, and turn them over and over. We see the deep marks in His wrists, so deep our little fingers touch and enter, and what we see causes wonder, not fear.

"And we sink into the soft folds of His robes and He bends His head to kiss us, one at a time.

"And we reach across and hold each other's hands, you and me, Priscilla-child and Cordelia-child. And we are safe. And we are loved, much more than we can ever love."

I waited.

I breathed in all that there was to breathe in.

And then I wept.

Part Three:

THE *ESCHATOS*

Chapter Twenty-Four

The journey overland to Corinth was much more difficult on Cordelia and Aquila than on me. He insisted on walking much of the time beside the cart and it was only with tears and sometimes threats as well that I was able to dissuade him. (Once I jumped out of the cart and sat beside the road until the cart had gone out of sight and cried until I saw them return in the dusk, a lurching wagon and lurching shadow people in a bas-relief with olive trees against a purple sky.) Only after that did he take a place beside Cordelia on occasion and allow me to walk alongside Baruch.

In other ways, though, these were days of rich, golden droplets of time as we made our unhurried way through a landscape that looked as if it had been drawn onto honey-aged papyrus that continually unrolled before our feet.

Baruch had inherited both his father's gift of effortless memorizing and his lanky frame that seemed to elongate each morning. And he was beginning to smell a bit, a man-becoming, a darkening on his upper lip, a lilt and a choking on certain words. Each day the two would walk, head inclined each to the other, repeating, repeating, the embraced and ingested words becoming their frontlets, on their hearts, as they sat, as they walked in the way, when they lay down, when they rose up; words wrapping around their hands and minds, words marking possession of every gate we passed, every doorpost we approached.

The journey was itself a *biblios*, written upon the mind of my son.

I was grateful that Ulpia had found employment with some new, wealthy converts in Ephesus and decided to stay, telling us between blushes and squeaking giggles of a widowed manservant there. I confess I did not miss her laughs; in truth felt guilty for not missing her at all. But Cordelia, after a few sighing remarks about what Ulpia would have said about this fig-laden tree or that three-legged goat, never mentioned her again either. We no longer had a child to distract, and now were lulled by the rhythms of the memorizing, of voices rising and falling and repeating, the passing of whispering, concurring trees.

Along the way, Aquila bought a flute. I could not imagine why he wanted it and barely tolerated the sounds that came from it at first, as he and Baruch took turns picking out the lullabies I once sang, the old songs of Pontus from the childhood of Aquila, the shepherds' melodies. But just as they could both memorize words, they both could hold song inside their heads. Soon, each night the perfect, plaintive notes hung in the air with the smoke of our cookfires.

One night as Aquila lay beside me on the ground, he turned his lips to my ear. "The flute is my gift not to Baruch, nor to myself," he whispered. I sought to see his eyes in the darkness, but could not. "I am learning to play it for you."

I lay in silence.

"I have made you a wayfarer, I fear."

Had he read my mind? What was beginning to bubble up from the water-skin of my soul that he was now carrying?

"This is my gift of art to you, my Priscilla. I know you yearn for art like others yearn for food." It was true. It was more than yearning. It was as near to coveting as anything in my life: my last treasured idolatry.

"I will give it to you," he whispered, "even in the wildernesses where there is none."

And from that moment on, wherever Aquila was, my hunger was slaked by the warm oil of his music that bathed me, deep inside.

The brethren in Corinth knew of our intentions to come and upon arrival we found a house ready for us, nearly inhabited already by the oddity of factions of visitors who each seemed to want to discredit the others with greater offerings. No bundle of flowers, no cluster of grapes, no handmade broom nor tight-knotted basket was unaccompanied by the merest brush of words and questions about others—to such a degree that we came to dread the cough outside the door that announced another brother or sister, even those we had known from our time there before. There was talk of liaisons and lawsuits, allegations and allegiances, always words aside, always hushings of one another, a sense that there was more unsaid and more to dread. We had scarcely settled in and begun purchasing our household goods and some fabrics and pelts to make tents, before the Jewish Sabbat. That gave us a few short hours before we were to meet with the brethren on the Lord's day.

That was the night which became a hinge on which my history, my life, began to turn. I believe the great battle of my mind began during the long months that we were in Corinth, began the night that I heard Cordelia first moan in her sleep and then at that moment I became committed to a nocturnal path where I awakened, drowsing, night after night, to company with her, to take the measure of her misery.

It was not the rasping of a snore (I came from a family whose night-sounds were a chorus) nor the empty chewing words of a dream talker. It was a steady rhythm of intaken air and then the release of it, time after time, as a sobbing that came from below even the stone child, as if her body cried out in protest against the weight of the lithos, the knife-pains of curving swollen bones, and released this with unutterable groans she somehow by sheer will kept suppressed during the daylight hours.

These escapees of her pain roamed our house each night when her mind lost her grip on them. Aquila and Baruch never stirred, and when I asked them circuitously if they'd heard anything in the night, their response was to check the perimeters of our rented house for signs of breaches—and of course there were none. The intruders were hostage inside her as long as she was awake, and they left no trace of the nights.

Corinth itself was charged like the air before lightning. I have never known such a place as we found this time: a church of maniacs and gluttons and saints. It was a swarm of beggars and pretenders and constant sound, ever and even at its best besieged by rabid Jews and urgent newcomers and blank-eyed, open-handed questioners.

The elders of this church seemed to have regressed in time and become children, tossed about by the prevailing winds of the city. Sometimes the greatest wisdom came from Gentiles who first observed the church. And, to my sorrow, what many saw the first time became the last time.

It was like a lake turning over in the spring, bringing up from its hidden, unredeemed depths all the unstirred opacity that had been covered through the winter.

We brought Paul's letter with us and whatever illusions I harbored of groups of people sitting respectfully and quiet to hear it—these were demolished like those two or three who, rising with familiar fury in the assembly, tried to rip the scroll from the hands of Aquila. People went hoarse reading it, wore it thin by copying it, wept and fought and sang over it.

And then there were all the wonders. I would have had trouble believing what I did not see with my own eyes, events that brought even the most jaded of the city to shut their gaping mouths and shake their shaking heads. This was the work of Jesus, Jesus, Jesus: His name formed on lips that tasted and considered. New languages erupted from people's lips like lava (and sometimes as erosive). Limp, grey children came back to life. The newly-hearing put hands over their ears and grimaced; pale new eyes looked from behind parted fingers shading from even moonlight. No one could deny the flexing limbs, the tumors that dissolved, leprosy that fell like chaff from pinking skin, the epileptics that sat clear-eyed and unafraid to tell their stories above the clamor, the clumsy dancing of straightened feet and legs. It was as if miracles had boiled down to a syrup and poured freely over this city.

And yet my Aquila hobbled and flinched.

And I saw Cordelia's eyes each time she saw such a wonder-person: a brightening of hope and then a fading like the sun's twilight rays, slow and irretrievable.

These two I loved were starving mendicants bringing succulence to others at a banquet: words that healed hearts, patience, kindness, the amnesia of wrongs. Even Baruch, his black hair behind his ears, his leaning to the young men, murmuring, became the embodiment of the words: bearing, believing, hoping, enduring.

He spoke earnestly of a tree that could sweeten waters, a handful of meal that was an antidote, footfalls in treetops, a curing, curling serpent, raven waiters, eyes seeing through clay bandage, shadows and kerchiefs that heal, what he had seen Paul do.

And yet none of Paul's words brought the offence that those regarding the breaking of bread together brought. This was the tender core of the Corinthians' fleshliness, I saw; the coveting of morsels, the elbowing of lessers, the wholehearted and focused idolatry of self with the new vestments of freedom once worn by a gone-away god.

And to my shame, the women were the worst, the fattened, still-ravenous who rose to power as their rivals died off.

"Don't they know," Cordelia asked me one day, "that this is not a game? Did they not listen to what Paul said about eating a meal with the Lord? Haven't they seen what happened to the others, men and women alike, who have treated this as some kind of competition, with laurels for the belching winners and hunger for the losers?"

I turned in surprise to Cordelia, at the vigor of her words. We spoke for a few moments about a way of beginning to teach these obstreperous women, about telling them this feasting was paschal, not like any other day's meal; about its proclamation of death, its own prophecy of a coming day.

"So many are Gentiles, they won't know about the Passover, about heritage, what it meant to Jesus," I was counting points onto my fingers, "about symbolisms and respect." When Cordelia continued in silence I did too, wondering how we would temper the aggression of these women before whom we had been speechless for months—Cordelia because of her self-deprecation, me because of my own inner battles.

"Perhaps they would understand if I read them this," she said, struggling to draw a large piece of papyrus from behind a rug. I blanched when she unrolled it, at the meandering of the letters, at her half-closed eyes as she read, at the bite of her words.

Oh, body of Christ!
Oh, body of Christ!
Oh blood-filled pores
Oh bones wrenched out of sockets
By its own newly-paralytic weight

I call on you, spittle-rankled skin
Outstretched, screaming muscles
Bones (unbroken, yes, but barely,
Barely);
Nearly-suffocating lungs
Wrenched, failing organs
Even veins and nerves with tremors

I call on all these
yellow bile black bile blood
I won't let go until You bless me
I'll wrestle Your strength until
You pull my hips all out of joint

Give me
Justice against my adversary
Give me what I ask in prayer

I swallow You whole

She ended her reading as matter-of-fact as if she had finished a market list, letting the crinkled paper pull itself back into a roll that she left on the table as she moved out into the sunshine of our courtyard.

Later, when we spoke to the women, she would read her poem, the sight of her twisted fingers guaranteeing that they would at least be silent long enough to learn what was written on the paper stretched and smoothed out painfully over her belly, long enough to draw deep breaths, long enough to visualize the wine as Blood-ransom, the bread as a Body eaten—and eating.

And things began to change. In our assemblies, the sounds of weeping instead of shouting. Faces of shame and hope. Embraces of robes that didn't match, would never have been found in the same home: threadbare and embroidered, shoddy and silken.

It was scarcely the same group into which our friend Timothy walked one day. He sat with newcomers at the back and we did not see him until Baruch ran to him, covering his cheeks with kisses as then did Aquila and Cordelia and I. His smiles and returns of fervent kisses to us showed us how he had missed us too.

But his news, delivered over wine and salted fish and bread in our home, sobered us. He was much thinner than the last time I saw him, and he ate cross-legged in front of a bench, with both elbows on it. He hovered over it like a banquet banner, scattering crumbs as he spoke, seemingly ready to snap down to the table against any predator more ravenous than he.

We listened, sometimes with our hands over our mouths, as he told us what had happened since we left Ephesus.

"Paul has been working hard to train the other disciples," Timothy said. "As you know, believers in the

Way earned a reputation for being 'unlearned' early on, and now there is such a need for writing down the experiences of those who actually walked with Jesus. So, Paul—and Tyrannus himself—have been training people in rhetoric, and how to write. Fishermen, tax collectors, everyone comes to him. The great and the small."

He looked gratefully at Cordelia who slid more bread to him from her forearms.

"But Paul has had to contend with that thorn in his flesh," he went on.

"Do you mean the illness he contracted while he was in Galatia? The swamp sickness? Has it returned after all these years?" I asked. I remembered hearing of the shaking fevers in Galatia that left Paul weak.

Timothy shook his head. "Not illness of the body, but the plague of people," he said. "When Paul speaks of his thorn in the flesh, Gentiles sometimes wonder if he has some hidden infirmity, but he is referring to what it says in the Law and the Prophets, of course."

Baruch's head bobbed up. "Yes, that's what Adonai said about the bad people in the Promised Land: they would become snares and traps and whips on the backs of those who would not drive them out as Adonai asked—and thorns in their eyes and flesh." He stopped and looked around at us, swelling at his recitation. Aquila nodded with a smile which Timothy reflected, and Baruch deflated back into a boy on his stomach watching his hero, his head held in his hands, his elbows on the floor.

"It is that Alexander again," muttered Aquila. "Metalworker. Malice worker."

I looked with surprise at Aquila. I had never heard him say anything that approached humor, and I could hardly take my eyes from him to hear Timothy continue. But Aquila's wit was apparently lost on himself and he looked toward his young friend as well.

"Indeed, that very Alexander," said Timothy. "And his companions—and there are many of them now. He incited the Jewish exorcists that wander the countryside, got them to challenge Paul. But our friend Paul prevailed." He was relishing the attention now that his hunger seemed to be slaked. Everyone in the room leaned forward to hear the story.

"Imagine this—the high priest, an oily man like Alexander"—and we all could fairly smell him—"has seven sons, all of them tricksters and pretenders. And they decide that they can profit from Paul's reputation. So, they hire themselves out to cast out an evil spirit, and they think to trap it inside a house."

Baruch sat up, rubbing his hands together.

"And like the priests of Baal these seven men begin to shout and jump around." He looked at Baruch with wild eyes and waved his arms, and Baruch giggled.

"And they say, 'We now assume command over you, oh demon, in the name of Jesus Christ who is preached by Paul.'" He paused dramatically.

"And what happened?" asked Baruch, breathless.

"The evil spirit speaks in a soft, soft voice."

Baruch's voice wavered. "What did it say?"

Timothy stood up and put one hand on his hip.

"It says, 'Now, Jesus I know.

"'And Paul I know.

"'But *who* are all of you?'

"Then the man who had the evil spirit jumps on top of them, and beats them! And then he tears their clothes off! And they keep trying to get out of the door of that house, and finally when they tumble out into the street where a crowd has gathered, they are completely naked and bloody!"

When our laughter finally subsided, Timothy continued.

"This loosened the tongues of many," he said gravely. "Not against Paul, as before, but people found the courage to ask questions about Jesus. And then their hearts were ..." Here he struggled for a word. "Stabbed. That's the only word I can think of. They saw the contrast between what they could be, and what they were, and they felt the only way to put their pasts behind them was to say what they were."

He held his hands to his ears, lightly, but winced. "And one of the sins so many wanted exorcised, so to speak, was that of dark powers. No one wanted anything to do with the kind of power that could batter those sons of Sceva. And so they took all their spell-books and burned them."

We sat sobered as he calculated the day's wages for 50,000 laborers, all tossed without regret onto a bonfire. I was carried away and wondered if the words screamed out into the tendrils of smoke as the flames licked away at them.

Timothy rubbed his eyes and stretched his shoulders. "One of the brethren just come from Ephesus met up with me here and told me of yet another event since I left. He said that the whole city was involved in a riot at the theater when some of the idol-makers saw that Paul was cutting into their business. Another close escape from the mobs there, and Paul has gone on into Macedonia and intends to return to Jerusalem."

It was with this last statement that I felt a clenching in my stomach and knew that our time in Corinth was nearly over, that we too were being dispatched again. I looked past Aquila to his flute hanging on the wall and wondered if its reedy walls would compass the only home I would ever have, from then on. Thus, it was no surprise when the next morning Timothy spoke to us about urgent needs in Rome.

Later that day the voyage was sealed when a new visitor from Rome brought Cordelia a letter that she took with trembling hands. She motioned to me and we walked back into the courtyard where she sat motionless for a long time, holding the letter in her lap.

"Miriam, servant of Christ Jesus in Rome, to our esteemed sister and fellow-traveler of the Diaspora, Cordelia, widow of Caius Clovius, grace and peace," she read. "It is with great sorrow that I inform you of the death of your mother and brothers."

Cordelia looked up at me with the same question as I had: Brothers? She knew only of one. She continued reading.

"Your esteemed mother, our sister in the Lord, died along with her newborn son the same week that your elder brother Lucius Septimus succumbed to a long illness that took him after a broken leg. Your father, the esteemed Kaeso Septimus, cannot be comforted and says that he will take peace only from you. He looks to any solace that will allow him to see them again and although he does not accept the teachings of resurrections from me nor any of the brethren here, we believe he may hear it from you. At any rate he is enfeebled and if you can come, we of the Church welcome you and will help you and him. We salute you in the precious Name."

I sat alone in the courtyard for a long time after Cordelia left it. I wondered how she would be received in the courts of Roman aristocracy, with her red hair now streaked with gray, with her crumpled limbs that all now bend toward her stone child, as if to say in her silence, look here, look what being a follower of that Man has brought me to.

In the weeks before, the Breath had approached me as gently as a suitor and again and again I had spurned Him, all but stopped my ears. Here in the coolness of the falling evening I could hear only Cordelia crying, telling her sorrow to visitors.

I pulled the garments of a vagabond around me and knew that I would wear them the rest of my life. Go to a land I'll show you, God had told Abraham, go to a land I'll show you, He had told Moses. Direction that would outstrip knowledge, and the requisite blind trust that provision, thrown ahead in the road, would outstrip need.

I remembered the story of Philip, when the Breath had picked him up and carried him from the Ethiopian's chariot; I thought of Ezekiel shoved through a hole in a wall, dumped insensate on a riverbank.

I heard a dove.

I dared the Breath to touch me.

Resolutely, I turned my face toward Rome.

Chapter Twenty-Five

On the sea voyage to the Seven-Hilled City I was not ill, not for a single moment, was perhaps as vigorous as I have ever been, for I was constantly on guard.

While the others wandered the ship or played games or memorized or read or dozed, I took my post, stock-straight each day at the railings, looking at the haze of blueness where the sea met the horizon. Only when I would turn away would I see, just beyond my outer lashes, the great fish that tracked the ship, just beyond sight but never beyond my fears. If the Breath could take the bodily form of a dove, He could inhabit—or, indeed, create—a sea creature enormous enough to swallow me up. Of this I had no doubt nor, strangely, any questions. I could even across the waves hear His sighing, His aggrieved wind. I told no one of this, not even Cordelia. By the time we caught sight of the shores of Rome I at once became more exhausted—and then, upon disembarking, more ill—than from any other voyage.

Even with my weakness I recognized that the road into

Rome was still mine: I not only still owned property there, but all the views on the road to it I found I still possessed as well, as if by remembering what lay around the next corner, the surety of memory, they had been deeded to me.

Our yellow house awaited us. It looked strange to me, like someone I'd conversed with but never looked directly into the eye. The believers who had used it to harbor those in danger had built a secret wall in the back, and when I saw it I remembered the airless camouflaged grotto in the stable of Caleb ben Azariah in Judea, where we had hidden after crossing the wadi so many years ago. I felt an ache in my knees and, leaning close to the wall, could all but hear the echo of breathless hearts beating against my own.

And surely such measures were necessary in Rome. Since the expulsion decree of Claudius against the Jews had expired, many Jews had returned. Though we were foolish enough to believe that our citizenship—mine, Aquila's, Cordelia's and Baruch's—were protection to us, we remembered the warnings of Paul to us. How could the prayer of Jesus be fulfilled in such a mess, I wondered: His kingdom was not coming, at least as far as I could see.

The city had the sound of a lion in it, in the evenings when the wind blew and Aquila played his flute, and often Cordelia and I would remember what Peter always said about the roaming devourer.

And yet, in what we knew of Jerusalem, the situation of believers was at least as perilous. I wondered if I would ever go back there. I wondered how I could tell the Hebrews there the truth of what I had learned: that whereas in their temple of long ago, God had funneled His infinite attentions onto a point just between the wings of cherubim and with His glory self-shackled looked out at His people through a crack in the great curtain, now that cube of gold, though thoroughly furnished, was nonetheless empty.

What would they say if I told them that the God of their fathers now looks through the eyes of His wounded One, His glory glinting out through nail holes and spear wound?

They wouldn't listen. Nor would I be able to tell them how I knew.

Nor was I willing to learn more myself, at least not then.

Cordelia went immediately to the house of her father upon our arrival, though she came daily to visit me to report upon her father's failing health. Sometimes she brought Miriam, our sister in the faith with her, laden with baskets of strange-colored fruits or gazelle steaks or honey candies her father's servants prepared in an effort to tempt his absent appetite.

That was the time of feasting for us, the time of the riches of Rome. Each day Cordelia brought more baskets and news of her father's urgent questions about Jesus. He was still able to visit the public baths and one day Aquila and Miriam's husband took him there and, because he was a weak old man who must be lowered into the waters, no one thought anything of what turned out to be a baptism.

Shortly thereafter he began to become golden—with yellow eyes and teeth, even his wispy hair the color of late wheat. One day he came to our house, and looked for all the world like clothing hung on the walls into which he all but disappeared.

Baruch and Aquila became the owners of the yellow house I had inherited, though it came to cost us dearly. The thousand or so women who were landowners in Rome avoided taxes, even in spite of the attempts of the Second Triumvirate a generation or so ago. But taxes and the fact that this transference put his name on the deed—and thus under the scrutiny of Roman tax collectors—might, we hoped, be compensated for by the fact that it might allow Baruch to use it for years as we had.

Deeds and fabrics, the rearranging of our lives like furniture—many of the things I remember about this time in Rome seemed to be concerned with a kind of housekeeping, as if our lives there were scattered shavings on a floor that we had come to sweep up.

One of those matters that had troubled me in my years away from Rome was uncertainty about young Rubria, my distant cousin whom I met after the funeral of my mother. I knew that seeing her might prove difficult, for the Vestal Virgins were property of the state, so to speak, both inviolate sweethearts and invested slaves. It would be impossible for me to summon her—she and her five companions were the most famous women in Rome. She would not go anywhere without a heavily-armed lictor guard.

I was unsuccessful in my first strategy, which was to contact her through the nurse, Philomena, who first brought her to me. Perhaps the waddling woman had died, I speculated, or perhaps Rubria's age—she must be thirteen or fourteen now—meant she no longer needed such a companion. At any rate, no one in Rome seemed to know where Philomena was.

"Perhaps we can go to Rubria," said Cordelia one day, as we mulled our options. The Virgins did not often appear in public, but any woman could go to the Vestal temple to request fire for cooking. As newcomers to Rome, we reasoned, our visit would be unremarkable—which was essential for Rubria's safety and our own. But the singularity of Cordelia's appearance caused her to beg me to go escorted only by one of the brothers and Baruch, who would, like all males, be required to wait outside the temple. They sat on a great grass-soft knoll, straining their eyes, and considered the fate of being required to stay so close to a hub of beautiful women.

My prayers to be able to see Rubria were answered, for when we arrived at the temple it was her turn to sit on the great marble bench, guarding the flame that represented Rome's well-being. She sat as straight as if strapped to an invisible post behind her spine. Her hair was ornately arranged and her face was patrician and so pale that at first glance she seemed a statue. Yet I knew it was Rubria—the same cheekbones, the same bottomless black eyes that seemed to focus past yours and onto a spot at the inside back of your skull.

"Do you remember me? I am Priska, your relative," I whispered to her as I bent toward her with a firepot, open to receive a glowing coal. Her hand holding the tongs stopped its motion for a nearly-undetectable moment.

"I have asked the goddess Vesta to bring you here." Her voice seemed restrained, as if it were tethered: nearly without emotion or timbre, low as the rush of the flame when the fuel fell and settled.

I did not know how to respond to that, so I backed up and waited, respectfully. Only two other women stood waiting for fire. After they left, Rubria pulled her *palla* shawl over her head and motioned for me to follow her through a door. At once, another Vestal (where had this one come from?) glided out of the shadows and hovered over the fire as we passed outside into the temple's gardens.

"We have only a moment," Rubria said, taking me to a fountain in a courtyard where she took a clay jar and filled it from the spring, the water splashing noisily over its narrow opening. As I bent to her to take it, she spoke again.

"No one must know we are speaking. If someone asks, you needed the water of the goddess for your new home." Her words were soft but hurried. "Know this first. My nurse Philomena paid with her life for her interest in the foreign god you serve. All that talk of eating the flesh of a god …"

She trailed the long fingers of one hand in a ribbon of light that spilled over the rim of the jar.

"And yet I yearn for contact with you, because I know you are the only blood relative I have."

I looked up and saw her face dissolve from Parthenos to pathos, unspeakable sadness.

"I have a son. You have a cousin, nearly your age." I whispered the words.

She blinked. But then she was rising, giving me the jar. She leaned in close one more time and said, "Write me letters that you sign: 'your cousin Livia Ocellina.' Tell me where you live so that I can find you if I must."

I was startled to hear my mother's name. I had not heard it nor spoken it aloud for years. Then she leaned back and without looking at me, motioned for me to leave; and I did. For fear of someone overhearing, I would not speak to the men until we reached the safety of our home.

When we arrived, a mule-drawn cart was tied near our front door. Upon entering I learned that Cordelia had that very day gone from widow to widowed orphan. Miriam sat with her arm around Cordelia. All around them were stacks of baskets, each covered with a cloth, and the smell of yeast and salted fish was in the air. I stepped around the baskets as I rushed to embrace my friend, whose tears fell in hot spatters onto the tiled floor.

She wept and sighed at the same time. But when she felt my arms around her, she stood up and brushed the tears from her eyes with the palms of her hands.

"He was lucid to the end, and generous." She motioned to the baskets and I wanted to ask just how many foodstuffs we could eat, but she was continuing on. "And at the end, he sat up, straight in the bed, Priscilla, and he pointed and said, 'Look! I see the Lord!' And then he laid back on his elbows and lowered himself to the bed so gently that I did not know where he could have gotten the strength to move so slowly. He closed his eyes, smiling and murmuring, and then the last breath … the last breath … the last breath was the last breath." Another tear rose in her eye and as it rolled down I caught it with my thumb and drew it to my mouth and kissed it.

And that was the last tear she ever shed for her father.

It was only when we began unpacking the baskets that I understood what she had said about her father's generosity. Beneath the breads and jugs of wine and bags of raisins and figs were napkins that hid strings of pearls, coins, ornate, heavy rings. Cordelia and Miriam and Baruch and I took them to the hidden room at the back of the house and by torchlight I saw them put it all into a space below a loose tile in the corner of the floor.

"Can you see, Priscilla?" Cordelia asked. I saw a glint deep in the space. "He has been sending such things here ever since I returned. And of course, I've passed along most of it with messengers, wherever Paul has said there is need. But this last my father swore me to use for what I could do in Rome." She put the tile back and brushed off her hands.

We returned to a room that now looked empty. I took the firepot and removed its lid and spilled the coal onto a piece of broken pottery we used to scrape the dishes. Its redness rose urgently with the air but within a few minutes it was grey and lifeless, collapsing inward onto itself. I threw it into the ash heap later that night.

Though Cordelia allowed a great funeral and feast for her father, she honored one of his last wishes which was to have his body interred as Christians did instead of cremated as were his ancestors. Only under the cover of night were Aquila and some of the brothers able to take the corpse to a new burial place recently built underground in a spot outside the city. While Miriam and others went periodically to put spices on the body, Cordelia felt that she must wait until going to pay her respects in the tomb.

Once we saw the emperor Nero riding through the streets in a chariot, wearing only a toga, when we were returning from the marketplace. I saw why Baruch had described the young man as looking like two twigs holding up a rotting apple. I can only describe his demeanor, even as a young man, as unpleasantness.

All of Rome knew the rumor that his mother had poisoned his uncle Claudius to gain him the throne, of his military campaigns. Lately people spoke of his conflicts—and perhaps his uncleanness—with his mother the round-eyed Agrippina whose extra canine tooth gave her the appearance—and some said the appetite—of a wolf. Now she had died after escaping from drowning in a boat her son Nero designed, and he had cremated her on a dining couch in his own quarters. It was as if that smoke lingered over the housetops of all of Rome for days.

Nonetheless the poor of the city saw him as a hero. He had censured lawyers and lowered taxes, after all.

The arrival of brothers with news from Paul made us hungry to see him and hear him. He was writing a letter to the saints here in Rome as soon as he got to Corinth, they said. I wondered how he would be received in a city he had chastened so severely. One of the new arrivals read to the large group in our home a copy of another letter Paul had written to the church in Corinth. People sat with their eyes closed, listening. Where they were imagining the men and women of Corinth hearing with satisfaction that they had been able to stave off the disaster of their souls, I saw only Paul, a grizzled old man inclining his head to the whispers of the Breath as he wrote.

When he wrote of a sentence of death that the court of his heart had handed down on his life, I understood. Like him, even as I labored for the Christians of Rome, I despaired even of my own life. The church that assembled under my roof grew to such an extent that with some of Cordelia's money we bought the residence next door and knocked down walls to house more refugees, harbor more Jews on the run from other Jews who saw them as traitors of their ancestry, and break bread with their broken hearts. And yet mine was ripping like a tent wall full-face against a persistent gale.

Aquila and Baruch and the other brothers and sisters who often gathered to argue the meanings of some of Paul's letters or to memorize the teachings of Jesus—none of these noticed that my soul was curling and withering.

Cordelia, of course, did notice. We returned one evening from the home of a recent convert to the Way whose son had been murdered after he announced at the gymnasium that he would do the same.

"Why are you not writing anything, dear sister?" she asked. After the cacophony in the home of mourning, here it was so quiet that the silence hummed in our ears.

I had been dreading this question and was prepared with what I hoped would so shock her that it would deflect the question.

"I have been memorizing the lamentations of Jeremiah," I said.

"What possible good can that do you, dear sister?" she asked. "They are on the scrolls, hundreds of scrolls. And there is so much to learn about Jesus. Nearly every week we meet someone who knew Him, who has a story to tell. Why not memorize those?"

I felt slight and somewhat soiled beneath her questions.

"You know Jeremiah, how satisfying he can be. Speaking of your bones cracking under eternal weight. Being bricked in and your prayers bricked out. Chains and wormwood and gall and your teeth broken by gravel." I thought I would cry, or that she would, as I spit the words out. But neither of us did.

"Or how about seeing yourself in a rain of arrows and finding out that as you run, the stola in which you have wrapped yourself for protection is a painted target."

She looked down.

"Listen to this," I said.

Heaven's lion has pursued me
And I coyly hid and cavorted—
Enjoying the chase
Even as I lost a finger or a toe;
Hanks of hair hanging on
Limbs I had left

Now
He has cornered me and
He is devouring my arms and legs
And the soft parts
Of my belly

And I have lost
The will to run

She continued to look down. But she did not leave.

"I tell you, Cordelia, about writing." My voice was spinster-thin in the room. "What I have discovered is this: every time I put pen to paper it is a holy act—holy in that it is separated from everything else. But what comes from the act of writing is not always holy, and not always good."

She looked to the corner of the room, to the clay vessel where my scrolls were.

"Surely you do not mean …"

"I don't know."

"But people have learned so much. So many of the Hebrew people have been able to see Jesus as an eternal high priest. They understand what God always intended them to understand about the tabernacle."

"We came this night from a senseless death. We can show people how to live, and how to die. We know that wickedness always brings punishment. But tell me, does good always bring reward? Did it bring reward for that family? For that young man killed at the gymnasium?"

Again she was silent.

"I don't want to talk about this anymore, Cordelia." I brushed something—her?—away as if it were chaff drifting on the wind toward my eyes.

"I have become a lamentation to myself. Leave me with that."

After she left, I looked at our hearth fire and the pot with the scrolls for a long, long while.

I cannot number the good people who passed through the gates of Rome that year, into our hands, into our lives, and on to unknown places. But instead of being the city of children suckled by a wolf, the city itself became twin devourers, the Jews who became more ravenous in their pursuit, and the Romans who grew increasingly wary of a sovereignty within their own walls.

Chapter Twenty-Six

Paul's letter to the church of our city Rome, sent from Corinth, finally arrived; and to my great surprise a substantial number of Jews who heard it simply laid down their debates and surrendered, as if they had been waiting for this one argument that neither they nor any Gentile could win. Now there were hundreds of believers in the city and it was as if each month the gospel was poured into reinvented ears.

The word is near you, I heard Paul saying, it is in your mouth and in your heart.

Cordelia and I now headed up a cadre of women and worked day and night, forming a network of bread bakers and fish-dryers and butchers and grandmother-laps for hungry and desperate and even orphaned newcomers who by one voiced statement—*Jesus is Lord*—often lost not just employment and homes but loved ones; and in an increasing number of cases, soon lost their lives as well.

I closed my eyes each time Baruch and Aquila left the

yellow house. We heard the stories, like those years ago in Jerusalem: The men of some believers' households sometimes did not return. One day a young Grecian woman who was ripe with her first pregnancy staggered into our house and sat speechless for an entire day and night. We learned that her husband had been dragged behind a horse when his parents learned of his decision to follow Jesus. When she finally arose from the stool where she sat, there was a smear of blood on it.

"She is not injured. It is the bloody show," said Cordelia, taking off her chiton and wrapping a clean robe around the blank-eyed young woman. "It's the sign that your baby is coming." She faced the girl, looking directly into her eyes. "We will help you." And indeed within a few hours the contractions began and her screams, and then the wails of her newborn, filled the house.

The next morning I awakened and I heard a whisper say, "Come away with Me."

I turned to my husband, but his bed was empty. I could hear his voice and that of others, speaking to one another in the predawn darkness.

I knew that this was the bloody show of the Spirit, and I did not know if I could stop the labor that must follow. I felt urgent movement inside of me, life inside my leather-stiffness.

I heard no more through the day, and late that afternoon Cordelia asked me to accompany her to the crypt of her father. Even though he had been dead for months, I had never been to his tomb and Cordelia had only been once.

"Come with me, my sister," she said, not meeting my eyes. We made our way to the faraway tomb complex outside the far wall of Rome, riding in a donkey-drawn cart that two of the brothers drove for us. They waited outside the entrance and I realized from the greeting that people called to them that this settlement of houses was new, and they were all believers too, perhaps with the ministry of guarding this place.

Some Christians had begun burying their dead in tunnels they carved in the soft volcanic rock called tuff, often burrowed through the rock like the tunnels of insects. After exposure to air, the tuff would harden. But this complex reflected an orderly plan, not haphazard like the family tomb of Pudens that sprouted new limbs with each generation. This one was laid out as if it were a city, with buildings and streets and intersections and squared corners. I half expected to see signs for the streets but there were none. One of the finished crypts, I noticed as we rushed by, had fresh paint on its border and a square of dustless space in front of it, as if an owner had swept his stoop.

In front of me, Cordelia walked with lame certainty, turning here, counting, counting, turning this direction, counting, counting.

As soon as I walked down the steps into the complex, I knew that a birthing time had come. The air was as still as the sucked-in breath of the wind before a storm.

We had entered into a metropolis for the dead. And I knew that its life was its meaning, and that it would soon engulf me. The stillness was like static and promise all at once.

I gagged at the death-smells all around, but Cordelia didn't seem to notice. Then I remembered: it was the same smell of Alexander.

One turn, count, count. Another.

We arrived at the address. I shuddered and helped her by brushing the lint-like dust off a great slab that covered the opening in the rock where the body of her father lay. Like the disk that covered the tomb of Jesus outside Jerusalem, I thought, and then knew it was no accident.

Cordelia must have ordered it fashioned so. She lay some fragrant limbs in front of the disk and bowed her head. I did the same. Then she began to sing:

Oh death, where is your sting?
Oh grave, where is your victory?
We will meet Him in the air
We will see Him together when He comes.

The flickering of the torch cast shadows into the other avenues and her voice was absorbed into the porous rock like water into sand. It was as if she and I were alone in a great, abandoned town that listened, greedy for the companionship, to every sound we made.

And then.

"Oh no," I said. "Oh no."

I had a sense of mindlessness, the feeling of missing a stairstep and finding one foot poised for impact and finding air instead.

The Breath was there in the sponge of that silence, and would not be denied.

Cordelia looked at me, and then touched her robe. She had no paper nor did I.

I was relieved. Perhaps there would be no message.

But then there was perfume, like the smell of olive flowers carried on salt breeze.

A set of images with words infusing them began overtaking my mind. I felt a twist in the axis of my being, as if I were being turned and reoriented like wet clay, and I struggled against it. But it was like labor, insistent unseen kneading. And this was its show.

Cordelia and I both sat on the floor. I propped the torch up against a wall.

I knew what the coming of God Uncreate could do, His blinding hot light from all directions with no source to see, His speaking into being of worlds and words. We shared history.

This I could not restrain.

The words we spoke came just like this:

Now faith is being sure of what we hope for and certain of what we do not see. This is what the ancients were commended for. This I can understand; it is proof of the invisible, meat and skin on the bones of wondering; our heritage, time-hallowed. By faith we understand; yes, it is the mechanism for processing, that the universe was formed at God's command, so that what is seen was not made out of what was visible. Yes, a type of the antitype of creation. I will concede that.

By faith Abel offered God a better sacrifice than Cain did. By faith he was commended as a righteous man, when God spoke well of his offerings. And by faith he still speaks, even though he is dead. It was faith, tangible as life, given voice.

By faith Enoch was taken from this life, so that he did not experience death; he could not be found, because God had taken him away. For before he was taken, he was commended as one who pleased God. Yes, I see that. It is good to please God.

I heard Cordelia moving next to me, touching me. Was she trying to restrain me?

And without faith it is impossible to please God, because anyone who comes to him must believe that he exists. And with what mental groaning and straining would one deny that? And must believe that he becomes a rewarder to those who earnestly seek him. It is the becoming part. The before and the after. A time when blessing is not and then it is. And the question is when. And where. And how.

By faith Noah, when warned about things not yet seen, in holy fear built an ark to save his family. And so it shows itself to be irresistible portage. By his faith he condemned the world. By contrast or by agency? and became heir of the righteousness that comes by faith. And so we inherit. But inheritance means death.

By faith Abraham, when called to go to a place he would later receive as his inheritance, obeyed and went, even though he did not know where he was going. Ah yes. Direction that would outstrip knowledge, and the requisite blind trust that provision, thrown ahead in the road, would outstrip need. I have lived this.

By faith he made his home in the promised land like a stranger in a foreign country; I have lived this. He lived in tents, as I have, in too many houses to remember the colors of their front doors. As did Isaac and Jacob, who were heirs with him of the same promise. For he was looking forward to the city with foundations, whose architect and builder is God. And I ask you, does this have any substance at all? Can I walk through its gates? Does it have a table? Does it have a bed?

By faith Abraham, even though he was past age—and Sarah herself was barren—was enabled to become a father because he considered him faithful who had made the promise. The crux lies there. Can a person sustain life on the invisible? How does one look at irredeemable loss and say, "It will change"? And so from this one man, and he as good as dead—and what is as good as dead? Can one be only partly dead?—came descendants as numerous as the stars in the sky and as countless as the sand on the seashore. Yet remember, remember Sarah who died only knowing her son, the lone childless Isaac with all those nations cached unseen in his loins.

All these people were still living by faith when they died. They did not receive the things promised; they only saw them and welcomed them from a distance. I stand in the near side of that distance. You are truthful here. And they admitted that they were aliens and strangers on earth. I know the disorientation of waking in the dark and not knowing what wall to face. People who say such things show that they are looking for a country of their own. I am in Rome and of no home. If they had been thinking of the country they had left, they would have had opportunity to return. No ship can take me to a destination I do not know. Instead, they were longing for a better country—a heavenly one. Therefore, God is not ashamed to be called their God, for he has prepared a city for them.

I sat, clear-minded, when He suspended: breath taken in but not breathed out.

Cordelia and I stayed leaning our backs against a stranger's uncut tomb in the fitful torchlight until it was just a glow and the men came to find us. We could hear them calling, far away at first with tiny voices, then sounds surging and ceding, taking the wrong turns and doubling back, then calling again, closer. By the time they reached us they skidded on the loose stones as they ran, almost past us.

I cannot say why she did not respond to them.

I know that I could not. There was more of me lost than what sat on the pumice.

I felt myself a field newly-sown with barley and wheat and it could not be harvested: I was a limp length of cloth of flax and wool, and they could not be unwoven because both were in the warp, and both were in the weft.

"I will write it all down and I will burn it." I whispered this to her in the cart.

She did not reply.

Chapter Twenty-Seven

In one of Rome's many marketplaces I stopped to watch a man preparing a mummy case portrait. Its owner, quite alive, was an Egyptian expatriate, and as she sat and he painted, she told him through stiff lips that this would accompany her as she took her final pilgrimage back to the Nile's birth-waters. Placed on her body after her death, through it she would look out at the world with the lustrous round eyes he was painting.

I saw her sunken cheeks, the way that the flesh on the back of her hands was held up by the bones like twigs holding the mossy knotted scum up out of a river's backwater pool. I wondered if she would survive the voyage.

I carried that woman's true portrait inside me for a long time—how she sat trying not to blink in a slice of light that came from between the awnings of the shop, fragile as a hollow-boned bird, silently begging for the grace of beauty to survive her, naked though clothed.

Those years. It was as if I had been trapped in my own wax portrait, like those of mummy cases from Egypt, painted with slick tempera onto my still-living but immobile face.

This was the wages I paid for the barricade of my soul. I lived the next two years in Rome through the eyes of others. Better said, for the most part I can only recount events as they affected those I loved or as they were told to me. I wear them still, the borrowed, second-hand experiences like the clothing of wealthy women we passed on to ragged refugees.

We did not see Paul again during those two years. After he left Macedonia, he went to Greece where a plot against his life revealed enemies like hidden creatures swarming out from under overturned paving stones; and they bred and appeared wherever he went, for the rest of his life.

I thought of Jesus' message (second-hand here, too) to Paul as he sat blind and dazed in Damascus: *I will show you how much you will suffer for My name.* Visitors from Ephesus brought tear-stained scrolls recounting his last visit with the church leaders there: a prophecy of merciless wolves that would shred them and leave them like ribbons on a fence, Paul's description of himself as wrapped and bound by the Spirit, on a journey to a Jerusalem whose chains rattled and beckoned to him, taunting him across the ocean.

I could hardly bear the last part of the story. When he got to Caesarea, a man named Agabus sealed the prophecy. Two witnesses, every word established. I can see it as if I were there:

Come here, Paul, you who are almost to this Jerusalem way station. Weary? Give me your belt, that length you wrap yourself in, how you gird those loins. Stand here before us with your robe shapeless around you. The Breath is talking to me and I will tell you what He says. See what I am doing?

I am wrapping this belt around my own feet. I am an object lesson for your undelighted eyes, like Ezekiel building the siege ramp, like Ezekiel making the detestable bread, like Ezekiel stiff, lying on one side. See how I sit crouched before you, my ankles kissing and constricted. Now I am knotting your belt around my own hands, the last of the length anchoring them to my feet as if I am an animal taken to market.

Here are the Breath's words to you, Paul the apostle of Christ Jesus. He says to tell you that the Jews will do this to you, and they will cart you off and throw you down in front of the Gentiles.

Paul, please don't go to Jerusalem, everyone begged him. And did that stop Paul from going? No. He just kept on his way, kept irritating people everywhere, never missing a chance to say, "You murdered, you murdered, you murdered," just like Peter; and was of course captured when he arrived in Jerusalem.

The Jews ambushed him in the Temple itself, dragging him out like a bundle of lightning-felled firewood. They shut the gates, quick-quick, take him outside, so he couldn't grab the altar horns for refuge: willing to murder but not to profane the courtyard.

(Did the forty starve who vowed not to eat until they'd killed him? No one seemed to know. And I kept asking. I see them in Caesarea still in my mind: each lying in his bed with his belly concave like a bowl, his ribs like fingers reaching toward it.)

They turned Paul over, of course, and he was in jail in Caesarea for months, years. The years of my famine of Rome years.

The years I did not look in the face and cannot remember; when I admitted that I had not received what I asked for in constant, urgent prayer, so much that I said the prayers almost without thought like a murmuring child whose mother has grown deaf to her cries. The years where I was looking for another country that our many travels would never find. My years, faster than a weaver's shuttle through the fibers that kept variegating themselves: Baruch's manhood, Cordelia crumpling as she moved here and there, just outside my field of vision, so many believers come to the city, faceless waves, so many believers gone.

Those years, the lacuna of my life.

Chapter Twenty-Eight

Paul once said of his friends that they were his letters, written on his heart. Whatever wrote those letters continued to chronicle without my help, I suppose, because during the time when I had no writing—nor indeed, no seeing—of my own, Paul said he never stopped praying for me.

In truth, I had during those years of my spiritual desiccation wondered if I would ever look again upon his face, or if I even deserved to do so.

The penultimate time he came to Rome, the time I refer to as "the gentle incarceration" two-and-one-half years before the Great Fire, some of the brethren traveled down the coast to meet him. They found his traveling group, including his guards, two days' journey out from Rome.

By the time Paul came to the great city, the Jews there had begun to murmur. Paul sent word that he wanted to talk to them; he knew that the republic excelsior would not abide the kind of riots that men of circumcision had caused in other places, and he spent days patiently answering their questions. In front of the guards, they pretended they had no animosity toward him, greasy as Pharisees trying to trap Jesus; and Paul, to his credit and much against his nature, did not deliberately inflame them. In such close quarters, so to speak, many listened but most refused to grant any sort of spiritual asylum to a fugitive messiah who would run into the arms of Gentiles after being rebuffed by his brethren and theirs.

In the end, Paul the old man with battered ears, sent them all away with a description of the calluses on theirs—and the watching Romans scratched their own, wondering no doubt at the peculiarities of this polyglot people and their clenched-teeth arguments over a dead criminal.

But the crowds of elbowing Jews had made the guards uneasy, we heard. They did not understand all Paul said, but understood well that they were not supposed to understand. It was two weeks before Aquila thought it safe for me to go and see him. Our citizenship was our password that gave us some relative safety.

It was cold that evening, and when we approached the entryway of his quarters, Paul sat with his back to us, the fire he faced looking as if it boiled in the basin of the oval courtyard. He leaned forward to raise his hands to the warmth and a wiry man next to him seemed his mirror image, leaning too, and the red light caressed the chain that connected them.

I held to Aquila's arm so that he would not announce us with a cough. Paul was speaking to another man on the other side of the flames, recounting the trip from Caesarea to Rome.

As he spoke, I felt water beginning to flow beneath frozen streams, for just the words in the stories he told were wondrous: the shelter of Cyprus as they sailed, Fair Haven's launch to a shipwreck, the tempest of Euroclydon, fourteen days of straining eyes and empty teeth, foresail to the wind and splintering planks run aground on snake-infested Malta, sailing again with the Twin Brothers Castor and Pollux, the sight of true brothers like the sun rising over Puteoli.

And there was what he did not say: the chains, the never being alone, the peril that inevitably accreted around his person.

His listener, a Greek with round, quick eyes, glanced up at us, and then both Paul and his guard looked over their shoulders to me. Then with a scrambling over the bench they moved in a clumsy partnered dance to face us.

Paul kissed us over and over and wept as he looked into our eyes, holding each face between what seemed like his three hands, the slab-faced young guard letting his shoulder go slack with Paul's motions and looking away with a mixture of disgust and, I think, longing.

Then he reclaimed his arm and we all sat down. Paul then continued to love us with an abandon of words, his left side as immobile against the guard as if he had suffered an apoplexy; and I thought of old Uncle Aaron leaning on the arm of young Jehu, standing at our door, asking for shelter. I looked at the guard and I wondered.

Looking back I realize that Paul had been dead since Damascus and only as a revivified corpse did he live on and reappear, always at the knife-edge of jeopardy, never quite dying. But it was a jeopardy he courted, and he often spoke of a blink of an eye in which all his risks would melt away. No wonder it didn't seem to matter to him but only to those who, with cool rushes of fear in their bellies, loved him.

There were more scars now, his puckered skin a net of pale and crimson ropes everywhere. When he spoke of being bound I wondered if it were not first inside his own flesh.

I must have been staring at his scars, his chains. He looked at me and said, "People can be bound. But the word can't be bound, you know." He looked up at the smoke curling out into the darkness, past the reach of the light of its own source, and smiled.

"Let me introduce you to one another," he said, gesturing first to the guard who blinked at us. "This is my shadow of the hour and companion Inventius Vedrix, minister of the justices of Rome, lately come from the household of our young leader, Nero Claudius Caesar Augustus Germanicus." In response, Vedrix narrowed his eyes, wondering, no doubt, why he was introduced before Paul's friends.

"Vedrix is quite adept at whittling with three hands but is not a very good resource for the spelling of words I might need." In response, Vedrix permitted a tiny smile.

"And this is our brother Onesiphorus, lately come from other wilds, those of Asia. Onesiphorus has his own self dislodged several pillars of the city to find me," he said and the other man threw his head back and laughed long. For the first time I noticed a great plate of food on a stool nearby and knew that such was not a prisoner's normal fare. The Greek gestured to it and we took a few grapes to eat. Paul continued, slipping a piece of bread bristling with almonds under his sleeve to Vedrix as if none of us would notice.

"And these are my most beloved friends Priska and Aquila, who keep the church out of ditches and me out of trouble." Again, Onesiphorus howled with laughter as Paul raised his shackled arm toward us and Aquila murmured, "Not a very good job on the second part, it seems."

As Paul continued I remarked to myself how apt his descriptions of Aquila were: A remarkable mind for memorization, stone-like in his loyalty, with cunning fingers in the fellowship of the needle, open-eyed bravery for his friends.

And then how strange his descriptions of me: a hearer of mysteries and a writer of truths; an heiress of what the Spirit, as executor of Jesus' last will and testimony, bequeathed in measures. A conspirator, with Him, of Breath.

"And how goes that conspiracy, my sister?"

My eyes narrowed like those of Vedrix and I looked down.

And here we all sit in triumph, I thought. A near-cripple, a woman desperate with sadness, a state prisoner, a guard whose eyes might never be able to blink away what he had seen at the palace, and a Greek who was delighted that he could smuggle in food.

"I tell you, brother, I have become wary of telling anyone that I pray for them; it seems a herald of disaster." I made my voice both linen and horsehair.

"Wary of the praying, or wary of the God?" I heard Paul's voice match mine, infused with the crackle of the fire. I felt the stares of the others.

"And others have felt this, have they not? A sense of an obdurate and flint-faced God?" I knew the words wounded. But I knew they were true and so I continued on with words from our profession, words from the prophets. "Above us, a ceiling of buckram. And when we claw that away, a ceiling of brass."

"Sister Priska, what if I told you that you can speak with perfect frankness here? What would you say?"

I looked at the face of Aquila, pale with fear for me. He nodded.

"I would have much to tell you."

"Then tell me."

"First of all I would say that Jesus' promise of coming

back quickly is one I do not understand." At this Paul dipped his head for me to go on.

"And the other matter, quite familiar to you, brother Paul. I have found that although God is quite plainspoken with me, I am apparently incapable of making the things that matter to me, matter to God."

"The old disappointments."

I dared not look at Paul's own body, nor that of Aquila.

"Take my friend Cordelia, for instance. No one has more faith than she. And yet you will be aghast when you see her. You know how a bean seed breaks the soil in which it first grows, leading with its back? That is Cordelia the servant of Jesus. She leads with the parts of her body which were never meant to lead—the twist and hunch of her back; that pitiful, insistent stone child within her."

Paul's head lowered. Perhaps I wanted him to feel the shame.

"I have touched the kerchiefs. The shadows have passed over all those I love. We have slept mere cubits away from you, Paul the miracle worker, for months and years."

"I know." The words had a sob on their outside edges.

"Is this what it means to be most favored?"

No one stirred to respond for a long, long time.

"Tell me how you see this favored status." Paul spoke across coals that surged hot light as a breeze passed over them.

I thought for a moment. "I can tell you who I identify with. I feel that fire in my bones like Jeremiah, but it is fire that is burning me up from the inside out and there is nothing left at my center place. I feel like John the baptizing one, who spent his whole life free, never seeing past the edge of an endless steaming desert horizon, the greatest one in the kingdom—yes? finding himself now locked in the murk of a cell and asking, 'Is this what we were expecting?

This?"

"I have heard that the Breath spoke to you of faith. Of its power in creation, with Enoch, with Abraham. Of its kinetic power." At Paul's words, I looked at him in surprise. How had he known about what happened in the city of the dead?

"Then let me tell you what the absence of faith looks like." I bit off my words. "It is like the death of a loved one. When he or she is with you, you can touch a cheek and hear a voice and smell raisins just eaten. And then a fraction-second of death changes everything. What you once loved, embraced, perhaps even entered or were entered by, now you do not touch. Not because of anything ceremonial. It is the demarcation of the beginning of you, without. And this is its irrevocable claim on you: the utter finality of mourning."

I think Paul groaned at these last words. When he spoke again his voice was lightless.

"Why do you see it as final?"

I waved an impatient hand before me. "For others, of course not. And perhaps not even for me. But it feels permanent. It feels like a lost cause."

Paul lowered himself from the bench, tugging Vedrix with him onto the ground. He rested his back against the bench with a sigh.

"It is that. A lost cause."

Everyone else turned to Paul in surprise except me.

"Which is why the story of the man crucified with Jesus is such a remarkable one," Paul said. "He alone of everyone there, he risked everything for Jesus. Jesus the lost cause. Jesus who could do nothing for him but promise."

"And I ask you, brother Paul, what value did that have for him?" I hoped the softness of my voice did not betray my feelings. "How can we tell someone who wants to know about this Jesus, what do we tell them is the advantage of this lost cause? Do we say, 'Come die an unjust death, too? Who wants to be first in line?'"

I saw Paul stretch his neck, heard the familiar knuckle sounds come from it. It was the sound of a wrestler who has won the match and now relaxes into the mat. His voice was so gentle it yawned.

"It wasn't that the thief on the other cross had nothing more to lose when he cast his lot with another lost cause, that likewise shuddering, heaving, near-corpse next to him," he said. "The thief's faith was in the only resource and hope he could have—a future. He put his eternity at risk for this lost cause—because he believed it to be more real than anything he could see."

Paul stretched both arms out front now, and Vedrix permitted his one arm to follow.

"As do we all, dear Priska. As do we all." The yawning veered toward a shudder. Again the coals flared and I saw his face, sagging and tired and old. "You are telling me that Jesus has not met your expectations. And you are telling me that you base that on what your eyes capture from between your eyelids. What you see. The tinglings of your skin, what you touch with your hands. And yet you admit that even what you know of Jesus is second-hand. What will happen to those who hear from you, third-hand, your second-hand accounts? And pass them on? Will Jesus grow dimmer like purple cloth washed over and over until it is dingy grey like all other old cloth?

"To answer your question, this is indeed what it feels like to be most favored. I, and the apostles, and anyone who has known Jesus, we stiffen words like the glued linen buckram you mention. We mold them around the realities which are gone from this life but will exist eternally: tabernacles in heaven, a high priest with an indestructible life, coming resurrections secured with the down payment of one superlative past event here on earth. An empty tomb."

Vedrix had his head turned all the way to stare at Paul, who seemed not to notice.

"You and I, sister Priska, are given a task. It is an urgent one. There are not many of us. We have little time left. We are given words, wondrous words; and as the Breath breathes, they stiffen into the form He wants, exactly corresponding to eternal realities. And then He takes His residence within them."

I opened my mouth to tell him that the last time the Breath breathed on me we wrestled like cyclones colliding over an open sea.

But the hour was late. And I was a woman. And I was a Gentile. And I could at that moment claim no credentials of faith, so I said nothing at all as Aquila played a simple tune on his flute for Paul.

There was much for the others to talk about and when they awakened me near dawn for our trip across the city to our home, I was angry that I had curled up and surrendered the entire night to sleep. I awakened with my jaws and teeth aching. None of the men seemed anything but refreshed, and a new guard, this one with adamantine joints, was a post around which Paul stiffly and cautiously moved.

When I approached him to bid him farewell, Paul looked again into my eyes. He said nothing. But I heard a sound, and it was that of a catapult stretching as it never had before, and I heard its song of eschatologies.

All through the day Aquila and I worked side by side. He told me of many things the men had discussed while I slept, but he did not mention any of my conversation with Paul. In fact, through the day my husband treated me as if I were unfired clay, or ill, or pregnant.

In the silent spaces, though, I spoke to myself. I said I had been stripped down to the bones of my soul. Sins I had not remembered in years came to me as if it were the night hours and coughed at my door. I sat beneath a withering gourd plant in blinding sun. I tucked my robe into my belt and ran for the desert, away from any mountain where miracles had happened.

When Aquila and Baruch left for the evening to meet with some of the brothers, I repeated to Cordelia the men's talk of the runaway slave of our old friend Philemon, and the twice-veiled imagery of a young beast that roared in the riches of Rome.

"Is young Rubria in danger?" she asked. I did not know. I prepared our dinner of boiled eggs and toasted over the fire some of Cordelia's bread with butter on it. She ate a few bites and retired.

In the silence of the yellow house I looked, really looked, at a just-peeled egg that sat on a plate with a curling plume of steam still coming from its white symmetry. I thought I had never seen anything quite so remarkable.

But then I heard the rustling sounds of the sea creature and knew it had come to shore before me. I had run as fast and as long as I could away from my Mount Carmel to a cave where I could mourn alone; had sailed in the opposite direction from my Nineveh, only to find that I had been swallowed whole by Rome.

Chapter Twenty-Nine

I wish I could say that while Paul was chained yet not imprisoned, I made the most of that freedom. I can only say that our lives, Aquila and Baruch and Cordelia and mine, became one emergency after another. This day it might be a new servant from the household of Caesar who, like Vedrix to no one's surprise came to believe—and thus to fear. Another day it might be a rumor that someone was writing down the names of all whose fingertips did not linger in passing upon the foot of an imperial statue. The Jews had their lists and their vows. And the sheer number of people in this cosmopolitan and international city who freely spoke the name of Jesus—no one kept such lists, and afterwards we were glad none such existed.

Thus I saw Paul only at night and only occasionally because we could not endanger the lives of the many who passed beneath our roof by visiting him. We read copies of his letter to Philemon and urged the slaves who appeared at our door at midnight to find ways back to their owners. I smiled when I read his letter to the believers in Colossae for I heard the Breath's unison with me and Paul as well, as he spoke of a Jesus who was the image of the invisible God; of feast days and moons and Sabbaths that were shadows of eternal things—just as the Breath had told me that the tabernacle was.

"You breathe with the Breath," he said to me on one of our rare visits. "We share this fellowship: you have it from the lips and nostrils of God."

I remembered what the Breath said: laws written on the heart and mind, that show His ownership. But I did not want to be owned.

When I began to protest, Paul raised his hands as if to put them over my mouth. With shame, I clasped his wrists, and dragging that of the guard with them, put his hands over my ears.

"Ah," he said. "Ah."

A few days later—or was it weeks? was it months?—Aquila told me of a village of women at the foot of the mountains west of the city. Some people called them the Amazons because they lived in a community nearly devoid of their men who had died or gone for soldiers or both. Even the majority of the children were females. One of the women had brought back news and scattered stories of a protector-Man Jesus, and without further teaching it had become its own tangled and shallow-soiled mythology.

Cordelia and Aquila could not make the trip to such a mountainous place, so Timothy and Baruch and I went to live with them and teach them for a week. For the young men it was an adventure with much preparation of hunting and stream-fishing implements. I took scrolls and good needles and fabric. So few of the women could read that I copied for them some of the teachings of Peter about Jesus to teach them.

I shall never forget the cleanness of the air there, like slices of cold melon, and as sweet, and the determination of these hardscrabble women to master the words I brought them: repeated in the kneading trough, shouted across rows of ox-broken soil, chanted to babies, murmured over caldrons of soup and tallow and gruel. After the week was done, I knew they could build other words, trustworthy words, on those I had given them.

I had never been so close to the great peaks of the spine of the land, and on our return trip I looked back again and again at them. Some of them still harbored snow that spilled in heaps from deep crevasses like a woman's breasts tightly bound to stop her milk. I thought of all the processes we women employ to stop the signs of life from us, of what I had for years now done to stop the life of Breath within me.

I had come to disallow ecstasy from him. It was as simple as that.

As if He had been granted permission by the mere thought, the Breath returned to me then, once again.

I sat alone beneath an olive tree of such age that I wondered if it had been formed at Creation while the two young men hunted the hares they wanted to take home for dinner. Its leaves began to vibrate, even though there was no wind, as if a thousand people held each leaf in their lips and hummed.

Whereas the Breath had come with a solicitous alert the time before in the city of the dead, so gentle that I thought of it as a bloody show, this time He came with the implacability of breaking waters from a ripened womb.

I had pen. I had scrolls. I listened as the Breath recited as if teaching me by rote as I had taught the women.

By faith Abraham,

By faith Abraham, when tried, offered up Isaac,

By faith Abraham, when tried, offered up Isaac, and he who had received to himself the promises offered up his only begotten son,

By faith Abraham, when tried, offered up Isaac, and he who had received to himself the promises offered up his only begotten son, as to whom it had been said, In Isaac shall thy seed be called:

By faith Abraham, when tried, offered up Isaac, and he who had received to himself the promises offered up his only begotten son, as to whom it had been said, In Isaac shall thy seed be called: counting that God was able to raise him even from among the dead, whence also he received him in a figure.

A figure: something that carried the authenticity,

By faith Isaac

By faith Isaac blessed Jacob and Esau concerning things to come.

By faith Jacob when dying blessed each of the sons of Joseph, and worshipped on the top of his staff.

By faith Joseph when dying called to mind the going forth of the sons of Israel, and gave commandment concerning his bones.

By faith Moses, being born, was hid three months by his parents, because they saw the child beautiful; and they did not fear the injunction of the king.

By faith Moses, when he had become great, refused to be called son of Pharaoh's daughter; choosing rather to suffer affliction along with the people of God than to have the temporary pleasure of sin; esteeming the reproach of the Christ greater riches than the treasures of Egypt, for he had respect to the recompense. By faith he left Egypt, not fearing the wrath of the king; for he persevered, as seeing him who is invisible. By faith he celebrated the passover and the sprinkling of the blood, that the destroyer of the firstborn might not touch them.

By faith they passed through the Red sea as through dry land; of which the Egyptians having made trial were swallowed up.

By faith the walls of Jericho fell, having been encircled for seven days.

By faith Rahab the harlot did not perish along with the unbelieving, having received the spies in peace.

And what more do I say? For the time would fail me telling of

Gideon, and Barak, and Samson, and Jephthah, and David and Samuel, and of the prophets: who by faith overcame kingdoms, wrought righteousness, obtained promises, stopped lions' mouths, quenched the power of fire, escaped the edge of the sword, became strong out of weakness, became mighty in war, made the armies of strangers give way.

Women received their dead again by resurrection

I put the pen down. I had heard witness of resurrection, but two of my children lay in graves a world away.

I knew of this faith, this done-unto-you-according-to-your-faith that came out in words that could drown mountains and expand the very universe and yet mine echoed on and on until they lost their voice in that vast void.

Baruch and Timothy returned with swaying, soft-haired lumps on cords over their shoulders. We took up our other bundles and began walking toward the walls of the city.

"We were talking, Mother," said Baruch, "about what Paul said, that everything in creation holds together because of the power of Jesus."

I thought of the buckram glue.

"Yes, my son."

"And we thought of what Peter told about the time on the boat when Jesus stilled the storm."

"Yes, my son."

"And Timothy told me—didn't you, Timothy?—that it was not just that Jesus could calm the storm. It was that He owned the storm."

"Yes, my son."

Beneath my shawl, I clutched the scroll with barely-dried letters on it. We walked on in silence toward Rome, and the gathering storm that Jesus, there too, owned.

Chapter Thirty

No one knows to this day why Paul was released so suddenly from his two-year captivity. I have wondered if the great maw of Roman jurisprudence had gagged on him and simply spat him out instead of trying to digest him. Aquila and the brethren put him on a ship for Spain before the Jews knew he was gone.

Such speed was necessary. Though Peter and others had wonderful accounts of release from prison in the early days of the church, we heard few such stories now. The Jews had learned how to manipulate legal systems throughout the known world, and hundreds—perhaps thousands—of our brethren were incarcerated or executed by them, or sometimes single-handedly by local government officials who saw danger in their growing numbers.

I did not know that the last time I saw Paul before he left for Spain would be the last time I saw him in this life. It was a late summer evening with a single tine of cold in the breeze. He was no longer chained to his ever-present rotation of guards, but they left their weapons on a table and ate with him. This time, when the guard saw Aquila and me enter, he inclined his head just slightly and walked outside to stand in the last rays of sunshine.

Paul was trying to push a stout needle through the sole of a shoe he held between his knees, and after he kissed us he resumed his repair.

"The Breath told me I will need these soon," he said, winking at Aquila. It was not that I disbelieved him but I had heard the sound of the catapult ratcheting and knew that his end was nearing. We sat down and I fussed with a basket of bread that Cordelia sent. I was filled with inarticulate sorrow.

"I've been thinking about the mistakes that Abraham our father made," Paul said. He reached to the table for the guard's helmet and used one thick ear flap to force the needle through the shoe leather, then replaced the helmet with a grunt of satisfaction. "We're supposed to walk in his footsteps, you know." He waved the shoe's sole at us.

"God gave him a bottomless purse full of righteousness, and no matter how far he dipped into it with sin, it never ran out," Paul said.

"But only because he believed," I said without thinking. The words from the last Breathing: *By faith, by faith, by faith.*

"Yes, sister. Only because he believed." He reached for his oil lamp and held it close to the shoe. "And this purse, so to speak—it was his before he was circumcised. When he was, we might say, a Gentile."

Aquila and I looked at one another and Paul didn't seem to notice.

"The point I am making, sister Priska, is that the good news is for the Gentiles now. Maybe only for them. And someone must tell them of how the Old Law had only one purpose—to bring everyone to faith in the One whose death guarantees the funds in that purse. Forever."

He put another stitch in and forced the needle through with a thumbnail as thick as the walls of the shofar trumpet. He smiled as it slipped through.

All well and good for Abraham, I thought to myself. For all those like him. He died old and rich, in his own bed.

"Nevertheless …" I began.

Outside the house, we heard Onesiphorus and some other brethren. When they entered, they were agitated. I cannot recall what the bad news was this time. Paul kissed us goodbye with his face wet and I thought we would continue later.

But we never did. In two days, he was on a ship bound for Spain, and my last word to him was, "Nevertheless."

His sudden leaving affected Cordelia more than anyone, I thought. Somehow a Rome that held Paul captive seemed less menacing than the Rome he walked freely out of. It was as if the Ark had left the Temple and all its golden walls resounded with noises of confusion and distress. It was to Cordelia that the women of Rome came with their fears and those fears began to rub her raw.

One night she had retired and I sat weaving, weary of waiting for Baruch and Aquila to return from a late-night meeting. She appeared at my loom disheveled and her eyes filled with worry.

"The Breath has a message for you, Priska."

I looked at her with surprise. This could not be good news. She did not know of any time He had spoken to me since that last time in the city of the dead. I had indeed burned my scrolls—all but the last one, from the trip back from the mountains.

In her hands were paper and a pen. I sighed and rubbed my eyes.

"Your hands cannot write it, dear sister." I tried to keep the edge out of my voice.

She looked at her hands as if they had just grown their tortuous angles and lumps, then back up at me. She handed me the paper and pen.

"It's only one word."

I shook my head, in disbelief, in bitterness. She drew herself up as straight as she could.

"'The Breath says to tell you, 'Nevertheless.'"

"'That is all? 'Nevertheless?'"

First, she shook her head, then she nodded. Then she shrugged and went back behind her sleeping curtain.

I held the paper and pen in my lap until my lamp went out. I refilled it and then pinched out the flame from the wick with my fingers. I was sitting there in the dark when Aquila and Baruch returned.

I knew that the labor that had begun with the bloody show and the breaking of the waters had only paused, contained by some unseen force, but now gathered and surged toward release.

Aquila lit our household lamp with his small one and looked at me for a moment. Then he kissed me and stumbled toward our bed, but I caught Baruch's muscular arm as he passed.

"Sit with me," I asked, and because he was young and unwearied and bright-eyed in the lamplight, he did.

I gave him the pen and paper. He looked hard into my eyes.

"'The Breath says, 'Nevertheless.'" I tried not to make my voice apologetic.

He wrote it down and waited; I do not know how long.

It began again with a gush.

and others were tortured, not having accepted deliverance, that they might get a better resurrection;

and others underwent trial of mockings and scourgings, yea, and of bonds and imprisonment.

They were stoned,
were sawn asunder,
were tempted,
died by the death of the sword;
they went about in sheepskins,
in goatskins, destitute, afflicted, evil treated,
(of whom the world was not worthy,)
wandering in deserts and mountains, and in dens and caverns of the earth.

And these all, having obtained witness through faith, did not receive the promise,

God told me the truth.

God having foreseen some better thing for us, that they should not be made perfect without us.

Nevertheless, indeed, I thought. This is my cosmos: and its citizens, the people of the nevertheless.

I opened my eyes and looked at Baruch. He was looking off in the distance, his eyes unfocused. I do not know how long the Breath had spoken nor how quickly. He held the paper he had written with trembling hands, but the ink was dry.

Without a word we both arose and went, he to his bed, I to Aquila's.

The next morning no one mentioned what had happened the night before. At first, Aquila read to us as he always did from one of the old scrolls, this time about the vision of Ezekiel who looked over a field of dry bones that came to life and became an army. Life from death, he said; and the resurrection of Jesus sealed this truth: there are no lost causes.

I turned to look at Aquila but Baruch had arisen to open the door to someone. The men spoke in low, urgent tones to a filthy-robed man who entered and then sat and gulped wine and stuffed handfuls of bread into his mouth and swallowed them nearly whole. Other than the condition of his clothing, he was like so many who came, almost every day, to our house. The men left for the bathhouse and Cordelia gave bowlfuls of flour to women who came throughout the morning. Each woman would help mill her own flour, and rattling grains soon quiesced into rivers of dust for dinner.

We were not alone until the time of the afternoon rest and Cordelia went to her bed and drew her curtain. I sat in the sultry shade in our courtyard and turned my face toward the small breezes that came through the door, my mind as blank as scrubbed papyri.

I heard Cordelia behind me and again, she held paper and pen.

I was too ashamed to tell her again that she could not write, too tired to tell her I did not want to hear any more good news from the Breath.

"I want you to write for me, Priscilla," she said.

It took a moment for me to understand what she said, but I took the paper and pen. She sat across from me and leaned her head back.

"I thought all morning about the valley of dry bones," she said. "And when we were grinding the flour, I thought of how these individual grains become part of each other, in the flour. And I have been trying to write something, in my head."

"Would you like me to write it down for you, is that what you are asking?"

She nodded, and began, and I wrote.

I had a dream and a vision
I was in a blistered valley
In Ezekiel's shadow
And when he said
"Sovereign Lord,

You alone know"—
Then he prophesied
And when the rattling began
And bone
Came to
Bone
It was your bone to mine
My wrist joined your hand and arm
My breastbone
To your shoulder
And the sinews that grew
Were the
Power
Of
God

You,
Bone of my bone
And flesh of my flesh
And I
We have become
The mighty army
And we chafe as
We await our marching orders

As I wrote, it seemed that the only sound in the world was her voice, but as soon as she finished speaking, I could hear the vendors in the street, the shouts of children, the urgency of traffic, coming and going.

I reached under a blanket and drew out what Baruch had written for me last night. She sat without looking at me and listened as I read.

"It began with 'Nevertheless'?" she asked.

"Not that word, but the idea, yes."

"'Nevertheless' means a contrast to something that preceded it," she said.

Reluctantly, I pulled the other scroll, what the Breath had said on the way back from the mountains, and read it to her, about Abraham and Isaac and Jacob and Moses and the conquering of kingdoms and glorious promises and resurrections.

"Now read the one from last night again."

I did so. The caves and tortures and destitutions and deaths. She looked up at me.

"Will you burn these scrolls, too?"

There was no breeze in all of Italy that could cool the shame on my temples and around my eyes. This time when I began to cry it was more than the gushing waters of labor, more than the torrents of the most malicious sea, more.

Cordelia pulled the tangle of her arms around me and she wept too, until we were spent. I slid to the floor and sat with my head against her leg.

She pulled a comb from her pocket and held it between two bent fingers and with its edge teeth began to tease apart the knots I had rubbed into my hair with my fists while I was crying.

"I was thinking, Priscilla."

I shuddered still.

"About Jesus, when He was overwhelmed."

I nodded my head.

"The time when He did not think He could do what He needed to do alone."

"Yes."

"In the garden of Gethsemane, do you remember? He asked His friends to stay with Him."

"Yes."

"And all He asked of them was to stay awake, and pray."

"Yes."

"And when He came back, twice, they were sleeping."

"Yes."

"Well, I do not believe myself to be better than those good men, our friend Peter among them. But I believe we can learn from what happened."

I rubbed my nose with a corner of my tunic.

"You see, when there are a group of people assigned to a task, we do not all have to do it at once."

"What?"

"When the disciples all fell asleep in that garden, it was a corporate failure. Some needed to sleep, but some, say two or three, could have kept each other awake until time for the others to take a turn."

"What are you saying, Cordelia?" I said. But I knew. *God having foreseen some better thing for us, that they should not be made perfect without us.*

"That you are carrying as much weight and sorrow as any of them, my sister. And you are trying to stay awake for all of us, and it has become too much for you."

"I … I don't know how to rest."

"It is because you are trying to find your own rest. Or create your own rest."

"What do you mean?"

"Have you forgotten what Jesus promised? He didn't say He would show you how to rest; He said he would rest you." Cordelia spoke in the *koine*, stressing the active nature of the verb He used.

"'I will rest you,' He said."

We sat there for hours, it seemed, as Cordelia combed all the knots out of my hair.

I gave her the two scrolls.

Then we prepared dinner, and the men returned and ate.

Chapter Thirty-One

And then He was back:

The Holy Inhabitant like a fire burning through my innards, glinting into every hidden, unknown interior place, disjointing my bones, thawing my marrow.

It was as if waters had broken, gushing forth with the message of saints saved and saints savaged; and then ceased—with the illusion that labor itself had arrested.

But when He returned, it was with all the ferocity of birth's wrenching to the stomach: implacable, irresistible, stone-faced refusal to be denied.

But before I myself felt the rise and fall of the first contractions, they came with a herald, as I sat with my family one winter evening with the notes of Aquila's flute still tingling in the air.

"Please tell me, Mother, why you think it is that some of the great ones of God were given some sort of earthly vindication, like the Josephs and the Abrahams and the Rahabs," said my son Baruch (and is it not a child who first feels the bearing down, even before the mother?) "and others lived in caves and wandered their whole lives without anything we would call a blessing?"

He held the two scrolls of the Breath's words in his hands. I could not answer. I was hearing the appeal of a dove, a voice beyond words, far in the distance.

I saw Aquila glance at me with a look of concern but I was becoming untethered to the room. I knew with Agabus-certainty that blessingless death awaited some of us in that room and this knowing robbed my limbs and lips their volition. At the edge of my vision I noted with dispassion as if the room and the people were a memory, that Baruch had stretched a clean, new parchment over a slate and sat cross-legged and leaning forward, ready to write.

The Breath began wringing me like a woman who begins at the middle of a roll of cloth to remove every mist of moisture from it.

Let us also therefore, having so great a cloud of witnesses surrounding us, laying aside every weight, and sin which so easily entangles us, run with endurance the race that lies before us,

And in that instance I saw it; I know the others saw it: a ceiling of aching faces above us. And I knew that Cordelia was right, without them we are not; that Paul was right, this body of parts arches across the expanse of heaven and time, and would be lame and blind and crippled without each single one.

looking steadfastly on Jesus the leader and completer of faith:

And He, the excellence and truth of the tabernacle, the pinnacle of priesthood, the summit of every mountain of revelation

who, in view of the joy lying before him, endured the cross, having despised the shame,

And I thought of the theatre of remorse, the flushing face of shame *and is set down*

It is finished. Finished.

at the right hand of the throne of God.

For consider well

Consider well, I repeated to Baruch, Consider well.

him who endured so great contradiction from sinners against himself,

He, the hinge of history, the consummation of space and time, dying alone on a cross when He was heir of glory.

That ye be not weary, fainting in your minds.

Ye have not yet resisted unto blood,

And yet I knew we all would do so: Baruch, Cordelia, Aquila,

I.

wrestling against sin.

And ye have quite forgotten the exhortation which speaks to you as to sons:

And daughters:

My son, despise not the chastening of the Lord, nor faint when reproved by him;

I could focus. I looked at Baruch. You are my son, I said. We are all His legal heirs; He declared it inescapably so.

for whom the Lord loves he chastens, and scourges every son whom he receives.

Ye endure for chastening, God conducts himself towards you as towards sons; for who is the son that the father chastens not?

When Baruch and Aquila looked at one another, their eyes were two mooring ropes and they drew their ships together.

But

But

if ye are without chastening, of which all have been made partakers, then are ye bastards, and not sons.

And I heard the voice speak of fathers and Father, chastening and holiness.

And then the seed-laden core of the message:

But no chastening at the time seems to be matter of joy, but of grief;

but afterwards

yields

the peaceful fruit of righteousness to those exercised by it.

And then I heard the voice of Cordelia, urgent as labor herself.

"This is shared history."

The Breath had inclined His lips from me, His exhalation mixed with her breathing.

"He asks us to accept a view of reality that is outside our own experiencing." Her voice was like softness itself.

I looked at her twisted body and wondered what it would take to live outside that prison while nailed to its inside walls.

And then He was back, and the fullness of His message to me was crowning, and I leaned forward to birth.

Wherefore lift up the hands that hang down, and the failing knees;

and make straight paths for your feet, that that which is lame be not turned aside; but that rather it may be healed.

And I knew the healing would not be that of bodies.

Pursue peace with all, and holiness, without which no one shall see the Lord:

watching lest there be any one who lacks the grace of God; lest any root of bitterness springing up trouble you, and many be defiled by it;

And I reached inside to strangle that root that had wrapped itself around my entrails for so long, hearing the Breath breathe of the utter loss of birthright sold for belly-fullness or even eye-pleasure, of exile in a province beyond the borders of repentance; and I knew I must turn my back on even that country's boundary stones, forever.

Then the Breath was artist, painting a heaved-up summit

that lost itself in clouds.

For ye have not come to the mount that might be touched and was all on fire, and to obscurity, and darkness, and tempest, and trumpet's sound, and voice of words;

Not to the tangible

which they that heard, excusing themselves, declined the word being addressed to them any more:

Saying, as I had, No thank you, to an invitation to a touch that could kill.

but ye have come to mount Zion; and to the city of the living God, heavenly Jerusalem; and to myriads of angels,

the universal gathering;

and to the assembly of the firstborn who are registered in heaven;

and to God, judge of all;

and to the spirits of just men made perfect;

To invisible infinities more powerful than muscles and stone and steel

and to Jesus, mediator of a new covenant; and to the blood of sprinkling, speaking better than Abel.

It was done but not yet done. I reached for the two other scrolls sitting beside Baruch. I took the pen from him and began striking through all the Esau words I had mingled with the Breath's.

I looked up to see the others each nodding at me.

"We knew not to memorize it yet," said Aquila. "We knew you must circumcise yourself out of the Breath's words."

I blinked at him. I pushed myself against the wall of the room to rise and then sank down onto the bench again. The birth was finished, but the afterbirth was coming.

See that ye refuse not him that speaks.

For if those did not escape who had refused him who uttered the oracles on earth, much more we who turn away from him who does so from heaven:

whose voice then shook the earth; but now he has promised, saying, Yet once will I shake not only the earth, but also the heaven.

I heard the Breath for the last time speaking for my ears alone.

But this Yet once, signifies the removing of what is shaken, as being made, that what is not shaken may remain.

Wherefore let us, receiving a kingdom not to be shaken, have grace, by which let us serve God acceptably with reverence and fear.

For also our God is a consuming fire.

God, a consuming fire.

With that knowledge, that God Himself is conflagration, I give no credence to the rumors that it was Nero who started the Great Fire in Rome later that summer. Some say he only wanted to rebuild the city in his own image, and began it with the implacable burnings inside himself and let it singe others who would set torch to over half of its buildings.

We felt the presage of it, or at least Aquila did and told us of it. Through the springtime that was so hot it crisped tree leaves and withered their aborted fruits within their leathern blossoms, we heard news from Paul in Macedonia, in letters to us and to Timothy that read like wills. Here is what must be done, he said, teach this, appoint this, set things up according to this.

Paul's urgency was a contagion. In the evenings in the late spring, Cordelia and Aquila sat with me and from their memories resurrected the scrolls I had burned, all the Breath's words. Baruch mouthed the words with them and wrote them in his fine, clear script on parchment.

I had believed I had spilled these words onto the sand, but they had flowed through it into the aquifers of their minds and they brought them back to me. And, when they were complete, Aquila rolled up our household goods with the scrolls.

"We must go to Ephesus to help Timothy," he said, sweat dripping from his brow in the buzzing summer heat.

"How can we leave all the brothers and sisters here?" Cordelia asked. "And what about Rubria? When last I saw her she began to ask me questions about Jesus, and I fear that madman Nero—"

Aquila did not let her finish.

"The Breath is sending us."

And so we went, on a voyage on a sea so serene that its winds seemed only to kiss our sails but not to touch the water.

Our time in Greece was a portend of finalities. It was there that both Cordelia and I ceased our menstrual cycles, ending as we had for years now on the same date and, then, never beginning again.

We had only been in Greece for a month when refugees from Rome brought the stories of the Fire. Over half the city lay like Gehenna in ever-smoking ruins.

With the suffering of pagan and Christian alike, we dared not ask about the yellow house. But its precinct was one of the few left untouched by the flames. We were glad, because we heard that so many left without homes could use it, sleeping in rows like rolls of fabric on our shop floor. How many hid in the secret room? I wondered.

Many more had joined the cloud-ceiling of witnesses. The laughing Onesiphorus, a whole household of women that Cordelia had taught to support themselves, everyone who named the Name in Caesar's household, the village of people who guarded the underground city of the dead, others more each day, it was said.

I think it was to protect my mind from the unbearable grief of loss that I began to think of them as rosters of the dead, only given faces that I could see as I looked up, seeing them chin-first.

At night, the Fire shrieked in my dreams.

Nero told his people, we heard, that purging the city of the fire-bringer foreigners, the Christians, would renew it. Perhaps he knew that blood cleanses, perhaps he had heard that from the lips of those who died before his very eyes. Perhaps that is why in the spring he sent for and brought Paul back to Rome, this time in death-chains.

We learned of this in Paul's last letter to Timothy, devastating news to the young man who had been working so hard in that city, had himself so narrowly escaped death in that city and had himself been imprisoned. In Paul's letter was a resignation we had not seen before, a desire to stitch together the ravelings of his life. He spoke of its rips: of betrayals and illness of his friends, and his hopes for others.

And its warnings: "Take thy share of suffering, Timothy."

And a plaintive request from the most favored man alive.

"Bring my cloak, Timothy," he wrote, "and the scrolls, especially the parchments. Try to get here before winter."

The threadbare cloak Timothy now held before him, draped over one arm that he held over his stomach as if he needed its warmth, as he read Paul's letter to us.

"Scrolls?" he said. "All I have are the letters he has written to me. The other brethren have the scrolls with the Old Law. Why would he want us to send them from here? And we have no parchments."

Aquila turned slowly to look at me. "I believe he wants the writings the Breath gave to Priska, for the Hebrew brethren. But they are just sections, not a letter. And we will want to make a copy for ourselves."

"Of course." Timothy's voice was that of a son. "I leave as soon as I can get passage to Rome, and I will take them with me. Keep them here until I am ready."

"Wait a moment, before you go," I said to Timothy. "Several of the women had been working on a cloak for Paul," I said. I brought out a length of padded fabric. "One of the sisters from Egypt had the idea to pad it, see, almost like a mattress." I held the quilted surface up for him to see and he turned it over in the lamplight.

"Well, tell that sister that Paul will be honored and grateful," he murmured.

I rubbed a thumb over the unfinished hem.

"Oh, that sister awaits us in heaven," I said. I held up a corner. "As does the sister who began this design here, and another who bought the binding. In fact," my voice caught as I smoothed the fabric, "everyone who worked on this is now dead. But I will finish it."

After Timothy left our home that night, I sat looking at all the Breath-words on the parchment. Aquila put his arms around me and held me as if we were bidding farewell to a child; and indeed, it felt that way. But then with a shudder he moved away from me and I could see he no longer rested his eyes on me nor on anything in the room.

I heard a hollow-throated sound, like wind passing over the narrow opening of a deep vessel.

"It is the Breath, speaking to you," I said.

He nodded. "Call Baruch and Cordelia. This is for them as well."

And with that I knew that just as I had birthed the message of the Breath, these who had protected it must protect it again and swaddle it for travel.

I took a piece of parchment and wrote as they, Aquila and the Breath, began to speak as fathers.

You have fed too long on milk; seek meat, they said. You have a foundation—do not think to lay it again but build on it.

They spoke of fertile fields gone fallow, of thorns and

briars that choke men's souls; of hands equipped to crucify Jesus again and again. Watch yourselves, they said, sound the alert of these hidden dangers to others. You are the festival that people come to see: tell them that being plundered is not the worst thing that can happen to you.

Take courage: *The just shall live by faith;*

Take warning: *and, if he draw back, My soul does not take pleasure in him.*

Nurture brotherly love, share your homes because sometimes angels come without you being aware of it. Protect the marriage bed, be content with your possessions, remember that Jesus stands with you.

for he has said, I will not leave thee, neither will I forsake thee:

A Savior-friend who stands at your side, flinching with your pain.

Make yourselves mirrors of the faith of your leaders, the Breath and my husband said. They are the sentinels of your souls.

I felt as if warm oil were flowing from my head to my feet, as if the whole room were light, as if we all were suspended in honey that would preserve us like amber for posterity, for

Jesus Christ is the same yesterday, and today, and to the ages to come.

Strange doctrines are winds that can carry you away. But you have an anchor and it is not the tabernacle but the reason for the tabernacle.

It is Jesus,
it has always been Jesus
and it will always be Jesus.

If He walked outside the camp, to the place of reproach, will you not walk with Him? You want to sacrifice something: give Him first your words, the bubbling up of what you think and what you are.

And now, the ending of this. Pray for us to come to you, brethren and sisters of the Old Law and New.

But the God of peace, who brought again from among the dead our Lord Jesus, the great shepherd of the sheep, in the power of the blood of the eternal covenant, perfect you in every good work to the doing of his will, doing in you what is pleasing before him through Jesus Christ; to whom be glory for the ages of ages. Amen.

And when I joined my voice to theirs, I wondered if the faceless readers would feel the Breath across their cheeks as they read.

I had only apologies and farewells for those who would hear my words:

Forgive me, I said, bear with my earnestness and pleadings and the brevity of this all. Goodbye, goodbye. Timothy has been set free and he is coming. And I shall come too, if I can. Those here from Italy salute you: the only salutation of this letter its farewell as well.

Grace be with you all
Grace be with you all
Grace be with you all
Amen

Chapter Thirty-Two

The only miracle that passed from God through me happened so quickly that I scarcely knew it.

When Timothy came to our house that last time in Ephesus before boarding the ship, Paul's ragged cloak was over his shoulder and his face was the color of prison dust on leather sandals. He tipped the wineskin he carried to his lips and winced as he swallowed, and I recalled how he had held Paul's cloak to his stomach.

"May I offer you some of Cordelia's herbs for your pain?" *A little wine for your stomach and your frequent illnesses*, Paul had advised.

Another dear friend that Paul did not heal, I began to think, and then remembered about sonship. *The later, much later, harvest of righteousness, for those who have been trained by it …*

Baruch came into the room, his eyelashes still carrying a tear suspended on them, but he did not want Timothy to see him cry. He held the parchment scrolls and he began to thrust them toward Timothy.

"No, let your mother hold them one more time." I was startled, not knowing that my grief at letting them go was so visible. So I took them gratefully and stood, letting the smell of the parchment fill my nose and throat. I had made a case for them, and after a while I rolled them together and put them into the cylinder I had made, then wrapped them in the padded cloak with the stitches of so many dead women, and tied it all with a leather strap.

It was with the simple act of putting the bundle into Timothy's hands that it happened. It was like a shooting star which passed as soon as it caught my attention, like a sudden blow to the tender bones of the elbow that carries pain to the fingertips, like a rasp of fear that sings through the ears.

Timothy's eyes widened, and then they began to soften and lose focus for a moment until they closed. When he opened his eyes, his was the face of one who had been comforted.

"I have no pain."

When he departed, he left all our tears and the wineskin behind.

All of us sick with crying, Baruch and Cordelia left Aquila and me alone to work, and I stabbed at fabrics with ferocity all through the morning. After a while Aquila touched my arm.

"What is your anger, my wife? You must let the writings go, you know."

I wrested my wrist away from him.

"Why could I not have healed you? Or Cordelia? I have vomited out prayers for your healing and yet when I am able to do something, it was not for you!"

Aquila's slow considering came to speech.

"If it were a matter of compassion only, there would

have been no one unhealed in Jesus' day."

I thought about that for a while.

"The wonders have ever been for the confirming of the Word," he said. "Now *your* words. God Himself just confirmed them."

He quoted from the scrolls. "'*God also bearing witness both with signs and wonders, with various miracles, and gifts of the Holy Spirit, according to His own will …*'" Then he reached for his flute.

I wove my thoughts into the notes of Aquila's music, hanging in the stillness of the room.

After lunch Cordelia and Baruch came into the room, and he gestured toward them.

"These, your family, have protected those words, even from you. Those words cannot be restrained now. They are seeds that will grow in the minds of all who hear them."

"You say that because you love me and my words," I said, but even as I spoke I knew the Breath-words to me had been like a blade deftly trimming gristle from my own thoughts.

"Or maybe you just say that because of Timothy's healing," I pursued.

I heard the stir of questions from Cordelia and Baruch but Aquila ignored them to answer.

"I say that because the words themselves have power. They carry more than they are. They are like wide-shouldered porters, and what they carry is truth."

"They carry facts." It was Baruch's man-voice, with authority. I turned to look at him.

"It's true, Mother. These words do not convey emotion, though they can cause it. But more important, no matter where Timothy and I take these words, they will carry facts that people need to know. Listen to this, just the beginning of what the Breath told you." He tipped his head back, just a bit, and recited. "'*In the past God spoke to our ancestors through the prophets—at many times and in various ways. But in these last days he has spoken to us by his Son, whom he appointed heir of all things, and through whom also he made the universe, sustaining all things by his powerful word.*'"

We waited expectantly, Cordelia and Aquila and I.

"We can see that God has mind, and He can communicate that mind to people."

"Yes," said Aquila.

"And He is comprehensible when He speaks. Not the ravings of a priestess sitting over the fumes of Delphi."

"Yes," said Cordelia.

"And what He has to say, He has mediated through humans."

"And not through auger bones or sheeps' livers." Aquila brightened as he spoke.

"Yes," said Baruch, his excitement growing. "And that message isn't bound—won't ever be bound by time, because His message is eternal. Nor bound by any culture."

"'Many times, various ways,'" said Cordelia.

"Such as by creating the universe—or speaking through the Son," I said.

"Which means of course that God is greater than the universe He created." Baruch was spreading his arms.

"And not bound, Himself, by it," Aquila said.

"And even those things we think of as insubstantial, like voice or word, He uses to actually sustain and support the universe."

And by the time we finished, our sorrow at Timothy's departure was dimmed as Baruch tallied facts the scrolls conveyed, keeping count with marks into the wall plaster with a nail, seventy-seven in all, lights and perfections.

"I can see what you are saying, but has anyone considered the problem with Paul sitting in that hole of a prison with the scrolls?" I hated to bring a shadow to the shimmer of words in the room.

The others looked at me expectantly—and with sudden uncertainty.

"Have any of you thought what will happen if Paul does not survive this imprisonment? And have you thought of how he promised that the scrolls would be protected by Timothy and Baruch?" I gestured toward Baruch, who drew himself up in pride, then looked down. With a wrenching in my heart I wondered if I mourned more the knowledge that the scrolls had passed forever from my hands—even though I had a copy that Baruch had made, I knew that there would be no more Breathings to add to them—or the certainty that my son would likewise soon pass from my life as well.

I knew this because of the convulsions of the great Fish that had pursued me and devoured me and drenched and infused me with all His inner juices and which would now vomit me up onto a final earthly shore. I could feel the ripples of heaving and nearly said out loud, "Which shore?"

A man came to the shop door and Aquila went outside with him. When he returned he had a strange look in his eyes, a longing, yearning, painful look; and as I gazed into them I understood that he knew, too. He cleared his throat.

"I must go to Corinth," he said.

"We have not yet been here a year." At my words, he hung his head.

"You mean we all must go, of course." I pushed, resigned.

"No." His voice was flat as suede. "It is hard to think of myself as a leader, an elder, but that is what is needed there right now. Someone who can stamp out some things for the last time. Besides, there is news from your relative Rubria the Vestal, words not consigned to writing because of great danger," he said, his voice husky with something that never escaped his throat. "She sends you two messages: first, she seeks the God of Philomena."

"Who is the God of Philomena?" Baruch asked.

Cordelia and I looked at one another with puzzlement that grew into joy. Her nurse Philomena, Rubria had told us, paid for her newfound faith in Jesus with her life. Could it be that Rubria wanted to believe as well? I could scarcely believe it.

"And she sent another message. 'Urgently I beseech you to come, for the great artist has noticed me.'"

I sucked in my breath. That could only mean Nero Caesar, who fancied himself an actor and musician and athlete but most of all a patron of the arts. Many commoners loved him because he built fine public buildings and held festivals and athletic contests. But the worst thing that could happen to anyone—commoner or nobility—would be to attract his attention, for even his relatives died at his hand, and his sexual depravities were legendary. But a threat to a Vestal Virgin, symbolic guardian of the nation's purity? Surely not …

And such were the perils of his own countrymen, but to be a subject of the unseen Heavenly King in the shadow of the emperor of the Seven Cities meant death.

"I must go to her," I said.

"I know," he said. "You and Cordelia and Baruch. I will join you there as soon as I can."

And thus it was that I was called back, spat out for the final time on the shore of a Rome that was all her own unguents gone rancid, to a city whose torch-smoke held the stench of Christian flesh.

The three of us arrived here after a two-month journey in the middle of which we left Aquila in Corinth. As if compensating grace, the sea had lulled me each night and the stinging salt of it pelted me each day as if I were meat to be hung for a distant winter meal.

An unearthly cloudscape hung around this city of Rome, with clouds as spiked as eel skeletons stretched across all its horizons. That which was rebuilt in the city in the districts of Rome destroyed by the Fire, had been constructed quickly. Even just entering the city I could not recognize landmarks because they simply didn't exist anymore. Both Cordelia and I found ourselves in the middle of new avenues peering toward the ancient hills to orient ourselves until at last we saw architectural survivors.

We knew the names of our noble forebears and birthplaces to be more valuable than the scant money we carried. We wore Roman clothing; *Civis romanus sum*, *Civis romanus sum,* I am a citizen, we are citizens, the young man owns a house near the Aventine Hill.

My yellow house was the color of long-neglected brass. Months of distant fires which never touched it still produced smolderings that gave it a patina of umber soot that came off on your clothing if you brushed against it. It was inhabited all by strangers, wary-eyed people who looked at our robes and asked many questions before they allowed us to enter our home. The canvas banner of a church that had once snapped in the winds of Rome now apologized for itself, for its torn ribbons, for its raveled selvages, for its limp hiding.

"So many died after the Great Fire," said Cassipor, a freed slave smelling of sweetnesses—was it flowers?—who seemed to be their spokesman, "people you know like the nobleman Pudens, your friend, executed because he tried to keep Paul out of prison; and many others. Months of horror, months. People being drenched in oil and then tied to posts and set afire for banquet lights."

I heard the intake of breath, a chorus of it, from

Cordelia and Baruch and me.

"It took us weeks to find each other, the Christians who were left," he went on. "We harbored many here, and some escaped to other cities. Others saw the wisdom of just giving up the faith, or at least swearing some allegiance to Caesar." He pursed his lips together like menopausal knees during a cough. "Paul continues to send messages from prison, encouraging people to keep faith. And since he arrived last month, young Timothy attends to his needs. It is as if he is invulnerable—Timothy comes and goes as he wishes from the prison, and about the city. Once he hears you have arrived, he will come here."

"Peter? What about him? He is still here in Rome?"

"Peter, that's another story. No one has heard from him for a week now. He must be in prison, or dead. He swore he would not leave Rome alive."

I noticed that the others did not speak when Cassipor spoke. He bustled through the house after our meager supper in the rearrangement of bedding to accommodate the three of us. Cordelia was out in the courtyard for a long time, and when she returned she spoke to me in whispers. Once it was dark, she and I and Baruch walked outside.

"We must watch this Cassipor," she said. "The advantage of being a cripple is that people think you're deaf and blind too. I heard the others talking about how he seems always a flurry of activity, but actually does nothing. I watched him walk from room to room carrying one blanket as if helping, but he just ended up throwing it into a corner when he thought no one saw."

I was surprised to hear this swift assessment from Cordelia.

"Are you sure?"

"I saw something tonight, too, Mother," said Baruch. "I saw him eat the heart out of the melons and then give the rest to one of the women to cut up for everyone's supper."

"Ah," I said, yearning for Aquila. "Ah."

I wondered if the tile in the secret room still had Cordelia's inheritance below it. "Look and see tomorrow," she said.

When I arose in the morning, Cordelia was trying to help one of the women with her bread, which seemed to be as heavy-hearted as the woman herself. While they struggled with the dough, I slipped into the hidden room, past all the piled-up baskets that disguised the entrance. There in the close gloom I moved aside a sleeping mat to find the tile, and looked down to see that the hole's contents reflected back my lamplight.

I was anxious to get to the Vestal temple, and with one of the coins I brought from the hiding place, Cordelia hired a cart to transport us and wait for us. The temple we had visited years ago was destroyed in the Great Fire, but Nero had rebuilt it. We left Cassipor giving advice to the flour-dusted woman and instructions to Baruch and the others about some errands, and inspecting a pair of sandals a vendor brought to the door.

When we arrived at the temple with our firepots the virgin attending the fire, a woman in her thirties, had reddened eyes and streaks on her cheeks.

I hazarded a conversation. "We seek hearthfire. And we seek the Virgin Rubria."

At this she sighed deeply but said nothing, putting a coal into each of our containers. I looked around cautiously and winced at my coming lie.

"I am her relative, Livia Ocellina."

She looked at me sharply, then grasped my wrist and pulled me behind her as if I were a child being led to punishment, and Cordelia limped along behind us. After many long passageways, we entered a room with a sleeping mat on which something bloodied lay.

"Well, she is no longer virgin," said the woman who had led us there. I heard bitterness in her voice. "Our great Caesar called for her, and though we tried to dissuade him, he wouldn't be denied. And really, perhaps she deserved this. Those in his palace say that he screamed all through the night, telling her over and over, 'This is how … this is how … this is how … a god begets a child with a virgin.' And when the screaming stopped—his screaming, for she never made a sound except for some low talking no one else could hear—they called for some of us to clean up the mess. He wanted us to see."

Cordelia was stroking the cloud-white and purpled shoulder that was exposed by the covering sheet. On Rubria's clothing, blood had separated and the clots smeared onto Cordelia's robe but she didn't seem to notice.

"And we didn't know what to do with this body," continued the woman. "We don't want to give her a funeral like all the Virgins of our heritage since she announced to us two days ago that she'd been washed clean of all our ancestral gods, the ones that protected her, and that she believed in that corpse Jesus." She spat on the rips of the embroidered chiton as some other women, silent as ghosts, glided into the room.

"So now you have arrived, and I thank the goddess that we don't have to make that decision. You are her relative, you decide what to do with this trash."

With the women stood a very young girl, young as Rubria had been the first time I met her, pale as winter breath. I looked directly at her.

"Please, be gracious enough to tell someone to direct the driver of the cart with the roan horse outside the main entrance where he can bring the cart to help us with a bundle," I said gently. She bolted from the room. Soon, some women servants appeared and managed to put the body into a stretcher that they carried with cadenced and, it seemed, reluctant steps. Cordelia and I followed them without another word, afraid that someone would change her mind.

None of the Virgins came with us. But I became aware of someone walking just behind us as we followed behind Rubria's body.

"I must tell you of her last days." A voice was in my ear and I began to turn.

"Do not acknowledge that you hear me or it will cost us our lives." At this the servants with the stretcher slowed their pace even more and we moved through marble-cold, columned rooms as if in a dream. The unseen voice spoke again, just behind me.

"Someone gave her a dangerous scroll, a letter by a man named Paul to the city of Rome. This scroll cost her life, but she said it gave true life to her."

"Where is the scroll? Did she write anything down for me?"

"The other Virgins burned every scrap of parchment and papyrus she owned. Everyone was frightened. So yesterday she made me memorize three things to tell you."

I saw daylight in front of us and knew we were approaching the gate where the cart awaited. The woman's voice was urgent.

"The first: 'The resurrection means that anything can be resurrected, thus there are no impossible tasks, no lost causes.'"

I was so startled by that, "lost causes," that I stopped walking altogether. A hand urged me on.

"The second: 'I will see you again.'

"The third, and I confess I do not understand this last: 'I go with joy.'"

In the bright sunlight of the open air, one of the servants put a clean, rough-woven covering over the body in the cart. The driver never looked around, afraid, I suppose, that he might be asked to help. One of the stretcher-bearers and I boosted Cordelia onto the cart and turned to see who had been speaking to me but no one was there. But from the shadowed portico I heard what sounded like a sob or a cough, and then nothing.

At first I directed the cart driver to take us to the yellow house, but at Cordelia's counsel gave him directions to the underground city of the dead instead. In the rocking cart I leaned close to Cordelia to speak.

"Once you left the old gods, you threw them over your shoulders and ran away, just as Rubria did, and never looked back."

She nodded.

"But I didn't. I ran, but with them still strapped to my back and they sang their sweetest songs in my ear, for years."

She nodded again. "I have wondered, Priscilla. I have wondered if all the prayers we prayed in the old days to the old gods ricocheted off them and were deflected to the true and living One? If maybe they were flat rocks that skipped along the lake of idolatry until they reached His shore on the other side? If He redeems everything, could he redeem all that lost devotion if it were finally turned to Him?"

"I do not know." I looked at the covered husk between us and earnestly wished that could be true, that all of Rubria's lifetime of serving could count for something. Was it just the changing of symbols?

"I tell you what I know about the lure of idols," said Cordelia. "I think we welcome our desires and assign them to gods with mirrors for faces.

"I think it begins in the first breathtaking feelings, like

our first sexual desires, and we believe that we have invented this, that no one ever felt this way before and our knowledge of this makes us powerful. We can protect cities with a hearth fire. We can ward off danger with chants. And we can know the future, and bless or curse others.

"And Rubria, of all, must have known the cost of giving up something so ordered and resplendent for an intractable God only accessible through words and water, and blood and wine and bread."

"Is it about changing symbols, then?" I asked.

She silently swayed with the motion of the cart so long that I feared she had fallen asleep under her mantle. But then we arrived at the village that guarded the city of the dead. The cart driver left us and the body there at one of the houses—fortunately, someone there remembered us—and then he went back to the yellow house with our message that we were safe and would return after midnight.

Then we washed the ravaged remains with water and our tears, a body so light it seemed only feathers and bones, as if the soul that departed it had been all its weight. Two of the men accompanied us into the tomb complex after dark. I was startled to see how many had been occupied since our last visit, many of them sealed with plaster still damp in the middle. They showed us an unclaimed tomb and there we laid the body of our sister Rubria.

The monster had not touched her face, and in the torchlight it was as serene as dawn.

We thought that by starting our journey back to the yellow house so late in the night we would not encounter many people. But as we neared the Circus Maximus there was a churning of people in the streets. There were many torches and the smell of smoke and fear and intoxication everywhere.

High on the Palantine Hill was a platform like a stage

and at first I thought it had a gallows on it. People milled around the base and I could see bonfires leaping and ripping in the wind. Then I could see a crossbar and thought it was a crucifix. I had not seen one for years—perhaps because Aquila always saw them first and directed my eyes elsewhere.

"There's something wrong with the cross there," said Cordelia, her face close to mine, her voice hoarse. Indeed, it seemed constructed wrong, with the crosspiece too low. As we neared, I could make out the body on it, upside down, then looked away quickly.

We hurried on, our cloaks over our faces, hunched down in the wagon like escaping slaves. Then the waves of sound began, voices chanting in the choking darkness, as if the crowd repeated a joke that I could not understand, at least at first.

"This is how …

"This is how …

"This is how …

"you kill a rock."

Thirty-Three

Cordelia and I awakened the next morning with throats of rusks and ashes from crying. We had been here in Rome only two days and both Rubria and Peter were dead, and we had no idea where Aquila was nor when he would come. Baruch joined us in the courtyard, his jaw jutted forward, and put his arms around us both. The three of us sat in silence as the sun rose.

Others in the house began to stir but its rhythms were different. When I asked about Cassipor, the woman with the breadmaking woes said he left the day before soon after we did, carrying a heavy bundle that Cordelia and I deduced to be just about the size of the secret compartment.

"No matter," said Cordelia, wiping her face. "God's household of mouths cannot live on bread alone, so we must get the tentmaking shop established." She patted her purse hanging from her belt. I praise God that I had brought as much out as I did, before Cassipor disappeared. By that afternoon we had enough fabric and leather to begin a small tent as a sample, with orders from the fabric merchant for more; and Cordelia had fine flour, raisins, and honey. The more we looked like a business and the less like a refuge, the better for the people who came and went through the way station of our home. And for a while it seemed that as long as the Christians under our roof seemed employed they attracted less attention, even on the Lord's day when some others like Timothy joined us.

But others in the city have not been so favored, and out of that has become my present vocation. It began when Cordelia and I realized that now only a few of the believers in Rome were citizens who have the freedom to move freely through the city. The apostle Thomas, the Twin, like many others has gone on to other cities: believers scattering like beads dropped on pavement.

After our interment of Rubria, Cordelia sent word that our brothers and sisters should send her a message when a believer died. Thus, she and I joined the fellowship of those who, like wide-pupiled Joseph of Arimathea and Nicodemus who took charge of the body of Jesus, like spice-laden Mary and Martha and Mary Magdalene, could prepare corpses for burial. I can say "corpses"; neither Cordelia nor I ever had the ancestral Hebrew squeamishness about bodies. We still mourned the fact that unbelieving hands buried Peter's body and would have done it ourselves if we could.

"Perhaps the Lord will come back soon. Even if not, we put all our hopes on the fact that these corpses will rise again, with the Body that rose again, those thirty years ago," said Cordelia one day, pragmatically, as she looked at a bolt of winding cloth she had just bought in the market. That was during the first weeks after the death of Peter and Rubria, when we so foolishly thought that those few who died of illness or age and were buried intact in daylight funerals perhaps presaged a coming time of relief for the living, a honeymoon with the earth before eternity.

But as the Israelites in the desert who never had a day without a funeral, soon it came to be for us. One morning, still crusted with the blood of others and weary from the long trip across the city to bury a friend and some strangers, Cordelia reassessed for us. "It must be that our illness, suffering, trial, anything that impinges on our senses, is given to us to help us remember that we were not built to live on this earth forever." She looked at me with her head turned to the side. "Weaned away. As when you weaned Baruch, remember? You put vinegar on your breasts."

I remembered the stinging and the tears, his and mine, then looked away and wondered with shame if Cordelia could ever know what it felt like to have meat and drink flowing out of one's body, what it felt like to have one's breasts prickle and moisten even now at the crying of an infant.

But she was continuing on. "I remember what Jesus told Peter," (and here her voice caught), "about how the adversary wanted to sift him like wheat. And what the Breath told you, that everything was going to be shaken and only that which was solid, anchored, could remain. And we're all being shaken, are we not?"

"But you have never wavered, Cordelia. I feel sometimes like I am a hillside eroding into the sea and when I look at you, your courage, your peace, you are a tree whose roots spread inside me and hold me together."

She held out one hand and I blanched at how much it looked like a gnarled branch. But she was smiling.

"Faith is perhaps simpler than what I thought at the beginning," she said. "Perhaps its sum total lies simply in giving God the benefit of the doubt in every circumstance."

"But I hate this circumstance, Cordelia! Has there ever

been anyone as evil as Nero?" I was crying the hot tears I hate.

"But look what we learned from the Breath," she soothed. "All those men and women who lived in horrible times, to whom did they look for examples? No wonder people call them pioneers. It is as if faith were an undiscovered land and they were the first ones to hack into its wild-grown forests and its matted undergrowth to find a way through. Should not our faith be greater than theirs, our lives more exemplary than theirs? The paths they made are worn smooth. We know so much more!"

"Apparently, we knowledge-filled, blessed ones are chosen to be the examples for today." I was bitter. "Look at the favored one, Paul. We hear only of his suffering in that miasmic pit of a cell, not news of his triumphal release. How do you feel about that? Do our lives have no more meaning than to be lessons for others?"

She settled against the wall, but the curve of her back made it only possible to do by turning sideways. Her arms negotiated around her belly, one above and one below, and I noticed how thin she had become.

"I have run out of resources, dear Priscilla," she said. "All I have left is my example. Even just by standing still I can demonstrate unseen realities to others. This wretched vinegar body can be a symbol for someone else. And if it does not, it is a symbol for me. I can subdue it, even if I can't change anything outside it. It cannot make me do anything faithless. My circumstances cannot make me do anything faithless. Only my mind can do that."

"And you just decided not to be faithless?" I tried not to sound aggravated.

"All of faith, the Breath showed you, is just each person's exercise of her will to access something that connects the seen and the unseen. And this connection is real enough—it has evidence, it carries conviction. You have to decide, consciously decide, whether what you see and hear and feel is more real, or if there are eternal realities that can demolish all we experience here. That is what the Breath was saying. Everything is made relative to God's reality: 'The better resurrection'—as if anything could be more wondrous than rising from the dead!

"We pick up bodies and wash them for burial because their living souls, awaiting us in heaven, are more real than their skin-bags. It is about which version of experience we choose to enthrone and serve."

I lowered myself to sit below her and put my head on the corrugation of her leg. "You remember what my mother said, that none of us would die alone in our beds."

"Ah, the wisdom of the prophetess Livia Ocellina." Her voice had changed and I realized she was laughing at me. "I've been thinking about witnessing with our deaths. None of us has any practice at martyrdom, and we only get one try."

We giggled like the young girls under the cypress tree, then fell silent.

"Sometimes, in those moments just before I awaken in the morning, I feel my body stretching," Cordelia said, her voice a whisper. "I feel like Jacob's ladder, with angels ascending and descending on me, like a bridge, or a conduit carrying something from those unseen realities to this. Sometimes I see myself in this dream, like the women who followed Jesus around, cooking for Him, listening to Him, and then coming to put spices on Him like the finest of breads for a king's table."

Her voice was slow, like a dreamer's now. "And everything we do for anyone, dear Priscilla, even when they are reduced to the least, the elementals of stilled blood and broken bones and skin, we are doing for this Jesus."

Sometimes, I think to myself, I can almost smell the oil that the sinful woman once put on His feet, when I wash their feet.

"Jesus," she said, her voice fading. "The one we never got to meet. The one we will meet soon."

Her voice was a murmur. "*Maranatha. Maranatha.*"

She was silent again, and when I turned to look up at her, she was asleep.

That night, two months ago, I had the last dream of the names on the sheet. And even as the dream commenced, I knew it would be the last one and the knowing filled me with a sense of incomparable loss. Exhausted as Jacob after the wrestling match, I was unwilling to let it depart without a blessing.

It was no longer the curtain of the Holy Place, but one of Cordelia's winding sheets. As each name appeared on it, a thunderous voice pronounced it: *Author and Finisher, Cross Endurer, Sitting Ruler, Contradiction Resister; Covenant Mediator, Better Speaker, Heaven Proclaimer, Shaker of the Earth.*

Ever the Same: Yesterday, Today, Tomorrow.

Sufferer Outside

Resurrected One

Great Shepherd of the Sheep.

And the names wrapped me, and I was comforted until I awakened.

The next morning Cordelia was up long before me. Only a couple of guests lay asleep against the walls, brought apparently by Baruch and Timothy whose sleeping mats held their snores and sighs. The two young men sat in the darkness in the courtyard, eating some of Cordelia's bread dripping with lily honey and laughing softly at one of her stories.

"I was telling the boys that several of our guests lately have ransacked the house," she said. "But ransacked it so neatly that one would hardly know."

I rubbed sleep out of my eyes. "I have seen nothing."

"I think they have been sent by our old friend Cassipor to see if he left any of our money behind. So, since I am sometimes here alone, I have given our funds to Baruch." My son—Was he through growing yet? He towered over even Timothy—jingled her purse from his belt and smiled broadly: a flash of white teeth and a face that had grown angles.

I felt a sudden panic looking at the slackness of the little bag. "So that is all that is left. Perhaps Baruch and I should work a bit harder until Aquila gets here to help with the tentmaking."

Cordelia leaned toward us, motioning, and our heads came together. "There is plenty more in a false floor of the old hiding place. The last place they would think to look." She chuckled, pleased with herself.

And so it was for the last few weeks we have had more than enough for our needs and those of anyone who has come over our threshold.

Once I saw an old woman sitting in the marketplace with twins—grandchildren, I suppose—playing at her feet. I stopped to look from face to face, each unremarkable except in its resemblance to the other. The Breath brushed against my cheekbone and I understood: This is the way we witness, the more we look like His face, the more people will stop and wonder.

To my surprise, the woman pulled the children close to her. "Get away. You are a curse. You were a curse from your first breath."

I looked at her for an answer.

"I have known your family all my life, served in your grandparents' house, and see what utter ruin you have brought it to," she muttered. "Even from your birth. You cursed your brother."

"Publius? I don't—"

She stopped me with a sneer. "No, your twin brother. Everyone knew if your mother had not been exhausted with pushing you out, her son would have lived. You were the price of his death. Get away from us."

I stumbled away from her. I do not remember how I got home. I remembered how many twins had come into my life: Tirzah and Shiprah, Thomas Didymus, my own Baruch and Tikveh, even the ships that brought Paul to us.

I remembered the twins in the marketplace, how I stopped to look at their plain little faces. How we look at resemblance even when individuality passes unnoticed.

I had no way of knowing when Aquila would come to us, though Timothy heard from a Corinthian sailor that he hoped to come soon. I did not yet know of the events of his life away from me, yet I knew, with a knowledge beyond informing, that thousands of contraventions would bring him back to me.

I yearned for him in every way: The points of my pelvis sought his flesh, I longed to taste his skin and savor his soul; I was the arcing branch that sought union with his earth and sky and cosmos. And yet such ripened love was beyond that of just the flesh, for even across unmeasured distance I bared the breast of my mind to his, and would have shed my own body to be reunited with him.

But one twilight when the air of the city seemed so thick it stopped time, I heard his soft, old-wood voice call my name and all the dead, sainted things in me returned to life, for he stood in the doorway of the yellow house and redeemed my being.

As I look back, perhaps it was my loud cries, the hoarseness of his responses to the tears of Baruch and Cordelia, the tear-drenched delight of homecoming that attracted the attention of some neighbor or sycophant.

Or perhaps it was just the final shuddering of the catapult for Aquila in the sling of God; and I know now for Baruch and Timothy, and for Paul, and for Cordelia, and for me. But that night, nothing could dim the glory.

"We must visit a new widow," said Cordelia after we ate. "And Baruch and Timothy, you must accompany me." Baruch protested longer than Timothy but soon the three of them were gone, with our houseguests grumbling alongside them, laden with baskets of bread and wine and fruit.

And the yellow house was ours alone, for golden hours.

There was a richness that rose off him, like a fragrance from a warming rock after dawn, without temperature nor clarity nor color. In my mind, I walked across row after row of brilliantly-colored flowers, across a landscape of distant, clear, bottomless lakes and intaglio clouds that rose and fell like tides.

At the end, my husband Aquila rose and stood over me, astride like the Colossus over the tides of its ocean harbor, and looked down at me with more fierceness, more compassion, more emptied-out devotion than he owned the words for; and his lank hair fell forward, and his tears fell from that height onto my face and hair and neck.

And when we awakened still damp in each other's arms the following morning to the yeast-smell of Cordelia's bread, and the rhythms of Timothy and Baruch reciting, and the street sounds of Rome, we almost believed that this would be our life.

Each day that Aquila went with Timothy, they danced the delicate passages that allowed them to visit Paul. After the first time, I saw in Aquila's greyness his concern for his friend.

"Maybe it is the screams of the other prisoners," he said.

"They never cease. And the smells of death. And we cannot see Paul unless we lower a lamp to him through the hole in the ceiling of his cell." He rubbed his knees and I saw the filth on the front of his robe and knew with a stabbing in my heart that he had lain on his stomach to talk to Paul.

"But we can still bribe the guards to let him have lamps and oil to read his scrolls and to write letters. And he is always so glad to see us—especially if his oil has run out," said Timothy, the optimist, who had been imprisoned before and been released. Perhaps he thought Paul's warnings about the shortness of life were just the bleakness of old age. I hoped that Timothy's inexplicable cloak of invulnerability would hold Aquila under it as it had Baruch.

Somehow Aquila's scarred body found the strength to help with the tentmaking business, and to keep visiting Paul, and each night to help Cordelia and me respond when tear-streaked faces appeared on our doorstep. Then we would go to the execution site—a public square, a coliseum, to the madman's own palace—and spare Caesar's men the distasteful task of cleaning up.

The only way we could do this, night after night, to handle torn flesh and bones and despair, was not to speak of the way the people had died.

We would separate out the pelts of animals in which our brothers and sisters had been wrapped before the dogs and wolves got them; or find a way to swaddle the ones who had been drenched in oil and set on fire, to keep the charred flesh from falling from our cart, and by an act of our will refuse to see in the ones crucified neither a reminiscence of our Savior nor a prophecy for ourselves.

Was it just a trick of the mind to see the worst of it, the limbs ambiguated, as meat that must be properly wrapped, as leather not yet tanned?

Sometimes there was no more than raw bones.

I do not know what the others thought because all the gathering was done without words. We knew well that the extension of the privilege of the gathering could be rescinded at any time, and were as workmanlike as we could be. But by the time we reached the city of the dead, there were quiet whispers and even caresses and tears before we placed what was left of believers in slots in the stone.

And as we walked away each day, I remembered the words of Isaiah: "The LORD will rise up as he did at Mount Perazim, he will rouse himself as in the Valley of Gibeon—to do his work, his strange work, and perform his task, his alien task." His task was justice; ours was mercy and mercy alone.

The last time Aquila went to visit Paul with Baruch and Timothy, the three of them returned with unfathomable expressions. Not until after dinner did Aquila bring out a small papyrus sheet, words shouted up from darkness, written in the handwriting of my son:

Paul, apostle of Christ Jesus to the esteemed lady Priska, sister and co-worker.

Grace and peace to you from God our Father and the Lord Jesus Christ. I praise God daily for you. It is with greatest sadness and yet boldness that I ask you and Aquila to join me in a task that will seal our hearts together. The Breath has told me that it is time for Baruch and Timothy to go back to Ephesus. They must leave at once. Your son Baruch, and the son of my chains, Timothy, as last ambassadors to the Jews, must take all my scrolls, for the Spirit tells me expressly that the day of my departure dawns.

The grace of our Lord Jesus be with you.

And they left that very night, their passage paid from Cordelia's cache. They tucked their forelocks behind their ears and tied them at the backs of their heads, but shaved their beards: Jews but Gentiles.

Timothy brought Paul's last letters and my Breathings

and the Law: books of the beginnings and the leavings and the ministerings and the countings and rememberings. He rolled the scrolls together into a scribe's leather carrier. And as I saw him making the roll tighter and tighter, my words with Paul's words with the oldest words of all, I understood.

My last memory of the two sons is of them standing in smoking lamplight over Cordelia and Aquila and me, their arms outstretched with their robes wings around us like the cherubim hovering over manna and budded staff and testimony.

I could not bear to see them step over the threshold of the yellow house, out, away, into a day that, for my heart, never saw light.

I do not know if Paul ever received my letter in which I told him that the young men left for Ephesus, that I loved him, that I forgave him.

Two days later I understood something new: why the very first time the psalmist used the word *Hallelujah*, it was breathed with a prayer for the destruction of the wicked.

Our brother Paul was beheaded along with three other Roman citizens who named the Name. Those who saw Paul's death reported that he caressed the block before he laid down his head, as a weary man would a pillow. They said Nero posed at the executioner's elbow, and with his own foot kicked the bodies one by one into an open pit.

With this event, something once held at bay escaped into the city, surging over that pit until it covered it and then spread silent as contagion through the streets, alerted, authorized, deputized.

Though there were often men under our roof, Aquila trusted no one with our safety. I ached for the braids of muscles in his neck as he watched the door, for the fact that he could no longer sleep without jerking awake again and again. And yet he went about each day as a man planning his own distant funeral.

"I would die for you," he whispered to me each night.

I looked him in the eyes, his face between my hands. "We die for truth, we die for Baruch, we die for our brothers and sisters, we die for Jesus," I murmured until his eyes closed.

For once in my life, that last night, I had fewer words than he, and he said only these: "Such a high priest who has passed through the heavens." The next morning he arose clear-eyed and greeted two brothers who awaited him in the predawn darkness. Both of them carried flutes like Aquila's.

"They bring news of Baruch, my Priscilla," he said. "He and Timothy made the journey overland and sailed across to Macedonia. They are safe and send you grace and peace."

Cordelia and I fell into each other's arms, sobbing with relief. Aquila encircled us and then waited for us to part before he drew his cloak over his head and slung the strap holding his flute over one shoulder: one of three traveling musicians.

"I have asked our visitors to accompany me to help some women newly-widowed," he said. I began to speak but he touched my lips and then played a few notes on his flute. "If nothing else we can collect alms as we play," he said.

With an embrace that sank into my chest like heat, like mercy, he was gone.

All morning I heard the wordless sounds from the Breath like moans or sighs of Someone too grieved to speak. I felt the advent of bad news, so when someone burst through our door at sunset I was at first relieved to see that it was Cassipor, until I heard him speak.

"They are all dead, lady Priska, all dead."

I did not need to ask of whom he spoke.

"Your lord Aquila and two companions—I do not

know who they were—were walking near the city wall when I saw an imperial soldier ask them to play their flutes."

I spread my hands, why, why, how?

"And he was … displeased … with all but Aquila, so he broke their flutes and ran them through with his sword."

I gasped. I still had hope.

"And then," Cassipor cast his eyes into the corners of the room, away from my eyes, from Cordelia who ran into the room when she heard the voices.

"And then he told Aquila to play a tune for Apollo, god of music, and he refused. By then the soldier realized why, and no matter how much he jabbed at him, he would not play. The soldier took the flute and flung it up onto the wall, where the strap caught; and then he told Aquila he could have his life back if he climbed up to get the flute and played for Apollo."

"He is in the prison. Say he is in the prison," screamed Cordelia.

Cassipor hung his head. "I am so sorry. I am truly sorry." He began to sob. "By that time a crowd had gathered. Your husband held his hands out to the soldier, and his face was so gentle. He smiled at the soldier, and kept saying, 'Sharper than any two-edged sword, the Word of Jesus! The Word!'"

I knew those words, and I knew their cost.

A sinkhole opened beneath my feet and I fell into a place that leeched the color out of everything. I could see only slate with etchings on it that moved like people around me. Later, Cordelia handed me Aquila's other cloak. It became sacred with the folding, with the putting away into a basket. Then we walked from room to room. Our garments smacked against our skin and stuck to it, soaked with tears.

Once it was dark, Cordelia and I rode in the cart to the place near the city of the dead where some other of the brothers had taken the bodies. Cassipor told me where to look to see the flute on the city wall, but clouds hid the moon and we barely could keep the cart on the road. I realized that the new widows must have lived nearby. I wondered where.

The people who always helped us with the bodies stood in a line outside one of the homes, as if it were already overfilled. Inside, the three men lay side by side, each covered to the chin with his cloak. The other two rested as if asleep, their faces impassive, but my husband's jaw seemed set, as if he were in an argument. Underneath the cloak, bulges tented the cloth.

I felt Cordelia leaving my side and I found myself alone in the room. I turned first to the other men, to thank them for going with my husband, to ask their forgiveness for it, too; for only until I had dispensed with this could I kneel beside Aquila. But my voice would not work right.

I drew back the cloak. I saw more clearly in the light that his whole body seemed fixed, his arm across his chest and his legs buckled, as if a sculptor had been given the assignment to idealize pain and this was what resulted. When I touched his arm, though, it softened and slid slowly down to his side, and his legs relaxed as if he had been waiting for me. His clothing was clean and undamaged, and I thought of someone washing him as we had done for so many others.

I do not know how much later in the night Cordelia awakened me and drew my arms from around him. The other two bodies were gone. Some men came in and carried the body to the cart, and we followed like somnambulists through the avenues and intersections of the catacomb.

I do not recall how they placed his body in the crypt, only that someone hung his cloak over the opening. Hope keeps us from mourning like the pagans, someone said. We will see him again. Someone else said something about his name, like an eagle, and mine, steadfast; then Cordelia was singing one of the psalms.

I wondered what he had looked like when he was a little boy.

I heard in the market yesterday of rumblings and smoke in the city of Pompeii, and in one Breath-sight I saw its painted grimaces peeling from the wall, its underfoot mosaics gone to sand and ash that spreads over the whole nation.

Today, everything is charged with meaning.

I walk through the city of Rome with no fear now, though I hear the brush of Peter's lion's stiff fur against me as I walk, hear the echo of its voice from the catacombs as it feeds its own hunger and rage with the saltwater of blood that makes it more ravenous, drives it mad. And the city is its own founding wolf who suckles no one but pulls at the breast of the church until it draws blood. These are the wild beasts, Caesar has none like them.

"I am no longer afraid," said Cordelia yesterday in the coolness of the infant morning's air.

"So much is uncertain," I said.

"Is it? What is uncertain?"

What was so certain, so noble about two old women left alone? I wondered. I pulled at a piece of fabric in my lap and saw that I had stitched a long seam with no thread in my needle. I thought of patterns and seams and things unraveling, and a line of tiny holes that held nothing together. Had my life been the needle unthreaded?

Cordelia saw me looking at the fabric, saw the empty needle. After all these years, no words were needed.

"*By faith, by faith, by faith.*" Her words were music. "Nothing impressed the Lord Jesus except faith. No good deeds, no heroic deaths," she said, her voice trembling and her eyes afraid I would cry again. But I did not cry, had not cried since I came back from Aquila's burial.

"I tell you what I would write to everyone, if I wrote on scrolls as you do," she said. "I would write this: 'I serve a mysterious and terrifying God of love. I have plighted my troth to a resurrected Man, the Lord Jesus Christ. And if some other god sends me to his hell for that, he will just have to do it. I will be faithful until I die. And I will help you to be, too.'"

"Just like that?" I asked.

"Just like that." I heard her old laughter again. "It would be a very small scroll."

I put the cloth down and sat again at her feet, resting my head on her leg once more. I thought of what she said years ago when she read one of Paul's letters that said the church was the bride of Jesus. "I knew it, I just knew it," she had said.

"This is how we overcome," she said, stroking my hair with two bent fingers.

"If God makes someone into a symbol, He gives her the power to cope with any circumstance. No matter how hard. In fact, the circumstance seeps back into the symbol. It is absorbed by it. All that we endure becomes part of that symbol, stronger, richer than it ever was alone."

"And we are all symbols?"

Her voice was soft. "And we are all symbols."

We sat in the silence, my friend Cordelia and I.

It was not yet light, yet someone coughed outside the door. In the room behind us, two women—a dark-skinned mother and a daughter, I thought—who had arrived after midnight, frantic with fear, now stirred. Hide us, keep us hidden, they had begged.

"We are not yet dressed," I called out toward the door. Cordelia pulled the wide-eyed women from their sleeping mats and silently showed them to the secret room. I heard the soft crackle of baskets striking the wall. People asleep in the other rooms did not move, in this house where each day tides of guests ebbed and flowed.

Two were outside the door. I recognized the first one, a Roman slave named Marcipor, a brother. The other I did not know—he looked like a Jew yet he had no beard and his hair was ragged and clipped short as his hurried words.

"Greetings, I salute you," he said.

"Sister Priska, Sister Cordelia, this man needs our help to bring his family from outside the city. His name is Kohath," said Marcipor.

"A Levite," I murmured and saw his startled look. Then he nodded. He took a piece of Cordelia's bread from her contorted hand and stared at it for a moment before eating the bread.

"But my lineage no longer matters," he said between bites. "There's a new priesthood, a new order, a high priest we all can trust, unassailable, someone whose power comes not from lineage but from his indestructible life, you see. Like Melchizedek, you have heard of him, the priest of old? This is what I have learned about *Yeshua HaMashiach*, and is it not wondrous? No matter how far we are from the temple, He stands and intercedes for us! At a heavenly altar, eternal. God has declared the Law satisfied."

Marcipor looked up at me, his eyes bright, and out of the corner of my eye I saw Cordelia move to touch my arm, to say, this woman knows more about these things. But I stopped her with a look.

And then I felt sweetness near my ear.

"Listen, listen," said the Breath. "See? See? Breathe!" And I did, deep into the veins and catacombs of my lungs, I breathed.

"Breathe," says the Breath, "We breathe together, now

and forever."

I thought of the scrolls, in the trajectory of the Breath's catapult, vaulting over land, people, ages. They are the treasure from the sea, brought on birth-waves to shores I will never see.

Cordelia was speaking to Kohath. "We have funds to hire a cart to go get your family," she said. She gave a glance at her rising bread and I nodded.

"I will show them who to hire. And I will get more cloth while I am out," I said. More winding cloths, I meant, but I did not say this.

She did not look at me as I put my mantle over my face, so I kissed her goodbye with my eyes. I was not gone long. Soon Marcipor and Kohath rumbled away on a cart and I brought the cloth back like a saddle across our mule.

When I entered the yellow house, it was silent, as if it had been turned upside down and all sound emptied out of it. All the wall hangings lay in heaps on the floor, the baskets and my bolts of fabric were a jumble, and Cordelia's rising bowls lay on their sides with crusting strings of dough stretching from them to the lumps on surfaces below.

I sat down hard on the floor. How long I was there, I do not know.

This is what I have to cache in my mind, I thought. This is what Aquila would want me to do, what Cordelia would want. This inventory is what Baruch and Timothy know, the message of my scrolls.

All of human history has been an army of archers, letting fly its arrows only toward Bethlehem and Golgotha.

All of human history has been staged to get our attention: people, things, events. The tabernacle was never about the tabernacle; it was about what it housed. Its furnishings are just copies of originals somewhere else. Why would any thinking person not want to see the originals?

The laws were never about the laws or systems; they were about the excellence of oaths, and Oath-maker.

Priesthood—mysterious, unmanageable, autonomous —persists, but with only one Officiant. He is the point of everything. From first to last. From beginning to end. Eternity to baby to corpse to priest.

Faith is commodity. It transports the intents of God and slams it into the joints and marrow of earth-life. It changes reality.

People are created to be symbols, like altars and lampstands and chests. They are cargo ships of meaning. They most often cannot carry explanation.

If there is explanation, it is only in the aggregate: *only with them.*

Only with them.

I felt secret caverns collapsing within me.

Some time later, when there were long shadows outside in the courtyard, I heard a rustling sound from the baskets behind me. I realized that I had been speaking the inventory aloud, over and over.

"Who is there?" I asked. The two dark women came from the hiding place, peering around corners and stepping over everything on the floor.

"The soldiers took them all," the mother said. "To the Circus Maximus, they said, for the games tonight, the great lions." She shuddered, and I did too.

"Everyone?"

"We stayed in the hiding place, and they came close but didn't find us. But we could hear. They came for your friend Priska, and I am sure she went, because we could hear her talking to them about Jesus."

"Priska?" I asked. The woman's speaking my name hurt my ears.

The woman looked unsure of herself. "The soldiers

called out that name, and your friend, you know, the hunched-over one who was with you last night when we came, answered them. 'The follower of Jesus?' she said, and went with them, talking the whole way out the door."

I thought of judgment day. Tens of thousands of voices claiming only one name.

The two women looked at one another, perhaps because of my silence and my tears. They sat down in the floor with me.

"Hallelujah," I said, when I was able to speak. They looked at one another again. I suspected they did not know about the Psalms.

"It may not be safe for you here anymore," I said after a while. "Soldiers will be back if they see lamplight in here." They looked at the disarray around me. The bread had risen and fallen again and the smell of yeast was pungent, bitter. They closed the door without a sound when they departed.

Long after dark, I loaded the donkey again with the new winding cloth I bought, and put all the rinsed-out tent pieces into the stained floor of the cart. I went back inside to wait to see if anyone would come to help me, but no one did.

But when I arrived at the dumping grounds outside the Circus Maximus, men and women emerged from pillars and walls as if they were branches and arches themselves, and two other carts appeared. As always there were no words, only the touch of a forearm on my shoulder, a kiss on my wet cheek.

It took all of us, loading and sorting in the last spitting light of imperial torches. Even some of the lions had killed and eaten one another. Other than that, hardly anything—anyone—was identifiable this night. I have seen the insides of people now, and know that there is nothing there that attaches the soul to it.

The cart is loaded up with the animal skins and the trash, and mine and another carry the bodies. We take separate routes through the city.

Tonight, the mystery of Cordelia's child is revealed: heavy and rounded, perfectly detailed, a child curled asleep, white as chalk, hard as stone. I feel an honor in carrying it, though my arm can hardly bear it.

I mourn a different mourning as I pass my mother's house and the cypress tree where Cordelia and I laughed and dreamed.

As I walk, I think of Job's plea: Give me the consolation that I will not deny the Holy One. I wonder what the old prophets would say of me. Like Ezekiel and Isaiah and Jeremiah, I have been a voyeur of heavenly things, felt their fire in my bones.

I share the fellowship of the ambushed with Paul. I wonder if brother Luke wrestles with being a second-hand witness. *Many times*, I say aloud. *Many ways*.

At the city wall the moon brushes clouds off its face and casts a cool brilliant gaze onto Aquila's flute hanging the height of three men above. I see it from a distance, and the nearer I come, the slower my pace, because it seems disloyal to walk past it. But the moon is overcome by the clouds, and I am not sure when I pass the flute because the light of my torch will not reach it.

I think about the fact that the pivotal event of all of history—the bursting-forth of a corpse from a tomb—happened in the dark, with no witness to its event but only its subsequents. I hear the truths in Cordelia's voice, as she would talk to me:

Someone came from a realm beyond my experiences and yet decided to pick them up like ill-fitting garments and try them on for size. The size of sickness, regret, death. Now, He says, let us trade. I tried all yours, now you try on eternal life. And while you are waiting for that, give Me the benefit of the doubt. Take My word for it that all the sins of your ancestors only bring death. Take on their experiences as if they were your own. You were a slave in Egypt. Let Me rescue you.

I think of the little words the Breath used, over and over: *thus, therefore, because.* They welcomed from a distance. We look back.

When I reach the houses where the burial brothers and sepulcher sisters live, the others who were at the Circus Maximus have come and gone. Only one brother waits, yawning, to help me. I see that there is no winding cloth anywhere and I wonder what they used for the other bodies.

We take the body parts from my wagon and wash them and wrap them in lamplight that makes everything look like bronze. He has a clean cart to take the bodies to the catacombs but awakens another man to help him load and unload them, and through the doorway I see the eyes of his wife and children staring out at me. May I borrow a comb? I ask. He brings it and tells me that his family will be moving into the city soon, that so many people are coming to believe in Jesus that they are needed there, and that others will take turns with the catacomb duties because there are so many new believers.

So many. So many. The words echo in my head as we chant a psalm. The men are Romans, I notice, and do not know the words to the psalm but are reading it with relish from a piece of vellum they brought from a niche by the entrance.

"I am the resurrection and the life," one says. We put all the wrapped pieces from my cart into one large crypt. *Sabbath rest, Sabbath rest,* I think. Someone has been carving out these large openings and an entire boulevard of them stretches as far as the lamplight will reach. I remember

Cordelia's poem about Ezekiel's vision, and bones joined to bones.

I ask the men to leave me, and show them that I have plenty of oil in my lamp. They know that I have been here enough times that I can find my way out unaided. They look at Cordelia's baby lying on a folded cloth on a ledge, and they leave.

I take the length of winding cloth I carried over my arm and rip it into strips, and begin to wrap the baby, but my tears make the swaddling hard to do. I talk to him, for it is a boy, and wonder about his name.

Then from the bundle of cloth I take what I found as we were washing the other bodies. It is a matting of Cordelia's long hair, red streaked with grey, still damp from my washing. I sit cross-legged in the dust, stretching my skirt across my thighs to form a table.

I hold the end with one hand and comb Cordelia's hair until it behaves. Then I wind it around my wrist in a circle that touches my pulse. Pulling it off, I tuck it into the folds of the baby's wrapping and push it far back into the opening with the other bodies.

I wonder what some distant person will think when they find Cordelia's baby among the bones when they come to reinter them. Like Melchizedek, without genealogy. Like my scrolls, with no provenance.

On the way out I pause before Aquila's crypt. The cloak is gone and it is sealed with fresh plaster. In it, someone has inscribed his name and an anchor. The crypt next to it has a barrier of sticks across it that say: do not use this one. There is a smear of fresh plaster above it with the same anchor inscribed.

I walk back out into the sweet night air to the house where my mule and cart are tied, and lay the comb atop a jug. I release the mule and lead him to the pen where the families' animals are, and then I begin walking back into the city.

As I pass through the gate it is almost as bright as daylight, as if the moon has rebuked the clouds. I turn around and I can see Aquila's flute, moving slightly in the breeze, and I can hear it too.

I cannot bear this, I cannot.

Is there no wrench that can turn the cosmos back?

But now it is not music, but the voice of my husband breathing through it.

"Come my beloved, let us go forth to the field …"

And I am remembering our first night as I lay my face against the stone of the wall.

A group of soldiers marches by, and I turn my face away. In my mind I see the faces of the twins in the marketplace—was that just this morning? An eternity has passed since then. I think of how Rubria and Peter departed this life at nearly the same time, of Paul and Aquila in pairs, and now Cordelia.

Jesus said that He would shorten days for those who love Him. This killing-age of my life has been purposefully compressed, I see; and I think of my scrolls being wound tighter and tighter with the other scrolls. The thought comforts me as I walk up the Caelian Hill.

A wall of an estate has a cleft in it, and the soil is soft there, as if the owner had removed a shrub or tree. I sit and push the small of my back up against the smooth stones and look out over the city, and breathe prayers that the Cassipors and Alexanders of my life be given another chance. I look toward the palace and wonder about the twisted things there, the festering. I cannot ask that he be forgiven because he did not know what he was doing. I shudder and forgive him myself.

I think about the message of the scrolls and wonder if

the people who hear it think it will not apply to them, if the Gentiles will think it is just a book for Jews. I forgive them for that, because they cannot know. I hope they understand that some triumphed here and some lived in caves in this unworthy world and both are sonship.

I wonder if they will know that my letter had no intention of preparing them to cope with this life, but to help them cope with the implacable eternal realities. I wonder if they will feel the fellowship of the Breath, if they will believe that He will give them words, too, in their times of danger and loss.

Suddenly I am being pressed back into the space in the wall, and covered over so that I cannot see. At first I am hollowness, reduced to a child within my own self and He, Holy Parent, sets about rearranging my innards and feeding me. The Holy Inhabitant is preparing me.

Then I can see, and something is passing in front of me, terrible as an army with banners, stately as a great ship in majesty upon waters. The great High Priest has wound the sash around Himself and walks back and forth before me, calling out all the names on it, all the Breath-names from the scrolls.

I awaken, and it is still dark. I touch the rocks and wonder if they have enough inner vibrations to cry out if I am silent.

I know that He had been with me in the Judean desert, on the seas, in the godless cities, in birth, in death.

He will be with me as I light every lamp in the yellow house.

I am stripped down to my soul's bones. I am washed with blood, scoured with sand, thoroughly rinsed, and dried in blasting light, ready.

I know who You are, I say to Him: revealer of mysteries, bargainer with Abraham, wrestler with Jacob, Breath drying the fleece. You honored the woman who wanted crumbs, You rewarded the widow's persistence.

My eyes and my heart are clear.
I know Your names. I come with joy.
I come with joy!

About the Author

Latayne C. Scott, PhD., is the recipient of Pepperdine University's Distinguished Christian Service Award for her writing. She has authored more than 20 published books with over 150,000 copies in print through Zondervan (Harper Collins), Baker, Howard (Simon & Schuster), Word, Moody, Trinity Southwest University Press and other publishing companies, as well as hundreds of magazine articles and shorter works. She has won national awards for poetry, humor, and other genres.

Author's Note

I am very grateful for Sharon K. Souza, Celeste Green, Ryan Scott, J. Michael Strawn, Dave Leaumont, and Phil Silvia, as well as all of my family for their help, comments and support.

If you'd like more information on the opening scene of the novel as well as other details of life in Rome, I highly recommend *The Bone Gatherers: The Lost Worlds of Early Christian Women* by Nicola Denzey.

In supporting the premise of Priscilla as the author of Hebrews, I stand on the shoulders of giants. Around 1900, renowned German Bible scholar Adolph von Harnack published several scholarly documents citing ancient sources, asserting Priscilla's authorship; and his work and that of many other scholars is chronicled in *Priscilla's Letter: Finding the Author of the Epistle to the Hebrews* by researcher Ruth Hoppin. I have leaned very heavily upon Hoppin's detailed work, and will give only the briefest account of the case she makes.

First of all, the theory of female authorship of great works of ancient literature is well-documented. Socrates says that the author of one of the greatest discourses of the ancient world, the "Funeral Oration" of Pericles, was not Pericles but his lover and mentor, a woman named Aspasia. Samuel Butler, the Victorian translator of other ancient classics attributed to the poet Homer, insisted—and had considerable scholarly support in his theory—that the *Iliad* may have been written by a man, but that the *Odyssey* certainly was not. (Having read both recently, I can see the value of Butler's argument.) Finally, the late S. D. Goitein theorized that *The Song of Solomon* may have been written by a woman.

I am no Greek scholar, but my own reading of Hebrews causes me to agree with Harnack, Hoppin, and many others who assert that the *koine* of the Epistle to the Hebrews is unique (thus, not Pauline). And of course, many emphases of Hebrews (Melchizedek, for instance) don't appear anywhere else in the New Testament.

In brief, as outlined by Hoppin, here are some reasons why Priscilla could legitimately be considered the author. Hoppin has convinced me that Priscilla had the right abilities, the right connections, and was at the right place at the right time for everything that would qualify someone to write Hebrews. Here are some (not all) of her conclusions:

1. Priscilla is never mentioned without her husband Aquila in the seven times they are named in the New Testament. (Four of those times, quite remarkably, her name is listed first and thus she is given preeminence by both Luke and Paul in their writings.) Thus, it is reasonable that through her epistle, she refers to "we" and "us" as well as "I" and "me."
2. The author could not be Paul, an eyewitness of the Resurrection of Jesus, because of what Hebrews 2:3 says: Jesus spoke, some heard, and then those confirmed it to the "us" of the Epistle to the Hebrews. In contrast, Paul met Jesus on the road to Damascus and then was privately tutored by Him in the desert (Galatians1:12). Certainly, thus, Paul was an eyewitness, unlike the Hebrews' author.
3. The author was a colleague and co-worker with Paul and Timothy.
4. The overt mentions of women of faith—Sarah, Rahab, women who received their dead back (the

widow of Zarephath? The Shunammite woman?), as well as men notable because of women's roles in their lives (Barak owed his victory to Deborah, Jepthah is known for his daughter's sacrifice, Samuel entered ministry when dedicated to the Lord by his mother)—all of these could point to female authorship. (But as I mentioned in the introduction, since I assert verbal inspiration, it could perhaps more properly be seen as the Holy Breath's concession to the fact that He was collaborating with a woman.)

5. The author was trained in rhetoric, literary devices such as type and antitype, and quoted from the Septuagint (the Greek translation of the Old Testament documents). She must have had great intelligence to teach a luminary like Apollos (Acts 19). Priscilla is an aristocratic name, and according to Scripture, she had enough resources to have a church meet in her home.
6. Apollos and Barnabas, because of their intelligence and training, have been proposed as authors of the Epistle. But Hoppin argues, if such a well-known man as either of them wrote this epistle, why was no name attached to it?

One of the arguments against the authorship of the Epistle—to me, the only one that could possibly hold water, is an obscure grammatical one: the use of a male participle the author used of himself/herself. However, Hoppin convincingly shows how non-agreement of the gender of a participle and its noun is not unique in Scripture, and could have other explanations as well. I'll let her book do the heavy lifting on this point.

Did Priscilla write Hebrews? I think she could have. I think she probably did.

Of course, my book does not pretend to be anything but fiction: exploring what it would have been like for a woman, a Gentile in the midst of the suffering "most favored generation," to receive revelation that would be canonized for millennia as the Word of God.

CPSIA information can be obtained
at www.ICGtesting.com
Printed in the USA
LVOW03s1512231017
553451LV00001B/304/P